Bloom *books*

Dear Readers,

It is an amazing thing to be able to open a book and escape to a new world. A place where the pages become a comforting blanket of adventure and excitement. The only thing that could possibly be more magical is getting to create that world of comfort and adventure for you. Thank you each a thousand times for being a part of my story.

ALSO BY JENEANE O'RILEY

The Infatuated Fae

How Does It Feel?

HOW DOES IT FEEL?

JENEANE O'RILEY

Bloom *books*

Published by Bloom Books, an imprint of Sourcebooks
P.O. Box 4410, Naperville, Illinois 60567-4410
(630) 961-3900
sourcebooks.com

Originally self-published in 2023 by Jeneane O'Riley.

Cataloging-in-Publication data is on file with the Library of Congress.

Printed and bound in the United States of America.
KP 10 9 8 7 6 5 4 3 2 1

To you.
My hope is not that you finish this book
but that this book finishes you.

AUTHOR'S NOTE

I want you to enjoy this book with every cell inside of your body. I want you to escape to a magical, villainous fairy land full of fun, but not at the expense of your health and well-being.

Please be aware this story contains content that might be troubling to some readers, **including but not limited to violence, abuse (physical, mental, emotional, verbal), kidnapping, death and dying, gore, mental illness, bones, hospitalization, profanity, snakes, sex, poisoning.** If you decide to proceed (cracks knuckles and turns to face you in a large, ominous desk chair), then please enjoy book one of the Infatuated Fae series.

Jeneane O'Riley

PLAYLIST

"Like A Villain"—Bad Omens
"The Death of Peace of Mind"—Bad Omens
"You've Seen the Butcher"—Deftones
"Black Honey"—Thrice
"Make Believe"—Memphis May Fire

CHAPTER 28:

"Reach"—Eternal Eclipse
"Inferia"—Eternal Eclipse

CHAPTER 29:

"Born from Ashes"—Eternal Eclipse

PROLOGUE

CALLIE

THE DAMP FLOOR OF THE DUNGEON MADE IT HARD TO KEEP the tiny cuts of cheese on my mini charcuterie board. I suppose it was less of a board and more of a loose brick from the back wall, but the rat that visited this cell wouldn't mind.

I laughed out loud at how cute it looked with the little bits of cracker and honey saved from my meal yesterday. My muscles froze. I immediately berated myself for the laughter that had slipped out.

It didn't like when I made noises. When I made noises, it woke up. It had told me they would hurt me again if I made any more noise. I pressed my body into the faulty shelter of the dungeon's shadows.

My fingers poked the open, bloodied wound on my head as a firm reminder of its horrible capabilities.

A deep inhale stretched my sinewy ribs as I imprinted my fingernail sharply into the wound. I bit the iron cuff around my wrist to muffle my cries as the metal tang of blood swirled with the bite of iron in my mouth.

Good; I still felt something. My taut muscles relaxed the faintest amount.

The iron chain between my cuffs clanged loudly against itself with my slight movement.

Blackness immediately consumed me as my eyes shut so tightly that tiny flecks of light speckled the back of my eyelids. The hard stone wall dug into my flesh. I pressed harder, willing it to swallow me up so I would no longer be inside the fear-laced cell of this dungeon.

Had I caused him to wake?

A few stray tears escaped my eyes as my body trembled.

Fuck. Fuck.

I shook so hard, I threatened to wake him simply with the rattle of my bones.

Be quiet or it will wake and hurt you again.

CHAPTER 1

CALLIE

I SLID MY HANDS OVER THE SUN-WARMED LEATHER OF MY Chevy with an influx of small prayers.

The old truck gurgled and shook at my attempted coaxing. I heaved out a sudden breath of relief, sliding down in the seat a few relaxed inches. I wouldn't ruin my record. No late days, no call-offs.

I was doing a good job.

The tires crackled haphazardly over the stray twigs that littered the gravel of my driveway as I pulled out of the winding trail and headed away from my beautiful cottage. Okay, maybe calling it a cottage was a stretch…and maybe so was calling it beautiful, but "cabin" made me think of some old hunting shack in the middle of nowhere. My house was much, *much* cuter. I'd bought it two years ago for a steal from a potbellied widower with a bald head and a penchant for pulling too many whitetails that he didn't have tags for. Was he trying to bribe me? Possibly. It was rumored I was dating the game warden, Cliff, and in a small town like this, the folks would do anything to get a leg up, especially when it came to deer tags. I almost couldn't blame them, except that tagging was set up specifically to help control the wildlife population, and when people took it upon themselves to judge what numbers were okay to kill, the rehabilitation efforts and statistics always got skewed and caused problems. It didn't matter because Cliff and I weren't dating anyway...and also, Paul the widower had died a few days after I had bought the house.

My grip on the leather steering wheel tightened at the thought of Cliff, but I quickly brushed it away. In truth, we had never even been on a date, and we never would. When the state had hired me as the park's environmental scientist, Cliff was one of the only kind faces to greet me. The small hole-in-the-wall town did *not* take kindly to a stuck-up fancy-pants scientist riffling around in their business (I actually heard this one with my own ears at the Sizzler in Maulberry), coming to their beloved town and ordering them to stop pulling out their milkweed and tightening the parks hunting regulations. Being the only woman to work the parks, besides Cecelia at the wildlife rehab center, most of the men didn't take me seriously, and the ones who did were accused of having an affair with me. That was small towns for you.

Though I couldn't remember my hometown having the same mentality, I was practically a child when I left.

At twenty-nine years old, with no children, no husband, bright blond hair to my waist, and a decent enough figure (you try hiking these hills all day), the women of the town seemed to think I had a secret vendetta to steal their out-of-shape, misogynistic, husbands or take all the available Wrangler-wearing, dip-chewing men. It was actually kind of flattering when I thought about it at first. Until two years went by, and I still had to think about it. Then it grew less flattering and more...lonely.

I debated stopping at the local gas station for coffee but decided against it. I really didn't want to risk the truck not starting up again. The coffee wasn't very good anyway, even for gas station coffee, and if I had to sit and listen to the locals talk any more about "Crazy Earl", the town drunk, and his quest for Sasquatch, I was going to quit my job and move.

Thankfully I was usually with Cliff when we stopped, and he would quiet them down a bit. For whatever reason, he hated Earl. I'd never formally met the town drunk, but I'd heard enough stories to write a book.

I mentally made a note to check the woods behind the gas station for Amanita muscaria. They were poisonous mushrooms that, if eaten in small enough quantities, might not kill you but made you act out of sorts...like Crazy Earl. He was always in the woods out back of the old gas station. I was about to turn around to inspect my hunch when a long-necked bundle of brown feathers shot out across the road in front of me.

My aging truck screeched to an abrupt halt, protesting with a puff of black smoke the size of an elephant and shutting off. Temperamental hunk of metal and bolts—it was worse than a man.

"Gosh *dang it*, Dorothy!" I slammed the truck door closed behind me as I walked across the dirt road to the turkey hen that forever stalked me.

Thankfully I was on the long driveway of the rehab center, so I would just deal with my dilapidated truck later. Dorothy was flopping around wildly in a patch of cattails like a toddler who had just escaped their parents' clutches. She was lucky I hadn't hit her with the truck, and it was only her bum wing causing her to chaotically dance about like a poorly choreographed Zumba instructor.

I made sure no cars were coming, pretty certain they wouldn't be because it was the back entrance to the wildlife rehabilitation center. I plopped down crisscross-applesauce style on the dirty path and tried not to look at the smoking truck to my left. Maybe if I didn't think about it too much, it would start up again.

No sooner had I sat on the dusty gravel road than I was accosted by the large adult turkey trying to nest in my lap. Happy squeaks and grumbles filled her long neck, and I couldn't help but smile at the goofy bird as she nestled into me. She was one of my patients at the center. It wasn't really in my job description to work on the animals, but with only one vet in the building, I ended up helping with the injuries more often than not. I didn't mind; I much preferred the company of animals to people as it was.

"I was just coming to see you. You didn't need to break free again. You're lucky I didn't run you down," I chided as I nuzzled the beady-eyed turkey, tightening my hold on her body as the crunch of gravel sounded behind me.

I lifted the giant bird, being careful of her bad wing, and moved us out of the way. I didn't bother to look up, assuming Cecelia had just come to look for her.

"You owe me five bucks," crooned a male voice.

I knew before I looked at the game warden's truck whose voice it was.

"I don't owe you anything, Cliff Richards. If you're stupid enough to bet with Cecelia, then you should owe me five dollars," I said with a big smile before scooting over toward the gray Ford truck with the handsome man hanging out the window.

We couldn't have looked more different in our khaki-and-green uniforms if we had tried. Mine hung over me like a too-big shirt I stole from my dad, while on Cliff it clung to his athletic body like he was some L.L. Bean catalog model.

He peered over the top of his gold aviator sunglasses as he reached out to smooth down Dorothy's neck feathers. She flustered and bobbed her head away but eventually let him pet her.

"Never seen anything like it," he said matter-of-factly, a hundred-watt smile plastered to his unshaven face.

Sometimes he reminded me so much of my best friend from back home. Something about the friendly smile, or the charismatic attitude he carried, always made me think of Eli.

"Seen anything like what?" I asked and looked around us.

The amber glow of the sun had begun to heat, and little beads of sweat had started to collect at my hairline. I was ready to get Dorothy back inside the air conditioning or in the shade of the woods. It was going to be a hot one today, and the crevice between my boobs was already filling uncomfortably with pooling sweat.

"Like you, Callie. Everything wants to be with you, even the wild animals. You're like a goddamn Disney princess." He smiled, and the look he was giving insinuated that more than just the turkeys wanted to be with me.

I shifted uncomfortably and tried to think of how to politely tell him I'd rather date Dorothy than him. It wasn't anything against him; he was a great friend. I just had no interest in being trapped in this town forever, and I was not in the habit of having relationships with coworkers.

"She's hardly wild," I said as I nuzzled the large bird.

She had been raised from a poult at the center, born with only one good wing. I was making great progress with her, though, and had a few more things I wanted to experiment with to fix her wing.

"I gotta get Dorothy inside. I'll see you later?"

I began the walk toward the new building when I was cut off by the back of Cliff's tailgate as he reversed the truck in stride with us.

"How you gonna get home, scientist? You gonna build a set of wings and fly home? That truck of yours is done for. I told you last month it was too dangerous to be driving." He raised his eyebrows cockily as he continued to slowly back up, maintaining eye contact with me.

"Well, it's a good thing I don't listen to everything you tell me to do," I grumbled.

"Get in. I'll give you two a ride back," he said as he stopped the truck, blocking my path.

Dorothy flustered once again inside the truck, but it was a short drive up the road to the center, so I knew she'd be fine.

We pulled up to the back of the building two minutes later. The painted white brick beamed in the sunlight. Only two other cars were in the front parking lot, one being

Cecelia's. I got out of the truck to find I had turkey droppings all over my pants.

Perfect.

I set her on the ground and scowled at the fluttering bird as I wiped myself off, making certain she knew I wasn't happy about it.

"Where you headed? To the lake?" I asked Cliff before I realized he was on his cell phone.

"Don, she did it. It finally broke down." He turned to look at me. "I know, tell *her* that. She won't listen to me for shit. How's about you send Wally out to get it? C'mon, man, do it for me. Git that old thing runnin' again, and I'll take you both fishin' next week. To my *special* spot." He rolled his eyes in humor before hanging up the phone. "There, now you definitely owe me dinner." He grinned, making his tan face look extra charming with just a dash of arrogance.

"Forget about dinner. I want to go see this honey hole of yours. You know the bass are projected to be at a thirteen percent underpopulation next spring?" I accused.

He rolled his eyes. "I'm not taking *you* to *my* honey hole. Especially if you're not gonna let me fish!" he shouted with mock exasperation.

For being the head game warden, he was actually incredibly lax about the conservation of wildlife. It was no wonder they had to hire me.

"You're ridiculous. I'm not going to stop you from fishing. I want to study that spot. If it has a lot of activity, we may be able to re-create it and encourage reproduction." As I said the words, my face began to heat and blush. "Thank you for calling Don. Last time, he told me he'd light it on fire before he towed it again." I smiled at the memory from last year.

"Ya know, the state isn't so bad. I know they'd *happily* give the fancy-pants scientist a vehicle to drive if they thought she might stay for longer." His voice was gruff, with just a hint of an accent clinging to the ends of his syllables.

"Ahh, but the migratory flight patterns of the monarchs

wait for no one." I brushed a stray feather from my sleeve. "As soon as I get the call, I'm off to Mexico, baby!"

Even as I said it, I could feel the energy shift within our conversation. I remembered why I didn't make friends when I moved around.

They never understood when you left.

I had made it up the concrete steps of the back entrance and was about to breach the large aluminum doors when Cliff continued. "I'll pick you up at six, Callie Peterson. I'll have Tom drop off the Jeep here if you need to get out and about. He's just closing the gates at Clover Park now."

"If Tom's bringing the Jeep, then what do I need you for?" I smiled at him as I pulled the big metal handle to shoo Dorothy inside.

She patiently waited as her human servant widened the door to make room for her large, feathered body and waltzed in as though she owned the place.

"'Cause I'm taking you to my honey hole tonight. Get all your nerdy notebooks ready, I'll throw in a fishin' pole for you too. You want pepperoni on your sub?" he shouted as he backed up to leave.

I rolled my eyes so hard I thought they might get stuck. "Extra pepperoni if you're buying!"

I didn't want to lead him on or give him the wrong impression, but my friends were few and far between, and though I did try to keep everyone at arm's length, sometimes it got lonely.

"Callie Peterson, quit flirting and get in here!" Cecelia's old voice echoed through the back building with a hint of distress.

"I'm coming. What's going on?"

I scooted Dorothy into her open playpen, noticing the loose feathers on the ground. She must have flown out of it to escape, which meant the tincture I developed last week might actually be working.

I almost skipped on the way up to the front in my excitement as I shoved through the double doors—just before letting out a scream.

CHAPTER 2

CALLIE

M Y SHRIEK WAS ENOUGH TO MAKE CECELIA DROP THE clipboard she had been holding. It hit the ground with a clang as the gray-haired woman clung to the large metal desk in shock. The mailman behind her visibly jumped with the clamor of screaming women and clipboard dropping.

"Mother Mary! Will you stop screamin' and take your damn package?" The old woman's voice sounded harsh, but I swore there was a glimmer of amusement in her eyes.

We had an interesting relationship, Cecelia and me. She acted like I was a nuisance, and I acted like it bothered me. Truthfully, she had been nothing but a sweetheart to me since I started at the rehab center. I would even call her a friend, but I'm sure that wouldn't look very good to her fellow townies, so occasionally, she pretended to find my bubbly nature annoying. At least, I thought she was pretending.

"My microscope!" I squealed, running over to the large brown box that waited for me on the desk.

Golden light from the heavens beamed down dramatically over the package as angels sang a victorious tune—at least in my head.

After dramatically picking up the abandoned clipboard,

Cecelia finished her task and handed her signature back to the shocked mailman.

"Told you she was off her rocker," she shouted dramatically as he hurried out the front doors.

I scooped up the large box and ran back to my office to open it up. I'd been waiting on this equipment for nearly a year. A year! My hands began to tremor, and my vision blurred from excitement. This was better than any Christmas morning I had ever had, even though those had stopped when I was a young kid anyway.

The ALMScope B/20c was the best in-field compound microscope available. When Stanley, my boss, told me to just "deal with it" after I had begged for a new microscope, I decided to take matters into my own hands. Months ago, the old one had quit working completely. I had to have one though. How else would I find *them*? Plus now, when I get called to Mexico to help track the monarchs, I can take it with me.

I was glowing, I was sure of it. Like someone had poured a fresh pitcher of hope into my system.

I set the box on my small metal desk, ignoring the adorable cage of brown and gray baby bunnies to my right. They were ready for rerelease today. I made a mental note to get Cliff to help me rerelease them in the meadow today before we did anything else. I also needed to check through my books and letters for any more details from my family on when I might get the chance to see them.

I was readying my glass slides, about to take them for a trial run, when my cell phone rang. The sound of Vivaldi's *Four Seasons* played loudly from my dark-green backpack on the floor.

With the temperament and mentality of a pouting toddler, I carefully—yet dramatically—set my new slides on the desk and made certain they were secure before I pulled the moth-covered iPhone case from my bag's front pocket. I didn't recognize the number, so they would get my very official and professional salutation.

"Hello, this is Cal–Callie Peterson?"

"Callie, it's Mary again. How are you?"

I froze, afraid to move for fear the tiniest shift in my appendages would alter the course of this conversation. Today *was* going to be the best day ever.

"Mary, oh my stars. Mary from the Lepidoptera Migratory Society?"

This was it. The call I had dreamed about for years was happening.

The other woman chuckled. "Yes, the butterfly lady. Listen, I just reviewed your work from last year's Actias luna migration. We had no idea they were so abundant in Willow Springs. Your thoughts on using mycelium to eradicate the Compsilura concinnata are absolutely astounding."

I shifted to sit in my chair, attempting not to make a sound. My body hovered for a second, praying the ominous screech from the wheels wouldn't ruin this dreamlike moment.

"Oh, thank you! Ever since I was little, I've had somewhat of an obsession with winged creatures. If I can do anything to help them, I'd love to dedicate my time to the cause. We ran a few similar trials with the Pteropus scapulatas, and the megabats showed significant promise with parasitic immunity." I let out a breath.

Did I sound too eager? I needed to follow these monarchs; the luna moths were proving to be leading me nowhere.

"Well, listen, I know that this is important to you, but… it's just—how do I say this?" The woman's alto voice would forever be etched into my memory.

Please let this be good news!

"Say what?" I asked as I attempted to steady my voice from raising seven octaves due to the excitement of what I was certain was about to be said.

"You know that if you get the position you requested in Mexico, you'll be in the field…for years? Some of the others are concerned that a young, pretty thing such as yourself might…well, might end up wanting *more* than the lonely field life of chasing butterflies. It's not as glamorous as a lot of people think. You don't have kids or a husband, and I don't mean to pry, but don't you think that's something you'll want? Especially at your age?"

I tried to breathe but forgot how. Darkness crept into the edges of my sight. I could hear the rejection lacing her voice.

"No," I said, feeling frustrated. "I don't have kids *or* a husband, and I won't be getting either. Just because I'm twenty-nine doesn't mean my hormones have gone feral and I feel the need to reproduce, Mary. I-I know what I applied for, and I plan to see it through." Did I sound too stern? I added a huffed laugh, just in case.

"Believe me, honey, I know. It's just, most of the people doing this project are older, with grown children, or retired. You know how it is. We've already lived, so it's easy for us to focus on the work at hand. Listen, I think you'd be great. The theories you have sent over here were more amazing than anything I've seen in a really long time. It could be life-changing to the conservation of Lepidoptera, and I don't care about your personal life. I'll do what I can to sway the others."

I wasn't sure what to say. "Umm…thanks."

Words eluded me, and the wind had been knocked out of me. The awkwardness in the conversation hung thick like a damp blanket now.

"The Actias luna should be making their way to you in the next week or so, isn't that correct? From what I understand, they have been hit pretty hard with the Compsilura concinnata as well. Be surprised if you even see any at all again this year, but if you do…anyway, I will let you go, Callie. I'll speak with the others and tell them how committed you are. Send me some pictures of the moths if you get any good ones!"

The woman's voice overlapped my worry.

"Okay, Mary, will do. Please keep me updated."

I tapped the end button and tossed it onto the desk, not caring if it shattered into a million tiny pieces. I turned my head to stare at the new microscope. The glowing light and angelic sounds had receded and were now replaced with the anxiety of how much I'd actually spent when I should have been saving my money to follow the butterflies.

I wasn't getting the position, and I knew it.

I swiveled my chair around, no longer excited about my new toy. Little squeaks greeted me as I watched Dorothy weakly flap out of the metal playpen and trounce into the open doorway of my small office. I wheeled over to her and stroked her back feathers.

"Well, look at you, miss *two*-winged hotshot," I sang to the sweet bird.

Cecelia paused in the hallway to lean against the metal of the tiny office door frame. "Is it broken?" she asked, nodding to the microscope sitting on the cluttered desk.

She crossed her wrinkly arms over her chest. Cecelia reminded me of a mother watching her children pout. She brushed her grayish-yellow hair out of her face and back into the fluffy mullet it had fled from.

"No...well, I don't know. I didn't finish opening it. The butterfly lady with the group in Mexico just called." I tucked my knees to my chest in the chair to get more comfortable as Dorothy pecked her way around the various cages and stacks of boxes in my office. It was a very small space filled with red-and-yellow speckled floors, white cement paver walls, and one shrouded window that looked over the woods and parking lot to the side.

My coworker shifted at my mention of the butterfly lady like she was secretly excited too.

"Well? What did she say? Are you going to Mexico and leaving us?" Her gray eyes peered over her glasses with the focus of a hawk.

"I don't think so." Saying the words out loud made them real, and I instantly wished I could vacuum them back in. "She didn't say no, but...I guess the other scientists are concerned I'll abandon the project halfway through to get married and have babies. Apparently, I haven't lived enough at twenty-nine years old."

I couldn't look her in the face. I was too afraid of seeing someone else that agreed. I just wanted someone on my side for once. Why did everything feel so hard?

"Well, good," she bit out defiantly.

"Good?" I said, looking up in surprise. "I've spent my entire life devoted to the saving of wildlife, and I'm about to get refused my *dream* position of saving more wildlife because I've done just that," I huffed. "Instead of going out on dates, I stayed up all night researching. Instead of spending my weekends with my family, I propagated milkweed for the monarch butterflies, and now I'm going to miss out on my dream because I was too dedicated?" I stood, nearly screaming.

"Oh, so what? I, for one, am glad they don't want you. I'm tired of you thinkin' you need to go all the way to Mexico to make a difference. Look at what you've done here in this hole-in-the-wall. You've done more for the wildlife around here than all of us combined, and I'm glad you're not leaving." She finished her speech with an actual harrumph.

She meant well, and if I were a normal person, it would have warmed me, but sometimes it was like I could only feel with half a heart.

I had a plan, and I wouldn't let anything stop me from achieving my goals. The chance to work with an organization filled with special details of where the winged butterflies and moths migrated was a part of that.

"Well, she didn't say no yet. She said she was going to talk to them, but I could hear it in her voice. Maybe it's a good thing I'm staying," I said in an attempt to comfort both of us.

"Yeah, fuck 'em!" Cecelia shouted, making me jump.

"Geez, Cecelia!" I blushed at her aggressive swearing.

Call me old-fashioned, but Callie Peterson certainly wasn't the type to use such crass language. I was a scientist, not a sailor. Was that childish? Either way, it made me feel like I was hearing something I shouldn't be.

15

"You don't need 'em. Save our damn butterflies. Show 'em what they're missing." The course woman turned and walked back into the hallway, smiling.

"You're right. I don't need them!" I said, feeling a little more resilient.

I had moved here to follow luna moths and hadn't seen one yet. Maybe this was a sign to focus on what was in my own backyard.

I rested my hands on my khaki-clad hips and turned to look at the wandering turkey and curious teen bunnies that watched me.

"I'll show them. I'll save our own damn—" I coughed and mumbled like a child. I really couldn't swear. "Our own darn butterflies! Well, moths, to be precise but..." I was quickly losing steam, and I turned to finish unwrapping my new microscope. "I am going to find and save the luna when they come to Willow Springs."

CHAPTER 3

CALLIE

Y OU'RE DOING WHAT NOW?" ASKED CLIFF AS HE STOOD OVER me in the deep green grass.

"Don't move. You make them nervous," I reprimanded the hovering man as I tried to shoo the teenage bunnies into the grassy field.

They didn't seem interested in leaving. All five brownish-gray rabbits continued to play and bounce about my legs as I sat stretched out in the grassy field.

"They don't look nervous to me. They look like they don't want to leave you, Disney princess." I could hear the smirk in his voice without looking.

"I'm going to—" I started before Cliff cut me off.

"In non-nerd terms, something I can understand, please." He smiled down at me. His golden locks were covered by a worn ball cap, leaving just a few tufts of disheveled, sun-drenched hair to pop out wildly.

I had goals and dreams, and they didn't involve love. Love made you hurt. Love made you distracted and inevitably sad and empty when it fell apart.

"Ouch!" My love-hating thoughts were interrupted as one of the small bunnies took a taste of my finger.

I loved animals. They couldn't drive. They couldn't crash rushing home to see you. They couldn't leave you with an empty hole in your chest. I missed my family so much.

Why weren't they running off into the field like normal wild bunnies? They hadn't been at the center for very long and had been cleared and ready to be off on their own.

Instead of running free the moment they were let out into the wide-open meadow of the large state park, they bounced around our legs in circles playing happily. I wasn't in a huge rush, and they were a beautiful distraction. Although, I *was* rather eager to evaluate the infamous honey hole and see what I could do to help the bass of Lake Blackwing, if anything.

"I'm going to save the moths. I only took this position because it was on the migratory pattern of the Actias luna. Several, if not all, of the lepidoptera are in danger of extinction due to the Compsilura concinnata parasite. I hypothesized that by infusing the water source with the mycelium of the Amanita muscaria, I could reestablish their immunity, thus creating a continuation of—"

"I said in terms a normal human would understand, Callie," Cliff interrupted as he tried to shove a few of the fluffy bunnies off into the field.

I rolled my eyes so hard I was surprised I didn't see my brain. "The big green moths that come here have a parasite that's killing them. Parasite bad, moths good." I grinned at a fluffy bunny in front of me. "I'm going to take the pretty red mushrooms and make a drink for the moths that will kill off the bad parasites, allowing them to thrive."

"You mean the big red mushrooms with the white specks? I thought those were poisonous?"

"Well, to us, they can be *highly* poisonous, but they also contain trace amounts of psilocybin, so people have been known to party with them. Foolishly too, because too many and they can easily kill you."

I had started walking in wide circles, trying to get the

bunnies to wander off. It looked like a bad magic act as they followed absentmindedly behind me.

"Geez, Callie, you really are different," Cliff said with a sincere look as he watched me now try to outrun the bunnies.

"What do you mean?"

My mouth felt dry and thirsty as I stopped running and crossed my arms. The sun would be setting soon, and if the bunnies didn't get out into the woods before dark, I would have to take them back to the center. How in the heavens would I tell Cecelia *another* of my releases wouldn't...release?

"I ain't pickin' on ya, Callie, I mean it. You're smart enough to be some big hotshot scientist at a big company making tons of money, but instead, you're in bum-fuck Willow Springs running from rabbits with a hundred-year-old truck, livin' in an old hunting cabin that stinks of piss. All 'cause you wanna help moths. You're as sweet as they come, Callie Sue."

"Thanks, Cliff, that's sweet. I just want to help the creatures that can't help themselves. I'm nothing unusual. Look at you. You're the game warden. That's a big deal." I smiled broadly at the man in an attempt to refocus the conversation, waving at the bunnies. "If they don't leave soon, I'm going to have to take them back to the center with us. Go! Go now, sweet bunnies! It's time. If you ever need me, you know where to find me, but right now it's time for you to go," I shouted at the bouncing cotton balls, suddenly wishing I could leave this situation. Maybe going fishing alone in the dark with Cliff tonight wasn't such a good idea. He normally was really nice and a great friend. It was usually never weird, but lately, he had been putting the flirting in overdrive.

All the bunnies froze to watch me as I scolded them. It was quite comical. Then, as though commanded, they each bounced happily off in different directions. Some into the woods, and some into the thicket of the field as though they had simply been waiting for my word.

Cliff and I looked at each other.

"Wow," Cliff murmured to himself. "Disney fuckin' princess."

"Okay…well, I guess we can go now. Do you mind running me over to Don's so I can pay him, on the way to my house?" I asked as we walked out of the field and back to Cliff's truck.

That was one of the major perks of working at a national state park—you could drive your truck all over the paths. Small perk, sure, but when you had to walk all over the eight hundred and twenty-nine thousand acres every week, it became a massive perk.

The air was already starting to cool, and the sun had only just begun to creep lower. That meant fall was just around the corner—my favorite time of year and the perfect time for harvesting mushrooms for the luna moths' anti-parasite cocktail.

We settled into Cliff's truck and headed through the familiar paths back to the main road. "Just grab what you need from the center, and we'll head to the lake. You don't need to bother stopping at Don's; I took care of it," he said, not taking his eyes off the road ahead.

"What do you mean you took care of it?" I asked the side of his face as I stared at the bit of stubble he had missed shaving.

I knew he was trying to be nice, but I didn't need anyone to "take care" of my things, and it bristled something deep inside me to have anyone get that close.

"It's not a big deal. I traded him some fishin' tags he needed," he said, his face still stoically turned toward the road.

"That sounds like either a stupid deal or an illegal one," I said, raising my eyebrows at him. "Thank you, Cliff, but I'd rather just pay him."

"Suit yourself, Callie," he said with a shake of his head, his body stiff.

We had pulled into the empty parking lot of the center. I ran in and finished the last bit of tidying and locking up that I needed to do before quickly returning to the shiny gray truck.

"Would you mind just taking me home, Cliff? I think I'm going to pass on the bass tonight. I don't want the town talking, and I really do have lots of things I need to get in order if I'm going to have this mycelium set up and harvested in time for the luna moths," I said with a sheepish smile, the same as I had rehearsed inside.

He clenched his jaw but didn't say anything. He'd known me long enough to know arguing with me would go nowhere.

"Whatever you want," he said as he abruptly slammed the shifter into drive. "Stacy Perkins has been dying to see my honey hole…and I kinda wanna see hers too." He grinned childishly, his stare holding mine a moment too long.

He was hoping to make me jealous and get a reaction out of me, but unfortunately, the only thing I was severely jealous of was that Stacy's family had a very secret morel mushroom patch they refused to share the location of.

"Well, I hope you have a lot of fun; you deserve it. If you want, I can get a ride with Hank or Cecelia tomorrow morning," I said.

Had I refilled the deer feeder in my back lot? Poor things were probably hungry. I added that to the mental checklist of things to do when I woke up the next day.

Cliff huffed a loud pouty breath but remained silent until we pulled into the winding gravel drive of my lot. I couldn't help but admire it every time I came back to the house. Of all the places I'd moved to, and there were a lot, this was by far my favorite.

Tall oaks and maples scattered the forest on either side of the long, curving driveway in a warm, picturesque way. I only owned two acres, but the woods surrounded it for about twenty acres on either side, lending to the cozy illusion. It was incredible, quiet and solitary, laced with a special warmth and character that I loved.

The gravel crunched and shifted under the tires as the

small house came into view. It was only a one-bedroom cabin covered in mismatched brown and tan siding and a black-shingled roof. No frills and absolutely nothing I didn't need. One shuttered window on either side of the front door and a bright-blue tarp that I parked under attached to the side. I loved it. Every type of wildflower I could find was scattered across the property. I had large beds of pollinator-friendly flowers strewn about, as well as several mushroom patches and a few deer gardens. I didn't bother trying to grow anything for myself here; animals were ever-present on this property, and I was more than happy to help feed them instead of myself anyway. Sometimes they felt like the only real friends I had, and they couldn't run to Tate's grocery like I could when I got hungry.

I waited as Cliff turned the truck around in the small gravel rectangle next to my house. "Thanks again for the ride, Cliff. I really do appreciate it," I said with a smile and stepped out of the truck.

"Yeahh, whatever," he said. "Hey, you know who you should talk to about those 'shrooms you're looking for?" he added as he popped a fresh toothpick into his mouth.

"Well, I'm not looking for them yet. They are predominantly found with birch and a few diverse conifer trees—"

"Talk to Crazy Earl. If they have the stuff that you get high off of and are around here, that bastard will know where to find 'em," he said as he chewed on the end of the small wooden stick.

"I knew it!" I shouted so loud Cliff jumped, dropping the toothpick from his mouth. "Sorry," I said apologetically as I calmed my voice, attempting to harness my excitement.

Earl probably did have a field of psilocybin-loaded mushrooms behind that gas station.

I said goodbye to Cliff and continued inside my home, setting my bag on the glossy cream tile just inside the front door. I unbuttoned my stiff khaki shirt. A few of the brightly colored patches had begun to peel up from the firm fabric.

Inside the bathroom that led to the only bedroom in the house, I paused in front of the mirror to assess the ironing that would be necessary.

I smiled at my reflection. Large ball lights cast a yellow hue on the big smile of straight white teeth that stared back at me, the result of three years' worth of incessant orthodontist appointments. My pale, dirty-blonde hair had bleached out this summer, giving me natural highlights along with a tan face full of freckles. I would wake up early and fix the loose patches on my work shirt. No sense in waiting for them to fall off. I made a mental checklist of my duties for tomorrow. Well, I made a mental note to write myself a checklist, I should say. I was a fool for lists. My entire being revolved around notes and checklists.

I washed my face before patting it dry. I scrunched my face in the mirror and made myself smile.

I was happy with who I was. Things were often hard, but I knew there was a light at the end of every tunnel. If the Lepidoptera Migratory Society didn't want me, that was okay. I understood not wanting someone to flake halfway through a long project to go have a family. But them assuming that was something I would want or do, made me sad. I could never whole-heartedly love someone, not after everything that had happened in my past.

I would prove to them I was serious about the conservation of moths and butterflies, and they would accept me eventually. They had to.

How else would I find him?

If the society members took one step into my house, they would know just how serious I really was about butterflies.

Photos of wings lined every wall in my small home. Beautiful feathered falcon wings backlit by abstract colors. Realistic paintings of every species of bat and bird wings lined my entryway. I had even added a photo of Dorothy the turkey's now not-so-injured wing to the kitchen wall collection. Some from my family's postcards with wings, several from antique stores.

I had dedicated the last ten years of my life to following the Actias luna, or luna moth as most people called it. The parks sent me an email after seeing a TED Talk I had done on the importance of integrating wildflowers and pollinator gardens into rural and residential properties. Several places with growing luna moth populations had reached out, and Willow Springs State Park was one of them. They said the job offer was a long shot for such a small state park, but when I googled where it was, everything changed.

I had been mapping the luna moth's migratory patterns for years after my best friend had piqued my interest in them. There was one place in particular that always seemed to be a hot spot for the moths, but it never made any sense. I was specifically looking for where they gathered, so this was intriguing.

What was it in the small area of Willow Springs, Michigan, that drew such a large luna moth crowd? Well, I had to find out and see them for myself, so I emailed an acceptance letter the very same day. Do I regret being so rash? Not at all. It was incredibly unfortunate that their numbers had dwindled so low the following year that I hadn't actually been able to see any, or even one for that matter.

I would see them this year in person. I knew it. There were certain things that drew them to this area, and I needed to know what they were.

I looked at the painting of the cloudless sulphur butterfly on the bathroom wall, and recalled Cliff calling me "different". My butterfly and moth obsession started when I was little, before I even knew what a scientist was.

One day, I had been out playing in the meadow behind our old house. I was seven or eight years old. My younger sister had been out with me, following me around as I picked dandelion bouquets for my mother.

A sharp pain seared through my chest at the memory, like the pain was looking for them but could only find an empty piece to land on. I gripped the smooth vanity counter and breathed through the feeling. It hurt like the very day it happened.

The day the car accident ripped my mom and sister from my life. The only real family I had.

But this was before that horrible day. I could see the sunlit field as if it were yesterday. Dandelions were the chosen flower to pick for my mother until I happened to see little bell-shaped mushrooms. I instantly decided that Mom would be delighted to have a bouquet of smashed bell mushrooms and dandelions combined. This was where things started to get odd. The tiny mushrooms were strewn through the tall grass, a bit past where we were supposed to play, but Mom was inside, and I had decided she wouldn't mind if I wandered a little in an effort to get her something beautiful.

As I collected an exceptionally bright and beautiful mushroom, a tiny glowing bug stood beneath it. Only, once I had moved closer in an attempt to get a better view of the odd bug, I realized it wasn't a bug at all. Stunning golden wings fluttered behind the tiniest person I'd ever laid eyes on. I had read the tales my mother gave me, they were some of my favorites, and I knew I had found a fairy. Her entire body had shimmered gold in the amber sunlight, and her orange and yellow butterfly wings seemed to be illuminated. Even her tiny dress had hung from her dainty body like a glittering ray of sunlight. I could still recollect the intricate updo of coiled golden curls that had rested upon her head. Her tiny eyes gleamed as though they were little citrine stones framed by delicate features and a tiny mouth. I was in complete awe.

I threw my bouquet to the ground, save for the tiniest and most pristine of the dandelions I had picked. That one I pulled free and rested at her feet as I had lain upon my belly to chance a better view of the beautifully winged creature. I was set to make my plea, asking how I could become a fairy as well, when a sudden gust of wind, quite unlike anything I'd ever felt still to this day, flung me several feet away from the tiny fairy and onto my back. I remember it like it was yesterday. I had landed on a stick that dug viciously into my baby-skinned palm. It had even left a tiny, jagged scar that I still possessed in the shape of a small V by my thumb. I remembered looking at Adrianna and making certain my baby sister was all right. She was unfazed and playing with a toad she had come across. When I had turned to check on the fairy, a large wispy-looking crow, bigger than any I had ever seen, swooped down at the speed of a torpedo. I cried out in pure horror as the giant black bird flapped viciously as it tried to kill the golden fairy. Don't ask me how I knew it was trying to kill it. I don't have a solid answer other than I could feel it. The golden fairy brought feelings good and wholesome, of tenderness, while the horrible crow emanated a sort of evil and vile response.

I ran as fast as I could to the helpless fairy and covered it with my own small body. I could see the glow of light bouncing upon my stomach and chest as I shielded her from the bird. It had continued its attack, only my back and head were then targeted. It flapped so wildly, so intensely.

I remembered looking up and crying, wishing with every fiber of my being that the bird would leave us. Then, a mere second later, with a puff of unnerving black smoke, the bird had transformed into an entirely different creature. Though about the same size as the large bird, this creature was more human than not. It had a similar build to the golden fairy, but instead of beautiful delicate butterfly wings, this creature carried inky black wings that looked to be made of macabre black smoke. The wings seemed to be longer than they were wide and were attached more to her shoulders than her back. The wings, no less beautiful, were different in their own right. Everything about the creature was. Where the golden fairy had oozed happiness and smiles that made me think of sunshine and summer, this creature made me feel only terror and fright, like death watched over my shoulder. Smoke seemed to flow from nowhere, surrounding her long black hair. A chill had cascaded down my spine as she stared at me with absolute hate.

What happened next, I couldn't tell you. I must have passed out because I woke up later in a small hospital room surrounded by every family member I had ever known hovering over my metal-railed bed. When I tried to tell them what had happened and find out if the golden fairy was all right, they laughed and cried, their faces full of regret.

Apparently, the beautiful bell mushrooms I picked had been highly poisonous, and the toxins had seeped into my little hands, causing hallucinations of astonishing proportions. At least, that's what they had said.

It hadn't mattered. What I had seen (or not seen) changed my life forever. From then on, I was obsessed with winged creatures.

I ran my thumb across the tiny V-shaped scar on my palm as I revisited the memory. I never got into drugs or parties, so I had no basis for comparison to my experience.

I met my best friend Eli shortly thereafter, and he had believed me. He had even encouraged me to follow my passion for wildlife.

I would see the luna moths this year and help rid them of the parasites that claimed them. Then I would get to see the treasures they held in all their glory.

CHAPTER 4

CALLIE

FOR AS IN SHAPE AS I WAS FROM ALL OF THE HIKING, I WAS still *just* out of shape enough that the monthly feed refill was every bit as hard as it had been the month prior, and the month prior to that.

It was still early morning. The beautiful birds chirped and sang their happy wake-up calls of tweets. The grass held drops of dew along with the orange blanket of a rising sun. The unmistakably crisp morning scent clung to the air like a promise, a whisper of fresh stars and pine.

I was attempting to quickly refill the various animal feeders I had placed across my property upon moving in. The fifty-pound bag of corn felt closer to three hundred pounds after all was said and done. I had finally arrived at the large black barrel resting on the far back edge of my property. Without the off-roaders to drive like at the park, I had felt the burn of the short hike more than I cared to admit.

"Holy stars, I need to start varying my workouts," I reprimanded myself as I tossed the feeder's lid aside and ripped open the woven plastic bag of feeder corn.

I needed to be quick if I was to be back at the house in time for Cliff to pick me up for work. A call from Don at the repair shop last night solidified my regret that I spent every penny of my paycheck on a field microscope—and that I got the "deal of a lifetime" on the old, used truck. I should return the microscope. I knew I ought to, but would I? Heck no, I wouldn't. Because that baby was going to help me secure my place among the Lepidoptera Migratory Society (okay, can we just agree to call it LMS from here on? That's quite a mouthful) and follow my dreams.

After dumping the bag of dried corn into the feeder, I replaced the lid. It locked into place, and I swatted away the barrage of dusty corn smoke that clouded my vision. All the deer feeders were stocked, the bee feeders hung, the hummingbird feeders refilled, and the bird feeders all loaded. Everything should be fed. All that was left was to quickly water my bird baths. I turned to head toward the back of my house, where the spigot was located, when I stilled.

No more than seven feet from where I froze stood the most beautiful red fox.

It was small but proportionate, its slim body giving the cute fluffy illusion of a house cat or pet dog. A large, fluffy, black-tipped tail, so full of fur it almost looked out of place, hung from the back of its smooth orange-red body. Small black paws completed the adorable ensemble of fur leading up to its fluffy head and pointy black ears.

My breath caught in my chest.

The air felt like it would rip through my sternum if it couldn't locate an exit from my body. This fox's features were unlike any fox species I knew, and I knew them all. A white patch of chest fur was topped by a slyly pointed V-shaped nose. Black whiskers and a wet black nose at the end. Normal enough. But it was the eyes. Something about the creature's eyes seemed to speak to me in a language I wasn't fluent in. It watched me completely still and motionless. Those golden eyes never once wavered from mine. They weren't just golden, they were every shade of yellow and brass ever known. The sharp eyes of liquid honey held mine, and for a blip in time, I felt a sense of familiarity, but the feeling was gone before I could pull anything further from it.

Foxes were not generally a predator to humans and were known to be quite skittish. The only time anyone came into contact with a sly fox was usually as it tried to steal their chickens or if it had gone rabid.

The dappled morning sun had begun to grow stronger and brighter. The amber glow shifted ever so slightly, or had the wind in the treetops picked up? Whatever the reason, it had caused the morning sun to shine directly on the back half of the beautiful fox, where another startling discovery awaited.

A million tiny fragments of gold seemed to reflect and sparkle from its fur as if golden shards of glass blanketed the mysterious animal. How could that be? How was the light producing that effect? On fur, no less?

My knees trembled furiously, and I was forced to shift my body weight to lock them in place so I didn't fall over. My small movement had already happened when I quickly froze, afraid my motion would scare this...thing away. I was breathing so intentionally that the act caused my eyesight and head to shift slightly.

I watched and waited. Silently readying myself for the exhale I would release when the fox inevitably scampered off, startled by my stirrings, in a flurry of red.

Instead, the fox sat.

It sat like a proper, elegant fox would sit as it wrapped its large fluffy tail around its round black feet. The sunlight blanketed every hair on the magnificent creature's trim body, and every one of those hairs glimmered in the light as if someone had thrown a jar of gold dust on it. I reached up slowly and rubbed my eyes to refocus them. Surely it would run from me now. A sparkle of awareness gleamed in the creature's beautiful eyes as it tracked my body, starting at my eyes and trailing down to my feet slowly.

I would have bet my entire house with everything in it

that the fox smiled at me. Like it was laughing at me. My mouth fell open, unsure whether to be startled or in awe.

It took a step forward, coming closer.

My heartbeat began to pick up its pace. What should I do? *Was I hallucinating?*

Could real foxes sparkle and smile at you? *Was I imagining this?*

I was about to find out. The fox took another slow step toward me.

"Callie, do you need any help?" Cliff's loud voice rippled through the woods as its owner walked into the clearing.

I glanced from Cliff back to the fox, readying myself to shout at Cliff to be quiet and look, but it was too late.

The fox was gone. Only the tiniest bit of black tail remained visible in the far-off brush.

"Oh, you already got it?" Cliff motioned to the empty plastic tub I held as I continued to play back what I had just witnessed, frozen in shock.

"Yeah, thanks," I murmured, still partially dazed.

"What's going on? You okay? You look like you've seen a ghost," he said, eyes concerned as he bent down, positioning himself directly in front of my face, blocking any other view.

"I uh...I just saw a fox," I mumbled as I shook my mind out of its blur and absently wiped the stray hair away from my face.

"Red fox? Which way did he go? Was he just passing by?" he asked nonchalantly.

I began walking back toward the house. Twigs and leaves compacted into the grass below my boots with each step as I tried desperately to make sense of what I had just seen.

"I guess. He went off that way." I pointed in the direction of the now-absent fox. "He just kind of...watched me, frozen. Then he started to come to me when you showed up. It was the strangest thing though, somehow the sun was refracting...shimmer-like prisms off his body." My voice trailed off, waiting to gauge his response.

"It what? Callie, he sounds rabid," Cliff snapped.

"It wasn't rabid. It was…it was beautiful," I tried to argue.

"Well, a fox wouldn't be that close to you without running if he wasn't rabid. I'm going to put out an APB for the boys to take care of it," he said sternly as he pulled a black walkie-talkie free from his pocket and pressed a few buttons, inducing a loud beep that abruptly unsettled the peace of the forest.

"No! I said it wasn't rabid, Cliff! I'm sure it was just curious!"

We had stopped our trek back to the house to stare at each other.

"Callie, you can't save everything. If the boys see it and suspect it's rabid, it dies."

His voice held a tone of arrogance I loathed the very second it hit my ears. How had I never noticed it before?

"Please don't."

Why was he not more curious about the shimmering? I had said it out loud, right?

The rest of our walk was in silence. He suddenly seemed cruel, and I didn't feel comfortable sharing anything more with him. I wouldn't let them hurt that fox.

I hurried to throw away my trash in the outside cans before I locked the door from the outside, not wanting Cliff to have a reason to go inside.

"You don't need anything inside?" His voice held something unfamiliar. Something not quite new but something I guess I hadn't paid attention to before. "Need me to look at anything for you?"

Was he trying to get inside my house?

"Nope, I'm good. Listen, if it's out of your way at all, I can just get Cecelia to grab me on her way. Actually, that's probably a lot easier, isn't it? You're not even going to the center other than to drop me off?" Damn that old truck, this was becoming another problem I didn't need.

"I don't mind. Stop shoving everyone away. Now get your Disney princess ass in the truck before you're late. Who even feeds all these animals anyway? You know they're wild, right?" His smile flowed into his words, and back was the friendly man I had come to heavily rely on.

Maybe depending on him had been a mistake.

≈≈

"Crazy—" I hacked and coughed with embarrassment. "Earl, how are you? Can I help you with those books? That's quite a stack you've got there," I said. My face had to be the same color as a beet.

"Miss Callie, how ya doing?" The man stepped up the cement step to stand next to me. "Oh, don't you worry about it, they call me Crazy Earl 'cause they don't know what else to call someone like me, it's just how they remember me," the rosy-cheeked man said with a kind smile as he straightened the leaning pile of paperbacks.

His warm eyes contained a yellow copper tint with specks of green and brown.

"I'm sorry, Earl, really, that wasn't very nice of me. Let me help you with those." I tucked my iPhone into my front pocket and took a few of the books from him.

His smile noticeably widened a fraction.

"They're right about you, you know that? Twenty-seven years, ain't nobody ever said sorry for callin' me crazy." He chuckled so hard, I thought he might drop his books.

I glanced down at the pile of books to spot a few I recognized.

"*Entangled Life? Mystified Morels?* Earl, are these all books on mushrooms? I didn't even know Willow Springs library had some of these. What are you doing with all of these?" I asked as I stared at him.

The man positively glowed. Did this have anything to do with his partying? Cliff had said to talk to him about mushrooms...

"Help me take these to the car, and I'll tell you all about it. Matter-a-fact, why don't I just give you a ride? I heard your truck was still at Big Don's. That's what you were doing on the steps anyway, huh? Tryin' to find a ride?"

More perceptive than I would have thought. To be fair, I had only seen him in passing a few times at the gas station, and I was surprised he even knew my name. My first week here, he had tried to talk to me about the trees talking and forest bogs or something. After Cliff had told me of his unstable chaos and drug usage, I had avoided him. It was easy enough to believe from his unkempt appearance. It wasn't that he looked dirty or anything, there was just something in his appearance that made me sympathize with him for not being quite "all there." Though were any of us really all there?

I followed him across the parking lot to a small white hatchback. I hesitated to respond because, quite frankly, I was shocked that Earl read or drove. I had never actually spoken to him after that first day, so I'm not sure why I was so surprised by how articulate he sounded. I shouldn't have passed judgment on him simply from the words of others, mostly Cliff. And I did need a ride today.

"If you're sure I won't put you out?" I asked as I handed him the last of the books to be placed in the back seat of his car.

"Not at all! Happy to have the company of a fellow biologist for a spell, and a pretty one at that," he said with a smile as he got into the front seat.

Okay, I was intrigued. I'm quite sure I've never jumped in a stranger's car faster. "Fellow biologist?"

He chuckled warmly. "You know any other nut that checks out eight books on mycelium and six on the genealogy of bullfrogs?"

Why would no one have told me this? Surely Cliff knew. Why wouldn't he tell me Earl was a biologist too? I would have loved to talk to someone in my field.

"Forgive my surprise, Earl. I just had no idea. Are you still working?"

"Oh no, I umm…was let go. A hundred years ago, least

that's what it feels like now, I worked as a microbiologist for the state. Where to?"

I had been so busy bug-eyed staring at him that I hadn't realized he had been patiently waiting at the library exit for more instructions on where to take me.

"The rehab center, if it's not too far. I need to grab some equipment. So, you worked for the state?" My voice was rising to higher pitches with each new surprise.

I coughed to try and control it better. I had no one to talk to about work. Not the complain-about-who-stole-your-leftovers talk, Cliff got those, but the "oh my god, have you seen the cercariae in the lake that's giving everyone swimmers itch?" type of talk.

"No problem at all," Earl said as he took a right onto the main drag. "Yep, I was a professor of biology at a university for ten years before Michigan offered me a job. After twenty-three years, they...let me go." He stiffened his back and shoulders.

I noticed the slight shift in his eyes as he tightened his grip on the steering wheel ever so slightly.

"Wow, that's quite an accomplishment. I was told I was Willow Springs State Park's first biologist," I said, silently hoping I hadn't taken a job he had tried to get or replaced him and he was mad.

"Well, so far as I know, you are. I worked in a small group with the government. They hired me to explain a few odd things they'd been finding. It's how I ended up here as well." He tipped his head to me and smiled kindly.

It was gentle and honest, and I found myself liking him more by the second.

"Really? I thought you were from here."

I glanced around the cluttered interior of the car like a sleuth. Old mason jars, food wrappers from the local Chinese restaurant, endless balls of wadded-up paper littered the floor and back seat, and a few notebooks, but nothing out of the ordinary.

"No, I was brought out here for work, much like you, and guess you could say I got stuck. Cecelia said you got a new microscope?" he asked, eyebrows peaked with interest.

"Now, how is it this whole town knows what I had for breakfast or what's inside my packages, but I've never heard any of this about you?" I laughed, instantly hoping he didn't ask what exactly I had heard about him. "Oh, I know what you've probably heard about me," he murmured with a sheep-ish look. "It's okay, one day, I will prove to them all that I'm right."

"What microscope did you get? I'm shocked they finally broke down and bought one, tight as they are with their conservation funds. Usually, all the money goes to hunting and fishing. They'd rather spend money to kill nature than restore it." He shook his head gently as he stared at the road ahead.

I twirled a frayed thread over my stiff khaki knee. I'd never really thought of it that way, but it was true. Cliff and his boys got so much money for the things they needed. Even if they "needed" new Ford trucks, while the conservation depart-ment was so severely lacking that I had been forced to buy seeds myself this year as it "wasn't in the budget."

"Well, actually, I got the ALMScope B/20c. I bought it myself thinking it would be an investment toward my move to Mexico, tracking the monarch butterflies." I could feel my cheeks turn red.

"*The ALMScope B/20c*!?" Earl slammed on the brakes.

The action sent us flying forward abruptly before I slammed back against the seat, flinching. Dramatic much? He stared at me with the same expression I would have expected if the ghost of Abraham Lincoln walked past the window in a cowboy hat and tighty-whities.

"Yeah, I know, it was ridiculously expensive—"

"That's the best compound field scope available! Do you know the things I…ugh…you could see with that!? It has a double-layered mechanical stage! Four objective lenses! I could finally test them!" He was close to screaming now. If he hadn't looked so happy, it would have been incredibly frightening. "Would I be able to borrow it just once? Of course, if you'd like to come, that would be even better. My eyes aren't what they used to be, and I'm going to catch them this time." He stared off absently.

This was a way better reaction than Cliff's, though. Why couldn't everyone be so happy for me and my new microscope? And I was gaining a field buddy? This was quickly turning out to be one of the best days I'd had in a very, very long time.

"Of course you can use it!" I was screaming now too, apparently easily affected. I cleared my throat in an attempt to bring down my pitch as we stared at each other in the middle of the road. If he had been ten years younger, this would have been one heck of a meet cute. "Come inside, and you can see it!"

Both of us sat excitedly in the car for precisely another seven minutes until we pulled into the center's parking lot.

We both jumped out of the car like kids in front of a candy store. I took the lead, running up to the door and letting my new friend in. This felt very much like in the first grade when I found out my cubby buddy *also* liked rainbow unicorns, and I just had to show them my very best one. Maybe this was better than that.

"Hi, Cecelia!" I shouted as I ran through the doors into my office.

"Hi, Cecelia!" Earl shouted excitedly, following close behind.

"What in the hell's going on? Callie, why you runnin'? Earl? What in the hell are you doing here?" Cecelia shouted back, gawking at us.

"Callie's showing me her microscope! Why didn't you tell me it was the ALMScope B/20c!?" Earl yelled before entering my office.

"Tell you what now?" she said, clearly confused.

"Cece, do we have any more of those cookies in the front?" I called, turning back to Earl as I pulled out the sturdy black case and unlocked it on the table. "They're *really* good. Sometimes she even adds chocolate chips. Here, take a look!"

I stepped aside so he could take the seat nearest the microscope and handed him a few of the glass slides I had prepared earlier. The toilet water sample from the Piggly-Wiggly was still my favorite.

A hush fell over us as he set up and dialed in the apparatus. I could tell by his practiced movements he was quite used to being around one, and my body began to hum with the anticipation of his reaction. How amazing today was turning out to be!

"What scope do *you* have, Earl?" I asked.

"Don't have one now. My salary at the gas station doesn't really give me the means to buy such a fine microscope, and what I'm looking for, well, anything in my price range wouldn't be of help," he said, one eye pressed to the lens.

"What type of things are you working on that require such a microscope?" I asked.

There had been far too many books in his car for it to be just a hobby. Plus, microscopy as a hobby?

He gently moved his head away from the lens and sat back in his chair. He had a worn-out appearance, but I had no doubt he had likely been very popular with the ladies in his younger years. He had flipped his hat around backward to look in the eyepiece, and the position of the ball cap brought focus to his honey-colored eyes. Eyes now bloodshot and cloudy, nestled in wrinkles of time. I could tell he had been incredibly handsome once. Unkempt ash-gray hair clumped over his ears, pressed at odd angles from the ball cap that only seemed to add to his disorderly appearance.

"Some odd years ago, the state sent me here to look into a new genus of fungi that has only ever been found here, in Willow Springs." He caught his breath with a long pause as if deciding how much to say. "I saw some of the most peculiar

38

things when collecting data for this odd mushroom. We tried to cultivate it with no success. It has yet to turn up anywhere else but here." Immediately, curiosity trickled into my system. "I have seen things from the areas where they fruit that would make you fear the woods. It's as if something inhuman floats around it." He stood from the chair and smoothed his wrinkly orange T-shirt. He stared at the microscope on my desk.

"Sounds like a really intense find. What did they discover about it?" I crossed my arms and leaned against the cold wall as fascination overtook me.

He was an odd fellow, but that's what everyone had thought about me when I was a child and had insisted I saw fairies. Maybe there was more to this.

When he spoke, you felt his friendliness, could hear his articulation and intelligence. But just looking at him, he gave off an almost wild and "not all there" vibe. The whole thing was so peculiar, I couldn't help but unravel it a little more.

"Nothing. Years I worked to find everything I could about this mystical fruiting body. Eventually, the state incinerated my notes and fired me. Claimed I lacked the mental capacity to continue." He looked at the ground, unable to keep eye contact. "Maybe they were right."

"I don't think they were right, Earl," I said as I walked closer to pat his bony back.

"I wouldn't be so sure. You haven't even heard what I've seen." He replied, a tiny sparkle of hope in his cloudy eyes; it looked like it'd been a while since it had been there.

"Well, I'd love to hear more. I'm sure I don't know near as much about fungi as you, but I can hold my own on a foray. I'm actually collecting mycelium for a project I'm currently working on. It's to save the luna moth population," I murmured as I watched his face.

If he really did know as much as I suspected, then I wanted to get his help finding what I needed.

"Really?" He perked up like a golden retriever being handed a ball. "What are you looking for? Maybe I *can* help,

I'm practically a fungi map of Willow Springs at this stage." He smiled, just like I imagined a golden retriever would smile.

I pulled a stool out and sat down. I grabbed a thick manila folder of papers and handed it to Earl, who took them eagerly. He pulled a pair of readers from a case in his back pocket and began to look them over.

"Well, that's one of my problems," I stated, and my pulse quickened. "You see, I'm using the 'roots' of the mushroom's fruiting body, the mycelium. I need the highest levels of psilocybin possible to dose the water where the moths will drink. I'll place special feeders at the locations where the larvae have been predominantly hatched in the past, ensuring they are thirsty and will have the need to drink. The mycelium water will provide an eighty-six percent immunity growth from the parasites that are wiping them out."

I smiled so wide it made my cheeks hurt. Usually, no one understood how exciting this was. They just heard "make mushroom water to feed moths, and they will get better." I knew Earl would understand. The more moths, the easier it would be to track them.

"Holy shit, Callie," he murmured, staring wide-eyed at me from his seat. "That's absolutely brilliant. What's the problem?"

I tried to calm my smile.

"Well, the only problem is I need the highest levels of amatoxin possible in the mycelia, and the only mushrooms I've found that would work weren't plentiful enough and have already died out. There are only a few known varieties that even have that amount of amatoxin. The luna moths are expected to be here in less than a month, and I don't know of anything strong enough that I can get in time. I don't have time to spawn anything—"

"I know where you can find some now."

Goose bumps ghosted across my skin. It was almost too great of a coincidence. I looked up, feeling as if the world were in slow motion, and expected to see the happy golden

40

retriever again. But his face was somber and still as stone, but his eyes brimmed full of something I couldn't quite place. Regret?

"You do? How would I not have seen them?" I asked, feeling suddenly wary.

"Because they don't show up for everybody." He swiveled his chair to look at the microscope. "I know where to find them. It's the fungus that has ruined my life. They have only brought me heartache and distanced me from my loved ones." He cleared the emotion from his voice. "I hope they're what you need, Callie."

"Do they have a name?" I asked curiously.

The mushrooms that would help me the most were only rumored to even exist. I could use a less potent variety, but I wasn't entirely sure how well it would work.

He turned to me with a tired and heavy expression.

"Destroying angels."

CHAPTER 5

CALLIE

IN THE FEW WEEKS SINCE WE HAD OFFICIALLY TALKED AT THE library, Earl and I had been getting together daily. It reminded me so much of how I had been drawn to Eli. Sometimes he felt like a magnet that I just wanted to be near. It had been so long since I'd felt that comfortable with anyone. Since Eli had left, no one felt safe, especially after the deal I made with his mother.

What an odd string of events to have unfolded. Maybe it was all the incredible gems of information that he carried and my hope of finding the very thing he claimed to have been ruined by, but every day I grew closer to Earl, and for once, I let myself.

Our age gap alone could make our friendship a little odd, but if I was being honest, Earl was on the fast track to being one of the best people I'd ever known. I loved bouncing ideas off him. It felt so nice to share those parts of me and feel understood. Though I didn't completely understand some of the wild things he claimed to have witnessed (a horse made of only bones and a rosebush that farted and answered all his questions had been my favorites so far), I still thought of him as one of the most good-hearted people I had ever met.

Weren't all great scientists a little quirky? Isn't that just what a lot of brain power did to you? I would ask him about getting a haircut today. He deserved to feel good too.

Yeah, a haircut and some new clothes would help. I would do whatever I could to help the town see what a wonderful person Earl really was. It wasn't what I should be focusing on, but it wouldn't hurt. If all went well with finding these mushrooms, I would be leaving again soon, and I wanted to leave things nicer for my new friend if I could.

With our supplies loaded into the back of Earl's car, we headed out to the far edge of the state park. Equine and hiking trails ran throughout the grounds, but the western edge was left mostly to Mother Nature. There were no paths where we were headed, which would be both good and bad. A greater chance of mushrooms being left undisturbed, but the hiking was a lot rougher.

Approximately a hundred acres of dense woods and wildlife took up the majority of the property we would be scouting today. I didn't have a lot of reason to work in these parts, and it was always exciting to explore new places in the park. I was pretty familiar with Willow Springs State Park, but when Earl parked his car on the edge of the road, I couldn't remember this section.

"I know they are this way, I can feel them," Earl said, pausing with his door open to sniff the air like a dog.

"You said that about the last three spots," I said, smiling at him.

Truthfully, I was starting to lose a bit of hope. It had been foolish to think he had the answers to all my problems. My whole plan to find the luna moths and the destroying angel mushrooms seemed to be slipping further and further away, but at the same time, I was having some of the most fun I'd ever had foraging with Earl.

"They are hiding from me," he said, locking his car and grabbing his walking stick.

It was a beautiful light wood staff with designs carved

43

intricately throughout. Swirls surrounding wild-looking butterflies and a fox covered the top third with a beautiful sun carved neatly into the tip. He told me the fox had taken him nearly two months to complete, to which I told him what a fool he was for working at the gas station instead of selling his carvings. They were glorious. He had just chuckled and said the gas station gave him free coffee.

"Maybe *I'm* scaring them off," I said as we began our trek into the forest.

"It's much more likely that they hide in pity so that I can spend more time with you." He laughed.

It was close to three o'clock when we had gotten deep into the land. The sun beat down brightly above our heads, though we wouldn't have known it other than the heat it cultivated, for the trees had grown so large and thick left to their own devices that they blocked most of the light save for a few patches here and there filtering through the trees. We had been at it for a while, slowly walking around all the different trees in an effort to find the destroying angels. Earl was a great storyteller, so it was never dull or boring. I had grown so comfortable with him in the hours spent together the last several weeks. His wild stories were like balm to my soul.

"Earl, I hope you won't take offense to this," I said, readjusting my long hair into a big floppy bun atop my head, "but what do you think if we got your hair cut and some new clothes? You know I don't really care about appearances, but I guess…" I struggled to find the right words now that they were forming outside of my head. "Well, I guess I just thought that maybe the town would see how great you are if they weren't so focused on your appearance." I nervously turned to watch him circle a nearby oak, praying I hadn't offended the closest thing to a best friend I'd had in a long time.

"What do I care what everyone else thinks of me?" he said, keeping his honey-flecked eyes on the forest floor.

"Don't you get lonely sometimes? I know you have people that are nice to you in town, but…did you ever have the urge to get married and settle down? You and Cecelia get on nicely."

"Me? No, Cecelia is just a friend." He stopped, seemingly lost in thought. "Once, a long, long time ago, when I was a very foolish young man still living under my parents' roof, there was a girl. Back then, things were different though. She was from another country, and my family, being influential in the world of academics, believed her family and culture beneath us." He smiled boyishly at me and ran his hands through his hair. "It didn't matter in the end; I gave myself completely to work. We were only ever friends anyway, but I still think about her."

Suddenly my brain flooded with thoughts of myself in Earl's place forty years from now. Obsessed over my work, mad with it. No family, no loved ones. Only a town full of people who thought I had lost my mind.

My chest suddenly felt hollow. As if all the air had been sucked out. That would be me. I would be "crazy Callie".

"You okay? What's wrong, Cal?" Earl said, grabbing my elbow.

His grip was surprisingly strong for his bony frame.

His wrinkled face was close enough for me to see the gold specks that mingled with the warm honey of his eyes. I was flooded with sympathy as I watched his gaunt face search mine. Thin, wrinkled skin hung down from a jawline that once would have been sharp and masculine in his younger years. He was still handsome, but in the way I thought of when I saw old war photos of friends' grandfathers.

"I just was wondering if we both work too much. It's been ages since I got all dressed up, and I don't know, I was thinking that maybe we both should get cleaned up and have a night on the town."

I smiled at him so wide, I could feel the forest air hit my gums.

"Then a night on the town it is. I'm never one to turn down a pretty girl. You pick the day, and I'll be ready. I'll even get my hair cut just for you." Earl chuckled pleasantly. "I know just the—no."

I abruptly stopped to locate where Earl was and if he was okay.

To my right, about twenty feet near a few deciduous logs, Earl stood, his face frozen and downcast, looking to the ground.

"What is it? Are you all right? Did you find something?" I asked, feeling my stomach fall to my feet.

His face was frozen. No expression. No movement.

I made it to his side in a moment, only to suck in enough oxygen to fill a hot air balloon.

"They are never far from me, even when I wish they would be," Earl said as he stared at the perfect white mushroom, and a puzzling expression crossed his face.

"Oh my god, is this it?" I asked, my voice barely above a whisper, apparently worried I might spook the mushroom.

When I looked at Earl, I expected to see a big smile on his face staring at the large mushroom.

Instead, regret and misery overlaid his worn features as he stared at me instead.

"Yeah, this is it."

Unsure whether he was sad to be near the fungi that had seemingly haunted his life or possibly the realization that our forays were over now that we had found our prize, I grabbed him into a big hug.

"Thank you so much! Now we really will have something to celebrate!" I cried as I squeezed him.

He had found it.

I looked around the trees, suddenly hopeful. The lore was that the luna moths and butterflies were drawn to this specific mushroom, and I had begun to suspect that was why they happened to be so concentrated here as opposed to everywhere else.

I saw nothing, but the luna moths were nocturnal and wouldn't be here yet. I peeked around, unable to stop myself from searching for any other winged creatures but came up empty-handed.

"Yes, I suppose we will. I really have enjoyed spending this time with you so much, Callie," he said, squeezing me back before he released me.

"I promise this isn't the last of our forays." I moved back to look into his cloudy eyes. "I need more mycelium than this one mushroom as it is. Hey, look! Nothing spooky around here now," I said confidently.

With some of the stories he had told, I half expected a monster to leap out from the patch behind the mushroom.

He smiled weakly at me but seemed to shake himself out of whatever sadness had clutched him. "You must be lucky," he murmured as he looked around.

"How great! Let's collect this, it's getting dark, and I really want to use my new microscope before we have to leave!" I practically sang. "Let's come back tomorrow and look for more, you free?"

By this time, the dense forest had grown dull with slate-gray skies. The air felt suddenly thick and mucky. I didn't see a storm in the forecast, but nature had no rules. No one knew that better than me. This was strange though. It was almost…a feeling. Something felt wrong, but I couldn't put my finger on it. It was exceptionally odd because I had just felt so happy. This mushroom could potentially be the answer to all my problems. So why did I feel like I wanted out of here as fast as possible? I couldn't help but look around the darkening forest floor as a feeling of dread began to overtake me. The giant trees hemmed us in as the whispers of fear began to trail across my skin.

I was being ridiculous. There was nothing here.

I placed my pack on the floor, but my body screamed at me to hurry and gather the sample so we could leave.

Something brushed against my arm as I knelt to pull out my equipment.

47

I leaped sideways to get away from it, nearly crushing my microscope as I clumsily fell on the ground next to it.

"Fuck! What is it, Cal?"

Earl launched toward me and helped me up with shaking hands. The harsh tone didn't sound like him, and it only made me more uneasy.

"It's Callie, not Cal," I said under my breath after thanking him for helping me.

He straightened his suspender strap and knelt to help me with the equipment.

"You feel it too, don't you?" he asked, looking at my face.

I really didn't want to admit it to him, but yes, I felt it too.

It was the shadow of a skin-crawling feeling, the leaking drip of terror before the true fear engulfed you. The feeling was so sudden and disturbing—I felt like we were marinating in it. It was like the feeling you get when you're alone and you know someone is watching you. No sounds to tip you off, no warnings, just a feeling. Except instead of feeling eyes on me, I felt...pure evil and darkness. Something hovered threateningly in the air that told my body to get away as fast as possible, that we were not safe.

Any other time, I would have searched nearby for more destroying angel mushrooms. Typically, where one mushroom grew, there were plenty of others hidden, and I needed to find a patch of several, but my mind was forbidding the thought of staying a second longer than necessary.

"Yeah, I do. Are we safe?" I asked, sort of embarrassed to be asking it out loud.

"For now. I'm really sorry, Cal. I hate that you are around any of this." He stared at his feet.

The expression was as forlorn as if his favorite dog had died. I felt terrible; I wanted to help him.

"Are you kidding? You have helped me in so many ways. You have been the best friend I've had in a long time, and I really needed a good friend," I said, hoping to make him feel better.

I really was grateful, but this ominous feeling was messing with my head. Was any of what he had said true? I pushed it into a compartment to dissect later, half expecting a black unicorn to trot out in front of me.

We finished collecting the slide samples and packed up quickly. The entire time Earl seemed to be regretting the decision to bring me here.

Under the microscope, the spores of the destroying angel looked unlike anything I could have ever imagined. Where spores normally looked like tiny beige bubbles or eggs, the destroying angel spores looked unreal, like black smoke trying to escape the glass. My blood was pounding so hard in my ears that I had barely heard the thunder that began to rumble.

"We gotta get out of here. I can't do this!" Earl shouted as a wild gust of wind dove violently through trees, shoving our jackets and clothes wherever it commanded.

"I just need to collect the whole specimen!" I shouted back.

The sudden aggression of the wind made it so I had to yell. It was only one mushroom, but I wouldn't risk coming back for it. I needed it now. Branches bare and full of foliage alike smacked and slammed the bodies of neighboring trees with each ominous gust. Earl's cap flew off, now a prisoner to the wind.

Normally I enjoyed storms. I liked the patter of rain on my windows and the peaceful rumble of thunder. I'd fallen asleep to it many times.

But not here and not now. This was anything but peaceful. Though there was still no rain, the smoky gray forest seemed to pulse as if readying itself for something evil. I've never felt anything like it. I was a practical woman, so it was even more unsettling to have my body suddenly react the way it was. I saw no threat, nothing but a storm. Nothing to provoke these feelings of...darkness?

A loud clap of thunder sent me nearly out of my boots as I jumped. Seeing Earl jump didn't make me feel any less scared. I nearly fell, scrambling to shove items back into my pack with pure determination to leave.

I had a fleeting thought before I placed the mushroom in the container and in my pack. Was this a bad omen? I typically wasn't superstitious, but I couldn't help feeling weird about what was happening.

Mere moments after I pulled up the mushroom and a few thin roots to cultivate, the oddest thing happened.

The gray began to clear from the sky above like a light switch had flipped.

The air began to clear, suddenly feeling less thick. It was as if we had popped the cork of the storm's drain and it slowly dissipated in front of our very eyes.

"C'mon, Callie. You got that one? We should go; they aren't ready," Earl murmured, looking around with an uneasy look on his face. "This was a bad idea. I shouldn't have told you about this."

"What do you mean they aren't ready?" I asked.

"They form a circle of mushrooms when they're fully grown. This must be the beginning. They call them fairy rings," he said, looking around nervously.

My body stilled but for my shaking hands that touched the V-shaped scar of my memories. "Fairy rings?" I asked cautiously.

"Yeah. They believed they were a portal to the human world from the other worlds, that the fae used them to travel. You've never heard that?" he asked, looking at me as if I were daft.

"I'm not sure..." My voice trailed off.

"I've seen some dark things around these particular mushrooms, though, so if it were a portal, it's definitely to somewhere evil, not like the agaric mushrooms I've seen."

I stared open-mouthed at him as I attempted to sort my thoughts out.

I suddenly felt sick; my nerves had gotten the best of me.

I needed to talk to my family, to the sweet woman who

was the closest thing to a mother I had since my own had passed. I needed to ground myself, get a firmer grip on things. I'd been working too much, and now it was catching up to me. Had they written? It had felt like ages since I'd heard from them.

Though the air had almost fully cleared, Earl began to shove things in my bag in an attempt to hurry me along. If someone wanted to shock my nerves and frighten me into a heart attack, now was the time. My body was so on edge, I nearly forgot how to zip my bag, unsure of what was real anymore and what wasn't.

We threw our supplies on our backs and quickly headed out the way we had come. Only the hurried footsteps on the forest floor sounded as we quickly shuffled through the wild forest to get as far away from the area as our feet would carry us.

Neither of us spoke the entire way. My mind was too full of questions to sort out a sensible one to ask Earl. It wasn't until we were in his car on the way home that I settled myself enough to speak.

"You're not crazy, are you?" I asked quietly. "I want to know every unbelievable thing you know about the destroying angels. I believe you," I said with a shaky breath.

I could easily understand how Earl had been trapped by his dedication to find out more about these mushrooms. It had been two hours in the forest, and my mind was in overdrive, trying to make sense of everything.

"No," he stated. His wrinkled face looked tired now as he stared at the road ahead.

"No, what? No, you're not crazy? I know, I don't think I ever really thought you were. I think we should contact the North American Mycological Association and see if they can send some others out this way to locate more—" I rambled.

"No. I don't want you telling anyone about these things, and you won't be working with me on them anymore. I'm sorry. This was a mistake. I thought I wanted you to see them, but I don't. I don't want you anywhere near the darkness," he stated, not removing his gaze from the road.

The air went out of me like a balloon. Did he just not want to share his discovery with anyone else? I was stubborn and knew I would wear him down so I brushed it off, not wanting to upset him further. He seemed really upset ever since we had been near them. I would convince him at dinner tonight to let me help.

"Let's talk about it at dinner tonight. We have so much to celebrate. We should go to Marion! I know it's two towns over, but they have that good steak house, and I really want to get dressed up!" I said excitedly.

The gloom and unsettled air were brushed off completely.

His demeanor instantly shifted from grumpy statue to boyishly charming. "Roadhouse? I can get us a senior discount there! You sure you want to waste a dressing up on me? I'll be the luckiest man in Marion," he said with a wink.

"Do you have anything nice you can wear?" I asked, hoping it didn't sound too harsh.

"I have a suit I haven't had a reason to wear in years. Taking a smart, beautiful, kind woman out to dinner sure seems like a good reason," he chirped, still smiling. "But, Callie," he said, his face suddenly falling. "Don't go back to those destroying angel mushrooms, okay? If you do, I'll never forgive myself. We will find another way to get you what you need," he cautioned.

I nodded, knowing he was just worried and looking out for me. I already had all the information I needed, so there was no sense in upsetting him.

"Earl, if you were thirty, heck, twenty years younger, I think you would be causing me a lot of trouble right now." I beamed at the older man as he puffed his chest out a little.

Earl dropped me off at my house and left to get a haircut straightaway with the plan of picking me up for our fancy dinner at eight. I offered to borrow Cecelia's car and pick him up, but he vehemently declined, muttering something about women driving a man around in his day. I couldn't help but feel like a burden making him drive me all around town, even though he said he enjoyed the company. Aside from being thin, though, he did seem to be incredibly healthy, and the few times I'd needed help from him, he was surprisingly strong despite his frail-looking features.

My boots were already half removed by the time I stepped onto the cold white tile of my entryway. The backpack landed with a thud as I neatly tucked my boots under the bench by the door and continued onto the surprisingly light pack, removing the specimens that needed refrigeration. After putting away what was absolutely necessary and electing to leave the rest for the morning, I hurried into the shower.

I was oddly eager to get dressed up. Maybe it was the fact that I hadn't seen myself in anything but pajamas and a khaki-green uniform in a long time, but I was thoroughly looking forward to going out and feeling like a normal human for once. Maybe it was also the fact that I could get as glammed up as I wanted, and I knew my date wouldn't assume it was so he could have sex with me. Yes, that was a definite plus.

An hour later, I had gone so far as to paint my nails a deep red (it was the only bottle of polish I could find, and likely from when I was sixteen), my hair sat patiently in giant rollers as I perched atop the bathroom counter, and I attempted to finish my makeup. The YouTube video I had watched said a smoky eye was easy, but I earnestly begged to differ. I had already scrubbed it off and started over at least three times, concluding I had looked like a bandit-eyed raccoon. Eventually, though, I accidentally smudged in the right spot, achieving a sultry, smoke-like appearance that I was pleased with. I wiggled my loose wisdom tooth back and forth with my tongue, a new nervous habit I had picked up. I swore I would get it pulled soon before it grew more painful, but I never found the time, and the thought of being all loopy from anesthesia made me nervous. Next month.

It took me an agonizingly long time to dig about my

closet and find the box I was searching for. Several boxes littered the edges of the small closet, and the one I wanted was hidden farthest in the back.

I set the beaten cardboard container on the bed with a small grunt. The box had been through a lot of moves, and to be honest, I didn't know why I had even kept it. More likely than not, I had assumed it was full of training equipment or something. I liked pretty dresses and fancy hair and outfits, just not on me. What did I need to dress up for?

I supposed the box in front of me answered that question.

I grabbed one of the blades from a scattered training box and cut open the lid to rummage through the clothes, setting out a few on my bed that could potentially work. Thankfully I was an excellent packer and had vacuum sealed each item because I wouldn't have time to wash them. I snorted at the slutty ones I would never actually wear and fruitlessly attempted to remember how I had acquired them. Some of them seemed ridiculously small.

On went a pair of black pumps with an elegant yet feminine pointed toe. Claire, the lady that cared for me after the accident used to wear a pair that looked just like these. With the memory of my family and a squeeze of my heart, I walked to the small wooden desk in my kitchen and opened the large leather-bound book that rested atop the worn surface as I checked for new letters and pulled an unopened envelope from the first page of the book. I shuffled back to the brightly lit bathroom to finish my tasks while I read over the latest letter from my adoptive mother. Plans of travel and enchanted little places she could take me to, whenever I was able to visit, were scribbled across the pages and followed up with a sparkling butterfly stamp near her signature that I knew she had added just for me. She was so incredibly sweet and thoughtful. I startled out of my cozy reflections with a glance at the time.

I pulled off the perforated plastic of a red "all day wear" lipstick tube and read the instructions before painting it on my lips. It was most certainly expired, but I would try and ignore that as it made my lips look pouty and voluptuous. I snorted in the mirror and tried to wipe it off, but true to my usual luck, it wouldn't budge.

Debauched red lips and over-sexed smoky eyes stared back in horror as I rubbed vehemently to remove the red lip to no avail. What was in this stuff? Maybe I should put it under my new micro—

My microscope.

Oh my god.

I had left my microscope in the forest.

No.

The case hadn't been with me in the car. I painfully remembered everything I had hurried to place in Earl's car in our rush to leave the forest, and the hefty black case had not been there. I needed to call Earl and check.

I was *so* close to reaching my goals. How could I mess up like this?

But then Earl would have to stop what he was doing to take me over there and hike into the woods again. That had to have already been so taxing on him and his aging body.

How *embarrassing!* This isn't how you treat equipment with the price tag of a car. He would think me unprofessional, and then he *definitely* wouldn't let me work with him on this new mushroom adventure, and I *needed* to find more of those mushrooms.

But how would I get there? The back end of the park where we had been wasn't *actually* that far from the end of my property if I went through the woods. I would have to. I couldn't leave it out there to get ruined.

There was only one way I could think of to get that far back into the woods and back before anyone knew I was gone.

CHAPTER 6

CALLIE

Callie: Running late, can you pick me up at 9?
Earl: No pomegranates.
Earl: No pomegranates.
Earl: No problem. Damn phone.
Earl: Sorry, dang phone. Forgot you hate swearing. No pome-
granates, I'm sure you have some girly beauty things you
need to do. See you at 9.
Callie: you caught me;)

※※

"OUCH!" I GROANED, TRYING TO COVER THE TOP OF MY FOOT with my hand. It burned from the intense heat of the engine torturing it. My shoulders tensed as I placed my cell phone into the cup holder and continued through the forest on my lawn mower, all the while wiggling my loose back tooth like a nervous madman.

High heels were not advisable for driving a tractor. Thankfully the storm had passed and it was still light enough out to see clearly and navigate. Otherwise, the trees would have caused me an incredible amount of trouble.

The tinted evening air softly rustled the pine branches in warning, and I suddenly remembered exactly where I was headed. I shivered with the thoughts of how horrible that forest had made me feel. Goose bumps pebbled my skin, and I instantly regretted not bringing a warm coat.

I pulled the large curlers from my hair and tried to calm myself. Thank god I didn't have neighbors close by. I was trembling and clammy. I'm quite certain I already had mud all over my tiny black dress.

I would just call and cancel dinner. Earl would understand.

"Ouch!" I moved my burning foot so the heel took the brunt of the heated assault.

The forest was quiet and calm, save for the roaring John Deere, but aside from that, it was actually really refreshing to be in the thick part of the forest this late at night, alone. Owls hooted to each other in the distance in sync with the crickets. I loved the night; it always gave me a sense of calm.

With a heavy sigh, I pulled my phone from the side cup holder of the tractor.

Callie: I'm so sorry, but I have to cancel. Something last minute's come up. Will call tomorrow. Sorry for everything!
Earl: What's going on? Is everything all right?
Earl: Cal?
Earl: Cal?

I tucked the phone back into the tractor's cup holder after checking my coordinates on the park's GPS app and let out a breath. At least I wasn't under a time constraint now. I was equally glad Earl wouldn't see me in this dress. Had I known it was this small and tight, I wouldn't have even bothered to put anything on. I should have grabbed the sparkly pink one off the bed before I ran out the door. Then I would have at least felt like tractor Barbie, which sounded more fun. As it was, I looked like some type of James Bond spy girl or something, though I seriously doubt a spy girl would ride a beat-up old tractor to her destination.

The forest was completely dark now. Shimmers of moonlight blanketed the trees like a spooky movie. Only cloaked in a silver sheen, it reflected off some of the pine trees and merely silhouetted others, leaving my mind to question the depths of what I actually saw. Maybe it was my mind playing tricks on me, but I swear I could already feel the terror from earlier creeping into my bones.

Amber orbs of gold flashed as lightning bugs danced along the trees like mystical Christmas lights. It seemed like there were hundreds of them, formed almost in a trail of sorts. The hair rose on the back of my neck. Something didn't feel right about the way they all trailed toward something.

I straightened my spine. It was only fireflies.

Even though it was just the quiet forest and myself, I tugged down the *very* short black dress, suddenly feeling quite silly and uncomfortable. My breasts were shoved together so high, I thought my nipples might pop out, so I yanked up the fabric masquerading as a chest covering. The dress rose higher up my thighs with the action. It was like a terribly slutty game of tug of war.

Pull up to cover cleavage, and the dress would rise to scandalous heights on my thighs.

Shove down to hide legs, and the treacherous dress would threaten to throw a nipple overboard.

Perspiration began to gleam across my forehead with the struggle. I had to be close now. All-in-all the tractor was going much faster and more effici—

My body lurched forward as the tractor's tire caught in a root.

I was so angry I nearly swore as I attempted to reverse the mower. The action only caused the tires to whip moss into the night air and trench farther into the soft soil of the forest.

Mother forking crap on a cracker! I was stuck.

58

"Nooooo, please no!" I begged the tractor as if that would help.

A curious raccoon wandered down a tree in front of me to watch the show.

"What are you looking at?" I shouted aggressively as I got down from the yellow seat and attempted to pull all my hair out in frustration.

"I'm sorry, you didn't deserve that," I mumbled at the trash panda apologetically.

He didn't. He was just being curious.

Angry and frustrated, I grabbed a pair of rusted hedge clippers from the tractor. I didn't think I'd need them because there were no real threats out here, but just in case. I huffed and stomped off back on my trail, now more determined than ever.

And when I say stomped, I mean on the balls of my feet because I was still very much in high heels.

"Uuugghh, maybe that stupid mushroom *is* bad luck," I grumbled and growled at the animals that walked with me.

A skunk had joined the team, with whom I avoided making any eye contact. Finicky things skunks were. I loved all animals…well, except snakes. Don't ask me why, but I am petrified of snakes. The slithering, the hissing—they've never bothered me, and I never bother them.

It was comforting to have the company of the animals in the dark forest though. Animals had always been oddly unafraid of me. I have no memory of it any other way. Had they not been more distant when I was with other people, I might not have ever realized they didn't usually get so close to humans. Whatever the reason, I was grateful for it. It drove me to want to do my job to the best of my abilities. All creatures deserved to be loved and taken care of.

That didn't mean I wasn't still wary of the skunk that trailed behind me.

A few creatures scampered beside me along the way as I stopped every few feet to pull a high heel free from the dirt. Walking on the balls of my feet was exhausting, but I refused to take my shoes off. You'd be shocked at the number of poisonous insects that littered the average forest floor.

I began to sing some old fluffy songs in a weak attempt at soothing my frayed nerves. I was just about to pick up a new melody when the ground scuttled with the sounds of my forest friends suddenly running to hide. I turned, startled at the sudden movement behind me.

And then I saw it.

The first living luna moth I had ever seen.

The creature I had moved across the country to find.

I nearly fell to my knees at the sight of it. They were early.

Three weeks until they were supposed to arrive in Willow Springs.

The large moth fluttered silently behind me before it landed on a nearby tree. The slow flap of its pale neon-green wings taunted me. A long tendril trailed behind each wing. These tendrils were part of what made them so rare, somehow adding to the majestic beauty of the mysterious luna moth.

In a trance of wonder, I moved closer. Two long fern-like antennae rested atop its fluffy body, only adding to its adorable aesthetic.

Something moved nearby, and I had to stifle a scream as my pulse quickened. I turned, catching the movement with my peripheral.

Another one.

I gasped as another luna moth fluttered past me.

The one on the tree took off, flapping with his companion.

I clamored to follow them, still in somewhat of a shock.

Tuna-teeth! These high heels were going to kill me! I was moving quickly to keep up with the moths as they floated along the twinkling trail of the fireflies. My cheeks felt hot even though my skin was chilled with the cool night air as I breathed heavily. Several parts of my body were exposed from the dress now, but I didn't care. I didn't care about anything as I chased the moths.

Several more luna moths glinted under the moonlight up ahead.

"Holy esophagus…"

I was shaking with excitement now.

It was stunning. More and more lightning bugs flew to the area, twinkling all around me and the beautiful moths in a mystical display.

It was so magical looking. I needed to get closer.

I reached for my phone to take photos—

Except I'd left my phone in the tractor.

Poop.

Okay, it'd be fine. Alone in the woods in a hooker dress and high heels with no ride or phone. *Perfect.*

I turned down a deep bend past a large hemlock as I followed the golden trail in an attempt to get a better look at the moths that fluttered ahead of me.

My lungs filled sharply with cold air. I had to grasp ahold of a nearby tree to keep myself up.

There had to be a hundred of them.

They all had stopped in the same area.

Pale-green wings seemed to reflect brighter under the sultry glow of the moon. Dozens and dozens of wings flapped slowly. Most of them had collected on the bark of trees or fallen logs surrounding the area. A few fluttered by in the air. They seemed to have gathered in a large circle deep within the depths of the forest. The large gap in the center of the trees gave way to silver mists of moonlight casting down gracefully upon them. It was beautiful, ethereal. Enough to distract me from the doomed feeling hovering over the area like a foreboding blanket.

A shrill scream sounded somewhere in the distance, severing the doleful quiet of the night.

I know that sound. That's a—

Suddenly it was before me.

A fox.

A red, snarling, angry fox.

I screamed, nearly falling backward in surprise. Normally a fox would not hurt a human, but this was not a normal fox.

It was the very same glittering golden fox I had seen before. I backed away from its snarling red and black face.

It wasn't glittering now in the darkness—not exactly. When the moonlight hit its fur unshadowed, it looked... magical? It seemed to ghost a golden glow that I couldn't quite focus my eyes on. Was this all my imagination? Was I really starting to lose my mind? Was it the mushrooms?

In a startling move, it nipped at my foot, and I leaped backward toward the center of the gathering of moths with a shriek.

My action only seemed to cause it to act more frantic. Was he hurt? I shifted back along the ground, suddenly very afraid. I'd never had an animal act like this toward me. Maybe he thought I meant him harm?

"It's okay, I won't hurt you. I promise. What are you?" I cooed at the reddish-orange creature.

His bushy tail flicked at my words. I'd never heard a fox snarl before, but it was terrifying. Shrill, more high-pitched than a dog's growl, but every bit as fear provoking, maybe more so with his pointed nose wrinkled up in anger. I moved to step around him. I needed to get to the moths.

I *needed* to see more.

"What the fork!?" I screamed as it went to rip my ankle off, barely missing.

The fox's amber eyes stared at me as he pinned his ears back, away from his bushy red and black face. White patches blended with rust-colored fur. He was beautiful. Don't ask me how I knew it was a he. I could feel it. Just like I could feel that he wasn't quite normal. Even if I couldn't see the shimmering gold fur in the moonlight, there was something in his eyes, something unlike anything I'd ever seen. I should have been running home now, but I couldn't. It was like I was hypnotized. I felt such a harsh pull to see the moths. I couldn't have ignored it if I had tried.

Most of my life had revolved around the hope of this very moment. If this glowing fox thought he would stop me, he had no idea how determined I truly was. I stepped back.

He snapped at me again, growling, this time, shoving his trim, fluffy body into mine and knocking me away from the moths.

He was trying to block me from the circular clearing where the moths and lightning bugs waited patiently.

"It's okay," I cooed again in my softest voice. "You have a family in there, don't you? I promise I won't hurt them. I just want to get a better look at the luna moth, okay?"

It began a high-pitched whine. All the while, his amber eyes continued to look frantically between me and the small clearing.

I stepped around him in a hurry, quickly walking toward the mystical hole in the middle of the forest where thousands of moonlit green wings flapped and fluttered a song all of their own.

I tripped and fell, quickly collecting myself, but not before I realized the fox had lain on my feet, whining with long, painful cries. It was incredibly eerie and unsettling.

"Okay, one thing at a time," I mumbled, quickly scooting away and walking toward the open circle.

I just needed to get a better look at what was going on. Then I would see how I could help the shimmering fox. The fox who was probably a figment of my imagination anyway.

I dodged him as he went for me, faking right and going left like a trained football player. I ran until my body brushed the circle of trees. I felt a slight pinch as the fox broke the skin at the back of my calf.

"You turd face, you got me," I hissed at the edge of the clearing, lifting my bare leg to look. Sure enough, there was a small bite.

Crap.

"You better pray to your forest gods that you don't have rabies you...you..." I angrily murmured as I turned to face the orange bandit, but he was gone. "Geez. What kind of luck am I having today?" I mumbled, turning back to the open space and trying to make sense of everything.

It was nearly a perfect circle of moss and dirt resting inside the large ancient trees. Hundreds, if not thousands, of luna moths fluttered and clung to the trees. Golden flashes from the lightning bugs lit the air like magic.

When I didn't think I could ever see anything more magnificent or magical, I saw them.

In the middle of the mossy floor lay another perfect circle.

A complete and perfect ring of destroying angel mushrooms. The clean white flesh of the mushroom caps shone brightly under the moon's silvery glow.

I sucked in an amazed breath. The scent of pine and earth filtered through my nose, and I heard only crickets and a distant high-pitched whine.

I took another step into the clearing. The thick moss gave way under the pressure of my black high heels.

Then I felt it.

I tightened my arms around myself as if that could protect me from the feeling.

It was the same grim vibe in the forest with Earl. Only now, it felt intense, like we had only sampled a taste earlier, and this was the entire feast.

Goose bumps bloomed across my arms and legs as the hairs on the back of my neck rose.

I had the immediate urge to scream and run. To get as much distance as possible between me and this weird circle of mushrooms.

But that was stupid. These were moths and mushrooms. Needing to show my courage, I took a few more steps into the space until my feet nearly grazed the large circle of mushrooms.

How could they form like this? I'd never seen anything so perfectly uniform. Moths fluttered around the small space, soaring in front of my face. Were these mushrooms causing me hallucinations?

Flashbacks of my childhood incident flashed in my mind.

I looked at the small scar on my hand. "Grow up, Cal," I reprimanded myself, feeling my heart flutter as I took in the many sets of wings surrounding me.

I dug my thumbnail into the V-shaped scar until it left a dent and a reminder that I needed to get it together.

I shivered and adjusted my black dress nervously. I picked up my leg and stepped firmly into the circle.

It was as if the ground were made of water. Nothing held under my foot inside the destroying angel circle. I tried to regain my balance and pull myself back out, but with nothing to hold onto, the rest of my body fell into the circle in an ungraceful stumble.

Sharp pinpricks covered my body. Thick black smoke suddenly swirled around me, choking my lungs. My eyes clamped tightly in fear as I fought to regain any balance I could. I was still falling.

On and on, I continued to fall.

It felt as though my body had been thrust into a black hole, tumbling and flipping slowly into the abyss. My arms and legs flailed wildly, trying to grab ahold of something, anything to stop this feeling. It felt like my stomach was in my chest as I continued to fall, flipping and turning as I screamed bloody murder.

I collided with something hard. The force was like I had landed on a brick wall, like I had been in a car crash. My body clung to the ground as nausea overtook me and bile rose up my throat. My mind swirled chaotically, unable to stop the horrible spiraling.

I went to roll onto my back when the ground beneath me shifted, and I was thrown.

"What the—"

"It's landed on the prince! It's landed on the prince!"

"It is an attack! They are retaliating!" Male voices rang out in alarm.

I struggled to open my eyes, my body holding tight to the lingering feeling of falling. I opened my eyes, but it was too dark, and I could see nothing.

Suddenly I was hoisted up by my arms. My eyes continued to fail me so I could only hear whoever was doing it.

"How did they know, my lord?" Gruff shouts and murmurs echoed like waves around me in rough accents I couldn't place.

"Cut its arms off now! It's dangerous!"

The darkness settled in my vision, but I wished it hadn't.

Inky black smoke shrouded what looked to be hundreds of men in fierce black armor. All faced me. I screamed with the only bit of air I could collect and ran.

I blasted into a wall directly behind me with what felt like the force of a train.

But it had not been a wall.

He towered over me like death himself. The moonlight illuminated bits of the dark armor that cloaked his massive body. Foolish because he didn't look as though he needed any armor. Every inch of his frame radiated the power of a predator. Where a normal man's head would reside rested a dark chest covering of armor glinting with what little light the moon painted it. I lifted my eyes higher until my neck craned uncomfortably to see the face of death himself.

My blood ran cold. Every instinct within my body surged with a need to flee. My feet shifted away, toward the other villainous-looking men.

A sharp jaw contoured his backlit face as cold blue eyes bore into my body and through my very soul. Obsidian-black brows rested slightly above the terrifying pools of ice. Dark black hair glistened, almost invisible in the darkness had it not laid so close to the pale porcelain skin of his harsh face.

The monster grabbed me as I turned to run. I heard myself scream as though I were outside my body. I continued to struggle against the strong gloved hand that held my bare shoulder. I looked back in horror at the monster, only to realize it had one hand on the hilt of a jeweled sword as the other tightly gloved hand nearly crumpled my shoulder in its strong grip.

66

Almost impossible to see in the darkness, thick columns of smoke coiled and shifted in billowy plumes from his back, slowly taking the shape of wings. The smoke was thick and lively, but it somehow appeared as though if I touched it, I would feel the wings were somehow solid. The thick blackness seemed darker than the night that surrounded us. The wings of smoke flowed at least five feet out on either side of his enormous body. They were unlike any wings I'd studied before. More beautiful than any of the pictures that hung on my walls. Even the luna moth's beautiful wings paled in comparison to the dark, ethereal wings spread in front of me.

I realized I'd been frozen, gawking with my mouth open at the mysterious man's wings. How could those be real? They were smoke—they were incredible.

Without permission from my brain, my hand shot out to touch one.

The black swirls moved instantly away from my hand, just as smoke from a candle would, but with more intention. The sensation of cold vapor encased my hand, and instantly, the onyx waves swirled and coiled around my fingers, causing me to nearly faint in wonderment.

"They-they're beautiful," I murmured, likely too soft to be heard.

The giant creature watched me with obvious surprise as his brows creased deeply. He glanced at my face before looking at the whispers of smoke that danced upon my hand. A shudder seemed to rack his body before he roughly shoved me away.

He tilted his head up and squinted to see me beneath heavy lashes, and then he spit on me.

The hot wet blob slowly slid down my dirt-covered cheek. I screamed in surprise, but before I could wipe it off, he grabbed me again. The pain of his grip nearly buckled my knees as I cried out.

The monster slowly raked his empty blue eyes over me; my dress had pulled up to expose part of my rear. His horrible gaze seemed to hover over my skin before a scream ripped from me.

Smoky talons had formed at the end of his wings like daggers and pressed sharply into my shoulders. Warm trickles of blood dripped down my arm as he squeezed tighter.

I was fucked.

CHAPTER 7

CALLIE

IN MY WORST NIGHTMARES, I WOULD HAVE BEEN UNABLE TO imagine the feelings of pure fear rippling through me as the wretched creature dug the smoke talons of his wings deeper into my flesh. The darkness of the night muddied my view, allowing me barely more than a moonlit view of the horrible creatures surrounding me.

I couldn't see far in the darkness, but it looked as if I were in the very same spot in the forest. How was that possible? When I had stepped into the circle of destroying angel mushrooms, it was as if I had fallen somewhere. The spot in the forest may have looked similar, but *everything* about it felt off. It felt horrible and terrifying. Dense trees collected around the opening where we stood. What was happening?

Hundreds of dark, ominous bodies surrounded us. I'm certain there were more, but I could only see so far in the darkness.

It—for he was like no man—towered over me, easily six foot five or more. He wore armor similar to the others, save for the helmet. His pale face was smudged with dark dirt that seemed misplaced against his pale, porcelain skin. His gaze seemed to shine brighter under the moon, almost producing a silvery glow. He was no man. His shoulders seemed far too expansive to ever be considered one. Even through the countless layers of black leather and armor, his body was mesomorphic. Powerfully built to destroy anything he saw fit as a predator. It, without effort, produced an overwhelmingly intimidating effect.

I cried out as his menacing wings pressed deeper into my flesh.

"Kill it. Now." His voice was low and spine-chillingly soft.

He didn't even need to raise his voice to command an entire fleet of soldiers.

I couldn't speak, couldn't think. The searing pain in my shoulders owned only a fraction of my panic as the nightmarish scene played out before my eyes.

The man continued to stare down at me as he released his hold from my shoulder.

All of a sudden, forceful pressure stung tightly around my throat as I choked and wheezed in an effort to regain my breath.

I hadn't even realized I had attempted to flee. My body had moved on autopilot in a last attempt to escape before the creature grabbed my throat, keeping me in place. My fingers tried desperately to claw his hand free, but it was no use. He was too strong.

I felt the cold metal slide inch by inch into my back, sharp and cold. Every muscle in my body went rigid and stiff, horror-struck at the sight as the skin of my stomach stretched. The pointed tip of the sword ripped through the skin of my abdomen.

Only once I felt the raw, grating friction of the sword withdrawing and the hard dirt grinding into my knees did I realize he had released his grip from my throat and stabbed me straight through my abdomen.

I looked down, shocked at the gruesome wound on my stomach, still not quite registering what had happened.

Deep, dark burgundy blood cascaded down my body as I grabbed at the gushing wound.

My jaw slackened. I had no remaining conviction available to close it. How could this happen to me? I was a good person. I did everything a good person did. I was good! Good guys always triumphed, always prevailed while the bad guy, without exception, failed.

I stared up in disbelief. The villain had held my throat while one of his men had stabbed me clean through the middle.

How could this have happened?

My face began to tingle as the blood slowly drained from my face. No one could survive a wound like this. I was going to die.

The winged villain took a step forward, stopping once he hovered over my kneeling frame. His icy blue eyes took in the scene with a look of pure satisfaction—enjoyment even.

"Brainless humans. Dressing an assassin as a lady of pleasure. Though I suppose that was part of a weak-minded plan, to distract us with a fresh human whore."

He kicked me hard in the chest with the bottom of his boot, and I fell backward, sprawled on my back in a helpless pile of blood and pain.

"Please—" I gurgled.

Hot liquid had begun to rise in my throat, slowly hindering my ability to speak. My back grew wet with puddled blood, and nearly as much covered my front. My vision came and went like a sadistic strobe light, and I closed my eyes in an attempt to steady it.

I felt no pain now; I suppose my body had gone into shock. I struggled to think of what I would do if this were one of my animals at the center, but the feeling of despair hung heavy on my soul. I knew it was too late. There would be nothing I could do to save myself from a wound like this.

At the sound of my gurgled voice, the giant devil's

eyebrows bunched slightly together as he tilted his head, looking at me with a confused expression.

I was almost dead, and he would be the last thing painted across my eyelids as I closed them forever. I could feel the sins from my past and the hopes of my future settling over my chest like a cloak of shadows.

I inhaled through my nose, coughing instantly. My chest, with all of its effort, struggled to rise and fall.

I estimated I had only three or so minutes until my heart gave out.

Faint voices and stomps echoed around me in the distance.

"Pack it up. Give the message to the queen. They obviously expected us," growled the smoke-winged nightmare in a displeased tone.

"What the fuck happened!?"

"We opened the portal, and *that* landed on Prince Mendax. They were obviously more prepared than we thought they were."

"Look at her! Did you see her reach out and touch the prince's wings? Touched the shadows of the gods with her own damned fingers! I've never seen anyone so fearless of the Smoke Slayers in all my time!"

"Well, it's only Mendax and the queen who are touched with the shadows now anyway. Blessed thing you stopped her, Fish. She was clearly an experienced assassin."

"Skilled but no match for me blade—well, and Prince Mendax holding her. What we doin'? Just leavin' the body? The wildwood creatures will eat her. Though her human cunt is still viable, dead or not."

"Leave the human, it'd probably rot your dick off."

"Yeah. The queen and prince would bag me if they'd known I'd touched one of 'em. King Marco would'a let me. Hell, he'd have kept her for himself—"

"Don't speak about my dead king unless you want to die alongside the human. Get moving! Leave the trash, the creatures will tear her apart before we make it back to the castle."

The murmurs and footsteps slowly grew farther and farther away, but I was unable to tell whether they had left the area or if I had, in fact, just died.

I struggled to open a slit of my eyelids. The small act felt like the hardest, most laborious movement I'd ever attempted. The puddle of hot liquid I lay in quickly grew cold as the forest's chill commenced. One of my eyes won the fight and opened for the briefest of moments. Only long enough to see I was alone in the dark circle of trees.

It looked similar but not as…happy as before I'd fallen. Several luna moths hovered on surrounding trees in significantly fewer numbers. Everything looked different. The forest trees looked older with more character, as if they themselves were monsters. The night felt darker and more malevolent even though the same moon spilled the same silvery-blue light upon the forest. Somehow everything felt scarier.

I was going to die all alone with only an eerie darkness and an overwhelming sensation that I was a sinking ship.

Something soft and spongy rested under my cheek. What had I lain on?

I had no chance of moving my hands, so instead, I attempted to move my head with the hopes I had lain on some magical key that would save me if I wasn't already destined for death. I was only able to move my heavy head a few inches to the right.

My face lay on a destroying angel mushroom—how poetic.

It felt like someone was slamming a hammer into my heart. *Thump…thump…thump.*

It was too hard to breathe now. It was time. My heart was giving out; I could feel it. I could no longer swallow through the blood that rose in my throat.

If I weren't already dead, I would be any second. It was harder to tell than I imagined if I were alive or dead.

I crunched a handful of dried leaves at my side and braced

myself for death. My biggest regret was that I hadn't seen my family again, Eli, Seneca—no, no, that's not true.

My biggest regret was never getting to feel love wholeheartedly.

Thump...thump...thump.

I never even had a chance.

Thump...thump.

"Holy suns! She's injured, hurry! She's not going to make it! Look at what they've done to her!"

Something sniffed my face, and a tickle of fur brushed against my cheek. Or at least I thought it did. I must be dead? What side had taken me, heaven or hell?

A soft pressure rested on the tops of my cold legs. It felt like a warm fur blanket covering me, just heavy enough to comfort me a little in my last moment.

"You're no better than him—" The voice sounded like silk wrapped in sunshine, even through its accusatory tone.

"Bite your tongue. I know what I've done," came an urgent raspy voice.

"Hurry!"

Something soft and velvety ran over the wound on my stomach, and warm droplets of something fell upon my skin. It felt as if the sun had melted and oozed into my flesh. At first, I could hardly feel anything but warmth, but then a sharp stinging sensation ran through me with a wild passion. A fire blazed through my insides, unraveling them one by one only to melt them together once again.

Thump...thump...thump...thump...

"It's working! Thank the gods! Her heart is beating... as well as it can. We need to leave here now," came the silky, womanly voice.

The harsh fire running through me jolted me with intense pain, but the thing on my legs and stomach bore down, keeping me still. Was there something fluffy now under my head?

Tiny prickles coursed through me, similar to when my

foot fell asleep, only these rushed through the inside of me like a river. My eyes bolted open in shock as if someone had used a defibrillator on my heart.

The fox lay on my legs and stomach as tears fell freely from its beautiful amber eyes onto my skin while it licked fervently at my wound.

"That's enough," scolded the silky voice next to my head. "It's already too much, she will be affected, and then *you* will be killed!"

"No one will ever know what I've done—including her. As for you, you will be quiet or *all* of our lives will be taken," the male voice growled.

"Enough, brother, we leave now! We must not be here!" the female said with panic, her stoic voice cracking.

The beautiful fox locked his glistening eyes with mine, giving my wound one last lick before gently standing up and stepping from my stomach.

I sat up with less of a struggle than I could ever have imagined and watched the fox stealthily canter to what appeared to be another smaller fox. His eyes locked with mine until he reached her. The only sound of their movement was the soft crinkle and crunch of dried leaves under their small feet.

"Wait...I...where am I?" I mumbled incoherently in their direction.

The pair stopped their trot to look back at me before immediately snapping their heads to the side in unison. They tilted their heads, leaning into their oversized ears just as a dog did when listening intently. In the blink of my eyes, they sprinted away with unnatural speed, even for that of a shimmering fox.

"Please! Wait! I need to thank you for-for whatever you have done! For saving my life!" I shouted after them, but it was no use because they had vanished completely.

What in the world had happened? I was alive. My body felt like a semitruck had blasted into it, but I was alive. Was that fox from here? First, he showed up behind my house in the middle of the day, then attacked me before I fell into the ring of mushrooms, and now he's saving my life? Magically healing me? I must be hallucinating again.

I shifted to my knees. One of my shoes had fallen off and laid a few feet away, my black dress had bunched around my chest, and I was caked in blood and dirt.

So much blood.

Unsure of what to do and needing to get away, I straightened to pull the dress over my head as I remained on my knees. I didn't care if I was naked. I was alive and needed to get the sight of gore away from me. Each move my body made felt like an electric shock to my system, but I didn't care; I just needed to get it off.

After several minutes of frantically trying, I finally gave up. It was plastered to my body like bloodied papier-mâché. This was not what I should be wasting my energy on, plus the black thong and bra I wore underneath were far too small if I happened to find others that could help me. Besides, I wasn't sure where exactly I was and that could put me in more danger.

I shifted, pulling the black dress back down over my legs. I shivered as I felt the frayed hole of fabric in the back and front of my dress where the blade had pierced it—and my body. The skin under it felt soft and tender. It was hard to see through the mess of blood, but the wound now appeared to be closed.

It couldn't be.

It was the palest pink with blue and purple veins around the scar, but it was closed? I no longer had an open wound. The fox's tears and licks had healed me, brought me back from an almost guaranteed death somehow.

In my fog, I had missed the sound of footsteps approaching until they echoed directly behind me. I remained kneeling on the forest floor, unsure of what to expect and now too frightened to move. Was this one of the forest creatures they had spoken of?

"Well now, for a human, this is quite impressive," rumbled a familiar deep voice.

I turned as fast as I could, which wasn't very fast at all, and scrambled to the aid of a tree that held me up. The wide oak's bark pressed comfortingly into my back as I held it tightly for balance.

The man stood in front of me.

He crossed his arms nonchalantly over his chest while glaring down at me. He harshly raked his unkind eyes over me with a faint glimmer of amusement, pausing at the hole in my dress for a moment before continuing their ascent.

One corner of his mouth lifted in a smug, vengeful smirk.

I was able to get a good look at him now, standing in the moonlight. He was beautiful. There was no other way to put it. Gorgeous in a hauntingly evil way with the bone structure and build of a Roman god. High cheekbones and a sharp jawline, skin as clear and smooth as porcelain. What kind of monsters looked like that?

Obviously, only the worst kind.

"Wh-what are you?" I asked shakily as my tremors vibrated my vocal cords. "Where am I?" At the sight of him alone, my body convulsed so hard with dread that I feared I would fall to the ground.

"Absolutely brilliant," he whispered. "And here I was wondering why the humans sent a useless weapon such as yourself. I was just returning to collect your head and send it back."

His voice was so deep and quiet that goose bumps prickled across my arms at the sound of it. Eerie and venomous, like it could put me under a spell if it wanted to.

He stalked toward me, slowly. Each step delivered with the intent of causing more fear. The right side of his grin had pulled so high a dimple formed on the stupidly attractive cheek. On someone else, it probably would have been cute, but on him it looked unhinged and sinister.

He continued his steps until he had hemmed me in against

the old tree. My back burned from pressing so harshly against the tree bark. Even this close, the darkness seemed to merge with his skin, blending us both into the darkness of the night.

"No one has sent me. I was in the forest alone and fell. I landed on you somehow—I suppose—I'm so sorry, but there's been some kind of mistake. I mean no harm, please, *please* just let me go. I'll find my own way back. You will never, ever see me again, just please don't hurt me again," I begged near silently as fear strangled the words before they could reach a normal volume.

Tears trailed down my face, falling off my chin in a waterfall.

His cold blue eyes stared. He looked so stoic he was nearly lifeless save for the predatory pleasure his features briefly expressed when he had struck me with fear. His body slouched as he leaned against the tree on either side of my head. I always thought of myself as a smart person, but in that moment of fear, barely a thought went through my mind, let alone a plan to escape. I'd never felt such terror in my life. I could barely speak because I was so frightened. This was the man that had dug talons into my shoulders and held me while another had run a sword through my body.

"Oh, you're good, I'll give you that," he purred.

A dimple popped as he grabbed my waist with his gloved hand.

Without thinking, I slapped him across the cheek. Hard.

It was purely a reaction.

I covered my mouth with my shaking hand and waited in horror for the reaction I knew would surely come from the monster.

He looked back at me slowly; his face had turned from the force of my hand. The view of his profile was like a painting of a Greek god.

"I'm so sorry," I mumbled as my jaw shook, making it hard to talk.

He grabbed my jaw with a large, gloved hand.

A small whine escaped my lips as I tried to shove him away, but his chest was firmer than the oak pressed against my back.

"Please—" I cried.

His sky-blue eyes twinkled with a menacing sparkle that hadn't been there before.

"They are getting smarter," he purred against my ear as he held my face firmly. The black leather of the glove did little to soften his demanding grip, and his muscular body was a vise that squeezed me against the dense tree. "You've no need to play dumb *human*. I'm quite interested in how you're not dead. Obviously, you're not as foolish as I had originally thought," he said, disgust coating every word.

His voice trailed over the dirty skin of my ear and neck, causing shivers to flow up my spine.

The giant of a man stepped back and let my face fall from his hand.

Just as I was about to breathe a sigh of relief when something cold and sharp stabbed into my chest, causing me to wheeze out a hoarse cry as I clung desperately to the tree behind me.

Black smoke swirled densely from the cretin's back. His right wing flowed thick and wispy behind him, the edges fading softly into the night.

His left wing swirled wildly with soot-black smoke, shaped like a hand against my heart. The "fingers" were pointed, knives of smoke that dug into my skin.

I cried out in pain, swatting wildly, searching for anything I could do to move the horrid thing's grip on my chest, but it was pointless. My hands flowed through the wisps as if they were the smoke from a campfire. Not faltering for a moment, the pain grew sharper as he dug the dagger-like talons of his smoke farther into the depths of my flesh. All the while, his face glimmered with a sadistic grin.

"Tell me how you survived that, and I'll remove my grip from what remains of your damaged mortal heart." His soulless eyes slightly darkened as they grazed over my exposed body. "Tell me, what's it feel like knowing the humans wasted every breath you've ever taken by sending you to kill a man who can't be killed?"

I fell to my knees, unable to comprehend what was happening or deal with the pain any longer, for that matter. Certainly no one in their right mind would believe me an assassin. And why would he think that humans had sent me? I would have laughed at the thought had I not been in such pain. I didn't dare continue to deny it, though, as that only seemed to anger him more. The last thing I wanted to do was put the foxes that had saved me in harm's way, but they were hopefully far away now. My head continued to pound, ceasing any further thoughts, no matter how helpful they might have been.

"A fox," I wheezed out breathlessly, shifting my loose wisdom tooth back and forth in a nervous frenzy.

He froze suddenly.

Even the inky smoke seemed to stop its swirling. Had I not seen him move earlier, he could have easily passed as a statue without question.

Concern and confusion muddled against his dark brows as they creased slightly before he dropped his grip on me.

I fell to the dirt with a thud, and my chin split as it bounced roughly off a nearby rock.

My body hurt in places I had never imagined being able to hurt. I was covered in dirt and blood. My blonde hair felt matted and sticky. I was clearly having a delusional episode because I had no idea how I could be seeing a giant, muscled, evil Calvin Klein model with wings of smoke right now. Not to mention a fox that shimmered gold in the sunlight, tried to attack me before I fell into another evil world, then followed me here and saved my life. Yeah, okay.

I couldn't even cry. I was too numb.

I sat up, wiped the blood from my chin, and clawed at the dirty black fabric covering my chest.

No exterior marks from the horrible smoke talons on my skin.

Well, what a horrifying trick.

I knew he could have easily ripped my heart out had he wanted to. I had felt it. For some reason, the mention of the fox had made him uneasy. I glanced up to see his eyes taking stock of my every twinge and wince like a hawk. Something flashed in his eyes briefly as I adjusted my dress to cover my rear yet again. I don't know why I bothered since it had been hanging out most of the time anyway.

Was that...fear that flashed in his eyes? Was he afraid of me?

At this thought, I did begin to laugh.

"What did the fox do?" he asked as he leaned in again.

At his movement, my laughter immediately left my body, replaced now with only fear. I wouldn't survive another near death.

That was something I certainly never thought I'd say to myself.

For whatever reason, this creature was uneasy about the fox, and I needed to do whatever I could to survive and get out of here. Whatever that meant.

"No."

"No?" He raised his dark eyebrows in surprise.

"Where am I? Who are you?" I asked. My words filled with a confidence I didn't feel.

I felt so very weak. Could I survive if I made a run for it? Could I locate another portal? Were there even other portals?

He stepped closer than he already was and gripped the hair at the back of my head, painfully twisting my head as he hovered to look down at me. I could feel the anger rippling off him as he glared.

"So we play this game again, huh?" he growled angrily as he wrenched my head farther back like a rag doll.

"I'm not playing a game!" I cried, finally having snapped completely.

"Prince Mendax is something—"

A large, round man in dark armor stopped abruptly after seeing the aforementioned man fisting my hair.

"Everything is fine, Dirac," the *prince* said, never once taking his deranged blue eyes from mine.

"Everything is not fine, Dirac!" I shouted at the brown-haired man that stood to my left. I couldn't tell much more about him as it was still dark, but I could feel him gawking at us. "Tell your disgusting boss to stop throwing me around like a dog and let me free. I'm not an assassin! I wouldn't hurt a fly!" I screamed and immediately began to flail my arms and legs at the man they called Prince Mendax.

The vile prince looked to his comrade and grinned.

"How did she—how is she alive, sir?" the unhelpful man named Dirac asked.

"It seems she's had help. Why *they* would help her and *how* they would have healed her is beyond me. In fact, I'm not certain I even believe her. She also says she doesn't know who I am," he said, turning back to me with a grin.

The line of his smile creased so hard that one dimple popped out, causing him to look disarmingly boyish despite the rest of his cold features.

"So, what do you want to do with her? Kill or keep?" stupid Dirac asked, sounding bored.

"Killing her so quickly was a rash decision on my part. The humans somehow surprised me. Look at it, Dirac," he said, shoving me over and pushing my head down slightly so the other man could look at me. "If the humans were so stupid to send such a…"—his face wrinkled in disgust, but his pale eyes still lingered on my body— "foul and disgusting creature to kill me, surely it'd be a waste for someone not to use her before she goes back."

He smiled again, but this time, his eyes darkened before he dropped his grip on me, and I fell against the ground with a grunt.

"You're-you're going to send me back? Back home?" I

clamored on the ground, trying desperately to regain my stance.

"Of course," the terrifying prince said as he stepped back, beginning to walk away. "Dead, obviously. You'll be returned to the humans broken and used beyond anyone's recognition. A symbol of what will happen to their entire realm once we gain access. I'm sure there are a few kitchen ogres that wouldn't mind running you through before the forest bogs obliterate you," his deep voice muttered darkly as his eyes twinkled with the glow of menace.

"You will not touch me!" I shrieked.

The thought of anyone, especially him, touching me made me frantic with fear.

He smiled wide at my horror. His white teeth flashed, but his eyes, like before, never shared the sentiment. Black swirls of smoke continued to flow from behind his back in oversized wings, now seeming to emulate the shape of segmented butterfly wings.

"Pet, I would never debase myself enough to touch you, a human. The royals would rather burn than sacrifice our dignity by touching you. Others may find humans a rare delicacy, but the Shadow Slayers, we would forfeit our reign over the entire realm before we desecrated our lineage with the tarnished touch of a human. Don't worry, there are plenty of other creatures that I'm sure will ignore your species...if not, we will throw a bag over your head or something." He smiled eerily, obviously satisfied with my terror as he began to walk away. "Dirac, take her to the tower dungeon with the rest of the rats and vermin. I'm sure the queen will be quite pleased, no one despises humans more than Mother."

His frame faded into the darkness of the forest as he left.

"Please, I beg you! Let me go, I do not belong here! Please!" I pleaded to the man named Dirac. I continued backing away from him as he stalked forward, clearly annoyed at my attempts to flee.

"Well, you're right about that, you *do not* belong here.

83

Now come here or I will hurt you, and I give you my word that no fox will be able to save you where we go." He lunged and caught me with ease, throwing me over his shoulder as I kicked and flailed.

"Stop this, please! I meant him no harm! Please let me go!" I shouted and kicked at his armored body as my head rapped roughly against the armored back of Dirac. Like his *prince,* he was much larger and stronger than any human man.

"Please just stop, you know I can't let you go," he mumbled impatiently as he walked out from the circle in the forest and farther into the dark woods.

"Where are we going? Why wouldn't the foxes go there?"

"Because you are going to the dungeon of the Unseelie court," he mumbled, "and nothing can save you there."

CHAPTER 8

CALLIE

I T HAS BEEN TWO WEEKS SINCE I WOKE UP IN THE DUNGEON. Unless my calculations were off. I was going off tally marks on the wall and tracking the guards' shift changes.

At first, all I did was cry. I must've sat at the large iron bars of my cell and cried for days.

No one came to save me.

The police never came.

Earl, Cecelia, and Cliff never barged in, knocking down iron bars to set me free. My family never burst through the stone wall of my cell to get me out.

I never woke up in a sterile hospital bed to find my family surrounding me.

Deep in the marrow of my bones—something instilled in me since I was a child—assured me that someone would come and save me. That some type of guardians would come to help me, the police or firemen, the army or the FBI, perhaps a hidden sector of the government that I had never heard of before.

Someone would show up to help me.

A familiar face would suddenly arrive and draw me into a firm hug. My nose would fill with scents of comfort and safety from being smashed against their shoulder hastily. They would wipe my tears and tell me everything would be okay, that I would be safe. They would squeeze me tightly. The very moment their arms circled me, the tension would wane from my muscles because I would know that I was safe and that they would take care of me—that no one else could hurt me.

But no one ever came.

Sitting in the dark, alone in the small cell, I thought my mind had left me.

Days on end, I fasted, refusing myself the small meals of rice and bread I was given in the glorified hope of detoxing my body from whatever hallucinogens or poisons may have been in my system.

I wouldn't give up. For the family I still had, I would do whatever I needed to so I could return to them.

My name is Callie Peterson. I am a proud environmentalist and biological technician. I was walking through the forest to get my microscope when I stumbled upon an anomaly of luna moths and a perfect circle of destroying angel mushrooms. After stepping into the ring of mushrooms, everything else became…less real. I live at 4313 Sassafras Road, Willow Springs, Michigan. My name is Callie Peterson. Proud environmentalist and biological technician, walking through the forest to get my microscope, when I stumbled upon an anomaly of luna moths and a perfect circle of destroying angel mushrooms. I live at 4313 Sassafras Road, Willow Springs, Michigan.

I've repeated this back to myself hundreds of times a day, refusing to forget who I was. I pressed my back against the cold stone of the damp dungeon wall, and the rigid rock dug through my filthy black dress and into my skin. I closed my eyes with relief at the feeling. Any feeling other than fear and worry.

My hands had been chained together by large iron brackets with a long, heavy chain that hung to my knees in between. The always-cold metal bit into my wrists painfully, but again I welcomed the pain as a reminder that I was still alive enough to feel something.

There were no windows, no cracks that enabled me to see the sunshine outside, though a part of me doubted the sun would ever bother to shine here. Everything I had seen and heard reeked of gloom and darkness.

The dungeon was an accumulation of small cells with dirty stone and brick walls, each sealed in with a set of foreboding iron bars. Inhuman cries and noises echoed from the neighboring cells every hour. No one but the guards spoke. Everything was filthy and covered in a grimy brown tinge. The space was so dark you could only see a few squares of amber light on the stone floor as the hall torch shone through the bars of my cage. The only light in the cell besides that was a tiny sliver in the brick. The small fissure appeared to lead to a hallway or other room with a fire or torch of some kind that lit its interior. It was a small break in the wall, and the most I could see was a flickering change of light if I pressed my eyes against it long enough.

Shortly after I had found the crack, I was determined to find a way out. I spent all my time devising plans and working out theories on how I could tear down the wall and escape.

The only people I ever saw were the guards that commanded the dungeon or put the food plate in my room. If they hadn't decided to eat it in front of me that day.

Most of the time, they wore thick black armor that almost covered them completely and solid boots that beat loudly against the stone floor as they walked up and down, occasionally pissing or shouting into the cells. The cries and curses of the others would quiet in a slow wave as they passed the cells, the cries growing louder once they passed.

A few would regularly stop and stare into the bars of my cell. They never spoke to me, but I heard what they said to each other. From what I had gathered, they were fae but not the good kind. It sounded like they were closer to hell as far as the fairy realms went. I had only heard mention of the

Seelie and Unseelie fae realms, which is where I was. They despised each other. The Unseelie hated the Seelie fae even more than they hated humans, though, from a few conversations I'd overheard between two of the younger guards, no one hated humans more than the Smoke Slayers—the prince and queen of the Unseelie court. From my eavesdropping, humans were even seen as an exotic sexual delicacy by several of the other royals. Lovely.

One night I was startled awake by a snarl.

One of the guards stood outside the large wall of iron bars, nothing visible but a giant silhouette. At first, I thought the snarls had come from him, but immediately two other guards flashed to his side, appearing out of thin air to grab his arms and pull him away.

I noticed the short guard from the day prior lying on the floor in a heap of armor, snarling wildly in pain. That had been the sound that roused me.

The guard that towered outside my cell cried.

It sounded similar to the whine a canine or lupine would make.

I hurried from the cot to hide in the corner. I had no protection here, and the darkness that hid me only made me feel a fraction safer. As soon as I moved, the towering guard cried louder and attempted to pull the door to my cell open.

Two more guards appeared at his side. Four guards in total attempted to pull him away as he clamored to gain entry into the cell.

I shook so hard, I couldn't see straight. The mournful depths of his cries caused me to shut my eyes for a few seconds to try and trick my terror-stricken mind into thinking that it would be all right and he wouldn't get in.

When I lifted my eyes again, I caught the last moment before all the guards vanished, including the one on the floor. The large one in the center had pulled off his black metal helmet, and for a split second, I looked at the face that cried like a dog to get in and kill me. His face was covered in fur, complete with pointy wolf-like ears. It was as if he were part man and part wolf. The dark brown fur appeared almost like a beard that had gone wild on his face. His bright brown eyes stared pitifully into mine, locking onto me as if he could see right through the darkness and witness my every move. His expression of anguish both shocked and rattled me.

He looked devastated, not angry.

Where had they gone? It was as if they had been there, and then they…they just weren't. I stared in disbelief.

There was an ache in my heart seeing the giant guard's face. The same feeling that put my soul in a vise when I saw a wounded or hurt animal. The same feeling that overwhelmed me with the need to make sure they were safe and taken care of.

Feelings stirred in my gut that something was wrong with him, and I couldn't help. Why had he looked at me like that?

A harsh scurrying sound startled me from the numb safety of my thoughts.

A large brown rat squeezed itself out of the crack in the brick, scraping the greasy fur of its back as it squished its large body through.

Rats were nothing new; they constantly scampered around the cells. Sometimes I would have twenty or more in my small cell at one time. They were sweet, and I enjoyed the little company they gave, even occasionally huddling up to cover my freezing feet. They never stayed long, always running around frantically as if they, too, were prisoners and terrified of the guards. Maybe they were. That seemed like an entirely different type of punishment, being turned into vermin.

This one seemed different immediately. For one, it was much larger than the others. Instead of just walking through the bars, he squished through the crack in the brick; none of the others had come from there. I would have doubted they could fit, and his body seemed much too large to fit through the fissure, but still, somehow, it did.

I wasn't frightened. I'd never really learned to fear animals—other than snakes—as they had never been anything but helpful to me. They seemed to seek me out even, and I welcomed it. In truth, they were the only friends I'd had at times.

This one was different for another reason entirely, another reason I would soon learn.

He spoke.

Over time he frequently kept me company, warning me of the guards on duty and various other helpful tidbits of information he thought would make my stay easier.

One day I managed to save a portion of this super acidic, pickled dish that they frequently included in the meals. I allowed it to concentrate for a few days under my cot. I then took advantage of the highly acidic pickling ingredient they had used and created a paste that slowly ate away at the brick's mortar near the crack the rat always squeezed through. It took days to complete, and I barely had enough for even this little task, but the thought of hoarding enough so that I could escape stayed in my mind.

I never got his name because he would leave as soon as I asked, so I quickly stopped, in the hopes he would stay with me longer. He later told me not to ever ask another fae their name or it would get me killed.

To them, a full, true name held a very strong, very easy-to-command power that they shared with no one. Not even husbands and wives typically exchanged this information.

Occasionally the other rats and hidden creatures would get too plentiful in the small cell so brown rat would arrive to shoo them away protectively. Sometimes it saddened me to see them go, but brown rat never seemed to like them near me.

One day I heard the scrape of the brick being shoved out of place, so I ran to the dark corner, excited to see brown rat.

He rushed through, out of breath.

"It's coming. It's coming, and I can't protect you!" His

small but deep voice was filled with panic as he struggled to catch his breath.

I paled. My heart felt like it stopped beating as I processed the look on his upset rodent face.

"You must listen, it is coming, and I *can't* get them to stop it!" He climbed up my shoulder and down the other side in a nervous scamper.

"What is coming?" I asked, my voice nearly nonexistent from fear.

"The forest bog. The prince has ordered it to be moved to your cell!" he cried as he pulled his little whiskers in distress.

"What is a forest bog?" I whispered shakily.

Just then, iron clanged, and the sound of heavy footfalls echoed from the opposite end of the dungeon. The screams and cries of the other prisoners only amplified as they continued down the stone aisle. Slowly the footsteps grew louder as they neared my cell.

"Oh! I have failed you! No matter what, be silent! It *will* hurt you! Oh, stars!" brown rat cried as he opened his mouth to tell me more.

The iron bars of my door gained a few silhouetted shadows, and I stared at the realization that they were here.

I moved to place brown rat safely behind me, but he had vanished, already gone to wherever it was he went.

My eyes returned to the bars from where I sat huddled in the dark corner of the cell. A stubby, round creature came into view, stepping arrogantly into the cell as soon as they opened it.

The creature's eyes immediately went to the dark corner where I hid and it began laughing a cold, grating laugh.

Could they all see in the dark?

I pressed my back harder against the cold wall behind me, wishing with everything I had that it would magically give way and I would fall through the other side to safety. What did safety even look like here?

The creature was about the height of a human man,

maybe six foot or so, round, with a greenish tint to its grimy-looking body. It looked like a cross between a toad and a human with no hair on its head. No ears that I could see, but giant bloodshot green eyes stared back at me with a look of wrongness. The eyes of someone who only held malice in their heart. They reminded me of the prince's cold blue eyes.

"So the prince left me a present after all," the voice croaked out, sounding infinitely more frog than human.

It smiled the eeriest grin I have ever seen as hundreds of needle-like teeth lined its mouth, with no space left for a tongue as it was filled to the brim with rotten yellow spikes of teeth.

I screamed, unable to stop the cry as I recalled brown rat's command to be silent a little too late. I slapped my palm over my mouth, praying I could go back in time and muffle the sound.

The forest bog trembled at my scream. It dropped to all four abnormally long limbs and careened its round green head to one side. Red flickered in its eyes before they returned to green while he continued to watch my every move.

"So he *is* trying to win me over after all," the bog chuckled to the guard. "Her terror is so palpable I could spend an eternity in this dungeon simply for the delectable scent of her fear," it croaked hoarsely.

"Prince Mendax said he doesn't care what you do to her, but once you are close to ending the assassin, His Highness demanded he is called upon to make the killing strike," the guard mumbled matter-of-factly as he locked up the bars behind the hideous creature. "Watch if you shift to an animal, Bog. We've been having problems with the animals and shifters being drawn to her. The assassin is dangerous, that's why Mendax is gifting her to you," he mumbled, double-checking the security of the sturdy iron lock.

"Drawn to her? What do you mean? She is human, I can smell it. Not even the weakest of the Unseelie would be drawn to a human." He spat the words out with obvious disgust. "Other than to hear their weak little mouths scream in pain." He lowered his voice an octave to growl the last sentence in my direction.

"I don't know, Bog," the guard said, sounding bored and confused. "Even the guards that shift are having problems." He leaned in closer to the bars now as if letting out a secret. "Captain Walter had to be forcibly removed. He was trying to get her out, can you believe that? Captain Walter, the prince's best friend, attempting to free the assassin?"

The bog's eyes went black for a second before it shook. It returned to stand on two feet as he turned to stare at the guard with an odd expression.

"*Captain Walter?*" It turned from the guard back to me, confusion marring its hideous face. "Just for that, I may keep you alive." It smiled eerily, licking one of his muddled eyes with a disturbingly long tongue. "I loathe that man." It snapped its neck as if stretching it to the side to get the kinks out, but it remained hanging grotesquely to the side as if it were broken.

I screamed before both hands flew to cover my mouth. Even without my scream, my heart pounded so loudly I was sure the creature could have heard.

The frog-man got down on all fours again, his eyes flashing red. This time the burning red of his eyes took over the green completely, and the creature let out a moan. It shuddered wildly as it crouched low against the ground, its robust belly pressed against the stone floor.

"Yessssss. I haven't tasted human fear in eons," it moaned, holding its head up and closing its heinous eyes. "I doubt I'll be able to keep you alive till the end of the week."

Its green belly dragged against the ground as it crawled closer. I was paralyzed with fear. This was it; I was going to die.

Its back legs dragged across the floor with an awkward gait as if only his arms functioned.

"Please don't hurt me! Please!" I cried, tears dripping from my eyes and heating my cheeks in warm streaks.

I checked to see if the guard was still outside the cell, but he was gone.

The bog's eyes flared even more red than before as it closed the distance between us before he stopped himself only a few paces away.

At my pleas, it shuddered and began to writhe against the floor.

The slimy-looking creature ground its pelvis against the floor salaciously as it stared at me, open-mouthed.

I screamed again, unable to hide the horror from what I saw.

"Fucking hell, that's good!" it croaked as it ground against the floor aggressively, never blinking as its red eyes stared at me. "I'm gonna empty that weak human skull of yours and fuck it. I'll be hearing your delicious screams until it overflows with my seed. You'll be screaming for a week, begging me to kill you." He seemed to be having trouble moving as his lower half slapped against the ground.

He was literally getting off on my fear.

I tried to stifle my panic, but no matter how strongly I tried, small terror-filled noises still sounded from my mouth.

I shoved my dirty dress down, desperate to cover my body from the disgusting creature's view, though I knew the skin that showed wasn't what was getting him off.

It was my terror.

I finally succeeded in silencing my whimpers. This monster would not get anything more from me. I *would* see my family again. I would leave this place. I refused to allow myself to believe anything else.

I shook like a leaf in a windstorm, causing the frizzy bits of loose hair around my face to tremble violently in my eyes.

The monster ceased humping to narrow its vibrant red eyes at me.

"You think you're well-fortified, huh? Human assassin or not, your fear is tangible. For this gift to my essence, I shall allow Prince Mendax's army through any forest he so wishes.

94

Though, I will most assuredly *not be* allowing him the killing blow. No, that is mine also." The creature flung out his clawed hand and clasped it around my head tightly.

I had to bite my hands to keep from screaming, knowing it would only fuel his need. The metallic tang of my blood filled my mouth, scaring me still more.

I was going to pass out.

The thought of what this creature would do to my body if I lost consciousness sobered me.

It was too much for my human mind; I was crumbling with fear.

I closed my eyes and pretended I was no longer in the dirty dungeon cell but instead, running through a field of wildflowers. I lost myself to the imagery. Sunshine warmed my skin as I twirled and frolicked through the tall array of brightly colored flowers. I imagined what the red poppies might smell like if I pressed my nose to their paper-like red petals, that the tall grass felt like tickling the sensitive skin of my palms.

From my mouth a scream so loud shot out, it made me light-headed.

"There it is," rasped the disgustingly warped creature.

One hand still gripped my head, its claws penetrating the softness of my scalp. I flinched again. Its other large hand clasped my left thigh while long dirty claws hooked into the sensitive skin of my bare upper thigh. The skin tented as its hooked claws pulled across the surface. He rubbed himself wildly against my side now. His long green legs slammed against me as he grew more and more forceful. Suddenly his red eyes widened to the size of saucers as he slowly dragged his nails down my tented skin. The audible tearing of my flesh made an unfamiliar and foul sound in my ears. The creature's moans and curses filled the entire dungeon as its body unraveled with spasms.

Dark green liquid shot out from between his legs and splattered across my chest and face.

Tears ran like a river as sobs racked my shivering body.

How could this happen to me? I was going to die getting skull fucked, covered in monster seed.

Suddenly the entire dungeon filled with a thunderous, raging growl so loud and full of anger we both inhaled sharply. It sounded like it was close, the other side of the wall maybe. Another prisoner? I'd never heard anything so terrifying, even during my time here.

The forest bog suddenly froze and transformed, shaping itself into a boulder the size of a large watermelon. The brown boulder dropped from the air and landed on my lower leg, crushing it painfully with the weight of…well, a boulder. It thudded to the ground next to me as I whined in pain.

What had made that growl? Was something worse coming to get me? Why had the bog been so hurried to transform himself into a rock? Is that just what forest bogs did to hide? Not missing an opportunity, I shuffled to my feet, wincing in pain at the four long gashes that marred my crushed thigh. I grabbed the large rock with what little strength I had and slammed it to the ground, praying it would shatter.

It did not.

I tried several more times to no avail until I settled on rolling the rock to the opposite corner of the room behind the only other cot in the room.

As I was deciding how I could tie the rock up, it shifted again.

A short log-like creature no taller than my knees scowled at me from where the boulder had just been.

"Do not think you are out of my grasp, human. His anger may have saved you today, but your erotic terror is too delicious to be blanketed by it for long. Sleep well, *human*. Don't make a sound, or I will wake extra ravenous." The now log-like creature had closed its black eyes, done with the conversation.

I scrambled to the corner to hide again as I tried to stanch the blood, all the while waiting in fear for what else was to come.

CHAPTER 9

CALLIE

THE DAMP STONE FLOOR OF THE DUNGEON MADE IT HARD TO keep the tiny cuts of cheese on the tiny charcuterie board I had been making. I suppose it was less of a board and more of a loose brick from the back wall, but brown rat wouldn't mind.

I laughed out loud at how cute it looked with the little bits of cracker and honey I had saved from my meal yesterday. I quickly looked over my shoulder to see if the sleeping bog had heard me.

I hadn't slept all night, too afraid to close my eyes, for fear the forest bog would wake and fulfill his promises.

I gently poked the open, bloodied wound on my head where he had hurt me. Somehow my wounds had already started to heal, faster than they ever had at home.

I pressed my fingernail sharply into the wound and bit the iron cuff around my wrist to stop from crying out. The metal tang of blood and iron swirled in my mouth.

I still felt something.

The iron chain between my cuffs clanged loudly with my movement, and I stifled a cry as I squeezed my eyes shut and listened in terror.

Had I woken the bog?

A stray tear fell from my crinkled eyes as I shivered and quickly attempted to shove myself deeper into the dark corner where I hid.

All night, thoughts of how to escape the cell and the forest bog tormented me. All night I had watched his sleeping form for signs he was waking. Fear never left me, even as I tried to feed brown rat with a meal one last time. The bog would not sleep forever, and when it woke, it would kill me. I knew it.

I surmised that waiting for death to arrive was infinitely worse than when death would actually arrive.

Waiting, every breath in fear for when the monster would decide my fate. I'm surprised it hadn't risen already with the tang of my fear in its mouth, because it had only increased with the wait throughout the night. Maybe that was his intention. Smart.

I was shaking so hard I feared I would make noise.

Be quiet or they will wake and hurt you again.

If I hadn't lost my mind already, then it was happening now. My sanity had slowly snapped. It was like the threads being frayed on a worn and tired rope. I began to unravel as I watched the bog's dark lump of a body breathe in and out on the opposing end of the dungeon.

A moment of stillness passed, and I breathed out a silent lungful of relief and returned to my mini charcuterie board.

I could wait and see if they gave me more bread tonight, but I doubt they would even bother, assuming I was as good as dead now.

Quietly and with absolute care, I stepped over the rusted chain connecting my cuffs and pulled my hands taut on either side of my body. The thick chain pulled tightly around my lower back, silencing any further clangs. I moved the small brick of food to the crack in the cell wall where I had previously removed the brick. I sat my body down silently in front of the gap and waited patiently.

Within only a few moments, the rat came crawling in.

The light scratch of his claws on the musty cell's stone and the deep rhythm of a sleeping monster were the only sounds. Even the other prisoners were eerily silent as if they, too, were afraid of waking the forest bog. Either that or they were quietly listening for the entertainment from my inevitable death.

"Friend, I'm so glad you made it back," I whispered, finally feeling a tinge of fear vacate my mind with the presence of a friend.

The large brown rat looked to both sides of the cell before bypassing the brick of food and hurriedly scampering into my lap.

"You're still alive! How!? I told you to stop saving your food for us. I need to help you escape, not take your nourishment," the brown rat scolded quietly as he climbed onto my shoulder to nuzzle the crook of my neck.

His soft fur, pressed against my skin, so warm and dry compared to everything else down here.

"Take the food back to the others, please. I need to know you are fed," I pleaded in a breathy whisper.

He had assured me many times the castle rats were beyond taken care of, but I couldn't harbor the thought of any of the animals and creatures around not having food, especially him.

"Please be quiet. I cannot bear to see that thing hurt you anymore. Hopefully, I have convinced him to arrive before the bog wakes," he whispered even softer than before. He paused to look in the opposite corner filled with shadows before continuing. "I came to tell you that *he* is on the way! I have failed you—I just didn't know what to do! Please, please don't give up, I won't…I just know he can't possibly be so cruel to you. How does he not feel it? We will find a way—" Brown rat squeaked loudly before quickly running off my shoulder and through the hole again, just as a loud bang thudded and a large boulder slammed into the wall, just barely missing the rat's tail.

I leaped back without thinking in an attempt to put

distance between the monster and myself. I quickly stepped over my chain and brought it to the front so I would hopefully have more range of movement with my hands, maybe use the chain. Not that I could defend myself much. Callie Peterson was weak and defenseless.

"What did I tell you, human? What did I tell you would happen when you woke me?" rumbled a scratchy voice. It was haunting. Its pitch both too high and too low all at the same time. Nothing human sounded similar. But then, I suppose he was not human after all.

I stopped breathing for a moment altogether.

It shifted with a tremble and briefly transformed into a few other various creatures before turning into a squat, tree-stump-looking creature no taller than my hips. Brown bark-like texture covered its long body save for the angry tan face, arms, and hands. Dried green and brown leaves rustled loudly at the ends of his branch-like arms. Large black eyes void of any expression perched in the middle of his face. No other features gave way to his personality but for the large black hole of his mouth.

"I-I'm sorry. Please go back to sleep, please." I pleaded with the forest bog.

It trembled again, and this time, sharp branches sprouted from his sides, each covered in thorns of tall green spikes.

"I *will* go back to sleep after I kill you and use you slowly," the forest bog rasped as it stalked toward me.

The thorns shifted, growing longer and more frightening as every one of them angled toward me.

"Please!" I cried out as I pushed my back flush against the cold stone wall.

"So, you haven't killed her yet?" Boomed a disappointed voice as the owner opened the cell door with a clang of iron and stepped into the dark cell.

Raw power rolled off the towering figure. At least fifteen guards in shadowed armor stood on edge as the man stepped forward.

The bog across from me shrank away instantly, withdrawing all of the thorns as he shifted into a boulder once again.

"Sir, the assassin is not safe to be around! Let us get her. Please, leave her cell," one of the guards all but screamed as he scrambled quickly to step in front of the towering figure.

They all appeared large and omnipotent, but none seemed to come close to the bulk and height of the shadowed figure.

He seemed to suddenly remember himself and left the cell to watch from behind the iron bars. Five other guards entered in his place. I assumed it was the man I had fallen on when I entered the portal—the prince. There was an aura around him I didn't think possible for anyone else to have. He was terrifying.

"Please! Don't do this!" I shouted as several guards grabbed me.

They formed a complete circle around me with their bodies as they pushed me out of my cell and into the torch-lit aisle of the dungeon.

"Where to, sir?" a different guard asked as they huddled around me wearily. As if I were the most feared killer in all the world, all the while making certain they kept me far from *him*.

"To the chamber of blood. You've had your chance, Bog, now I shall have mine. I have grown tired of keeping her, and it's just the place to kill her," the prince said nonchalantly as if he were speaking about the weather.

The iron slammed behind me. I careened my neck to see where we were going, but I was unable to see anything past the cluster of armored bodies that surrounded me.

Several sentries held me up while they moved their tight huddle, shoving me forward. I tried to get a look at what surrounded my cell, to see if there were any exits or things that might aid an escape, but the guards kept tight enough to block me from seeing much of anything.

Even through all of the movement and forcefulness, you could sense their fear. A few watched me with such apprehension in their eyes that I couldn't stop myself from laughing at them, which only seemed to amplify their weariness.

My head and leg throbbed painfully. A warm trail of blood slid down my thigh from where the bog had ripped open my skin.

The dramatic entourage continued. I was pushed up a set of stone stairs, thirteen—fourteen—black boots encircled me, shuffling to stay tightly together. One tripped, and his feet appeared smaller than the rest, maybe a men's size eight? Was he younger? Lower ranking, possibly? Would he be more likely to help me?

A large wooden door with worn iron buckles opened, and I was shoved in as the guards remained outside.

I fell to my knees, and my dress shoved up, bunching tightly around my waist. I had no shoes now, and blood and filth caked my feet. Flakes of dried crimson blood and dirt sprinkled the floor where it had fallen from the fabric bunched tightly around my waist. The room was brighter than the dungeon. In fact, it was the brightest place I'd seen here. The floor was a beautiful white marble with red diamond tiles scattered throughout. A glance at the walls showed a pretty crimson wallpaper covered with elaborate gold designs. A large black crystal chandelier hung in the middle of the moderately sized room.

It was beautiful in a classical gothic sense.

"My lord, please—" I heard in the distance.

I turned as I struggled to pull my tattered dress back over my exposed body, hurrying to my feet.

I could feel him standing over me like a black omen of death.

My cheeks flushed with anger and embarrassment, knowing he had just viewed my bare ass and probably more. I snapped my head up to scream at him to set me free.

Instead, I gasped as I fell backward on my recently covered ass.

In the brightly lit, opulent room, I could see him clearly for the first time.

He was ethereal. There was no other word for it. His head was free from any helmet, armor, or mask. His skin was a stark contrast against his black-as-night hair. A lock of it fell over one of his eyes. In the light, I could see the color easily. Cold and icy blue. So light they almost appeared silver, but no, they were an unforgettable pale blue. No mistaking them. They glared at me with a force I was certain must have been laced with magic as they pinned me to the spot. His head tilted to the left ever so slightly, giving a predatory movement as he stared at me with a bored and irritated expression.

I'd never noticed a man's jaw before, probably because they hadn't looked like his. I couldn't seem to shift my eyes to anything other than his face and neck. He swallowed under my scrutiny as if taunting my obvious internal war. The action caused a feathering of muscle and a small dip of his Adam's apple down his masculine throat. Since when was I attracted to a jaw? Was this some fae trick? Some type of magic they used to trip up humans?

His body was much larger than any human male's. Were those his broad shoulders? How much armor did he wear? His waist seemed more trim than bulky, filled out with hard ridges of muscle. He wore no armor, yet somehow managed to appear more impending than those around him that did. Muscular thighs covered in black and burgundy leather armor stood confidently yet braced as if ready for a fight.

Fuck.

Somehow it was *so* much more unsettling and demented to have your mind be physically attracted, *even a tiny bit*, to the villain that was about to destroy you.

I gathered myself, remembering exactly why this monster had brought me here.

"Please," I begged. "I don't mean any harm, just send me back. I'm just a scientist. This was an accident, I am no one." Sobs racked my body. I couldn't help it. My mind was weak from the constant fear. "I don't even know where I am. I don't understand…"

"Still going with that story, huh?" His gravelly voice rumbled across the air as he took a step forward.

His wings were nowhere to be seen now, and if I passed him in the street, I might think him human.

No, that's not true.

There was just something godly about him, a rare air of sorts wafted from him, letting everyone in the vicinity know he was the most dangerous and powerful thing. It made the hair on my arms stand on end just being near him. No human would mistake him for anything other than a powerful predator. He was almost too beautiful to pass as a human. A dark glint in his eyes didn't seem to connect to anything within him. His eyes held no feelings or empathy, nothing that would give him pause before he killed. It was hauntingly ethereal in a menacing and frightening way.

I shivered.

"It–it's not a tale, I'm not supposed to be here," I stammered. This could very well be my last shot to convince him to set me free.

"Oh, do I agree, human. I will say it still pesters my mind just how the humans knew when we would breach the veil. They must have someone here working for them." He paused briefly to grin a small creepy smile. "If I find out who it was, I'll hang them by their ears and skin them. Shame I had to adjust my plans, but alas. The Unseelie will still claim the Earth as their own regardless. But don't worry, you won't be around to watch us destroy your family and friends. You'll be long dead by then," he whispered as he crouched down and rested his hands on one knee next to where I sat on the floor.

My body involuntarily leaned back to escape his closeness. At my movement, a guard entered.

"Sir!" the guard shouted, obviously alarmed by the prince's closeness to me.

What did they think I could do? He and every other male here dwarfed me.

"Why would you want Earth? Why do you hate humans so much?" I whispered, unable to silence my curiosity.

None of this made any sense.

He ignored the guards and stared into my eyes, a wrinkle of anger and curiosity furrowing his brows.

"Ple—" I began to stand, but not before the younger guard I'd noticed from earlier, size eight, suddenly rushed me.

The guard's palm slapped me so hard across the cheek that my entire body slammed down onto the white marble floor with a clap. Blood filled my mouth as something small and sharp stuck to my tongue.

It was my tooth.

The young guard had hit me so hard that he knocked out my loose wisdom tooth. I stared up at the two large males with fury, and I had to remind myself who I was—I was a helpless human scientist with no defenses against these fae. They could knock me around all they wanted, and there was nothing I could do. I was weak.

The prince, still crouched on one knee, glared at the guard who had slapped me. His gaze held an irritated look, like it had offended him that the guard had thought he needed help. The young guard nervously slid himself back and away from the glaring prince.

"The Unseelie realm will take Earth because it is due to us." He turned his eyes away from the hiding guard and focused again on me. "When our space was divided, tell me why the Seelie were granted access to earth but not us? Because we are filled with darkness and they are filled with light? Most humans' darkness could rival ours. The only real difference is we have the power and longevity of immortal life to back it up. Not fragile, impending mortality like you. So very easy to kill," he said softly.

A vein had begun to pop forward in his forehead, causing him to appear completely unhinged.

I didn't dare make a single move other than to tremble. How much more of this realm's terror could I take?

When no more hits came, I slowly rolled away from him but kept my eyes locked with his. I spat out the blood and sat back up, pressing my loose tooth into my cheek. Maybe I could use the calcium or phosphorus for something later, something that could get me out of here.

I laughed chaotically as my tongue trailed over my hidden tooth. The scared faces of the guards flinched with every move I made toward the towering prince, and I couldn't suppress the laughter anymore. It was absurd. My laugh grew hysterical, louder and louder as I watched their terrified faces. I did more than just laugh, though, I *felt* it. It was when I knew I had truly gone mad. That was the first time I had *felt* the madness.

"What's it like, Prince?" I smiled at him as I canted my head and blood dripped from my open mouth. "To have your guards terrified of an innocent, inconsequential human?" I shifted and rose to my feet, not caring how close I was to him now. I was going to die soon enough, so what did it matter?

He bristled and tensed his body as I quickly moved to stand next to him, so close I nearly brushed against his gloved hand. The timing left him still kneeling. As I stood, I looked down on him for a moment before I gave him my back. Tears leaked from my burning eyes even though a smile remained.

"You turn your back on a Smoke Slayer?" he whispered, and I heard him stand. "You're much dumber than I had initially thought. You didn't even try to block or overpower me. What a waste of time you are. At this point, I'm forced to believe the humans just wanted to be rid of you." His words echoed in the room like a sound system, full of power and arrogance.

Unseelie prince?

I needed to know. Even in my death and madness, my curious mind refused to comply.

"What exactly are Unseelie, and why do they need a prince?" I asked, turning back to face him.

His blue eyes flickered a moment with confusion as he tilted his head slightly and clenched his jaw. His full black brows pinched slightly before returning to their statuesque state.

"Why not, I'll play, assassin. You currently stand in the blood chamber of the Unseelie kingdom. The most evil and deadly fairies and creatures behind the veil bow only to me, their prince and soon-to-be king." His stance widened as he crossed his arms, the action pushing his biceps out even more obnoxiously.

And then I saw it for the second time in my life.

"Ohmygod," I gasped, inhaling sharply. "Actias luna…"

Had it been here the whole time? It fluttered its wings slowly as it rested on the shoulder blade of the cruel villain. I only saw the tip of beautiful green wings that stuck above his ridiculously wide shoulders. In pure awe, I forgot myself and scrambled to get a better look. I ran around to see his back before he could turn.

Three luna moths clung to the black leather of his large back. He turned quickly, and the movement caused them to flutter their giant green wings, always slow and controlled. Two flew off and landed on the scarlet walls of the chamber, leaving only one to crawl on his back.

"My god…" I whispered in complete amazement.

I had searched for years for them.

His brows drew together over his repulsed squint, and he shifted away from me in disgust.

"You act like you've never seen a luna moth before. I happen to know they are on earth and were waiting for me at the portal. I sent them."

"You sent them?" I scowled, knowing he was lying.

He brushed his shoulder as if to shoo the moth away. "Of course, they are the chosen symbol of the Unseelie fae royals. You wouldn't expect me to leave them behind when we took Earth would you?" He tsked as one flew to his finger briefly before they all fled to the crimson and gold wall. "They are drawn to portals through the veil, being from faerie."

For the first time, he looked at me puzzled, as though he was no longer completely sure that I was an assassin.

"They are the most beautiful things we have on Earth," I murmured, staring at their bright wings before I turned to meet his gaze. "Shame they came from someone so ugly."

Menace flamed in his eyes briefly. A corner of his mouth pulled up in a lopsided grin as he leaned slightly forward, nearly grazing my ear. "I happen to know the only place I'm ugly is on the inside," he whispered. His voice sounded sinister, like he knew *exactly* how evil and beautiful he was. He watched me for a moment with a grin. His pale eyes danced with caged madness. "Send in the cat o' nine tails," he shouted to the guards at the doorway.

"I've thought about you a lot these past few weeks, human. I've thought about how much I want to hurt you. How badly I *ache* to feel your weak neck give out and collapse under my grip. But then I was reminded how inferior you are as a human. I refuse myself the joy of killing you if I cannot feel your life fade away on my bare hands. Unfortunately, as a Shadow Slayer, I am forbidden from touching you. Forbidden against soiling my royal hands with human remnants." He flexed his gloved hands as if his restraint was fading already. "The only one truly fit to kill you is Lord Alistair Cain. The most feared monster we house in the Unseelie realm, next to me. He is what gives our monsters nightmares. My personal assassin."

A chill ran through my bones. The room felt like it grew smaller, the air harder to inhale.

"Why bring me out of the dungeon to such an elegant room just to kill me? Why not leave me in the cell? Much easier to keep the trash in the can, don't you think?" I bit out.

This didn't make sense. Why would they have brought me here? The room was empty enough, no weapons or torture contraptions, at least in plain sight anyway. The room was beautiful. Probably the most beautiful, opulent room I'd ever been in. The gold details sparkled ornately off the deep red walls in a beautifully elegant—

My stomach churned at the realization.

"The walls are painted in blood."

His mouth thinned as he smiled at me.

"Very impressive. One of the few to figure it out before their own blood paints the walls."

His watchful eyes were so penetrating against mine now I couldn't help but step away from him. My body's primal instinct set alarms and sirens off to get as far away from the look he gave me as possible. His every cell seemed to be on edge watching me. Like a hawk before it torpedoed to capture its prey.

"What is the gold then? Ground teeth?" I needed him to stop looking at me like he was.

I spat the tooth that I had been cheeking at him with as much force as possible.

A few loud slaps of thick glass sounded behind us as the guards drew their weapons. Weapons I didn't understand. Long bat-like sledges of iron and what appeared to be simple glass balls filled with black smoke.

With scary fast reflexes, he reached a gloved hand up and caught the tooth before it could hit his face. "Teeth? No, but your decorating ideas are truly inspiring. Maybe we have more in common than I thought." He looked at me another long moment and placed my tooth in the pocket of his black tunic. "No, pet, the scarlet is human and the gold, as I'm sure you very well know, is *Seelie* blood. Beautiful warm glint to it, wouldn't you say? Like liquid gold." He smiled at me, but it was only his mouth that held a smile. His eyes were once again empty and cold.

The way he had said Seelie left no need for interpretation about how he felt about the other fae.

"If you're Unseelie...and a horrible monster, are the Seelie gods? Is that why their blood is gold?" I asked.

I couldn't help it; my mind never stopped asking questions. It was part of why I became a scientist.

He growled at me. Actually growled.

I froze at the sound, my pulse in overdrive.

"I'm certain they think themselves gods. In a sense, all us old fae are gods in our own right, but no." He spit on the floor. "The Seelie are no better than us. They lie and steal just the same. Corrupt and ruin. They hide behind a mask of good, lying to themselves and everyone else in the light of day. We own our evil. There is beauty to be found in the dark, just as there is horror within the light."

I was going to throw up.

My legs were nearly unable to keep me upright. I stood in a room quite literally painted with the blood of their enemies. God only knew what the floor was made of.

I needed out of here and fast.

I began to panic. I didn't want to die. I needed more time to figure out how to get out of here.

"Please call off your assassin. If-if, in fact, the humans watched you wouldn't a human pet be a much grander display? Show them you owned and enjoyed their foolish threat." I was scrambling to think of anything, anything that would play to his arrogant nature and keep me alive long enough to escape and go home.

His head canted as a maniacal grin slid into place on his chiseled jaw.

"If you were more beautiful, I surely would have considered it, but you can't expect me to drag a human around that looks as you do? Fae are superior in every way, including beauty. Your boring features and ugly red hair pale in comparison to even the ugliest of female orcs. Disgusting really. The only thing a human is good for is the music their screams play just before they die."

He thought my hair was red from all the blood? "What about a—"

"Quiet. I've thrown away too much time listening to your plump mouth." He walked to the door, leaving me alone in the large room.

Just before he passed through the crowd of guards, he

turned. "This is exactly why Earth should be ours. What a waste you humans are. I hope Alistair enjoys killing you. I know I would."

The large door slammed shut, and I was left in the blood-painted room alone, awaiting the creature that would kill me.

Lord Alistair Cain.

CHAPTER 10

CALLIE

THE ROOM WAS STILL AND QUIET. I JUMPED WHEN THE WALL creaked behind me, and a panel of the scarlet and gold wall slid open as thick black smoke rolled into the large room.

I was prepared to run into the smoke with the thought of catching the assassin off guard but immediately rethought my decision upon remembering he was the assassin for the crown. I wanted to be as far away from him as possible.

My eyes darted about the elegant-looking room. It held nothing I could use as a weapon, not even furniture to hide under.

I hastily slammed into the nearest wall and flattened my body against it as I crouched low, praying I would get my wish and become invisible. I was so very tired of being frightened.

The black smoke swirled from the wall's opening as clouds billowed onto the marble floor.

Interesting, black smoke.

A hotter fire than normal converts more fuel into elemental carbon. That formed into tiny particles that absorbed light and appeared as black smoke. At least in the human realm, the blacker the smoke, the more volatile the fire, generally speaking. Most fires, like camp or kitchen fires, produced white smoke. I kept that knowledge filed in the back of my mind.

I careened my head to get a better look but could only see smoke-filled shadows. I knew he was inside, though, because the wall panel slid back down with a loud clang. The smoke billowed across the floor, but still, I saw no man.

A low, rattling growl sounded beside me as I stared at the wall panels. I spun, uncertain of how it had passed by me unnoticed.

The coat of the large panther glared blue it was so dark and velvety. Its head was aimed at me, lower than its body, ready to pounce. Large golden eyes gleamed against the shadowy fur on its giant face. Small black irises tracked my every breath, flickering slightly as my chest rose and fell rapidly. Long clear whiskers shot out from either side of his nose like a normal panther. Round ears sat positioned slightly away from me. It was going to pounce.

Up until this point, my mind seemed determined to categorize it as a normal panther. What a foolish thing to do in a faerie realm filled with magic and beasts. Where a tail might normally be, sat nine powerful tails. Each of them with a glistening tip, poised in an arch, aimed at random spots on my body.

It took me a moment of curiosity, wondering why they were aimed at random places, before I realized they were all the various points on my body where a puncture wound would kill instantly, especially after being injected with what I could only assume was poison dripping from the sharp tips. The sharp, curved points formed a threatening vision. They were all black but reminded me of liquid metal dipped in ink.

Had I seen the tail, I would not have been so stupid. I would not have been foolish enough to have attempted what I did, though, to be honest, I hadn't been thinking at all. My body simply reacted.

I reached my hand out quickly, without hesitation, and rubbed its furry black cheek.

My fingers rubbed the soft pad just under its rounded ear deftly, and suddenly, I had no fear. I only ever felt peace and magic with animals, foolish as it may have been. Even the scary ones were still in need of kindness. The moment my fingers touched the creature, all my terror seemed to evaporate. I supposed this was what true madness looked like after all.

The large black cat hesitated only a second after my touch. Before my eyes could open from their last blink, the feline shot its scorpion-like tails over its body, pressing each point firmly against my skin. One pressed lightly into the base of my neck, where my spinal cord met my brain stem. Two on my neck at my carotid arteries, two under each armpit by the axillary arteries, one at my heart, one on the right side of my body at my liver, and one on the side of my groin in the crook of my leg…*What was that?* Ah, yes, my femoral artery and then one on my popliteal artery just below that.

Interesting.

The sharp points pressed just enough into the skin to cause a small prick.

I looked into the panther's eyes, foolishly searching for comfort. I'm not sure why since he was the one about to kill me. I took a deep breath as I continued to rub his velvety fur, more to comfort myself than anything. Its yellow eyes darted back and forth between mine in obvious confusion.

Animals had always been a balm to my weary soul when I needed it most. This large cat did the same. If I was to die, let it be by him and end this once and for all. I was so tired of being afraid, and my body found some semblance of comfort in his furry presence. He wasn't evil, even with poison tips feathered against my skin. I knew he wasn't quite like the others. I could feel it.

I reopened my eyes, not realizing I had closed them, and the giant cat slowly retracted all nine of his tales. His golden eyes still latched onto mine, but now his furry features pulled together with concern.

"Your heart rate is slow, almost as if…" The large cat's

voice was deep, like a long rattling growl with the hint of an accent.

It's what I would imagine my grandfather would sound like if I had ever met him.

"My heart rate?" I questioned, feeling dazed.

Had those points already injected me? I felt cozy. It was taking almost everything I had not to snuggle up to the giant death kitty. Yes, my mind had definitely left me.

"You...you pet me?" he asked incredulously.

I hadn't realized, but my other arm had come up to stroke along his back while the hand that was near his ear had moved to pet the soft fur under his chin. For a split second, I swore he stretched his head up to let me get a better angle.

"I understand you are going to kill me," I said sadly. "I suppose I trust your judgment more than the others here. If you're going to, you must have a good reason to, right?"

The cat backed away from my reach and scowled at me as if disgusted that I had touched him.

"A good reason? You were sent to kill the crown prince, my lord. I need no reason to kill you, human."

He began to pace in front of me, back and forth just out of my reach. It reminded me of the panthers that paced the glass windows at the zoo.

"No," I stated, wishing I could get my hands in the soft fur again.

This was the longest I had been without some type of animal interaction besides the occasional visit from brown rat, and I couldn't help but realize just how much I relied on them for comfort. Animals felt like home. The rehab center had meant everything to me. It often felt like they were the only ones to make me feel safe. Yes, I realized the irony of that statement, considering that I included a magical-Unseelie-assassin panther in that statement.

"No?" he said.

His voice grew gentler the longer he watched me.

"No," I corrected him. "I was trying to get back to my

microscope in the woods, and I followed the moths into a ring of destroying angel mushrooms. I stepped in, and the next thing I knew, I was falling on your crown prince. I've not made a single attempt on his life or anyone else's, for that matter, yet I'm starved in a dungeon with a forest bog as a cellmate." I huffed, the frustration settling back into my bones as I vented to the cat o' nine tails.

He stopped his pacing and stared at me with a deep exhale and a tilt of his wise-looking head.

"Do you know who I am? Surely they told you before I entered. I am Lord Alistair Cain." He paused as if waiting for a reaction from me.

"Yes, they told me. Very prestigious sounding. Please don't kill me."

He curled his lip at my words, showing the whitest and possibly sharpest teeth. Maybe even sharper than the forest bog's, though not as plentiful.

"I don't understand," he said, plopping down on his side next to me. His tails flicked behind him. "I hunt by detecting rapid heartbeats, the music of someone afraid or running. It is impossible to hide from me. So tell me why you do not fear me. You, a little *human*, reach out and pet *me*, Alistair Cain? I'm half-inclined to believe you're an assassin and the best one I've ever seen just from the boldness you possess." He looked around the room as if this were some kind of prank about to unravel. "How could you not be afraid of me? I've killed *hundreds* of assassins from both the Seelie and human realms, and not one has ever reached out to…to pet me!" He began to pace again.

He seemed to be at a loss for what was happening. That made two of us.

A laugh snorted out of me at the thought of him also thinking I was some next-level assassin. What did they all think humans could do against fae that caused them to be so frightened?

He stopped abruptly at the sound of my laugh.

"There is something else about you. I am drawn to...to protect you, and I don't even know you. Tell me, you are not full human, are you?" he asked as he sauntered closer until he stood directly in front of me.

"I am human. I can guarantee that," I said sadly.

If I weren't, I wouldn't be here in this position.

He watched me closely in silence. I hadn't felt safe since I had been here, and my eyes began to flicker closed despite my best efforts to keep the lids open on my burning eyes. I was so tired.

"In all my life, I have never been inclined to spare a life, but I will not kill you, girl. Something I don't understand calls for me to spare you, and though I can do nothing to help you beyond these walls, within them, I will not harm you." His whiskers twitched. "You are in the Unseelie realm, child. There is not a corner you will turn that someone will not hurt you. What is your name?"

He lay down again, his body language more relaxed now. He was close enough that his long back draped over my bare feet and pushed into my knees. I sighed at the warmth and comfort of the action, grateful to feel any bit of warmth against my freezing skin.

"I was told by a friend not to give my name to the fae." I straightened as I remembered brown rat's words.

"Your friend is very wise, and they are a good friend to you. Do you know why you do not share your name, child?" he asked, reminding me of an old grandpa.

I absently reached out and began to stroke the back and side of the cat blanket on my feet. God, this was so nice. I could almost forget I was in an Unseelie castle surrounded by monsters that mistook me for a killer. Almost forget that I was pressed against a wall painted with blood as I petted a nine-tailed death kitty.

"He did not say why you don't give your name. I only see him for short times," I replied.

"They are not your cellmate?" he asked.

"No, my friend is a brown rat that comes to me under a missing brick in my cell to warn me when others are coming. The forest bog was chosen as my cellmate last night," I mumbled as I fought to keep my eyes from shutting in exhaustion.

"The rat speaks to you?" He sounded concerned.

"Well, yes, don't you all here?" I asked.

Though, come to think of it, brown rat was the only rat that had spoken to me.

"No. The rats are just rats. Whoever this rat is lies to you. They are a shifter taking the form of a rat. Animal shifters generally have incredibly close connections to animals. He is likely feeling the same foreign need to protect you as myself."

I froze. Brown rat wasn't really a…brown rat?

"I don't understand? Why would animals want to protect me?" I asked as I reached out absently to scratch under his chin.

This elicited a deep purr, making the fur above my feet vibrate softly.

"I don't understand it either. I've never heard or experienced anything similar and am hundreds of years older than you could even begin to wrap your mortal head around. As for the advice of your shifter friend, in faerie worlds, a name holds power. Giving your name to someone is like giving them a piece of your soul. Families often do not even share their true names. It gives another the ability to hurt you where no knife could ever reach. There are a few that could even control and kill you just by knowing your name. Only those that truly are so dark they have no heart or soul left to be hurt share their true name freely. Like me," he said, the purring suddenly ceased.

"Alistair Cain is your real name? Surely you have a heart and soul. Look at you. You spare my life and allow me a moment of comfort petting you."

"Not all Unseelie are evil, but we all bow to the darkness. I, like so many others here, allowed that darkness to enter my heart eons ago. It's how you survive here. Trust gets you killed, and love gets you hurt. Everything here is about gaining power in some way or another. There are few here who could hurt me anymore."

"Alistair—"

"I'd like you to call me something else when you are around me. Something untainted with pain and darkness. I haven't purred since my mate died. My name is permanently soiled with disease and despair, not fit for whatever it is that you are." He purred deeply.

His voice and eyes held a sincerity I was unfamiliar with. His words sent a shiver up my spine.

"Shivers." I smiled.

He sat up to look into my eyes, and the look portrayed more than words ever could.

"If you like it, then that is what I wish you to call me when I'm in your presence." He purred again.

"I'm Cal—"

"No!" he shouted. "Haven't you heard anything I've said, child? Pick something else, do not speak your real name here," he admonished, shaking his powerful head.

"No, I'm sorry. I heard what you said, but I will not cower from my own name. I am a simple human and will not be here long enough for it to matter, as I'll either be dead or returned home. Those that want to kill me already have the upper hand on me whether I give them my name or not." I straightened my back and felt my chin tip up defiantly, finally feeling a small ounce of control. "I am Callie Peterson. Proud environmentalist and biological technician. I was walking through the forest to get my microscope when I stumbled upon an anomaly of luna moths and a perfect circle of destroying angel mushrooms. I live at 4313 Sassafras Road, Willow Springs, Michigan."

Shivers moved his head away from me slowly.

"Foolish girl, do not give your real name to anyone else, or you will regret it. *Especially* not Prince Mendax. He is one

119

of few with the ability to control by name alone. He could force you to walk into a wall repeatedly until it killed you. He could force your mind to think it obsessed with him to the point that you could not breathe without his presence. All the while not lifting a finger from his hand," he said with a look of tortured bitterness that made his eyes squint above his round jowls.

Was he being controlled by the prince?

"Are you—"

Before I could ask, the dark cat stood abruptly and watched the door, and all nine of his tails sprang to life to arc toward the entrance. My heart began to race at the conflicted look that pulled at his features, his large body visibly tensed. I hadn't fully understood how gently he had been treating me until that moment. He was the chosen killer of this horrible realm's most awful monster, the prince.

"Prince Mendax comes alone." He looked at me sharply. "He comes with no guards because he thinks you dead. I will be forced to leave the royal castle upon his return. I have loyally served for a very long time, and he will not kill me because of our history, but he will know you are different and that something mysterious has taken place. I, like him, would never pass an opportunity to kill, especially a human. He will know instantly that something mysterious lurks within your soul." He bowed his head to me slightly. "Do not share your name with him, Callie, I beg you. He is filled with more power and hate than all of the Unseelie monsters combined. The sole reason he remains a prince and not a king is because he detests everyone to the point of unemotional murder. To become king and relieve his mother, the reigning queen, of her duties, he must be bonded with another to ascend the throne, but he has callously killed every prospect to the point that we allow him to govern us as prince without ascending. Wars began after neighboring royals sent their daughters to the prince in the hopes of an alliance only to have them violently murdered." He shook his head slightly. "You will need to fight if you are going to get out of here alive." He was talking faster, the rhythm of his shoulder blades moving quicker as he paced in front of me.

"I can't fight," I whispered. "I'm just a human scientist."

Fear misted across my skin once again, forcing it to pebble with goose bumps. Escaping this place seemed impossible.

"Fighting isn't only with fists, Callie." He flicked his tails, and the fire from the wall sconce glinted from the tips. "You're a smart girl. Use what you have. I fear if you don't, you will not last another night in your cell."

The iron knob jiggled outside the door.

Prince Mendax was opening the door.

I stood, forcing myself to step in front of Shivers. I would not let him get hurt because he had helped me.

"Go now," I ordered him with as much bravado as I could muster.

"You're protecting *me*?" The large cat watched me as awe pulled his lower jaw down slightly to reveal more beautiful white teeth.

"You've spared me, so now I'll spare you. Leave before he enters. Please, I cannot fight for my life knowing I have cost you yours," I whispered to the cat.

The large lock twisted with the sound of metal scraping.

The door creaked open, and the prince stepped in, shutting it behind him. His head remained down, not yet noticing the strange duo that stood to the left of the room watching him.

"Did she scream Alist—" He turned and halted as our eyes met.

CHAPTER 11

MENDAX

D ID SHE SCREAM ALIST—" I TURNED, CURIOUS WHAT TYPE of massacre Alistair would have left me with this time.

My eyes crashed into the still-very-much-alive human girl's.

I clenched my jaw so hard I felt the muscle pop, and my teeth ground against each other as I stared at her. The human stood proudly next to Alistair as if they were old pals. She looked ridiculous. Her red hair was tangled and matted against the sides and back of her head. She was so covered in filth that it was hard to see her skin color. Golden tan bits surfaced between the dirt and cuts. She wore the same whore dress as the night she landed on me in the forest.

It had been nineteen days since that night. Nineteen days I'd stayed as far away from her as possible, all the while hoping she would hurry up and die.

I hadn't even bothered to get a good look at her that night. Why would I? She was nothing.

Nothing.

In the light of the torches now, I could see the creature that had haunted me since that night, since I'd touched her.

Even under my glove, I had felt the charge of electricity

when I touched her. That had been shocking enough, but then her soft fingers had coiled around my wings and I felt...

I had rejoined the castle, unable to keep my thoughts from returning to her.

When I had returned to her body in the forest, simply to reassure myself that she was dead, I was startled to find that she wasn't.

Ever since, I'd avoided the human, unable to stop thinking about what her skin would feel like under my ungloved fingers.

The fact that she was even still alive was a mystery. She hadn't died from being stabbed clean through in the forest. I knew she would have died. I had watched the life fade from her pretty blue eyes after Fish had stabbed her.

When she hadn't died in the dungeon, I thought I'd send a gift to my assassin and finally get her away from me. Surely she wasn't that hard to kill. After all, she was just a human.

But as I stood in the room and watched her stroke my personal assassin's muscled back like a house cat, I couldn't help but wonder what was different about her.

Apparently, she was harder to kill than I thought.

"Cute. You picked up a stray," I bit out as I tried to school my shock.

How was she still standing?

She shifted uncomfortably, and the filthy dress rode up her thighs, showing the claw marks of the forest bog. I knew it was from him. Good. I knew everything that happened in the Unseelie realm, which was part of why they feared me and precisely why my family held the throne. Her blue eyes looked fiery, much different from the doe-eyed act she had continued to attempt ever since she came through the veil.

Such idiots.

The humans really expected that I, the dark prince, would be distracted by a pretty slut in a short dress?

It would be that much easier to rid the land of humans and take control if they were that stupid. It still puzzled me how they knew we would be attacking that night. How did they know to send her at that exact time? If I found a mole in my men, I would drain his family's blood as he watched.

"He's not a stray," she said defiantly. Her chin tilted up ever so slightly.

"I was talking about you," I stated.

Fire was building in my blood as I watched her, and I knew Alistair would be able to track my heart because it was so fast now. Good thing I owned him, and he wouldn't do a thing about it.

She shot daggers out of her eyes at me. What an interesting blue they were.

My pulse quickened.

"Tell me, Alistair, why are my eyes cursed with the pain of looking at this disgusting human alive? Do make it good, as your life does depend upon it."

The oversized kitten shared a look with the human before stepping in front of the girl and bowing down. "I will not kill her, Mendax. She has my protection in my presence," the royal assassin murmured.

Anger boiled under my skin. How dare he disobey me. His protection?

My smoke strained against me, eager to throttle both of them and be done with this.

"So you are a traitor then, Alistair? I offer you safety, even friendship, and you turn your back on me to help the humans? Have you been behind this all along? Perhaps it was you who alerted the humans of our attack. Mind your words, *cat*. My temper, as you are aware, is flaring," I said calmly, even though I knew he could tell how much rage burned inside me by the speed of my heart. He also knew what would happen if I unleashed it.

"Mendax, I am no traitor. I have served this court tirelessly. I cannot explain my draw to the girl other than to tell you there is something enchanting about her, but I can't place it." He looked down, embarrassed. "I will not harm her and will not let harm come to her in my presence," Alistair murmured.

I could see the struggle in his vicious eyes. He was at war with his decision. He was a killing machine, never hesitating. Why would he disobey me and spare her? This stupid, weak, full-lipped human?

"Then your presence has no more duty in this kingdom. Leave now before I forget what mercy feels like," I growled at my friend.

We both knew I wouldn't kill him. In truth, he was a good friend. Which made it that much more interesting that he refused to kill her. I knew he wasn't a traitor. He looked forward to killing the humans as much as the rest of us.

The back wall panel opened, cueing the cat's exit. He exchanged a last look with the human, as if he debated attempting to stay and protect her. I pulsed a warning at his mind, reminding him that he couldn't truly protect her from me even if he stayed.

Nine tails flicked lazily behind him as he left us with a parting look.

The room stilled. It was just her and me now.

I could taste her fear. It grew the longer she watched me.

"Intriguing. That's now two times you have escaped a death I've dealt to you." I spoke so she had to strain to listen.

I wanted her to pay attention but didn't want to get any closer to her.

"Let me go. Please." She droned on.

The doe eyes had returned. Such a shame because there was something intriguing about that fire she hid.

"Now, why would I do that? We haven't had a human in the Unseelie court for ages, let alone one that won't die. Seems like quite the good time I could spread around. It is *quite* unnatural for a mortal to stay alive so long here. Especially one as sweet and innocent looking as you."

There it was.

A tiny spark of fire in her eyes at the mention of looking

125

sweet and innocent. Did that anger her? Good. I stared her down until the fire left and fear took its place again.

"Please." She rushed closer to me and fell on the ground, her dirty knees brushing against my leather training boots. "Please let me go. I'm no good to you. I'm just a girl that was in the wrong place at the wrong time," she begged.

Tears flooded her eyes and began to drip down her filthy face. Even I could see the fear rattling her as she clasped her shaking hands together in front of me.

A thrum of excitement at the tiny human crying at my feet sent a jolt straight to my cock. My wings, constrained too long, shot out in a clap that shadowed my frame at least seven feet on each side.

Huh, odd.

At this angle, I had a clear view of her full cleavage.

Maybe the humans weren't as stupid as I'd thought.

"What do they call you, human?"

Why did I even care? She'd be dead as soon as I sent her back to her cell. The forest bog had raised hell at not having had a go at her, and I was starting to understand why.

Maybe she *would* make a fun pet.

She hesitated at my question a moment. She was a human, so she had no knowledge as to the reason not to share her name.

Her eyes held a singular moment of madness in them.

It wasn't surprising, but my interest immediately sparked. Humans could only take so much before their weak minds snapped and madness overtook them.

I think I would enjoy breaking her.

"I am Callie Peterson," she finally announced with a raised chin. "Proud environmentalist and biological technician. I was walking through the forest to get my microscope when I stumbled upon an anomaly of luna moths and a perfect circle of destroying angel mushrooms. I live at 4313 Sassafras Road, Willow Springs, Michigan," she recited.

"Your name is Callie?" I asked in disbelief as she nodded her head.

I filed it away for later.

Maybe she *was* just a normal human? No assassin would snap so easily, and I could see the madness growing in her eyes. I could feel it. Shame she wouldn't survive the night. I was almost jealous that the forest bog would get to thoroughly break her first.

I collected her with my wings; the tendrils of smoke shifted to wrap around her throat like a leash. The second it whispered across her skin, I jumped from the way my smoke reacted to the feel of her. I dragged her, still on her knees, out of the room back to her cell, growing more uncomfortable with what she was doing to me every second. Her choking sobs sent a fresh jolt of excitement to my cock as she fought against the smoke's choke hold as we went down the stone stairs. I couldn't help but scowl at the response she had pulled from me. I shook myself for even thinking about touching a human in any way other than killing them. It was disgusting and below me as a Smoke Slayer *and* an Unseelie royal.

I hurried my pace in the hopes of getting rid of her quicker as I heard her body thud down the stairs behind me.

The dungeon guards stirred with my appearance. I knew I could throw her to them and be done, but I needed to see that she got into the cell with the forest bog. That I would never think of her again after today.

Guards quickly ran to her cell at the far end of the dungeon. Ironically it was just on the other side of the castle's library where Walter, my brother, had been spending most of his time, but she would never know that.

I threw her into the cell.

She slammed against the gray floor, cursing like a demon, and I couldn't stop my grin.

There was movement from the cot in the corner. The forest bog was already on her by the time I looked back down.

A small flicker of something foreign passed through me.

Jealousy, I'm sure, from the fact that I wouldn't be the one to break her. Odd feeling. My hand clenched, fighting the urge to stop him. I turned to leave as something wet hit my cheek. I wiped it with my palm as I turned to see where it had come from. The forest bog was petrified of me and surely wasn't so stupid.

She stood, tears clearing the only path on her face not desecrated by filth and blood. She braced herself in the middle of the cell, glowering at me.

She had spit on me.

My wings pulsed with the need to slam into something, the sharp talons already forming a claw at the top corners.

I already had one of her teeth, which I had kept in my pocket. Maybe I should collect another?

"Do it!" she screamed, surprising me.

She balled her fist up as the forest bog rubbed himself perversely against the side of her leg, but she paid him no attention. Every drop of hate was aimed solely at me.

"Do it! End me!"

She stepped closer to me until she was so close I could smell her. I had to bend my neck down to look at her.

The fire glittered wildly in her eyes, and I had to bite my lip to steady myself.

The guards began to rush in, but I spread my wings, blocking the cell's entrance with my smoke.

I reached out with my ungloved hand and grabbed her throat.

I don't know what came over me. Touching her with my bare hand. I'd never touched a human with my flesh before, only my smoke or gloves.

My breath hitched the second I felt her skin.

She didn't flinch as my large palm wrapped around her throat. Stars, her skin was *so* soft. I could feel the bones of her jaw resting on my thumb and forefinger. Why was her skin so soft? I froze as I stared into her insanely blue eyes. The fire inside of them pulled me in and mesmerized me.

Her chest rose and fell with each angered breath.

I could barely pay attention to the spark in her eyes as the pad of my thumb trailed against her jawline. I watched her face, wondering what I was feeling; I'd never felt it before.

"Do it," she whispered, drawing my attention to her full bottom lip. "Know that even a weak, innocent human died unafraid of you!"

She was lying, of course. I could feel her fear—could taste its sweetness on my tongue. Absently, I brushed my thumb across her full lower lip and reveled in the feel as it moved against my pressure. Her skin was like nothing I had ever felt before. Silkier than the finest fabric, softer than anything had a right to be. The feel of it coated my skin with curiosity.

I liked her angry and full of madness. I could feel the fire she camouflaged so poorly. She bore little fear of me in that moment, only hate. Probably still riding the high of escaping death from Alistair.

What the fuck was I doing?

I stepped back, startled at my own actions.

I shoved her face back away from me with disgust as I stared at my hands, the feel of her still lingering on them.

She tripped and fell on the forest bog that was trying to poke his branches in her leg. He no longer dry humped her, likely because she was angry and not afraid. They were only drawn to fear, not anger. He would take care of that though. He'd make her so fucking afraid she'd piss herself.

I turned and shook myself out of whatever daze I had been in and walked out of the door, hardly able to believe what I had just done as I left the human to die.

By the stars, I would be rid of her and these treacherous feelings by tonight.

She would be gone, and with her, whatever poison she had put in my mind.

CHAPTER 12

CALLIE

I SCRAPED MYSELF OFF THE DIRTY FLOOR AND STARED IN A stupor at the closed cell door. What kind of an animal could hurt an innocent person like that? I had done nothing to deserve any of this! When he let Alistair go without killing him, I had my first glimpse of hope. Maybe he wasn't as merciless and unfeeling as he was rumored to be. I had heard the guards talk of him. How he ran the kingdom with cold efficiency, annihilating anyone that went against him. He was a killer. You could see it in the way his muscles formed, the way he carried himself with arrogant confidence. The man everyone seemed afraid of. Even the commanders of his shadow army, the men that were his closest friends, seemed to rightfully have a healthy fear of him.

The forest bog returned to stabbing pointed twigs and branches into my thighs. He was trying to frighten me again.

I stared through the iron bars at the ghost of the smoky prince. His face had been softer when he touched me, almost intimate. The way his eyes had tracked my skin with fascination just before his thumb had grazed it. Before he threw me to the ground.

I was tired of being thrown around like a doll. In the

human world, I was treated like a doll, always underestimated because of my face and body. Even here, I couldn't escape it. Only here, they treated me like a disgusting rag doll left by the trash, thinking they could do whatever they wanted. I almost wished they viewed me with a bit more beauty here. People were usually nice to things they thought beautiful.

They also underestimated them.

I caught the bog off guard when I kicked him in the face as he was about to shift. He grinned viciously at me but remained a child-sized log with rows upon rows of pointed teeth. Anything was better than the frog thing. His arms and legs were long sticks that kept switching out leaves for different-sized thorns. I had noticed he seemed to draw more power to shift when I was afraid. Now he kept warping slightly but not changing, as if he were trying to shift but was unable.

I ran to the dark corner and grabbed the spoon I had used to scrape out the mortar of bricks for brown rat.

"Hiding again?" the bog rasped. His voice quivered, causing the hair on my arms to stand on end. His black eyes glistened as he watched me. "First, I'm going to smash your pretty face in against those cell bars over there." He pointed to the bars at the front of the cell. "Then I'm going to dump my cum into your mouth after I fuck it raw," he hissed.

I ignored his threats and took my spoon to the front of the cell and began banging wildly against the bars as I shouted angrily. Mendax had only been gone a moment, and the hallway was long.

He would hear me.

I screamed and yelled as loud as my voice would get.

"Shut the fuck up! Fucking banshee!" the guards shouted at me, but no one bothered to come closer.

If I could get Prince Mendax back, maybe I could make a deal, some type of negotiation.

The bog had followed me to the iron bars.

My anger briefly stuttered when he stabbed me with his

sharp wooden arm. He had shaped it into a wooden blade and stabbed the meaty part of my ass.

"I'll fuck you he—" he started, but the spoon I used to dig out his eye must have caught him off guard.

It scooped out with a pop, and I emptied it onto the floor like a marble. I grabbed his wood legs and lifted him up, grunting with exertion at the surprising weight before I hit him against the iron bars like a baseball bat. Nothing shattered like I had expected. I dropped him to the floor with a sigh. He was much too heavy for me to hold.

He shifted into the frog creature. He was bigger than me now, and his one green eye flashed triumphantly, knowing he outsized me. The empty hole on the other side gushed black blood. I walked to my corner calmly and pulled out the brick from its place with a soft clang. I turned to go to the bog but was grabbed around the waist by his slimy green arm, and his sharp claws dug into my sides painfully as he somehow clamored up my body. He had begun to bite the top of my head. He licked the perimeter just before I felt the sharp stab of hundreds of teeth.

I screamed, using every chord my voice could muster as I slammed the brick into his head. He dropped from his perch, and I didn't hesitate.

I ran at him, aiming the brick at his chin. If I could hit his cranium hard enough with it, he would lose his balance—it didn't matter how strong he was.

He braced his branches, certain I was going for his stomach or chest.

I landed the hit against his chin, and he fell back with a sludge-filled thud. In a fury, I straddled his bumpy green chest and began to slam the brick repeatedly into his head.

Some time passed before I realized his arms were limp at his sides. I was smashing a gelatinous blob of black into the stone floor. The remnants of his face deciphered next to nothing of what type of creature he had been before, and it didn't even look like a head any longer.

I took a deep breath and shifted off the horrible monster.

Steadily my hands reached for the spoon that lay to the left of us.

I was so tired. I just wanted to be done and go home. I could rest once I was home.

I grabbed his green hand and inspected his fingers. They would work.

Maybe.

The index finger was similar to that on a human hand.

I grabbed the bloodied brick and slammed the sharp edge against the metacarpal until it severed, and I held the proximal phalanx in my hand. I peeled the green flesh away to reveal a grayish-cream bone. Yes, it would work.

I stood calmly and pulled my dress back down. I would *never* wear a dress again.

Back in my dark corner, I reached under the edge of my cot closest to the wall.

"Aggh, there you are," I hummed and pulled out the cup of sauerkraut I had left to work away more mortar from the wall.

I sniffed it. The pungent tang of vinegar burned my nose and made my eyes water instantly. Yes, this would work.

I shoved the short bone of the bog's finger into the pickled cabbage mixture making certain to cover it completely. There was barely enough, but it would have to work.

I had just returned the cup to its hiding spot under my cot when the guards suddenly swarmed my cell.

"What the fuck! Holy shit!"

"She killed him! She killed the bog!"

"No chance!"

"I told you she was the deadliest human assassin! I told you!"

Various shouts from the excited guards rang loudly through the hall as a few argued about who would go in and clean up the body.

Hours later, they had eventually decided not to come

in at all. Instead, they left the black, bloodied frog sprawled across the cell's floor. They had all shuffled away after a few higher-ranking commanders came to see what the fuss was.

In the quiet, I stared at the body, void of any feeling. Served him right. I had done what I had to.

I had no way to keep track of time other than when the guards switched posts. About three in the morning, as best as I could surmise, they would leave the dungeon for the night as long as everyone slept and there were no problems. I assumed that with all the chaos of tonight, they would stay, but they hadn't. The loud door closing shut rang in my ears as I lay on my cot and stared at the body before me. Was I even blinking still?

As soon as the door shut, I moved with intention.

I grabbed the sauerkraut cup from its hidden corner along with a small chunk of bread and moved to where the torch-light dappled into my cell. Walking to the cell door, I made sure one final time no one was around. I moved to the large iron lock between the cell bars that kept me from freedom. Taking the bread, I tore away a bit of the edge until I found the right density on the small roll and shoved it into the keyhole.

I waited a moment, continuing to press as hard as possible. I removed the now key-shaped piece of squished bread from the lock.

Returning to the center, I sat crisscross-applesauce style in the long rectangular light across the cell floor with my spoon poised in my hand.

I pulled the bone free from the kraut and tested its bend.

It was perfect, just as I had hoped. The acid of the vinegar in the sauerkraut had penetrated the bone and removed the calcium carbonate, causing it to be flexible like rubber. I held it carefully and began to carve with the sharp edge of the spoon, frequently referencing the shape of my bread key until it felt like my hands and neck might fall off.

Finally, it was done, and just in time. The bone key had

begun to absorb the carbon dioxide from the air and was becoming hard once more, making it difficult to carve.

I stood, cracked my neck, and readied for escape.

CHAPTER 13

CALLIE

I CALMED MY BREATHING.

I needed to form a plan. Where would I go after I left the dungeon? The only room I'd seen was the blood chamber, and I certainly didn't want to go there if Alistair wasn't there. Maybe I could open the wall panel he had exited through? The probability of that leading to anywhere outside was unlikely, and I needed to avoid falling into a maze of castle rooms. I would just have to figure it out as I went.

I stiffened at the sound of something moving behind me.

I knew next to nothing about magic or the creatures that wielded it, had the bog not really been dead?

"Where are you going? Oh my—" His startled, squeaky voice echoed off the stone. A small gasp escaped him as he passed the full gore of the bog's smashed head and walked to the center of the small cell. "Glad I'm your friend and not foe."

"Are you my friend...shifter?" I turned to face the small creature, my chapped lips pressed together in a sharp line.

I really could trust no one, and I struggled to remember that.

Brown rat, which felt like a good name for him right now, stood on his back legs just out of the shadows.

"Yes, and likely the only one you've got," he bit out in his squeaky rat voice.

I wondered if it sounded like that normally.

"Tell me then, if you wanted to help me as you say, then why not shift into whatever it is you are and set me free," I said angrily.

I didn't know who to trust. It seemed like everyone wanted me dead. Why would he be different? Everyone in this place was so full of danger and hate.

Everyone.

"Who spilled? Another rodent in the dungeons I should worry about?" he asked playfully, even though his deep brown rat eyes held a bit of sadness in their depths.

"A certain nine-tailed cat told me. He—"

"You saw Lord Alistair?" The rat raised his body in alarm as he scanned me from head to toe. "You couldn't have. You're still alive," he said in awe.

"I promise you that I did, now shift into something useful or leave," I bit out, angry that I had found even a small bit of comfort in him only to be deceived.

"You cannot leave this cell, Callie," he said with a warning tone from the floor. "I don't know how Lord Alistair didn't tear you to pieces, but I assure you that was a fluke. As much as it upsets me that you are in the dangers of this realm and court, it is far more dangerous outside of this cell without a way to get you to a portal."

"He didn't kill me for what I believe is the same reason you are here now. I understand it even less than you, but animals have *always* been kind to me and I to them. Maybe it's some sort of karma, I don't know," I rambled, beginning to grasp the oddity of all the animals' behavior to me over the years.

I didn't have time to worry about that now. I needed to get out of here before the guards returned.

I pressed the now hard bone key into the iron lock and tried to turn it with no luck.

It wouldn't catch.

I pressed harder, careful not to snap the end off in the lock. Sweat droplets beaded across my forehead as my panic began to flare.

"Shit!" I cried.

It wasn't working.

"Callie, please! You cannot leave this cell yet. It is not safe for you out there! I am doing what I can to convince him—"

"Convince who?" I paused and felt the blood drain from my face.

I turned to look down at the small creature.

"You know who," he stated. "I've known him longer than most, and he can be reasoned with. I just need to convince him to return you to the humans. I'm close, I know it. He will listen to me."

"Return me to the humans so I can be a part of the genocide when you destroy us and take over?" I said bitterly.

It all began to sink in. I had fallen into something much larger than I could have ever realized. Even if I managed to escape, for how long would it be? Was I even escaping them once I returned home?

A cold sweat sent chills down my spine.

They would annihilate everything and everyone in the human realm if I didn't find a way to stop them.

I fell back against the iron bars. My body slid down limply until I sat with my knees pressed to my chest on the musty stone floor. The distant rhythm of dripping water somewhere in the dungeon was the only noise.

"I can't let him take over the human world," I whispered more to myself than brown rat.

What about Cecelia? Earl? Cliff? They would all die. Everyone would die.

"There is something different about you, Callie. I can convince him to keep you alive. I just need more time. He's not as horrible as most think. Please give me time, do not leave the safety of this cell."

I stood back up on shaky legs as I heaved out a long, jagged breath. I removed the key, wiped the bone on my dress, then re-inserted it into the cell's keyhole. I needed away from these bars, away from this place. It was doing something to me.

I looked at the heap of green bog on the floor.

I pressed the bone key up, this time putting pressure on the top.

Clink. It had hit the tumblers.

The cylinder shifted, opening the cell door.

My mouth hung open.

I turned to make eye contact with Brown rat, his tiny mouth slacked wide as we looked at each other, shocked it had worked.

I bolted as fast as I could to the other side of the iron bars. The free side. I was at the end of the long hallway. Cells lined the left side while torches hung on the right.

Silence.

Everyone was either asleep or dead. I took my first breath of musty freedom. I was so close. I would get out of here and find the ring of destroying angel mushrooms—the portal. They would send me home so I could alert the humans. Tell them...

I stilled.

Tell them what? That there was another world full of magical faeries? That in that world, the evil Unseelie fae fought against the good Seelie fae for possession of our world? No one would believe me.

I ran for the stairs I knew would be around the corner at the end of the hall, the same stairs the prince had dragged me down.

A hard body slammed into my side, knocking the wind out of me.

"*Please* let me convince him to spare you, Callie. If he or anyone else finds you now, you *are* as good as dead," the tall brown-haired man spoke as he grabbed my arm and looked deep into my eyes.

Brown rat's eyes stared back at me from the large man.

I stepped back to stare at him. In this form, he bore no resemblance to a rat save for his dark brown hair and eyes. Easily six foot three with similar broad shoulders to the prince, though not as muscular. He still looked athletic and lean with well-defined abs visible under his tight tunic. It wasn't the same warrior body of Prince Mendax though. I scanned his features in shock as the recognition hit me.

"It was you. You were the guard they pulled from my cell!" I shoved free from his grip to take a few steps back. "It was you who stood and whined at my cell to get in and kill me!"

Pain filled his eyes. "I wasn't trying to kill you. I was trying to protect you. I had just come from battle with the shadow army. I had fought in my wolf form, which tends to be a bit more...primal I suppose. When I returned, my wolf found you, and I was overcome with the blinding need to protect you." He shook his head slightly, shaking his brown hair into his eyes before he brushed it back. "I only shift into a few forms other than wolf; rat is one of them. I just needed to do what I could to keep you as safe as I could until I could get you away from here." He shook his head and looked down, hurt and confusion marring his handsome face.

"You didn't keep me safe from Mendax or the bog," I retorted, trying to fight off a feeling of hurt. "Where were you when your precious prince dragged me down a flight of stairs to see Alistair?" I bit out angrily, my eyes no more than slits as I watched his face fall.

Were all fae so handsome? It was unsettling.

I stepped around him. "It doesn't matter anyway. I'm not your responsibility. Tell the rest of the Unseelie animals to save themselves and stay far away from me." I walked toward the stairs.

"I will escort you out. They will kill both of us if we are caught, but you stand no chance of making it out of here alive otherwise," he stated, grabbing my hand in his large palm as he guided me faster down the hall.

"Tell me your name. Brown rat no longer suits you," I said as I pulled my hand free from his, forgetting the name rule.

"I will not tell you my name now, nor ever for that matter. I want to protect you, but I don't trust you if the prince doesn't trust you, especially not with my name, but you may call me Walter," he said, gently grabbing my hand again.

He continued to pull me down the aisle of the dungeon. He was going to help me escape.

"What if they catch you?" Though I was upset with him, the thought of him getting killed on my behalf sat heavily on my chest.

"Then I will die, I suppose," he murmured as he pulled me behind him.

"Please don't do this, Walter, just tell me where to go," I pleaded to his back as he pulled me along.

I expected the stairs to be farther away than they were. They had felt a lifetime away from my cell when the guards had moved me.

We tore up the stone steps and out onto a small landing. It was obvious Walter was no stranger to the castle. What did he do here that afforded him so much knowledge of the layout?

"What do you do here? What is your position in the Unseelie court, Walter?"

Did he have ulterior motives, perhaps, and he wasn't actually helping me at all? He could be the court's executioner for all I knew. He had already lied to me once.

"Quiet. Stay in the dark as much as possible," he ordered after I saw his features tense momentarily.

I listened and pressed my back to the stone wall. His task of staying hidden seemed like an easy feat when all I could see was darkness in the crevice of his back.

His broad, tapered body concealed me as he tucked me

closer behind him and through a large iron and wood door. The air shifted, no longer smelling musty. Only then did I realize we had left the dungeon.

It was instantly brighter, though darkness still settled around us. It smelled luxurious with various almost spicy scents. The air even felt rich and warm in contrast to the dungeon's stuffy moist air. My feet felt the contrast as well. Smooth black marble with thin veins of white and gray slapped coldly against my feet. Walter stopped and turned his head to scowl his liquid brown eyes at me.

"If ever anyone believed you an assassin, they ought to listen to you walk, be quiet! We will never escape with the sounds of your troll feet clapping for attention," he scolded.

He was so tall he had to bend to whisper. Had I not been a prisoner in an unfamiliar realm, I would probably have looked at Walter quite differently. He was beautiful. All the fae seemed to be—even the prince was uncomfortably attractive.

We were taught as kids that evil is ugly and crass, and beauty is honest and good, but that is a dangerous lie. It's so much more unsettling for your villain to be ungodly good-looking. It made it even harder to decipher the obscure feelings they elicited from your mind and body.

I rolled my eyes at his words. Troll feet. I was too distracted by his nearness to come up with a retort. He was so different from a rat now.

Thinking of the rat reminded me of the fox. My curious mind forced me to ask in case I did die before I could leave the castle's walls.

"Have you ever seen a red fox that shimmers gold in the sun?" I whispered at his back.

He still held my hand as he guided me down yet another dark hallway, and I felt a sharp squeeze before he abruptly stopped. He turned to face me.

"Why would you know anything about that?" he asked me, and for the first time, I saw cold anger in his eyes, not unlike the horrible prince's.

His jaw stiffened as he inspected me as though if he looked closely enough, I'd give a secret away.

"I saw one back home...and here. I think it may have tried to stop me from going into the circle of mushrooms—the portal. And when I was dying in the forest here, I saw two. I think the one was the same possibly? I-I think it saved my life after the prince's men stabbed me. It cried on my wound, and-and I just came back with a fire in my veins," I whispered.

Saying it all out loud felt so very different from what I heard inside my head. Walter dropped my hand. His eyes widened, and his mouth was open so wide I could see the back of his throat. Obviously, he knew about the fox.

"That can't be," he murmured as he stared at me with open shock. "You saw the fox in the human realm *and* in the Unseelie realm? You are certain?"

Goose bumps trailed my skin at the harsh look he gave.

"Is that bad? What is it?" I asked.

The fox couldn't be that bad. It had saved my life and presumably had tried to keep me from the portal to the Unseelie realm.

A loud creak from the floor down the hall broke the silence that surrounded us.

Walter shoved me back the way we had just come as he grabbed my hand once more and began running us down yet another corridor I hadn't even seen. He pushed me into what looked to be a linen closet filled with laundry. The room was small, the size of a nice human bathroom. Darkness cloaked the room as he pulled the black door closed behind him. There was a small light that softly illuminated the wall. Did they have electricity?

The black marble floor's polish gleamed in the flickering amber light. The walls looked modern with a hint of a more traditional influence. All painted black with wainscoting trim and high ceilings. Almost too modern to be considered gothic, but a malevolent feeling hung in the air, something that shrouded everything, making it feel much more gothic than it initially looked.

Walter pressed in, holding the large black door closed. I stepped back to allow more space between our bodies, but a rack of fabric shoved into my backside. I opened my mouth to ask about their technologies upon seeing the light. At a squint, though, I realized it was a giant lightning bug that sat on a small bench upon the tiny gold platform where a lightbulb would have been. It was ten times larger than the lightning bugs at home. His face held a more sentient appearance. Of which I got to inspect further after it turned its head to me and held a finger to its mouth in the universal sign to be quiet.

I gaped at the fact that a lightning bug wall sconce had just told me to be quiet.

I looked up to see Walter chuckling as he watched me with glittering eyes. "I forget what a culture shock you must be going through," he whispered.

"Tell me about the fox," I whispered, not having forgotten.

I needed to know what was going on. Why would the fox seek me out? I couldn't form a plan to get back home if I didn't know all of the variables involved, and I had an odd hunch the fox was very much involved.

He immediately looked angry and stared at the wall opposite us.

"I tell you this as a friend." He stiffened, and I swear I heard a small growl from inside his chest. "The only thing I know that can shift into a fox is an old line of fae that I promise you want nothing to do with. I don't know why they would have an interest in you, but I can assure you, it's not a good thing," he stated through a jaw clenched so tightly it looked painful.

Whoever the line of fae was, it was clear he hated them.

"Why would fae be in the human realm? It doesn't surprise me that they showed up here, this is their home, but in the human realm?" I asked, still struggling to put the pieces together. It felt like a big piece was missing.

He moved from the door to step closer to me in the small room. Linen and soap fragrance wafted toward me with his move. It was a pleasant change from the musty dungeon scent.

"Quite the contrary. It's significantly more unsettling that you saw them here, in the Unseelie court. They frequent the human realm as *they* were given passage. The fact that they set foot on Unseelie soil uninvited and then used their powers to heal you is unsettling, to say the least. It seems they have forged a plan that involves you in some way, which is far more dangerous than anything your human mind will comprehend."

I narrowed my eyes at him. "I can hardly believe there is anything more dangerous than being a prisoner of the Unseelie prince," I whispered.

Something in the air seemed to shift. It was unsettling and caused my stomach to tighten.

"Oh, but there is. The only fae that shift into fox are the royal children of the Seelie court, and by Seelie law, you are now tied to one of them with your life. You're at their command until they decide to kill you," he said before he shook his head softly. "Those bastards will never let you free. It doesn't matter what realm you go to now—the Seelie own you. The only solace you have is that they did it on Unseelie soil, which violates a lot of rules."

I clamored back as I tried to get my bearings and accidentally knocked a glass jar off the small table behind me. It crashed to the floor and shattered, quickly ending our hushed conversation.

I looked up at Walter, knowing I had just doomed us.

CHAPTER 14

MENDAX

C OMMANDER, REPEAT THAT ONE MORE TIME. THIS TIME though, remember that as your dead father would attest, I am not the type of fae that finds humor in incompetence," I ground out, certain there was no way I had heard the head of my shadow guards correctly.

"The human bludgeoned the forest bog and has escaped the dungeon. The shadow guards haven't seen her leave the castle's gates. We believe she is still inside the castle." The stoic man tried to present himself as calm, but I could hear the tremble in his voice, the sour scent of his fear.

He was terrified, as he should be. No one was comfortable in the presence of a Smoke Slayer, especially one with no conscience or feelings. He and I both knew that of all the evil that resided in this court—*my* court—I was the last monster he should disappoint. Unlike the other heathens, I wasn't uncomfortable with my darkness. I reveled in it. I commanded it. Others' lives or feelings meant nothing to me. Friends or family, it didn't matter to me.

Nothing mattered to me.

I could feel nothing.

I'd sooner kill my mother than relinquish the power I

held over others and the fear I brought them. Why? Because I could. What did anything matter? The only time I ever felt anything was as I watched another suffer in the pain I caused them. I enjoyed that. I could almost imagine what it would be like to feel those same feelings toward something else.

"You are telling me that the assassin, the very same weak assassin sent by the humans to kill your ruler, now wanders about my castle?" I said incredulously as I watched his hand tremble.

He quickly moved his arms behind his back to hide the sheer terror, as if afraid I would feed off it. I wasn't in the least bit afraid of the human girl, but I wouldn't deny my intrigue. Her tiny mouth begged and pleaded, filled with nothing but helplessness every time I had seen her. There was no way she could have taken down a forest bog by herself, let alone one that had tasted her fear. Someone had helped her.

"Yes, sir, the shadow guards are searching the castle now. The only problem is—"

"What is the only problem, Commander?" I cut the stiff, gray-haired commander off.

I had quickly grown impatient, and the overwhelming need to watch something bleed increased with every syllable he uttered.

"Your moth—the queen—is having a dinner party in the ballroom, my lord. The guards are, uh, having a hard time searching that floor," he mumbled, looking at the wall behind me.

"So they are afraid of dear old mumsie, is that what you're telling me, Commander? Leave that floor to me." I chuckled at the thought.

If anyone rivaled my bad temper and vengeance, it was my mother, the Unseelie queen. Reluctantly, she had remained queen after my father died, though she no longer bothered with any courtly tasks or decisions. No, that was left to me. Though she threatens that if I don't marry soon and become king so she can be finished with her reign, she will bond me to another of her choosing. She would too.

I'm certain the only thing that has stopped her thus far is simply that she despises every spineless female here. If she bonds me to another, they get half of my powers, and she'd sooner feed herself to a pit of zombified humans than share our powers with anyone else, even though it's the only way I can ascend the throne. She loathes humans quite possibly more than anyone. Anyone except me.

I stood, and my leathers let out a few small creaks as I stretched to my full height. I mostly did it to remind the man in front of me how much smaller he was than me, how much weaker. I ought to kill him for letting her escape, but I won't. He expects it, and there is no fun in doing what people expect. Maybe I will kill his wife as penance.

"Who left her cell unlocked? Send them to the blood forest," I said as I pushed in the chair to my desk.

My blood had already begun to thrum with the excitement of hunting the girl.

"No one, sir. She severed a bone from the forest bog and somehow fashioned a key out of it. It was still in the lock when we arrived."

My boots stilled as I turned to face the armored commander. Intrigue tingled at the base of my skull.

"And how exactly did she kill the bog?"

Ice flowed through my veins. If he says—

"A brick, Your Highness. It had been chiseled out from the library wall. She beat him with it until he was unrecognizable," the man said, sounding slightly impressed.

It must have been a full-on massacre for him to sound like that.

"Call off the shadow guards, Commander. They are no longer needed," I said, towering over the large fae. "Our little whore had help, and I know exactly where he takes her."

"But sir—"

It was too late. I was already out the door of my war room and headed for the fourth floor.

Interesting creature, this girl. Assassin or not, she was very intriguing. Disgusting and deserving of only death, but intriguing nonetheless.

CHAPTER 15

CALLIE

W E NEED TO GET TO THE ROOF," WALTER MURMURED ALMOST to himself as he pulled me behind him.

He was fast, and I was having a hard time staying on my feet behind him. A few times, I tried to move to his side but was quickly shoved behind the protective wall of his back. I needed to ditch him, but the more hallways and empty rooms we ventured through, the more I worried about getting caught. We had already experienced a few close calls with servants wandering about the halls dressed in finery. The black suits they all wore reminded me of something between renaissance and modern formal wear.

It seemed counterproductive to be going to the roof, but I trusted he knew where was best to go. He continued to keep me hidden behind him. Though whether that was for my sake or his, I couldn't say.

Up yet another winding flight of stairs. This set seemed to climb forever, tucked into an intricate corner of a humungous room. I paused to take in the startling luxury of the large room.

White fur rugs covered the vast space between us and the large door. The ceilings had to be twenty feet high with beautiful slate-colored walls. Intricate crown molding lined the ceiling and various other nooks in the room. Several black crystal chandeliers hung in the center of the room. I could see another of the large sparkling crystal lights hanging outside the door. I gasped when I realized it was a bedroom. Against the far back wall rested a huge black canopy bed with a fluffy and prim-looking black and gray bedspread tucked neatly in.

Oh god. We were in someone's room.

My heart pounded so hard I could have passed out.

"Walter! This is someone's room! We need to get out!" I whisper-shouted.

The panic somehow seemed to grow. The anticipation of getting caught was seemingly more frightening than if I had actually been caught. Like a bad game of hide-and-seek, but if we were found, we would die.

"I know the owner, they aren't in it right now. He's helping a human escape," he whispered back to my gaping face as he glanced in all directions.

Holy shit. This was his room.

"If we can get through that hallway, there is a room just past the ballroom where we can access the roof." He grabbed my hand again, ready to pull me to the door.

I stopped him and pulled my hand free. I couldn't let him go any farther, I just couldn't. I didn't want his life held in my hands, and I didn't know how much I trusted him now after seeing his opulent bedroom. Why would he help me if he was this close to them?

"Tell me what to do after I reach the roof. You can't go with me any farther," I stated, not leaving room for discussion as we stared into each other's frightened eyes.

"I will show you. There is a portal on the roof. I don't know much about it, but I know that it will at least get us out of here, and no. I'm not leaving you. I need to know why my wolf is drawn to you, but also because my allegiance lies with the Unseelie crown, and I will not let you harm him should you actually be an assassin. I will die to protect him, so I will be your escort until you are gone from here."

My feet pawed at the soft carpet. The trail of dirt I'm certain I left would be enough to give away our location if I didn't get my filthy body off the soft white rugs.

I would lose him once I knew where the portal was, and he would return to the castle safely.

Walter pulled at me, but I took the lead and stepped into the hallway. My feet found the marble floor of the hall, and the cold they had felt in the dungeon returned. The hallway was large, still dark in color but brighter in lighting. I didn't have to squint and could see everything clearly. Instead of a door on the right of the hallway, large archways led to a black-and-white checkered floor. I ended up standing in the wide entrance of one of the entryways to the ballroom.

The ballroom was filled with dancing people.

They all gasped and mumbled at the sight of me.

I was too stunned to move.

Hundreds of pristinely attired fae stood in the expanse, watching me. My stomach fell through my feet, and the blood drained from my face. There was no escaping—they all saw me. There was no questioning I was a prisoner from my filthy attire, and there was no mistaking that I was human. Even the few that seemed to resemble a human vibrated that they were a different, more beautiful species. Wings, fangs, and claws snagged my attention like sprinkles of death throughout the crowd. Hate and destruction clouded the air immediately. Every single one of them had the look of a predator. Even the small friendly-looking ones held an air of mischief when their eyes caught me. If looks could kill, I would have disintegrated on the spot.

"Oh shit," murmured Walter, sliding in behind me as he looked out to the crowd of fae guests that watched us.

"It seems our first course has been delivered early."

The voice stopped the flow of blood in my veins. It was like terror had its own music, and she was the composer.

152

The crowd of predators parted, letting through the rhapsodist.

Glittering black vines from an onyx crown seemed to command their own respect upon her head. The vines dripped down her stunning face, snaking elegantly around her fragile-looking throat before blending into a black velvet dress that clung to her feminine curves. Blood-red lips pulled up in a sinister smile as if she truly had been gifted a present.

The woman took a step toward us. The dress elegantly trailed behind her as the people closest to her bowed their heads and stepped farther back. This continued as the crowd parted, and she walked closer to us.

"My queen, I—" Walter stuttered, placing himself between the two of us.

Closer now, her eyes scanned me, and her nostrils flared slightly. Something in her eyes seemed to light with fire suddenly.

Black wings, like those of a butterfly, shot out of her back, casting a menacing gray shadow over her face. She moved fast, instantly thrusting a bare arm toward me. Black painted the tip of her graceful finger, quickly bleeding as it grew down her hand until it dripped across her skin like she had dipped her fingers into ink. The air crackled with power. Smoke rose from her now inky hands. Her blood-red lips pulled into a malicious smile.

"Run," Walter whispered to me with quiet urgency as he shoved my shoulder so hard toward the hallway I almost fell onto the floor.

The action shook me out of my trance of panic, and I spared a last look at Walter. The smoke from the queen's black hands shot toward him. I heard a loud pop, and the sound seemed to shake my eyes as I watched Walter transform into a larger-than-average dark-gray wolf.

"Walter!" I shrieked, barely hearing my cries over the hard slap of marble under my feet.

There was only one opening at the end of the hall, and I

took it. It was another large archway that led to yet another luxurious and expansive room.

Shit!

I spun around inside it. It was just a room, there was no exit to the roof!

There! Tucked in the back corner. A small door to the roof.

My breath threatened to stop completely as I slammed into the door, and I struggled desperately to use my shaking hand and turn the knob. Finally, it gave way and opened.

My eyes adjusted to the darkness and saw a large flat roof surrounded by a portcullis, the gray stone now a charcoal color with the drizzle of falling rain. I closed the door behind me and pressed my back against it as I struggled to catch my breath. The roof was empty. I was safe for the moment.

The night sky was a dreary bluish gray, only brightened slightly by small eruptions of lightning that backlit the clouds with a warm yellow. The soft pitter-patter of rain filled my senses. It was almost peaceful. The taste of fresh air in my lungs felt invigorating. I was outside again.

I was so close.

Thoughts of Walter flashed in my mind. Was he dead? I callously shook the thoughts off. I needed to find the portal. He could handle himself.

I stumbled to the front corner and leaned over the portcullis to see what lay below the castle.

Panic shot through me, and I fell to the hard floor. My butt slid back against the rough rooftop as I scrambled to get away from the short wall. The drop was so much farther down than I ever could have imagined.

The castle was nestled against the farthest edge of a mountain. It was huge in and of itself but was made even taller and more frightening by the precipice of the mountain's edge.

Where was the fucking portal? Where was it!?

Nothing was on the roof but short walls and a drop to my death.

I pushed myself farther back, and the roof scraped against my rear as I sought to get farther away. I had expected it to be a steep drop, but I had no idea just how high it was.

I continued to scoot farther back. I just needed away from that ledge.

Please get me out of here, anyone—I just want to go home.

Sobs racked my body. The hot tears that fell down my cheeks were a startling contrast to the cold rain that fell upon the rest of my body.

A low note of thunder rumbled deeply across the expanse.

Goose bumps rose across my skin, paired with an unsettling feeling, as I slowly turned around.

A shadow fell over me, blanketing me with terror.

My eyes traveled up from his black boots as they dripped with the falling rain.

It was as though he had fallen from the sky silently.

Several black leather strappings and buckles covered his broad chest. A black cape billowed in the wind behind him as he watched me, his pale blue eyes pinned on me with icy ferocity. His wings were spread wide, taking up too much space on the rooftop. Raindrops fell through the black smoke as if afraid to touch it.

"No," I whispered, scrambling to get back on my feet. "No! No, please!"

He strode forward, his long muscular legs covering the ground too quickly. I spasmed with fear as I tried to scrape myself away from him, but he was too fast, too big.

His palm fisted my hair, wrenching my neck back.

I cried out as he yanked me to my feet by the fistful of matted hair. He roughly pulled me closer to him.

I looked up, fighting against the rain to look into his cold blue eyes. I tried desperately to kick and scream, but the few hits that connected against his hard stomach and thighs seemed to hurt me and not him. Even standing as he was, he towered over me as if I still lay on the ground.

"Please, you're hurting me," I cried, feeling completely helpless.

"Why won't you die?" His voice was so quiet and deep. It was like a tiger's growl, powerful even in a whisper.

My arms pushed against his chest as I tried to balance myself and ease the pain on my scalp from his grip.

His pale eyes flickered as I touched him. Something seemed to pull at them cracking his stoic expression. Confusion crinkled his eyes as he inspected my features, so close now I could smell his spicy fragrance. He was ungodly attractive, like an angel of death.

Out of nowhere, a gray blur slammed into him, loosening his grip and sending us both to the ground. My body moved me away from the predator before my mind had even registered the command.

A large gray wolf bit into the prince's throat.

Walter!

A yelp rang out as Prince Mendax slammed the wolf to the ground with a grunt.

"After everything we've been through, you betray me."

The large wolf got up and strode in front of me with a low growl, guarding me.

I couldn't let him do this again. I would not let him die for my sake.

"Walter! No!" I shouted as I attempted to move in front of him.

The prince straightened slightly as one small corner of his mouth curled up.

"How sweet." He looked from me to Walter. "The human assassin protects you. I wonder how far she'll go to save you, brother?"

Brother? Well, that explains the room.

A snake of black smoke shot out from his hand, wrapping around Walter's furry throat. It was only then I realized he hadn't really been fighting the wolf. Rather, he'd been playing with him.

156

"No! Please, let him go! Take me! It was my idea! I convinced him, it's not his fault!" I shouted as I ran to Walter.

The smoke snake wrapped around the wolf's neck drew a gargled choking sound from Walter as it squeezed, still attached by a smoky trail to Mendax.

"I must commend you. I thought it was impressive, the scheme you two worked out. Walter kills the bog while you fashion some sort of key? I'm just *dying* to hear all about it," Mendax said pleasantly as a twitch of his fingers caused the smoke snake to constrict tighter around the wolf's neck.

"Stop now! He had nothing to do with this! I killed the bog, I used the acid to soften the bone, I carved the key, and I escaped!" I cried, trying to break whatever hold the smoke had on Walter, but it was no use.

My hands swatted through the smoke as if it wasn't even there. All the while, it held as strong as steel against my friend's throat. I ran to Mendax and slammed my fists against his chest and arms, blinded by adrenaline and panic for Walter.

He chuckled lightly.

This was a game to him.

"When you told me all your theories about the human girl, I had no idea you meant to actually become a traitor *with* her," Mendax said, keeping his eyes pinned on the choking wolf.

He hooked his pointer finger toward himself, and slowly the smoke pulled the fighting wolf to the front of his boots. The horrible prince reached down and picked up the wolf by the scruff of his neck. The smoke dissipated as soon as his arm had reached through it, thoroughly commanded by him and only him.

Collecting a whimper from Walter, the prince lifted the large wolf as if he were a piece of paper. He moved swiftly against the pelting rain, lifting the lupine until he was high over the roof's edge. High above the empty precipice below.

Lightning flashed, silhouetting their bodies against the gray sky.

He was going to drop him.

"Please! No! Stop!" I tried desperately to tug Mendax backward from the edge.

"Finish him or I will," stated a familiar cold voice.

The queen stood in the center of the roof, her black dress shimmering in the shadows of the night. Several of the fae from the ballroom stood behind her as more poured in from the open door.

"Hello, mother dear," the prince bit out, a hint of irritation in his voice. "Why don't you go back to your little party and let me handle this," he said, still holding the wolf over the ledge.

"Well, it *is* my sister's child you hold over the portcullis," she said matter-of-factly. "And had you truly taken care of it, my party wouldn't have been ruined by a human."

She crossed her arms. They looked normal again, save for a small bit of black near her pointer finger that had just flared. "As a matter of fact, had you truly taken care of it, my love, there would have been *no* more humans," she sang, her voice dripping with hate.

The hulking prince rolled his eyes. "Get back inside, now."

The air rumbled with his words as raw power pulsed from him. Even the scary fae in the back shrank away with his words.

The queen flinched.

Holy shit, was she afraid of him?

"Not until you finish the traitor off. You see, my friends missed out on their dinner"—she looked me over briefly—"and I feel I owe them some entertainment now to make up for it," she purred.

"I have all kinds of entertainment for you now, mother." The prince grabbed a handful of my hair again. "You see, I've just taken a new pet." He looked to the wolf with a devilish smirk and a glimmer in his eye. "Don't worry, brother, I'll take *extra* good care of her," he whispered darkly as he looked back to me, and his eyes devoured my body as the rain continued to pelt us.

He opened his hand and dropped Walter.

"Nooo!" I screamed as I watched Walter, still in his wolf form, fall from the roof. Down, down, down until there was nothing left to see but darkness; his shape grew smaller and smaller until there was nothing.

I looked up in horror to see the dark prince staring at me, his smile now gone. His eyes traced every horrified line of my face.

"Move her cage to my room," he said loudly, his eyes still holding mine.

I gripped his arm in panic and tried to pull it free from my hair.

"Disgusting. I'd rather you throw her over the ledge too," said the queen, standing like she was bored at a BBQ. "Have your fun, but make certain she's dead before next week, or I will handle it," she bit out, each word laced with venom.

She turned and walked through the doors as the guards and the other fae followed close behind.

Mendax loosened his grip on my hair slightly, staring into my eyes as if he would find a secret hidden behind my pupils.

"You have turned my best men against me. First Alistair, now Walter. Somehow my men have failed to kill you now three times. I will not."

CHAPTER 16

MENDAX

I LEANED AGAINST THE WALL AS RAIN PELTED ME, HIDDEN BY shadows and smoke. They would walk through that door any minute now. Unless they didn't make it past my mother.

The door opened, and the girl practically fell onto the roof, sliding her small frame against the door as if her little body would keep it closed.

All my senses reached for more as soon as I saw her.

She quickly scanned the roof looking for something. The shadows cloaked me as I watched her large innocent eyes search in panic. She was breathing hard, her full chest rose and fell heavily.

It never ceased to amaze me what idiots humans were.

A thrum of excitement passed through me as I watched her. She had no idea her biggest threat lurked in the shadows, taking in her every move.

In truth, I could understand why Walter had been deceived by her. She was unlike any other creature I'd come across. On the outside, she appeared innocent and weak, but I knew better. I'd seen a fire flash in her eyes, a burning madness that threatened to push her to the edge. I wanted to be the one to shove her into the fire.

There was a pull to her that just didn't make sense. It was wrong for a human to have such an effect on us...on me. I knew she was affecting the animals somehow—that was why Walter, the ever-heroic man he was, couldn't help himself, same with Alistair. I had no animal in me, but gods was I effected by her presence. I hated it.

She leaned over the castle's edge and quickly stumbled back, falling on her ass. She sobbed as the rain poured down on her. The filth of the dungeon seemed to wash away from her skin the more the rain fell on her.

I shifted, needing a better look at the spots on her shoulders. The tiny speckles of sun. I had noticed them on her nose the first night I saw her—it was one of the few things I could see on her that night. In the darkness of the mangled forest, they had fascinated me. Even once I had returned to the castle, they stole my thoughts. So much so that I had to go to the library to find out what they were. We had a small bit of the sun during the day in the Unseelie realm, but it was more of a gray haze. Nothing that would cause what they called "freckles."

Walter had tried repeatedly to get me to free the girl, which was quite unlike him to favor a human. To say I was shocked when he had tried to break her free would have been an understatement. He had grown up here, a brother in every sense except blood. One of the few people I tolerated. I suppose he wasn't thinking, his needs too primal in the middle of his shift but maddening nonetheless.

I watched him go to her as a stupid rat and climb all over her little body, and she obviously enjoyed his company.

What would it feel like if she looked at me that way?

Imagine his surprise when one day he crawled out to find me. He told me wild theories of why she was different and that he couldn't help it, that he needed to protect her. I nearly killed him then.

She was mine—my prisoner.

He told me he would leave her alone, begged me to return her to safety.

Seems he had other plans.

He had no idea what he was doing. A brat ever since my aunt died and dumped him here. He thought he would get her past the guards and take her to the hidden portal. It didn't matter that he didn't know where it was or how to use it.

He was a fool and would pay for his mistakes as soon as I saw him, if the human assassin hadn't killed him first. That seemed unlikely. She trained with humans, so even as a skilled human assassin, Walter would easily overpower her.

I silently moved behind her and waited.

Her shoulders shook with her sobs. The rain pulled away the gray dirt of her skin, and her red hair was matted in such a dense ball it presented a patch of her smooth neck.

My hand clenched involuntarily at the sight.

The memory of how soft her skin had felt under my fingertips clouded my mind. I itched to see if other parts of her were as soft.

My wings unfurled silently, stretching wide.

Shit.

I clenched my fists at my side.

I would *never* degrade myself by touching a *human* in such a way. They were the lowest scum created, and I refused to debase myself with the thought of how delicately soft her skin was.

I reveled in the moment she felt my presence behind her.

She turned, and pure terror filled her sweet doe eyes.

My breath caught tight in my chest at the sight of her. Thankfully it was controlled, not giving anything away. The rain and tears had stripped the dirt from her face.

Was this the same girl?

The night she had been sent to assassinate me was a blood moon, and darkness shrouded the creatures of the night everywhere they ventured. No matter what realm, everything was darker and harder to see during a blood moon. It's why we had chosen that night. But with that cloak of darkness, I hadn't been able to see her face quite like I could now, with some of the grime and mud not camouflaging her features.

She was incandescently beautiful.

The kind of beauty you hear of but never witness. The kind that crawls inside your mind and haunts you until it destroys everything and consumes your soul.

Upon seeing me, she cried out, shouting as if someone would come and help her.

Apparently, she still hadn't realized no one was coming for her, nor would they ever.

She was mine now.

I was still frozen, caught up in watching her.

This would end now. This distraction would end now.

Angry, I stepped forward and grabbed her matted red hair.

"Please, you're hurting me," she cried.

Even the unique silkiness of her voice had crept inside my mind. I would rip her head from her shoulders for making me feel this way. *Human filth.*

"Why won't you die?" I growled as my frustration caused my wings to pulse.

Her arm pushed against my thigh in an attempt to free herself. The touch simmered through my leathers and forced me to wonder what her fingertips would feel like.

What has happened to me?

I was the Unseelie prince, soon-to-be king. I felt nothing for humans other than hatred. What—

Walter slammed into me with force, knocking us all to the ground.

There he was, traitor.

I slowed myself and let him feel like he was in control. He wrapped his jaws around my throat with a deep growl, and I had to fight back a bloodthirsty smile.

This was what I knew. These were feelings I was familiar with.

Killing.

He was like a brother to me, yet here he crouched with

his shifter teeth pressed against my neck. He had trained with me enough times to know better.

A yelp rang out as I slammed him to the ground with a grunt. That should shake him out of whatever delusion he held toward the human.

He knew better than most exactly how much I enjoyed inflicting pain on others.

His compassion and closeness to me were the sole reasons half of the people I ruled over hadn't been slaughtered. Yet.

"After everything, you betray me," I growled at him.

The idiot got up and moved his body in front of the girl's, blocking her protectively as he snarled at me.

Something foreign rippled through my gut.

I didn't like him near her, keeping her from me. It made me want to kill them both more.

She shouted something and ran to stand in front of him.

What the fuck? Why would she risk her life for his? He was weak but still much stronger than her.

"How sweet. The human protects you. I wonder how far she's willing to go to save you, brother?"

I never played well with others, and apparently, I wouldn't begin to now. If he thought he had a chance at taking something, *anything,* that was mine, then he desperately needed a reminder of who he was playing with.

I unfurled my fingers; my magic absolutely *itched* to see blood.

"No! Please let him go! Take me! It was my idea! I convinced him, it's not his fault!" she shouted, running to Walter's side.

What?

This human bitch was going to trade her life for a shifter she barely even knew. She'd only even been here a few weeks.

An ache pulsed through me.

Half the Unseelie realm would gladly die for me, but it would be from fear. Fear from me or whatever devastation would take them all once the Smoke Slayer was no longer here to protect them.

My fist clenched inadvertently.

My smoke snake wrapped around the wolf's neck, drawing a gargled choking sound from him as it squeezed tightly.

"I must say, I thought it was very impressive the scheme you two worked out. Walter kills the bog while you fashion some sort of key? I'm just *dying* to hear all about it," I said, a twitch of my fingers causing the smoke to tighten further around his neck. I wanted him to hurt.

I want everyone to hurt.

"Stop now! He had nothing to do with this! I killed the bog, I used the acid to soften the bone, I carved the key, and I escaped!" the tiny human cried, trying to break the smoke's grip on Walter, but it was no use.

Her hands swatted through the smoke as if it wasn't even there. That was stupid. Only Smoke Slayers commanded the smoke—didn't they teach her anything during her training?

The girl bravely ran to me.

She was so small compared to us. She punched and kicked at my chest wildly. It was kind of...cute. I couldn't help but laugh.

When was the last time I actually felt anything enough to laugh?

This was starting to get messy, and I needed to finish this.

"When you told me all of your theories about the human girl, I had no idea you meant to become a traitor *with* her," I said, never removing my eyes from the choking wolf.

I could easily tell if he was lying; he was the closest thing I had to a friend.

I summoned my magic to bring him closer.

His eyes held an innocent gleam as I moved him in front of my feet.

Something more was going on, and I didn't think he understood it enough to be capable of lying to me.

Shit.

The others were coming, their heartbeats flooding into my senses.

Well, I suppose now I'd have to be deceitful. At least until I found out more. I enjoyed killing. I enjoyed the way it made me feel, but I had *very* few people I could trust, and Walter had been one of them. It would be smart to learn more before I killed him.

Poor mother.

I grabbed Walter roughly by the scruff and lifted him over the roof's edge. His eyes went so wide the whites made an appearance from panic.

Be calm. My eyes silently spoke to his, the way only those closest to you could interpret. I glanced dramatically back to where the queen and her cronies began filtering through the door. He glanced back with a small nod of understanding.

It was performance time.

Lightning flashed against the gray sky.

"Please! No! Stop!"

The girl was physically trying to pull me away from the ledge. Gods, she was beautiful.

And stupid.

A small smile tugged at the corner of my mouth before I fought it away.

Walter saw it and drew his furry brows together in confusion. I never smiled.

"Finish him or I will," mother stated.

I rolled my eyes at her dramatics.

The queen stood in the center of the roof. I could see how conflicted she was. She was ruthless, but not to my extent. She liked Walter. Probably more than me, but reputation was everything here, and with such an audience, I knew she wouldn't show an ounce of weakness, or they would use it against us.

"Mother dear. Why don't you go back to your little party and let me handle this," I said, still holding Walter over the ledge as I tightened my grip on him.

"Well, it is my sister's child you hold over the battlements," she said matter-of-factly. "And had you truly taken care of it, my party wouldn't have been ruined by a *human.*"

She crossed her arms. She was angry, and her magic strained against her fingers turning them black.

"As a matter of fact, had you truly taken care of it, my love, there would have been *no* more humans," she trilled.

She despised humans. Possibly even more than the Seelie—maybe not.

She would do anything to ruin the Seelie since Queen Saracen had taken the throne.

Taking the human realm had been her idea. It burned her alive that the Seelie were granted access to the human realm and not us. That the Seelie were given something we weren't. She let jealously rule her decisions. Another reason she was a weak queen. Emotions and feelings had no place here.

"Get back inside, now," I commanded her, letting the tiniest wisp of power leak through my words. Enough that they would know I meant them.

"Not until you finish the traitor and the human off. You see, my friends missed out on their dinner"—she looked the human over briefly— "and I feel I owe them some entertainment to make up for it," she purred dramatically.

I wasn't certain I was ready to give up my new toy just yet—I still needed to break it.

"I have all kinds of entertainment for you now, Mother." I reached out and grabbed a handful of the human's wet and matted hair.

She tried to slap me away. Cute.

"You see, I've just taken a new pet." I looked back to Walter, his feet still dangling in the bottomless night sky.

With the slightest nod that he and only he could see, I spoke my message to him.

"Don't worry, brother, I'll take *extra* good care of her," I whispered, heavy on the theatrics as I let my eyes take in her tight body.

He breathed a relieved sigh so deep, I saw it in my peripheral vision.

Then, I opened my hand dramatically and dropped him.

I waited to feel something like a pit in my stomach, something like a feeling of regret, but as usual, nothing came. I shrugged, thinking surely I would have enjoyed that more. I usually loved dropping bodies from high places.

He didn't even know I'd dropped him into the hidden portal.

For all he knew, I was killing him.

I stifled another smile at the thought of him landing in the golden seas. It was Seelie, the only place this portal traveled, hence why it was never used, and only about a handful of our line's kings and queens had even known of it.

Mother and I did.

Now it was the human's turn to die, and she would not be so lucky.

The sharp wail of the girl pierced the pitter-patter of raindrops, startling me.

Why did she cry for him?

I watched as her eyes seemed to morph, the sadness seemed to wrestle with fire, and for less than a second, I saw a flash of her darkness.

It *was* her who had killed the forest bog. I had no doubt now. Why did she continue to act so sweet and innocent when obviously capable of something so impressive as severing a man's finger and carving it into a key?

My interest in the human flared dangerously. The thoughts of what darkness pulsed behind her large doe eyes were enough to cause a tightening of the leathers that covered my groin.

"Move her cage to my room," I stated to the guards that hovered nearby.

I couldn't seem to peel my eyes away from the dirty ball of flesh in front of me. I tightened my grip on her hair. What would my new pet look like after it had been given a bath?

Curiosity slithered into my mind like a snake. A little fun before I killed her wouldn't hurt me.

It would most definitely hurt her.

"Disgusting. I'd rather you throw her over the ledge too," said the queen standing bored. She knew I had just dropped Walter into the portal—her heart rate had slowed significantly. "Have your fun, but make certain she's dead before next week, or I will handle it." She turned and walked through the doors, followed by her guards and the other fae.

Despite the many mats, Callie's hair felt soft in my grip. I felt each wet strand brush the underbelly of my palm like a caress. My grip loosened quickly. Poison may as well have rubbed against my hand.

"You've turned my best men against me. First Alistair, now Walter. Somehow my men have failed to kill you now *three* times. I will not," I threatened.

I have never wanted to kill someone more in all my years. To be rid of this girl that has wriggled into my mind like a maggot. She was a *human*.

CHAPTER 17

CALLIE

N O FUCKING WAY," I WHISPERED TO MYSELF.
Bars of faint charcoal smoke walled a six-foot circle around me.

Time and time again, I had tried to force my body through the teasingly opaque wisps of smoke that formed my new prison. It was the worst taunting of hope imaginable. A prison of smoke that teased your mind with shifts and swirls, believing a weak point has formed only to touch it and be disappointed.

It may as well have been iron for all the more it gave. Anger and sadness ripped through me as a vision of Walter being dropped into the abyss flashed through my mind.

He died because of me. Because he *helped* me.

A prickle of dreaded understanding began to unfurl within me, like puzzle pieces slowly coming together. Things I had struggled to understand began to make sense the moment I saw the dark queen. Understanding began to crack like a vein through the broken glass of my mind.

How would I escape? Could I do this? What if I failed? At least I was free from the dungeon.

I sat against the smoky rail and pulled my knees tight against my chest. It would be all right.

It had to be.

The cage's ceiling was a peaked blanket of smoke that hovered and shifted hypnotically with the air. It was eight feet tall at least and didn't seem to take up a fraction of space in the obscenely large room.

It was similar in style to the one I had been in earlier with the staircase, with one large difference.

Actias luna—the beautiful sherbet green moths—clung to the matte black walls. Hundreds of them scattered and dotted the walls of the large room, giving the illusion of a beautifully contrasted wallpaper. They moved their wings slowly—not fluttering, but smooth and deliberate against the dark walls. Mendax had said they were his pets. How poetic to be caged with the creature I had chased for years.

My neck spasmed slightly as the kink of manipulation settled into my shoulders, heavy with burden. It was clear now. Why, all those years ago before he left, the man I had once trusted, the one I leaned on—my best friend—had fueled my interest in the luna moth. He knew my obsession with wings.

What a fool I had been.

Something blurred in my peripheral vision, and my body immediately tensed.

Prince Mendax waltzed into the room, dropping his cape on the giant black four-poster bed as he passed. His gaze was as harsh as it had been on the roof before the guards had hauled me here.

I looked away, not wanting to give him the satisfaction of seeing the fear that filled my eyes.

Instead, I took stock of the nearly empty room. Large windows that climbed floor to ceiling were the only real light, and even that was sparse. Long black draperies pulled to each side of the enormous windows. The light that filtered in as the moon illuminated the room was hazy and silver but much brighter than I would have ever expected. I could see details in the delicate scrolls of appliqués that laced the dresser and the chandelier's reflection off the shiny marble floor in the room behind me. Even the intricate gold details of fancy bathroom fixtures glimmered to life with the touch of moonlight.

"Callie, Callie, Callie." His deep voice sliced the silence of the room like a knife as he walked closer to my cage.

He stopped in front of the cage and crossed his arms with a smirk plastered on his handsome face. A cold sparkle lived in his eyes when he watched me now.

"I'd almost forgotten that dull name of yours." He took a step closer and bent down, squinting at me with theatrical concern.

I scowled back at him.

"No," he said as he stepped back and straightened to his full intimidating height again. His black shirt pulled tightly against the muscles on his shoulders and arms as he wrapped them across his chest. He rested his chin against the palm of his hand thoughtfully. "You still haven't realized how incredible it is that you gave me your name."

I pulled my dress down, trying to cover the bare flesh that I was flashing him. I had more important things to care about than my modesty, but I still didn't like the way the sharp lines of his jaw seemed to clench when he tracked my body's movements.

He was dangerous.

You could feel it like a suffocating cloud when he was near. It began to concern me more why he hadn't just dropped me off the roof with Walter.

"Do you know how many fae have the ability to impel? To seep into your mind and melt it as they wish?" He paused for a moment, then continued when no answer came. "Two." His eyes flashed wickedly. "And I killed the other."

My skin prickled with the thought of how powerful he must be to have killed the other. It didn't seem like that kind of magic would be given to someone weak.

I was doing my best to ignore him, to not give in to my

fear, but my eyes betrayed me. It was like a magnet pulled them to his features. The sharp, cruel lines of his face made it impossible not to stare. He was the most horrifyingly beautiful creature. You knew you should run and hide from him, but instead, he consumed you, occupying all your senses in beautiful wonderment.

"I hold your name as a whisper on the tip of my tongue, pet. One command, and you will pull your fingernails off. I could force you to beg for me until your voice gives out. I could manipulate your mind to crave me and melt it." He spoke confidently as power coated his words.

He wasn't making threats. Obviously, he wanted to gauge my reaction as he toyed with his mouse. I glared at him.

Those eyes. It was as if they could see into me.

"Then do it already. Kill me. Why drag this torture out longer?"

Fuck. Had I just said that out loud? Why did I taunt him?

His dark brow quirked slightly in challenge, but the evil tug that pulled at his lips was the most unsettling of all his movements yet.

"Because you, my pet, have a party to go to before I kill you." His voice even seemed to smile now.

Dusty, stale fear clung to my throat. A party full of clawed, evil fae.

Perfect.

I'd never make it out of that room alive with the hate these creatures held for humans. I was no match for their wings and teeth.

"Fighting isn't just with fists, Callie. You're a smart woman. Use what you have."

Alistair's words rang in my ear, fighting away the surrender that had begun to cloud my thoughts.

I would leave this Unseelie castle if it was the last thing I did.

I watched as the prince of smoke turned and removed his dark tunic, turning his muscled back to me as he continued to undress.

In the wild, animals didn't leave their back open unless they either trusted what lay behind them or considered them too weak to do any harm.

I made a silent vow as my eyes followed the pale silhouette of the man in front of me. I would do *anything* I needed to reach my goals, and I wouldn't stop now. I would figure a way out of this disgusting place of evil and return to my home of happy sunlight. No matter what it took.

"What are you staring at, monster?" I snarled.

The prince had turned back to face me bare chested, with his shirt in hand. He watched, differently than before.

His body was full of lines and dents where muscles I'd never even seen on humans cut into his body. My stupid eyes lingered on the deep V of that cut down to his groin area. *God,* what a waste of a gorgeous body on a monster like him. My primal insides stupidly didn't seem to care that he was evil. It had been a very, very, *very* long time since I had been involved in any coital activities. All I ever did was work, and now the feminine parts of my body—surely consumed with their own madness—took it upon themselves to whimper a breath of hunger.

If I could have suffocated that breath, I would have.

"Tonight, the entire Unseelie court will gather to look at my human pet, and I can't have you looking like that. Filthy human, you may be, but you *will* look your best as *my* filthy human pet." He walked close enough to the bars of my cage that the smoke reached out to touch him.

I scooted back until the wall of cold smoke stopped me.

He leaned in and gripped a bar in each hand just above his head. He pushed his head between the bars slowly, and the smoke whispered away, letting his face and chest into the cage. I was trapped.

A cruel look took hold of his eyes. It was almost sultry as the thin line of his mouth pulled slightly up at one side. His blue eyes were the iciest blue color, like water near an iceberg in the coldest sea. His black hair was tied loose in a knot behind his head, showing his pointed ears.

This close, I couldn't help but stare at his mouth. I was pressed as far away from him as I could get, but it wasn't far enough. Shadows of black stubble covered his sharp jaw and chin. I noticed a small scar on his left cheek where a dimple would be. There was a matching scar just into his left brow. When he grinned—even slightly—the scar produced a dimpled indent in his cheek, granting him a deceptively charming appearance.

"Does my darkness frighten you, Callie?" his deep voice whispered mockingly, and mischief sparkled like a fire in his eyes.

"No," I stated, lifting my chin. "You haven't even seen mine yet."

<hr />

Bony fingers dug into my scalp, scrubbing away dirt as though their life depended upon it. That would do no good since they were already lifeless shadows. Blue skeletal hands from under a ghost-like cloak of shadows washed me vigorously in the large claw-foot tub. They had removed me from my cage by simply walking through and carrying me to the tub with their deceitfully strong cerulean arms. They had no face or voice and didn't care how much I protested, though no one here cared about my protests.

The three shadow-maids brushed and pulled at my matted hair as spicy ambrosia-scented soap lathered around me. As much as I wanted to fight it, it felt like heaven. How long had it been since I had bathed?

My home flashed through my mind briefly before I forced it out. The framed posters of wings and creatures lining the walls and my favorite red mushroom mug all threatened to push back in, but I fought it. I couldn't let myself miss those things; they were no good to me now when I needed to be completely focused for this party.

I was beginning to actually relax and enjoy the bath when they scrubbed my back. When they shaved my legs for me,

I thought about taking them with me when I escaped. They swooshed around the large, dark marbled bathroom. The iron wall sconces flickered every time they whooshed past. They painted my nails and toes a deep black, the Unseelie's favorite color apparently, and even applied makeup to my face in a way that would have shamed makeup artists back home. Deep crimson lips paired with an almost cat-like smoky eye.

Was my hair brighter blonde, or did it just look that way against all the darkness surrounding me?

So much blood and grime had coated me even after the rain that they had to drain the tub and refill it three times with fresh water.

I stared at the mirror in petrified fascination. I had firmed up a bit. The terror-induced shaking must have been better exercise than I would have thought because my stomach muscles seemed a bit stronger, a bit flatter. Apparently, not gorging on hot Cheetos and ramen every day did this to you. They had served some human food nearly every day, so I hadn't starved.

Human food...something about that phrase tickled the back of my mind—a memory of green ferns and Earl. Oh, how I missed Earl. Even though we hadn't been friends very long, his comforting personality had grown on me fast, and I missed him dearly. Sometimes he reminded me so much of my best friend, Eli. His mother had forced him to move away, and even after I had made the deal with her, he hadn't returned. It had devastated me. I'd never had a close friend like that again until Earl. Misery threatened to strangle my chest at thoughts of both men.

Human food—fae food.

My mind flashed to the green ferns again. We had been at the park collecting samples of a mushroom we had hoped would work to save the luna moths—*damn moths*. I hope they all died now. Earl had been opening up about some of the crazy things he had seen near the destroying angel mushrooms. Black unicorns, something about a winged serpent? Fuck! Why hadn't I paid more attention! Had he been here?

I stood alone in the large bathroom since the shadow-maids had left, locking the door behind them. My long hair tickled my bare back as I paced in panic and frustration.

That day in the woods, he had said something about not eating fae food, that it did things to humans. It wasn't poison—what had he said? God dammit! Something else about drinking the faerie wine.

I slammed my fist on the marbled counter, shaking the large mirror. It rippled slightly. Of course it wasn't a real mirror. My fingers rose instantly to touch it, curious what its consistency would feel like. The white of my dress shimmered brightly against it.

The dress was stunning and fit like a glove against my curves. It was nicer than anything I had seen at the party last night, save for the queen's dress. The symbolism wasn't lost on me. Even the prince's garbage pet had nicer things than them.

It showed a lot of skin, but compared to the disgusting black dress I had been wearing, it felt like angels cloaked my body with clean fabric. It had thin satin straps and dipped low into a V in the front and back, exposing somehow even more cleavage than my small black dress. The deep cut in the back flowed into a small train of bright white fabric. When I moved, the panel of luminous silk parted in the front, exposing my legs clear up to my hipbones on either side. Beautiful rhinestone strapped heels sheathed my feet. It felt so nice to have shoes on again, even if they were high heels.

I moved my finger closer to the odd rippling mirror.

"I wouldn't do that if I were you," purred a gravelly voice.

The deep bass of it rumbled over my skin like thunder.

I pulled my hand away from the mirror as if it had bitten me and turned to see the prince as he leaned nonchalantly against the doorframe in a crisp black suit. He looked like some sort of Mafia boss, save for the black pointed crown sitting atop his head. Black hair hung sleek and straight down to his shoulders, tucked neatly behind his pointed ears.

I watched him with my breath still held tight in my lungs.

With a sharp gaze, he trailed his eyes up my body, starting at my ankles. Slowly he dragged them up my bare thighs across my waist until the ice in his eyes turned to fire as he took in my face. Reflexively I lifted my chin in quiet defiance.

He shifted off the doorframe and prowled toward me—and that's exactly what it was, a predator prowling toward its prey. My blood turned to ice, and I had to fight off a shiver with the threat of being unprotected in his nearness. He glanced at the liquid mirror.

It had stopped rippling and looked completely normal now. "It doesn't like humans either."

He stepped close enough I could feel the heat from his body. I stepped back instinctively, just as a cockroach ran from his boot. He grabbed my wrist, and a gasp fluttered from my mouth.

The prince's eyes darkened as he tipped his chin down to peer at me. The harsh line of his mouth flickered at my cry but remained stiff. His hands, free of gloves, felt like ice against my skin, contradicting the heat that came from his body. He stared at me—searing into me with his eyes. He truly *hated* me—loathed me.

"Your hair is blonde, not red."

Had his thumb just caressed my wrist?

He held my wrist up, ever so slowly, toward the mirror. His hateful eyes bore a hole right through me, but for some reason, I couldn't seem to pull away. He seemed to be devouring me. It was all-consuming.

I could see the slow rise and fall of his broad chest at the bottom of my vision. I inhaled sharply. He smelled like a forest fire doused in seductive, lush spices. Like pine and cardamom mixed with something deep and sultry.

Pain shot through my finger as he pushed the tip into the mirror.

I gasped and struggled against him, trying to pull my hand away, but he held it firmly in place.

Burning shocked through my finger like an electrical charge had caught fire to my skin.

He never looked away from my face, not once, and his face showed nothing. It was a statue as he watched me struggle against him. For some reason, I thought I'd see pleasure lining his features, but it was void of anything but a stern expression.

My fear quickly turned to anger.

"For such a powerful prince, you sure seem to be having a difficult time finishing me off. Taking me to a party? Are you trying to fuck me or kill me?" I growled in pain-induced anger.

Something flashed across his features, but it was too quick. When I studied him again, he had already shifted back to the calm and confident prince.

He moved my wrist away from the mirror slowly. The pain ceased immediately, so fast and completely that a small sigh slipped from my lips as I closed my eyes in relief.

When I opened them again, Mendax had somehow stepped even closer, the front of his body brushed against mine as he studied my face, still holding my wrist.

"I could easily kill you, but what fun is hearing half a pitiful scream before I kill you?" His head tilted slightly, giving him a completely unhinged appearance. "No, fun is knowing I can hear hours and hours of your screams whenever I want for as long as I want. But alas, pet, a good king shares with his people, and that is exactly what I will do."

I stepped back at his words, but his other hand wrapped around my hip, stopping me. His large hand against the silk of my dress sent a surprised shock through my system. Had it been anyone else, I wouldn't have been able to stop myself from pressing into the feel of them, but not this man. I felt my eyes squint with my own brand of hate as I glared into his.

"I wouldn't fuck you, human, if my own life depended upon it," he hoarsely whispered. His warm breath tickled across my face. "*Believe* me, you detestable mortal, by the end of tonight, you will beg me to end your life."

He released his hold on me with a cold look and walked toward the door.

My feet trembled, frozen in place with a heady mixture of fear and anger. I wasn't sure if I was supposed to follow or not.

He paused at the door and looked back at me, letting out a two syllabled whistle while he patted the thigh of his black pants. "Come," he commanded with a rumble and a smirk.

I had to remind myself that if I was ever going to get out of this place, I needed to lay low and not push back. He wouldn't hesitate to experience the joy of killing a human, and I needed to be smart about this. Use what I had.

I blinked the daggers away from my eyes and pushed my shoulders back to imitate a bit of confidence. I needed him to keep me alive long enough that I could escape and *finally* go home. He may be the first Unseelie I had ever met, but he was certainly not the first predator. I made a living researching predators. He was no different.

I made a show of it as I paused in the mirror to touch up my makeup, pushing my slightly curled hair back behind my shoulders. I sauntered over to the prince channeling every ounce of *Queen of the Damned* vibes I could muster.

I stepped close to the front of him, close enough that I could practically taste his power. I salaciously peeked at Mendax through my lashes before I lowered my head, averting my eyes in a blatant show of my submission.

There was more than one way to skin a cat.

In the wild, wolves respected the luna wolf because she was the leader of the pack in every respect except that she submitted to the Alpha wolf, and in return, the wolf pack held her to a higher respect and privilege than the others.

A moment passed as I remained motionless in front of him and did my best not to succumb to my senses and run.

The dark sleeve of his shirt rustled as he slowly moved his hand.

Ever so slowly, he placed his entire palm around my neck, moving my chin up so our eyes met.

Two sharp lines creased between his chilling blue eyes as he stared down at me with what looked to be pure confusion and anxiety.

A tremble quivered through my body as his thumb ghosted the hyoid bone just below my jaw.

His grip was gentle enough not to hurt but firm enough to let me know he was dangerous and could snap my neck in a second if he chose to.

Apparently, my body hadn't gotten the notice that poison came in pretty packages. It leaned into his grip ever so slightly and only a fraction before I forced it to halt, but it was enough to surprise me. I licked my lips, hoping I hadn't smeared the crimson paint that covered them.

His grip tightened for a second before he pulled away as if my neck had scalded his flesh.

I looked away confidently, feeling like I had won that round, only to feel a cold clamp of iron tighten around my neck. My hands shot up to try and loosen the metal grip.

Twists of heavy smoke clamped around my throat, trailing down to a leash of ashy-gray smoke that Mendax picked up with a smirk.

"You need a collar more stable than my hand, pet," he growled before he turned and left the room, tugging me behind him like a dog.

CHAPTER 18

CALLIE

I LIFTED MY LONG DRESS, CAREFUL NOT TO TRIP AS MY STEPS quickened to keep up with Mendax's long stride. Walking in high heels was much harder than I had remembered, having been without shoes for so long.

The dark castle seemed to shimmer with excitement and frenzy as we continued through the maze of opulent halls and passages until we stood in the same dark hallway from the night before. The same arched entryways stood tall, separating the grand ballroom from the hallway I had etched into my mind from my attempted escape with Walter.

Only now, the archways seemed to taunt me. Instead of beautiful architecture, they reminded me of open mouths that waited to devour me after I walked into their waiting gullet. It wasn't far off from what would probably happen.

Mendax slowed his steps prior to the entrance and handed my leash of smoke off to one of his men. He was about to walk into the dark ballroom and leave me in the hall when at the last second, he turned and abruptly took up the space in front of me. It was like a dark shadow coaxing fear from every pore, even as I feigned confidence. Still, there was something undeniably alluring about the way he looked at me—at least until he spoke.

"When you walk into this ballroom, remember that you are a sheep among wolves. Only these wolves *ache* for even the thought of tasting you, the thought of using you, consuming you. That is one of the many reasons the Unseelie are no longer welcomed on earth," he warned.

My eyes darted back and forth between his, deceiving my false bravado.

"Oh, pet, there any many, many ways to be consumed. Humans, though detestable to *my* lineage, are undeniably rare, a bit of a sexual delicacy among the fae." His words were coated with obvious disdain, though not enough to camouflage the long perusal he gave my body as he spoke.

"Why do you tell me this?" I clenched my jaw tightly.

It felt like I was walking into an overpopulated, starved lion's den with my back wide open and unguarded. He leaned in closer, his cheek almost touching mine as his breath whispered against the shell of my ear.

"Because I like to watch you shake, little lamb," he stated. "And this will be the last time I'm afforded that." He pulled back enough that I could see his small smile. "You will not leave this room alive tonight." He nodded to the tall fae that held my leash before he took a step under the great arched entrance. The evil prince turned back to me casually as if an afterthought had just occurred to him. "At least not in one piece."

The way his eyes and body were taut with tension gave me the impression my death would be quite a relief to him.

He turned and walked into the dimly lit ballroom.

I debated trying to run, but I had no doubt that the smoke chain around my neck, an extension of Prince Mendax himself, would love nothing more than to choke me to death should I try.

After a few minutes had passed, a thunderous rumble and cheer came from the ballroom just before the guard pulled me forward.

Dozens of black chandeliers hung from a ceiling that seemed to be an exact replica of the night sky, complete with bright, clear stars. A well-timed breeze blew the hair free from my neck and shoulders, leaving a faint scent of pine and crisp open air. It was unbelievable.

The rumble of voices fell silent. Only the sound of a few clangs of glasses could be heard as we walked into the center of the room.

Hundreds of finely dressed fae gaped at me, sending a cold sweat across my skin. I could feel some of their hunger just from their gaze. The guard that held my leash tugged theatrically as he guided me down a grand staircase that I hadn't even noticed was in the room yesterday. The guard's chest seemed to puff out proudly as he paraded me down like he himself were my owner.

A second wave of crowd amazement flourished when we descended the grand stairs. Fae stopped midsentence to turn and gawk at me. A few of the women seemed to squint their eyes in hate and disgust as I passed, while I saw several of the men track every curve of my body. Several nostrils flared and eyes darkened. That seemed like a bad sign.

I fell ungracefully to the ground as I stared at a particularly grotesque-looking man licking his lips. Yet again, the man who led me tugged on my leash, only this time it was too rough, too harsh. The horrible collar bit into my neck and pulled me to the dark marbled floor, cracking my knees against it like a hammer. Gasps and laughter rang out from the crowd. A few nearby women pointed and jeered.

How foolish of them to think they could possibly make me feel worse than I already had.

"Get up, bitch," hissed the blue-haired guard that gripped my leash.

Giggles erupted to my left from a group of young women dressed in frilly ballgowns. A few winged men clanked amber-filled glasses together as they watched me on my hands and knees.

I really was going to die tonight.

I had been lucky before. The fox saving my life, Alistair, the forest bog, Walter. I had been so lucky up until now.

The white silk of my dress chilled to match the cold ground under my legs, but that wasn't what elicited the shiver from me. I honestly felt my defeat for the first time.

Whatever was left of me wasn't going to make it out of here alive tonight. If I ran, an entire room of much faster, clawed predators would be at my throat before I even made it to the end of the hall. There was no way out.

My hands and knees burned along with my eyes as tears of defeat tore away any mask of confidence I so falsely wore.

My eyes caught sight of the queen in the corner, near the back of the room. She covered her mouth as her lavishly dressed friends chuckled and mocked me. My eyes fell to the floor briefly before I felt the magnet of another set pulling at mine.

Prince Mendax sat on a black throne of long inky vines and thorns. The throne was seated in the back of the grand room on a dais at the top of four stairs.

His blue eyes held mine from an expressionless face, like we were the only two in the entire room. His dark gaze only seemed to match the harshness of his foreboding black throne. He spread wide in the large chair, looking bored as four beautiful women pawed at him.

Even I could understand their attraction to him as he sat like a king on the throne. He was the most gorgeous man I'd ever seen. Muscles and sharp lines sculpted together with wisps of danger and power.

He ignored the women completely; their body language seemed eager for the attention he didn't give. Suddenly his expression darkened as he cracked his knuckles.

"The floor is no place for a beautiful woman, pet or not. Please allow me to help you up."

The tall stranger stepped into my view, startling me as he grabbed my arms and gently lifted me up.

185

I immediately shrank back from the man's touch. Like the other fae, the stranger was beautiful in an ethereal sense. Tall with brown hair and green eyes, his crimson-lined wings were out on full display. He had the kindest eyes I'd ever seen, and I instantly shifted toward him.

"Thank you," I said softly.

"No need to thank me, it's my pleasure. We aren't all wishing you harm." He smiled an unbelievably friendly smile as he leaned in closer. "Though I'm afraid most of them are."

His soft lyrical voice trailed over the shell of my ear, and for a moment, it almost brought me comfort.

The stranger's red wings pulsed briefly as their span widened slightly. He absolutely beamed, and I couldn't help but smile in return.

"Find your own pet, Andrey." The rough words rumbled against my skin, forcing the hair on my arms to stand on end.

The umbra's presence was like a knife held to my throat. Excitement and fear roiled through me as everything stilled.

Mendax's gaze burned like fire as he took in the gentle grip the other man kept on my elbow.

"I was only helping the beauti—"

Andrey dropped to the floor with a sickening thud. The crowd gasped as his face rolled to the side, his eyes empty and void of any life.

My eyes shot to the man hovering over me. Mendax was idly wiping a dagger on a black silk square from his pocket.

"You killed him!" I yelled, unable to believe what had just happened.

I hadn't even seen him pull the dagger out!

He looked up nonchalantly. "He was touching you."

"Son!" the queen shouted in alarm from across the shadowy ballroom.

"He...just...he helped me up after your guard made me fall!" I stared in bewilderment at the scene before me.

Not a second passed before he turned and slammed the freshly cleaned dagger into the unsuspecting guard behind me, and he fell to the ground, dead in a heap next to the other man's body. He hadn't even known what had happened.

"What the—" I struggled.

He grabbed my arm with his gloved hand and leaned in to brush against my ear.

"I've recently decided I don't like others touching my things, touching what's mine." His deep voice was barely above a whisper as he continued to clean the dagger and sheath it at his side.

He grabbed my leash and guided me to the center of the room, and I had to step over the two bodies that lay limply on the floor. I noticed he had stabbed the guard in the chest, but the winged man he stabbed just below where his left wing connected with his body. The wound seeped thick black blood.

The queen bristled at the edge, trying to get her son's attention, but even she didn't dare enter his space unseen after his recent wrath.

"Creatures of the Unseelie court." Prince Mendax addressed the crowd like a king among men.

Where was the king? Was there no king? Why did Mendax not take the crown as king, then? I stood behind him in the center of the ballroom staring at the dark marble floor, afraid to peer into the eyes of all the evil that watched me.

"I'm certain by now you've all heard the humans sent an assassin that has failed to kill me." His voice was even as he looked around the room. "As so many of you have failed to do as well." His eyes fell upon mine with heat. As he removed his gloves, his face was stern, but his eyes seemed to be in a silent war of their own. "But I have failed equally." He held out his hand, and the smoke that clamped around my throat fell from my neck into his hand in a smooth, wispy movement.

Instantly my hands flew to the raw skin of my neck.

"Three times I have tried to kill the human, and three times she has lived." His voice boomed, echoing off the distant walls and staircases as the crowd listened in silence.

187

Hundreds of hungry-looking fae stood frozen, hanging on the prince's every word.

"Callie Peterson of the human realm, as Prince of the Unseelie court, I offer you a deal."

My attention snapped to his face. What was he doing?

"What?" I asked unsteadily. Surely I couldn't trust him no matter what temptation he offered.

"I am a man of my word. I promised entertainment to my mother and people of this court."

Cold fear crawled like a spider up my spine.

"As a human, you shouldn't be nearly so hard to kill. Against my better judgment, I am quite preoccupied with you."

The blood drained from my face as I felt it too go cold. I was going to faint.

Nearly faltering, I accidentally leaned into Mendax, steadying myself with his forearm.

He paused his speech to snap his eyes at where I touched his arm.

I expected him to shove me to the ground and pull his arm away, but instead, he just stared for a moment and then continued, leaving my hand clinging to his forearm for support.

"I will hold nothing but relief once you are dead," he whispered, studying my mouth before his volume increased yet again. "A game," he stated. "I will attempt to kill you three more times, human. If, by some gift of fate, you should live past my efforts, then I will return you to the humans alive."

The crowd erupted into boisterous shouts and applause.

"No, please! I can't—I'm just a scientist! Please!" I begged him, grabbing both his arms in a frantic haze.

That damned dimple appeared on his face as he looked at my hands and smirked.

"The first of the three trials starts immediately." His voice boomed loudly as he held my eyes with his humorless expression.

His hands gripped my bare arms, mirroring my actions on him. His palm subtly grazed the skin below my shoulders as he stepped into me.

His voice was a soft whisper that only my ears could hear. "May your death be fast...for both our sakes." His gravelly voice rumbled across my bare skin.

He took a step back, and instantly the room began to blur and spin as the stars above soon blanketed my vision and complete darkness consumed me.

<hr />

Cold air blossomed across the skin not covered by my white gown. I opened my eyes to see the beautiful stars, the same that decorated the ballroom's ceilings. I shifted to sit up and waited for the nauseating feeling in my mind to leave.

I was sitting in the dirt outside.

Distant cries and shouts crept around me as I hurried to my feet.

Where was I?

This was not the forest I had been in prior to being taken to the castle. No, this one was much more daunting. The moss was still green across the floor, and the bark was still a shadow-filled brown, but the foliage of the many trees and bushes were all various shades of red and crimson. Like the trees themselves bled.

The blood forest.

It had to be. How could it ever be called anything else? I had heard mention of its horrors in the dungeon.

Red fog covered the ground like a gory haze of bloody vapor.

I jumped as distant shouts and laughter echoed somewhere. Was that the crowd?

This was the first trial. What wa—

Without warning, small sparks dropped from the sky and seared into my skin like a cigarette as giant shadows shifted the moonlight overhead.

I cried out in pain and fell to the dirt floor, clutching my arm.

Small glowing circles of whatever had fallen and hit my arm lined the forest floor. I screamed in shock, having lay right on a few of the weird glowing droplets.

Blistering hot acid burned as the small balls embedded themselves into my skin.

My high-pitched wail seemed to draw whatever dark clouds held the acid orbs closer.

I ran to a path between two trees as I struggled to remove the searing orbs of acid from my arms and thighs.

My legs carried me fast. No longer commanded by my mind but fueled only by the unalloyed adrenaline that coursed through my tired system.

I ran as fast as my legs and dress would allow into the scarlet forest.

Red leaves thrashed against my face and body with each step as wind and my heartbeat slammed a taunting tune in my head, drowning out any of my remaining senses.

The black clouds trailed me, raining more acid droplets in their wake.

A scream I had no business possessing tore from me as a drop of the acid fell into the flesh of my head, burrowing itself deep against my skull.

I faltered, plunging into a somersault and landing on my stomach. The pain was unyielding, sending sharp, blinding waves down the entire length of my spine.

No sooner had I hit the dirt than the large clouds covered me, dimming what little light I had. I glanced at the sky.

No!

It wasn't clouds that chased me. Two enormous creatures hovered above the tree tops pelting more acid drops.

Each one of their projectiles embedded deeply into my back.

They thudded loudly against my skin. No, that was my heart that pounded in my head.

I could hear them snarling—wicked hissing snarls all directed at me.

I tried desperately to get up, but my arms refused. My elbows bowed with pain slamming my cheek against the dirt.

Something sharp grabbed my head.

My spine cracked at the pressure, and another scream tore through me when I saw the size of the creature that had grabbed my head.

It was easily the size of an elephant. Long bat-like wings pulsed against the air enough to keep its large black body just above the ground. The air flapped at the surrounding leaves like a helicopter about to land.

Along its stomach rested line upon line of acid spheres waiting to be dropped. Glowing red eyes looked to the sky, not at me. It was covered in black feathers from the tip of their giant talon-encrusted feet all the way to their thin arms.

Two curved horns sat atop each of their long, feathered heads. One all black, while the other looked to have red tips.

They were giant. Their large wings easily commanded a twenty-foot span. Equally bulky as they were lithe and agile, as the one that held my head angled its long wings at just the right slant among the trees. Bits of skeleton inlaid the huge muscles and tendons that ridged its entire feathered body while sharp rows of teeth glistened inside its long skeletal mouth. They were horrifying.

I grabbed a hand full of rocks and threw them at it.

Fuck!

I hadn't even come close to hitting it as the rocks fell to the other side. Not that they would have done anything anyway.

Both monsters snapped their heads toward the sound of the stray rocks hitting the ground but returned their hazy red eyes to the night sky as if listening.

By sheer luck, I rolled at the same time and managed to not only free myself from the monster's grip but also catch the orb burrowed in my skull against the monster's talon, freeing my skull from the searing hot pain.

I rolled into the underbrush, tearing the entire bottom off my silk gown. I flung off the glittering high heels and pressed against the tree in an attempt to hide from the abomination of wings and claws.

If I was anything, I wasn't stupid. They were much stronger than me, and I didn't know how to fight them. I was a scientist. I worked with animals, not enormous monsters that pelted you with acid marbles. My eyes tightened shut in frustration and panic. How would I ever survive this?

Immediately I felt their presence over top of me.

My only choice was to run.

I collected my breath as the dark forest seemed to still. It smelled like musty, rotten leaves and blind fear. The only sound I could hear past the blood that pounded loudly in my ears was the crunch of dry leaves and nearby clicks.

I could feel their shadows even in the dark woods. Even for their vast size, the darkness of night and the red tint of the horrible forest easily camouflaged them. The moon still shone a silver cast, but the vibrancy cast red against the mist, almost like a spooky haunted forest with red fog machines and lights.

I bolted, hoping to catch them off guard. One stayed toward the top of the tall trees as the other trailed me.

Fast clicks between them sounded as I abruptly turned and circled back the same way I had come. I tripped over a stray branch and fell to the dirt. *Fuck!*

A small arm had shot out from the ground, no larger than a small child's, and grabbed ahold of my ankle, tripping me. Blood dripped down the pale gray arm and hand.

I shuffled back, only to be grabbed by more bloodied gray hands as they tried to hold me in place.

"What the fuck!" I shouted, briefly forgetting my need to keep quiet.

I kicked the small arms away and scrambled to stand before I felt the acid drop hit my chest.

I shook with defeated rage, and my fists balled, digging tiny crescents into my palms.

I couldn't continue. I was outnumbered in every possible way. They commanded this forest, and I had no idea of what dangers lay ahead if I continued to run, what trap I would waltz into. I was outdone in strength, size, and ability to fight—everything that would have kept me alive.

Heavy defeat settled like a weight in my chest as I pressed my back against the tree. I wiped my face with dirty palms as harsh realization settled over me for the first time.

Humans couldn't survive beyond the veil.

Even with the queen's protection, I would never survive in the world of fae.

I grabbed the tree behind me for support as I felt half of my heart break.

A distant crowd laughed. I could pinpoint the higher-pitched laughs of glee and the deeper male chuckles.

Somehow they watched me, laughing at my defeat.

I felt the heaviness of the monster's presence again as the air in the forest shifted.

I dislodged the burning marble from my chest and tore off just as both monsters shook the ground when they dropped down to grab me.

Click! Click! Click!

Blood poured painfully from my wounds, which now felt like they lined every inch of my body. The pounding of my heart as I ran only increased my blood loss.

Click, click.

I looked up to see the creatures easily trailing me in the sky again. They probably enjoyed this. This was easy pickings now that I was slowing, full of acid wounds. They knew I wouldn't be able to last much longer.

Click, click, click, click.

Wait—

I stopped sharply and ran in a different direction as silently as possible.

Click, click!

After continuing flight for only a second, they turned back to my location.

Click, click, click, click.

There was no fucking way.

Click, click, click.

Oh my god!

They were using some type of echolocation to track me. That was why they didn't look at me but watched the sky because they couldn't see me! They were sending out some type of sonar to locate me.

I laughed.

I laughed so damn hard that anyone who had doubted I lost my mind would no longer question it.

The clicks. They weren't talking to each other, they were sending out a sound, and the reflected sound waves told them exactly where I was. Just like bats or dolphins used.

The freshly oiled wheels of my mind began to spin as a flash of the winged man Mendax had stabbed popped into my mind, and I couldn't help but smile.

It was a long shot, but it was the only thing I had.

My feet slammed against the mossy dirt as I ran back to where I had started. To where I had torn my dress.

This had to work or else…or else…I'd never get to see Eli and my family again, and I'd die with a half-full heart.

Click, click, click.

No surprise they had found me as I was struggling to locate the strip of white silk I'd left in the brush. Where had it gone? I continued to spin and dash about like a mad woman on the hunt.

Like a beacon of angelic light, the fabric lay under the moonlight in front of me.

I grabbed it and ran. They could easily pluck me at any moment, but they seemed to be lazy and waiting for me to tire.

As if they had heard me, more acid drops pelted toward me, just missing me.

My legs continued to pump as I tore the fabric into strips. Thank god the dress was real silk or this wouldn't work. I needed to pull the fabric at exactly the right direction until I got it torn a bit and then turn it the opposite way. That should force a spiral in the strips of fabric.

The silk coiled loosely at the ends in both directions. It was perfect!

I took a sharp left and stopped. I needed to move quickly if this was going to work.

I searched the ground for the thickest and sturdiest stick I could find and forcefully jabbed until two holes formed in the back of my dress.

The ground shook as both beasts landed.

They thought I'd given up.

Quick as my hands would work, I tied the spiraling silk to the back of my tattered dress. Fighting the cramps in my legs, I took off again just as they drew closer.

Click, click, click!

The luna moth had gotten me here, and they would get me out.

CHAPTER 19

CALLIE

ONE OF THE MONSTERS TOOK FLIGHT INTO THE TREES AGAIN while the other chased me on foot, not near as fast as when they flew.

With all my studies and obsession with wings, the luna moth had always been one of my favorites. It was so easy to fall in love with them after Eli had told me about the beauty of the wonderful green moth.

I touched the V-shaped scar on my thumb as a painful reminder.

After I had come home from the hospital as a child, no one believed me, and I had started to feel crazy. No one believed my story about the tiny fairies, insisting that it was a hallucination from the mushrooms I had picked, but Eli knew I wasn't crazy.

Click, click, click, click!

Fuck, they were getting close!

I took a sharp right and pushed to run as fast as I could, the strips flowing elegantly behind me.

Luna moths are unique in that they thrive at night next to bats. They only live about one week as adults, as their sole purpose is to breed. Evolution needed them to survive and outsmart their biggest predator—bats—long enough to reproduce. Thus they were blessed with long spiral tails that acted as acoustic camouflage, bouncing the bat's sound waves in different directions, making them nearly impossible to track.

Click! Click, click, click!

It was working. The monster began to stray slightly as the silk of my new tails worked in a similar fashion, redirecting their sound waves.

The ghost of distant murmurs mumbled frantically around me.

The beast on foot was faster than I had thought and slammed its large wing into my side, knocking me to the ground in a muddy heap, and I nearly impaled myself on the stick I still held.

I saw a flash of white teeth surrounded by black feathers.

I steeled myself quickly and moved under the beast's giant wing. My hands shook with what I was about to do.

I gripped the bottom of his wing where it connected to his back and shoved it aside, stabbing my pointed branch in as far and as hard as I could.

Gasps echoed from the crowd.

The monster shrieked an agonizing scream, and I couldn't help but feel horrible about what I'd just done. Unlike the bog, I didn't think he was cruel; he was just doing what he knew.

The screams soon drew the attention of the second monster. I pulled the stick free from the tender spot where I'd stabbed the creature with a slick sound. I couldn't risk not being able to find another stick that was strong enough.

I ran to a nearby tree, but my body was quickly slowing with the loss of blood. I climbed the thick tree, biting down on the bloodied stick. Thankfully I had climbed many trees at the park in an effort to see something better, and this tree had an exceptional supply of branches. Otherwise, I would have been too drained for the climb.

The second beast landed with a low rumble.

Fuck! He was much, much larger than the other.

He crouched down to sniff his friend and let out a pained roar that shook the marrow in my bones.

What the hell am I doing? He is so big!

I couldn't climb any higher to jump on his back like I had hoped.

If I was going to do it, I needed to do it now while he was crouched over, and I could still move.

I jumped from the tree but missed his back.

I fell to the ground with a groan.

I moved to get up as fast as I could, but my adrenaline was waning. I had lost so much blood.

I was too slow.

The monster stood in front of me. A large snarling roar erupted from its toothy mouth as bits of spittle flew out.

He was angry.

It slammed a wing into my head and knocked me to the ground.

I ruined my last chance, and I wouldn't do it again.

I rolled under his widespread wings and clamored up the feathered body. Lifting the wing slightly, I found the same smooth patch under the other monster's wing. I rammed my stick into its body with everything I had left.

The beast roared and twisted, sending me sliding against the ground at its side.

It grabbed me.

Its large claws dug painfully into my side as it hunched over, muscles slowly relaxing, and I rolled from its grip.

It gave one last squeeze and shriek before succumbing to the apparent deathblow and melted to the ground in a heap of lifeless feathers and horns.

I quickly pushed myself away from its grasp. The cool dirt below me collected under my nails as I pushed myself as far away as I could.

The ground shifted, bottoming out from below where

I had sprawled. I fell backward as I struggled to keep consciousness.

My tired eyes flickered at the temperature change as dry heat covered my now damp skin.

Instantly I was back inside the castle. The same twinkling night sky filled my vision but was now surrounded by fancy walls and tapestries.

"I must say, that was quite impressive," sang the queen as she popped her pretty head into my vision.

I struggled to sit, realizing I was in the middle of the ballroom floor once again. The crowd gathered around me as I fought to stand. I was still in the presence of predators, and it was foolish to lie vulnerable beneath them.

My eyes immediately searched for Mendax, although I'm not sure why. I suppose I was curious to see if he was actually going to hold up his end of the bargain. He was probably stewing angrily in another room.

"Unless you all would also like to die tonight, get away from my pet," his voice lumbered at my back as the crowd quickly moved away.

"Take her back but get her cleaned up before she is returned to her cage. I don't want her soiling my rugs with her red human blood."

His words were said to someone else, but as he moved in front of me, his eyes held mine with something I couldn't understand. A look I hadn't seen from him before. He looked disheveled, his dark hair mussed about as if he had been pulling on it. Likely furious because I hadn't died like he'd hoped. Why did he hate me so much?

This time elfish-looking lady's maids came to fetch me instead of guards or the shadow-maids that had bathed me last time.

My body was about to give out, and the acid wounds still burned full of fire. I couldn't continue with the other trials if I died from my wounds tonight.

"Say it," I stated, though it came out with more gusto than I could have predicted.

Mendax and I remained standing, eyes locked. He hesitated a moment.

"Callie Peterson of the human realm has won her first trial," he said, humoring me, as a foreign gleam of respect flashed over his eyes and just as quickly left.

CHAPTER 20

CALLIE

K EEP YOUR FAE HANDS OFF ME!" I SHOUTED AT THE WOMEN in front of me.

They had been scrubbing and bathing me for over an hour and, even now, wouldn't let me rest as they groped my body with their cold, bony hands.

They were attempting to salve and bandage my wounds, but I couldn't take it anymore. My body was still in fight mode, unable to relax. They were all predators to me, no matter how small and innocent they looked.

"Miss, we need to apply the salve, it will heal you and stop the burning that I'm sure you're still feeling from the nocturneye. Please," one of the lady's maids asked sweetly.

So that's what those dreadful creatures were called, nocturneye.

The small silk nightgown they had put me in rode up my thighs, showing more sunken burns as I kicked her away.

"You will not touch me!" I screamed as I tried hopelessly to clamor off the floor while the others held my arms down.

"Miss! Please stop, or we will have to bathe you once more. You're bleeding everywhere again!" whined the small elfish woman as she looked to the others for help.

"Leave."

His voice was like a rumble of thunder breaking through the room.

"She is bleeding again, Your Highness. She will bolt if we let up—her adrenaline is still peaked," the red-haired maid pleaded.

"Leave," he repeated, not taking his eyes from me.

The maids didn't hesitate to follow their master's order, rising off the floor in front of my cage to sprint out quickly.

I leaped up, finding new panic at being trapped alone in a room with the prince.

As if by his command, the door closed on its own, and the clink of a lock echoed across the walls of the large bed chamber.

"Get out. Now," I commanded, frantically looking around for some type of weapon, but his room was empty other than a few basics.

I settled on a large bronze candlestick that sat on one of the nightstands, hastily collecting it in my trembling hands.

"This is *my* room," he stated, casually crossing his arms.

"Send the maids back in, or I will bludgeon you with your own candlestick!" I shouted wildly, feeling feral from fighting the nocturneye and the maids with no rest.

His beautiful blue eyes suddenly danced with challenge. His entire person began to fade as faint charcoal smoke rose around him.

My back was slammed against the wall, my arms pinned together above my head, as he reappeared directly in front of me.

"You—" I growled through clenched teeth as blood whooshed in my ears.

He pressed his body against mine as the wall dug painfully against the wounds of my back.

"How did you know to stab the nocturneye under its wing?" he cut me off.

His hard body dwarfed mine as his eyes trailed my mouth.

His face was still expressionless, but his eyes sparkled with a dangerous fire as he bent his tall, muscular form to further cage me in. Had it been anyone else in that moment, the steady pressure would have been a calming relief, but it wasn't anyone else. It was Mendax, and it somehow seemed to set me off more, feeling the heat of his hard body pressed against me. The contact sizzled my burned-out nerves.

"I saw where you had stabbed the winged man at the ball. They were both winged. It was a calculated guess," I bit out as I struggled against the palm that easily held both my wrists.

He smiled wide. The action changed his entire face into a disarmingly alluring man as the scar on his cheek dimpled. That was the most expression I had seen on him since the rooftop.

"That sounds exactly like something an assassin would say."

"I am not an assassin. If I were, believe me, I would have already killed you by now!" I shouted, pushing my body defiantly into his as hard as I could.

The closeness and feel of both of us pushing our bodies together felt like an electric shock to my frenzied system. I felt *everything*.

"I think I underestimated whoever sent you to distract me," he rasped as he continued to push his frame against mine.

My eyes flickered shut with the feel of his ungodly firm body pressing against me, and the clean scent of dark vanilla and amber clouded my senses.

"You ought to have allowed the lady's maids to help you. You're bleeding all over my wall." His warm wisps of breath ghosted across my face and neck as if it were fingertips touching my adrenalized skin.

"Good, I hope I stain it," I bit out softly.

"Get on the bed so I can bandage you, and you'll stop bleeding all over the place." His husky voice trailed across my collarbone like soft velvet before he cleared his throat.

"I will die before I let you touch me," I snarled, still fighting against what my body seemed to crave.

"As you wish, pet," he whispered as he pinned me tightly against the wall.

The hand that wasn't holding my wrists reached out and slowly parted around my neck like a caress, his thumb on one side, fingers on the other.

Reluctantly my eyes flickered shut at the contact. He began gently at my collarbone before slowly caressing his open palm up my neck and closing just under my jaw.

I wriggled against him, trying to escape his hold, but each shifting movement seemed only to encourage him.

My eyes flew open. When had I closed them?

The feel of his hard arousal pressed against my stomach, a startling reminder of what was happening.

"Touch me, and you *will* regret it," I threatened as his forehead pressed against mine.

Why did it feel so right being pressed against him like this?

"I believe that to be true with every fiber of my being," he whispered with a conflicted look.

The room blurred together as everything started to spin.

I was going to faint.

"Stop it! Are you trying to impel my mind? Stop!" I pleaded.

"I'm not, Callie. You're losing too much blood. Your human body has fought too long." He pulled away suddenly, looking concerned. "Get on the bed and lie down so I can patch your wounds. Do it, or I *will* make you," he stated, leaving no room for protest.

I had no choice anyway; I was about to collapse.

Only once he felt my body go slack in agreement did he step back so I could walk to the bed.

The edges of my vision blackened, and I lost the fight, dropping the candlestick I still held, and as I fell, my body went completely limp.

Strong arms caught me. My head lolled backward until something gently shifted, and my cheek brushed against warm fabric.

This close, his clothes smelled of black amber and cedar.

It felt like my body had been laid on a cloud. Maybe I had died finally. My body gave out, and now I was resting on a cloud in heaven.

"Stay with me, pet, your body is just in shock."

I peeled open my eyes to see he had carried me to his bed. The few candles that remained lit in the dark room illuminated the wrinkled displeasure in his beautiful, pale eyes.

"Why put me on your bed if it displeases you so much?" I breathed, still feeling his arms under me.

"Human's lives are so short and fragile. The weight of that has never quite occurred to me until just now," he whispered as if to himself. "Lie back now and let me dress your wounds or I will crawl inside your mind and force it," he threatened.

I had no choice. Not that I ever stood a chance of fighting the towering fae male, but now even less so. I wasn't certain I could even sit up as the lack of adrenaline sapped all my energy.

"Stay awake until I tell you otherwise," he growled irritably.

I startled, having drifted off.

I felt his warm hands gently ghost up my bare ankle.

"Stop. What are you doing?" A tremor pirouetted in my voice.

"I'm searching for your wounds. Settle down. You are safe now."

Why was his voice suddenly so rough?

"Yes, of course. Safe at the hands of the Unseelie prince who wants me dead and just attempted to kill me?" I scoffed, trying to pull my leg away from him while I fought to keep my eyes open.

"Stop fighting. I promise that your life is not at risk outside of the trials. The rest of the court would overthrow me if they knew I deprived them of the entertainment of witnessing you die."

I heard the smile in his voice. It sounded foreign, as if it didn't show up often.

"Besides, you are the one who aims to kill me. At least you shall be rewarded if you succeed."

"I am not trying to kill you, for the last time, Mendax, I just—"

Scalding pain shot through my body, jolting my eyes open. The feel of something cold dug against the wound at my thigh.

"I'm sorry it burns. It's neutralizing the acid. Otherwise, it will continue to eat at your skin," he said gently as he pressed a cotton cloth to another hole at the top of my thigh.

I fisted the black bed cover and bit down on my lower lip in pain.

"Why are you helping me when you are the reason I have these wounds in the first place?" I asked, rising on my elbows to get a better look.

He stood at the edge of the bed, holding my bare thigh, and my other leg lay just on the other side of him so that he was positioned right between my legs.

"I'm not sure. I can't seem to help myself."

His eyes gleamed in the candlelight. He set my leg down gently and replaced it with my arm.

"This is deep. I imagine it's going to hurt," he said, looking concerned.

I stared at him. His gentleness was a weapon I hadn't seen him wield, not even to his mother.

"Where is the king?" I asked.

His throat bobbed slightly, and his face flushed. "King Marco is dead."

That was not what I had expected. I moved to sit up while he held my left arm gently.

He bent down to kneel on the floor at the side of the bed. He was so tall he still easily reached me.

My foot pressed against his chest, and I moved it to the side on instinct.

I bit my lip when I realized I had just moved my legs to either side of him, basically straddling him while he sat on his knees.

His jaw clenched, and a muscle feathered at the sharp curve. His eyes paused at the shadow my nightgown had formed between my legs.

Smoke unfurled from his back, showcasing his wide wings.

It was intensely intimidating, but also...a part of me longed to touch his wings—they were *unbelievably* beautiful when you looked past the sharp edges. Like their owner.

What would it be like to have such a bad, heartless man want me? To come apart only for me and no one else. I shook the deranged thoughts from my head.

Desperate to dampen the heat lingering in the air, I asked about his dead father.

"I'm sorry. How did he die?"

"I killed him," he said calmly.

"Is that truly your answer to everything? Just kill it?" I asked incredulously.

He looked up from where he knelt between my legs and into my eyes with icy resolve. He rested my arm over his shoulder as he leaned over and pressed the compress firmly into the wound on my chest.

I hissed in pain and grabbed at his shoulder as I scowled angrily at him.

"You develop a taste for blood when you're constantly licking your own wounds," he stated coldly, still watching me.

His wings pulsed, and the dark smoke feathered but remained spread wide at his back.

He leaned back, still on his knees, and grabbed my waist. With one quick motion, he pulled me until my ass was at the edge of the bed, and he had nestled himself between my legs.

It was probably more terrifying to see him in such a submissive position, though I seriously doubted he wouldn't hesitate to kill me from where he knelt between my thighs.

He still held my waist as his chest pressed against my center, and my hands fought for purchase on his broad shoulders.

"Why did the humans choose you to destroy me?" he

asked, his voice void of all malice as his strong hands left my waist to dab more liquid on the bloodied rag.

I laughed despite myself. "They didn't." I rolled my eyes as I sat, looking slightly down at his face. "Trust me when I tell you, I am the last person the humans would send to disarm you."

His hand steadied warmly again at my waist. The other grazed the wound on my chest.

I grabbed his bicep and bit my lip to block out the intense pain.

His mouth parted as he paused to stare at my lips. "Then, like me, they would have underestimated you."

The room was quiet for a moment. I watched him work, unsure of what his words meant.

"Is it always dark here? Don't you ever miss the sun? How dreary," I asked, struggling to change the subject and not curl up against his large chest.

He was still a horrible monster even if he happened to be kind to me in this moment.

His hands splayed on the sides of my waist as he pulled me harder against his chest.

We were so close now I could see every gray speckle in his sky-colored eyes, feel every fold and wrinkle of his shirt against my body.

Tension crackled like fire in the air. Both of us fought against something forbidden, something wrong.

He cleared his throat gruffly. "It is never truly sunny, but not always night. Just as it is always different shades of day for the Seelie." He bristled at the mention of the other fae realm.

He reached up and touched the back of my head. His eyes flickered shut as he threaded his hands in the back of my hair.

"Until this moment, I didn't know you could crave something you've never wanted." His voice was thick like honey.

I watched his full lower lip and the creases that adorned

it as he spoke as if I'd been hypnotized. My thumb found his lips and moved lightly across the soft linear creases. He abruptly stood to his full towering height, startling me, and I shifted to get off the bed, unsure of what had suddenly happened, but he lightly tightened his grip, still in my hair. Threading his hands through my hair, he tipped my head up to look at him. I instantly tensed, ready to fight him.

"You have a wound on the back of your head. Be still, and we will be done quickly."

I relaxed, and he loosened his grip slightly.

"That's it. Good girl." His voice rasped down on me.

"I still hate you," I said calmly as I stared at the black fabric that covered his large chest.

"I still need you dead," he said, but his words were said without venom.

After a few dabs of ointment on my head, he finally let me up and guided me back to my cage.

"Take this," he said as he handed me the black cloud-like comforter of his bed.

I paused to watch him a moment before taking it into my cage. Was he truly giving me his bedding so I didn't have to sleep on the hard floor?

"It's covered in your filthy human blood," he said as he handed me the fluffy bedding.

"What are you—"

"Rest, Callie. The second trial is tomorrow."

He turned abruptly and left, not returning for the rest of the night.

CHAPTER 21

MENDAX

B E SURE SHE GETS WHATEVER SHE WANTS TO EAT. I DON'T
know the last time she's eaten," I told the maid as I walked
into the large kitchen.

"Yes, of course, Your Highness." The petite fae nodded.

What was I thinking?

I quickly raised my hand to reverse the generous command
but hesitated, and the lady's maid left.

What was I doing? Feeding her? I should starve her.
Get her away from me all the quicker. Still, I think it's been
a while since she's had a nice meal—it will give her more
stamina, which will provide more entertainment.

The moment the trial began yesterday, I felt nothing but
pure relief, believing this roach would be dead instantly.

It had been a sure thing.

No one, not even the fastest fae, outran the nocturneye
with their tracking abilities, let alone a human with no skills,
no strength, no magic, and no help.

"Food, sir?" asked the thickly mustached chef from behind
the kitchen fire, startling me from my thoughts.

"No," I snapped as I grabbed the nearest bottle of faerie
wine and poured it into a large glass.

I had told myself yesterday not to worry about my enticement with her. What was the point of worrying? She would be dead, and my people would be thrilled with me for the entertainment I provided them with. Only the latter proved to be true in the end.

I knew what she was.

I knew how trained she must be to possess such toned thighs. Even covered in filth, her silhouette was mesmerizing. No one but a trained assassin could possess such a figure. It was obvious she was chosen to be a trained killer because she was the most beautiful human created. Perfect for distracting and disarming.

I knew how successful she surely was in her position as a mercenary.

Never had I witnessed such a fast-working and clever mind as hers. They had most definitely trained her in the art of persuasion and seduction. Never had I been so captivated and enchanted in all my centuries. My suspicions were only further solidified when I watched her quickly alter her dress to avoid the tracking of the nocturneye. I watched her with pure awe when she knew exactly where to land the killing blow beneath the nocturneye's wings.

She wished me to believe her a simple, insignificant human, but anyone that looked at her could see she was so much more than that.

When I witnessed my little pet lamb execute the killing blow to not one but two aged nocturneye, my intrigue evolved into something much more dangerous. It only made me need her dead faster.

A chill overcame my body as I ran my fingers over the small tooth that hung from my neck. The molar was hers. She had spit it at me in all her fiery magnificence in the blood room. I had pocketed it without thinking.

Then later, arguably still not thinking, I had it made into a souvenir to wear always. A memento from this enchantress to remember long after she was dead.

She could not live, but already I feared I would not draw breath without a part of her near.

A shiver racked my spine, threatening to unfurl my wings.

Hours I had paced the halls, attempting to understand how this maggot had wriggled into my mind with similar fervor as if she had impelled my mind. The foreign feelings she sent into my mind were severe and intolerable.

Before I had entered my bedchamber after the trial, I had wholly decided that she would be moved back to the dungeon. To the stone walls where her scent of lavender and honey could no longer trail along and blur my senses. It was admitting weakness to send her away, but I was without choice. Her pure existence had somehow infused my mind in a way I couldn't tolerate.

But when I had opened the door and saw her lying on the floor of my bedroom under the duress of the other women, all I could think about was slitting their tiny throats for carelessly handling her.

I would be the only one here to touch her.

Even then, I had still planned to send her silky hair and soft flesh back to the dungeon. I would carry her myself if I had to and enjoy the last checked touch before she would be gone forever.

But then…then she had grabbed the candlestick ready to bludgeon me, and I saw a bloodthirsty fire burn like an unyielded torch behind her eyes—for me. No longer masking to be the lamb I knew she pretended to be. She revealed a murderous serpent every bit as dark as myself.

The thought of being the one—the only one—to control and feed that fire sent an absolute inferno through my mind, taking with it every sane thought I had held.

Then when her body had softened in response to me—when her muscles slackened, and the flame in her eyes settled at the touch of my hands—I was lost to her. It was as if a part I had never before utilized suddenly began to function. The thought of her soft, yet dangerous, body sleeping on the hard floor bit into my soul like a knife, and the next thing I knew, I was giving her a blanket—*my blanket*—to sleep on!

I was so distraught I had spent the rest of the night pacing the library, trying desperately not to think of the way her small hand imprinted upon my arm when she touched me. The way her fingertips felt as though they were lined with satin. If I wasn't careful, I would do something very, very stupid.

Like let her live.

The thought of her being gone already pestered me more than I could consciously admit.

I would not let her turn my brain into wreckage.

"You look like shit."

"As do you, Mother," I retorted before turning around and quickly tucking away the tooth under the edge of my tunic.

The queen grabbed my arm and guided me to her breakfast table by the expansive window that overlooked the gardens and the first edging of town.

I shook away her sterile hand immediately but continued to join her.

"The entire court, all of the Unseelie for that matter, are in an absolute uproar over the trial. Can you believe that dim-witted human did all that?" She gathered her large red dress to sit and immediately began to stab her fruit vigorously. She liked stabbing things.

"She is not dim-witted—" I growled before I caught myself.

My mother froze as if she had suddenly turned to ice, dropped the strawberry from her mouth, and stared slack jawed.

"The human is most certainly a very skilled assassin. The only reason she has escaped death this many times is that everyone continues to underestimate her." I tried to recover.

A smile crept onto my mother's thin lips. "It is true, then. You banished the maids tending her wounds so you could do it yourself? I refused to believe the story when I heard it knowing it to be false. In all my yearning, not once have you taken to anyone. Your father and I quit forcing the issue after you killed all those princesses. Shame we never procured those alliances. Quite the mess you caused our line back then." Her eyes danced in sharp fascination. "Tell me you didn't touch the human, Mendax. I don't think my mortality could take it. First, you refuse to take your rightful throne merely because you won't allow me to bond you with another—"

"That's not—" I tried to cut off her rambling, but she was much more skilled in that art form than I.

"To which I understood! The females here are severely lacking. But to then simply hurl your desires at a *human*? That is too much!" She laughed, but her cold eyes held a depth of seriousness.

"As you know, I will never take the throne and be king because I will never share my powers with another and, therefore, never bond to another, which furthermore excludes me from the ability to ascend the throne, dear Mother. I will admit, though, for the first time in my life, I am oddly fascinated." I rubbed my arm, still feeling where she had touched it. "Still, she will be dead and out of my system as soon as possible."

She stared at me, a wicked look on her face. She no longer did the work of a ruler, but she still enjoyed batting her prey around a bit.

"I could bond you to the human." She leaned in, inspecting my expression for cracks. "It's almost too perfect—I don't know why either of us hadn't thought of it." She stood abruptly, brimming with excitement as if she would burst if she didn't go to the window. "Your powers don't divide until the marriage ceremony, but the bonding is what has barred you from becoming king." Her blue eyes looked ready to pop from her face—the whites gleamed brightly against the dark walls. "Bond with the human and kill her before the marriage ceremony. It's perfect. It's never occurred to me before because we were dealing with immortal fae, not weak human mortals." She looked to me, hope manically pulled at her face.

"You're wasting your haggard breath, Mother. I will bond with no one, especially not the human that, may I remind you, was sent to kill me."

I rolled my eyes at her and shifted my body in the opposite direction dramatically. How could she even suggest this?

"The expelled fae will eventually come for the throne. You and I both know a lightmire will be the only one strong enough to take it from you." Her voice darkened. "If you think I will stand by and let a fallen Seelie take my kingdom before I would bond you to a human...you are a bigger fool than I thought."

"They wouldn't challenge a Smoke Slayer. Even the expelled aren't so stupid." I grunted, frustrated to be having this talk again.

"Don't be so sure."

I instantly craved blood at the mention of the expelled. No one wanted them. The fallen Seelie fae had been banned from their realm and somehow formed a rebellion here. They were rumored to be incredibly powerful and in pursuit of taking over my court.

I rose to my feet, pushing the chair back with a loud screech. "Well, Mother, this was lovely as usual, but I have someone I need to execute." My words dripped with sarcasm, and I began to walk away.

"At least do me the favor of letting her live long enough to compete in the second trial. The Seelie princes are rumored to attend, and I think it wise for them to see how you kill people that are sent to slay you," she said, raising her brow as she remained facing the window. Her command was unconcealed.

"Fine," I bit out as I walked away.

Someone else's orders upon my tongue tasted bitter and unwelcome.

I held out my hands and shadowed back to my room, eager to see my wolf in sheep's clothing one last time.

215

CHAPTER 22

CALLIE

I ROLLED TO MY STOMACH, AND SLEEP PULLED ME DEEPER INTO the abyss with the new position. My hands fisted the fluffy comforter under my head. I inhaled the sultry scent of the bedding's owner. I would never admit it—maybe it was some type of Stockholm syndrome—but I couldn't help but find excitement when I breathed in the spicy amber and cedar fragrance. I tightened my thighs together. The reminder of Mendax's muscled body pressed against mine flitted across my mind as though he touched me now. The excitement he got from me felt like a power all on its own.

If only he wasn't so vile.

My stupid body ached with the delusion of wishing he were touching me. What would it feel like to have the harsh, unfeeling man fall apart just because he touched me? Simple me.

Even the pain he had caused as he cleaned my wounds had somehow felt carnal and erotic. Like there was a forbidden layer of pain-laced pleasure I had never experienced.

The formidable prince of death had knelt on the ground before me. I would have given anything to know the last time he had knelt before anyone—and given them his bedding. He acted as someone would who had begun to care about me.

That was a foolish thought considering he was determined to kill me.

This was stupid to think about. I needed to get out of here before it was too late. If I couldn't get to my family in time—

The hairs along the back of my neck rose as a presence loomed behind me.

Cool air hit the back of my exposed thighs, and I remembered the tiny blue nightgown I had slept in. I went to roll over, realizing that my whole lower half had exposed itself. Strong hands pushed down my head, stopping me from flipping onto my back. The action caused me to pin my arms under the blanket they had been holding as a pillow.

"Get the fuck away from me, Mendax!" I muffled through the fabric.

I knew it was him simply by the way my skin seemed to tingle in his presence. I could feel his hand like a magnet above the skin of my ass, even though he didn't touch it.

"Say it again," he rasped, his voice thick and husky.

"What!?" I replied as my heart rate quickened. I struggled against the hand that gently held my head down against the blanket.

I shifted up on my knees to gain leverage, my ass high in the air before I realized what I had done.

He was absolutely unhinged. A dark and deranged man who enjoyed slaughtering others and…and touching me. I had felt the proof of his hard arousal last night.

Trembles slithered up my spine at the horribly enticing thought.

"Say my name again." His deep voice rumbled as his hand ghosted my butt lightly.

Goose bumps trailed my skin, chasing after his hand.

"Fuck you!" I shouted, attempting to cover up a breathy gasp.

He was pushing my head just enough that I was stuck but

not enough that I had any trouble breathing into the fluffy comforter.

"Say it, Callie. I want to hear the way it sounds from your filthy mouth."

I felt his hot breath on the back of my ass cheek. I could feel his body towering over mine.

My face flared red at the vision he was seeing. My entire backside was exposed and raised to the gods, with only a tiny black triangle of fabric covering my center.

I knew I was skating the line, but I was at war with myself between kicking him in the face and learning what my words really did to him.

"Fuck you, *Mendax!*" Why was I so out of breath?

"*Very* good girl," he rumbled as his rough hand ran up the inside of my thigh, feathering where the seam of my panties rested.

I gasped, biting my lip so hard I tasted copper as my eyes fluttered shut. I pushed my head harder against the blanket to make certain he heard nothing.

"Your flesh is the softest thing I have ever felt," he said breathily, almost to himself. "Tell me why you want me dead, little lamb? Don't be shy with me. I quite like the fire that you attempt to mask."

"For the last fucking time, I'm not trying to kill you! God! I'm pretty sure I would be doing a better job than this if I were!" I shouted.

His hand skated across my most sensitive parts, softly feeling the silk triangle.

I knew he could feel my desire dampening the fabric even as I bit the other side of my lip to stop myself from letting out an unwelcome moan.

With my head and hands held down, I couldn't tell what he was doing, I could see nothing. All my senses heightened, and my skin buzzed, waiting to feel where his hand or body would move next.

"I'll ask you again, Callie." He pulled the triangle to the

right, and cold air hit my exposed throbbing sex. "Why do you want me dead?" His voice was thick and sultry, as if he could barely restrain himself at the sight of me.

"I'm not an as—"

His tongue swept over my center from behind with one long swipe.

I bit a mouthful of the bedding and tried to rise, but the steady pressure of his hand pushing my face into the fabric stopped me. I needed to get away from him. I was unraveling at his fingertips—and his tongue.

Holy gods.

My thighs shook in anticipation, and I was thankful my face was hidden from view.

Mendax groaned a low reverberating growl that had its own effect entirely on my body.

"I am plagued by you." Another light swipe of his tongue. "I am vexed with the thought of you constantly." His lips pressed against me as he spoke, and I felt every breath and rumble of his mouth as it moved against me. "I beg the old gods that listen"—another swipe, this time his tongue deepened, and he lightly ran his teeth over my nub, following with his warm tongue— "that they will rid you from my system after today."

I could fight it no longer and pressed back against his warm mouth, shamefully begging for more with a deep moan. I couldn't think straight. The world seemed to swirl and blend away, and we were the only two left. Nothing mattered but when I would feel him touch me again.

He readily acquiesced, grabbing both of my thighs. The prince gently spread my legs farther apart before he cupped a large hand under me.

I was completely undone, arching my back and moaning. I felt hollow with a need for him to fill me, to feel that delicious friction filling my body.

"That's it, my little hellhound, rub that pussy against my face so hard we both forget how much we hate each other."

A low growl ripped from his chest as I did just as he requested.

I was so close—so close to coming.

A sharp, pleasant sting flared as he suddenly slapped my ass. His mouth and tongue continued to flick and suck in a wild, mind-numbing assault. It was like a starved man given food.

"Mendax!" I shrieked huskily as the sting of his hand bit into my skin sharply.

The sensation sent ripples of sensitivity through the rest of my body, and I writhed against his face feeling the rumble of his moans reverberate over me.

"Mendax! Oh god! Me—"

"Say it again, pet. Remind the gods exactly who you have bewitched."

I came so hard that stars flickered in my vision before I collapsed in a pile spreading my arms wide. Only then realizing that my hands had been free most of the time.

"I still hate you," I said as I looked over my shoulder and into the hungry blue eyes that towered over me.

In another world, I would have wanted nothing more than to curl into his chest and sleep. His face seemed so different and full of feeling as he watched me.

"I still want to kill you…maybe more now," he said, staring at me one last second before he turned and walked to the door. "The maids will be in to get you dressed. We leave for your second trial in an hour. The Seelie royals wish for a piece of the entertainment as well."

❦

"We must go now, miss," the lady's maid mumbled while she sprayed something from a small ruby bottle at me.

I sighed heavily. I still felt so tired. My wounds hurt even under the bandages that were healing them at an alarming speed.

Foolishly, every time my eyes opened from sleep, I found

220

myself searching for the light, for the place that would always hold a piece of my heart, even if I didn't make it out of here alive.

"We know you can do it, miss. The staff all root for you, oh—please don't tell the queen I said that," the small elfish-looking girl murmured.

Even she was beautifully ethereal, like everyone else I had seen on this side of the veil save for a few monsters. I couldn't help but wonder why Prince Mendax always seemed so disgusted by the females in his presence. Everyone was so gorgeous.

I studied her heart-shaped face in surprise. "You—what? I was under the impression you all liked Prince Mendax?" I rose from my chair, now fully dressed in a beautiful crimson gown that fell in a heap to the floor. It instantly reminded me of pooling blood.

"Oh! Miss—we do! We very much like the prince!" She scrambled, beginning to look flushed as the maids all exchanged worried looks. "We like him very much, which is *why* we champion for you to survive. Had Prince Mendax not killed his father—well, there is no telling what would have happened to all of us."

The small group of maids walked me toward the door and stopped so the one speaking could adjust the back tendril of hair that kept releasing itself from my updo. She looked exactly like what the human fairy tales assumed small fairies to look like, petite with slightly more angled features and incredibly pointed ears.

Eventually, she stopped trying to fix my hair and snapped her fingers. A large luna moth that had been floating through the room—they always seemed to be—flew smooth and unhurried to the back of my hair where it landed, holding the misbehaving tendril in place. Another came and rested on the top, fluttering as if they were excited for the task.

"If you are on Mendax's side, then why do you root for me?" I asked as I watched the maids all blush in unison.

221

"We have been maids of the Unseelie castle for hundreds of years, since His Highness was only a baby."

Hundreds of years old?

She continued, looking down in an attempt to hide her face under her ashy brown hair. "And he *never* laughs or smiles, never has. He is completely unable to feel anything but hatred." She reached out to put her small hand on my arm. "Please know that not all Unseelie are this way. We have normal and happy villages, much like I have heard of in the human realm."

"What does this have to do with me?" I asked, feeling a painful twinge at the mention of the human realm.

She moved close to my face, her brown eyes glittering. She reminded me of a giant doll that smelled like cupcakes, not at all what I would expect from a maid of the horrible Unseelie castle. "He likes you, we can tell. The prince—it's like he's numb all the time. Never changes expressions or seems to feel unless he is killing." Her round bark-colored eyes sparkled. "But he feels with you, his eyes dance when he looks at you, and he is constantly *watching* you. If…if he bonded with you, then he could ascend and take the throne as king!" she finished excitedly.

The other three had now joined her in quiet harmony as they smiled and whispered excitedly to one another pressed up against me.

So that was why he hadn't become king. Because no one wanted to be tied to him forever. I certainly wouldn't blame them for that.

"You are foolish. He doesn't like me. In fact, he despises me. You do remember he's trying to kill me with these trials, right? I'm sure there are plenty of shadowy maidens that would love to bond—or whatever—to him." I pushed back my shoulders and steadied myself for what was to come today, not liking the nonsense they spoke.

I didn't want to bond to anything. I wanted to go home.

"Oh, there are *plenty* of women who have tried

desperately to claim him, he has never entertained one that we are aware of. He says he will never bond to another and share his powers and will never become king." Her round eyes drooped in sadness, and a dramatic frown creased her doll-like face. "Though he thinks he will live forever, he will not, and as of now, who knows who or what will take the throne if he is gone! His people need him to remain. With the expelled fae holding rebellion, it's trying times to have an empty throne."

I shook the confusing words from my head. This wasn't my world, and I wouldn't get tangled up in any of this. I just wanted to go home.

"I think I should go. I truly am sorry about the troubles you all face, and I hold faith in the hopes that you find a solution that works. Are the guards coming to assist me?" I asked, stepping out of the door to an empty hallway.

"No." She smiled coyly. "The prince said that the guards were futile. That he would find you easily and enjoy the hunt should you try to escape." She covered her mouth, and I swear a breeze of vanilla cupcake wafted into my nose. "He and the queen are escorting you in the carriage to the Court of faerie themselves. Good luck." She smiled, and I found myself cringing away from it.

I stepped into the dark hallway and headed for the grand staircase.

As much as I thought I would hate so much darkness, the castle had a cozy feel as the amber flickers of light cast a warm glow against the dark floors and walls. Maybe I should paint my rooms at home black if I returned.

I had to clutch the banister at the top of the stairs and close my eyes.

Home.

What if I didn't survive the trial today? What if I never made it home again? Never got to see Willow Springs or Earl again? I would never see Dorothy the turkey or the cabin I had so newly called home.

I stepped onto the dark wood of the first step, trembling. This was real.

I could easily die today.

My chest tightened, and the crimson fabric sparkled with my quickened breath as I clutched the iron balusters fighting to keep upright but failing as I dropped to sit on the step.

I couldn't do this—I couldn't.

A solid hand gently pressed against my lower back.

"It's a good thing Alistair's not near to hear your heart racing, or he would go mad," Mendax whispered softly as he sat down next to me. The soft onyx-colored fabric of his pants and coat gently caressed the side of my thigh as he sat.

I hadn't turned my face from the stairs to identify who it was. I didn't need to. I knew it had been him before he spoke. My nerves seemed to itch for him when he was near, and that bothered me more than any of this. How could I feel that way about the man trying to kill me? He was the villain. I would only feel that for a hero.

"Will you truly let me go home if I survive the trials?" I asked softly, feeling vulnerable.

I turned to face him just in time to see a muscle feather at his jaw.

"Believe me, pet, when I tell you I want you gone—I need you gone." His low whisper skated across my clavicle, down to lower, more hidden, parts of me.

"Then just send me away now. Why kill me?"

Our faces had somehow gotten closer. Here I could easily see the rosy tones of his soft lips, the smooth skin that made the dark hair near his temple stand out in contrast.

"Because if you're not dead, I fear I will leave every-thing to follow you." His gravelly voice was barely heard as it ghosted across my lips.

One minuscule movement from either of us and our lips would press together. What would it feel like to kiss that wicked mouth? Something in my gut warned me it would be like a drug—that it would feel like magic until every part of me was ripped apart, unable to collect the pieces.

"You assume I'd be easily found if—"

"I would find you," he stated with a look that sent so many butterflies into my belly it made the moths in my hair flutter.

He lifted my arm as he stood, helping me up and setting it in the crook of his before guiding us down the wide staircase.

"If you die tonight and I never get to tell you, you are the most beautiful thing I have ever seen."

His kind words startled me, and I tripped down the step before he caught my waist with a firm grip. My long nails dug into his back for balance as I steadied myself. I looked up to thank him but stalled, finding his features afflicted with a look of torment.

I realized my nails dug into the spot where his wings would attach if they were out. The place I now knew was the killing blow of winged Unseelie creatures.

We both paused. He turned to face me, still holding my waist.

"I'm sorry," I whispered as I pulled my fingers away. They trailed down his broad back, and I felt every muscle tense under my fingertips. "It's the same for you, isn't it? The killing point beneath your wing? Why would you not wear armor then?" I asked. Somehow this felt incredibly intimate.

I took the last step and moved off the stairs needing space. I hadn't really expected an answer from him.

He grabbed my hand as I walked off the stairs and pulled me back against his chest. Something in his eyes looked dangerous and unhinged. His wings unfurled. This close, you could see they formed more of a physical substance than just wisps of airy smoke. I went to pull away. The sheer danger my body felt at the sight of his spread wings was enough to make me run. His predatorial side was in full effect, no longer hidden beneath the guise of a kind man.

He moved my hand to the place on his back just under his wing.

I gasped as he pressed my palm firmly against it, feeling the edge of skin and fabric that made way for the wings.

"Yes, lamb, a wound here would end me," he rumbled as he held me against his chest. I could see every tiny blue speck in his beautiful eyes. His body screamed danger, but something in his eyes was gentle, sad even. "I wear no armor because I don't need it. I accept the challenge of anyone foolish enough to attempt to end me. Most fae are too stupid to know I also possess the weak spot.

He pressed my hand harder on the spot. I felt the thick liquid-feeling of his wing press against the top of my hand as if in retaliation to my closeness to the spot. Only our eyes spoke as we stared, our bodies pressed together intimately.

He was being vulnerable with me.

He had to believe I wasn't really here to hurt him.

He seemed to shake himself out of it and moved forward, still holding my wrist as he tucked his wings away. We walked out the door to the largest, most horrifying carriage.

It was large and gothic, with black overlays covering the intimidating square frame. Rich red velvet screamed at my eyes when the door opened, but that wasn't the scary part.

Six large skeletal unicorns with glowing red eyes stomped and huffed angrily as they waited at the front of the ominous vehicle. That still wasn't the scariest.

"Get in already," shouted the queen from inside the carriage.

CHAPTER 23

MENDAX

I WATCHED CALLIE CLOSELY.

Every time the carriage hit a bump, her cleavage shifted, making it hard to think straight. Had we not been sitting across from my mother, I'm not certain I could have resisted her in the tight red dress she wore. It hugged every curve of her soft body like a glove. The parts it didn't hug, I imagined in my mind, and it was almost too much for me to take. She smelled like amber and spice, not her usual lavender.

They had accidentally used my soap on her instead of her own.

Gods, did I like the way she smelled with me all over her.

I especially liked how every other fae tonight would smell only me when they were near her. They would know she was *my* pet.

I was losing the fight my soul waged against her. Every breath she took, another strand of my fight seemed to perish. Her words—her mind—her soft skin, it was taking over all of me.

I had hoped after I got a taste of her, my mind would finally be free of her, but that proved far from the outcome. As soon as I tasted her sweetness, I wanted—*needed*—more. Each wall of the fortress in my mind crumbled with her presence no matter how hard I fought against it. It was maddening! If she didn't die soon, I feared she would be my greatest weakness, and I couldn't afford to have any weaknesses, especially not with the throne open.

Tonight's trial would be a fast, speedy death for her. Even now, the blood in my body fought against the idea of it. I had always wanted to feel something—*anything*. Then out of nowhere, this human sparked a fire of need inside me where it once had been empty and cold.

"Why again could we not have shadowed to the faerie court? The girl could have been driven alone," the queen grumbled as she scowled at Callie across the plush bench.

"Because, as you know, they have wards up to prevent us from shadowing in unannounced, and even though I'm still quite sure, as Smoke Slayers, we could easily breech it, tensions already run high with the elf and Seelie royals already there," I stated cooly, though my fist clenched just at the thought of the Seelie fae looking at Callie.

"I could do it right now," the queen said. Her eyes twinkled with mischief.

I knew exactly what she spoke of.

"You will do no such thing. I will *not* be bonded. Period," I barked back.

Callie froze at the mention.

Interesting.

The queen pursed her lips. "I don't need your permission, dear. As your queen, I can do what I see fit, whether you like it or not."

Still just a cat, toying with a mouse, even if the mouse was her son.

"I'm right here. Stop speaking about me as if I'm not sitting right in front of you," Callie bit out at the queen.

Gods alive, she was stunning when she let that fire flow. There was a darkness in her that fueled her flame, and I felt it with my soul.

"You won't be for long if you speak to me like that again," the queen growled.

Had I not been her son, I might have missed the flickered eyebrow of surprised respect.

"I will not be bonded to him. I'd rather die than be trapped here with *him* forever," Callie spat out.

"That's sort of the plan," the queen chuckled darkly before the carriage stopped.

Something uncomfortable bloomed in my chest with her disapproval of bonding to me. I strongly disliked it. Why was she so against bonding to me? How could a human not want the powers she would possess? Most would beg for it.

I quickly escaped the confines of the conversation and helped the women out of the carriage and into the sizable stone castle of the Court of faerie.

Immediately upon entering, I spotted the separation of the different kingdoms. The elves had surrounded their white-haired king and queen, every last one of them draped in flowing white and gold traditional robes. In the back were a few of the smaller royals, the less important ones.

My eyes caught with fiery gold stares as I took in the Seelie princes at the back of the large ballroom. Remembrance of Callie mentioning their golden fox forms saving her life flashed in my mind. Whatever they wanted with her, they wouldn't get. She was mine now. They practically glowed amber from being in the sunlight so long. After everything, I loathed them almost as much as my mother did.

I quickly scanned the area searching for the Seelie Queen Saracen or the younger princess but found only the two princes had shown from the Seelie royals.

Good. I didn't need to diffuse another war between the two queens today.

I sized up the two brothers. Aurelius was the taller brother, though still not as tall as me. Langmure was more muscular, but in a lean "I run away a lot" sort of way. They both wore the typical Seelie dress, all white with a gold crown atop each

229

of their obnoxiously blonde heads. I had refused my crown tonight. They all knew who I was, I didn't need a crown to evoke what their nightmares reminded them of.

Aurelius downright gawked as his eyes found Callie behind me. I watched as pure desire flooded his golden eyes. His flaxen-feathered wings popped out from behind his back, startling his brother and everyone else in the room as he stared at *my* pet.

A male fae's wings only appeared when they wanted to fuck or fight.

Darkness shadowed the light as my own wings snapped out. I stepped in front of Callie, and the action drew Aurelius's stare to me with a small smirk as he and his brother walked to the center of the room to meet us, wings still spread.

"So it's true then," Langmure stated as he glared at me. To his benefit, he didn't look intimidated like most. Idiot. "We heard that you held a captive human, but I thought even for you that was awfully low." Even if they knew more, they wouldn't admit to anything here at the Court of faerie.

"We hope that you have been treated well." Aurelius moved in front of his brother to take Callie's hand. His broad golden wings almost knocked his brother down.

"I, uh—" Callie stared wide-eyed before I shoved her behind me.

"I suggest you go to that far back corner with your brother and stop touching what's mine unless you want your throat slit, Aurelius. Whatever your interest in the human, it ends now," I growled.

Langmure's wings unfurled with a smile.

"How sweet, the monster has fallen in love with the human," Langmure mocked as he stepped closer to get in my face.

My blood itched—screamed—to break his neck, even though it would cause a small war we couldn't afford to be in right now. The Court of faerie was supposed to be neutral territory.

I had been so focused on Langmure in my face that I hadn't noticed Aurelius had moved behind me and pulled Callie to his side, gripping her close.

Her eyes connected with mine, full of fear and something else I couldn't place.

"Remove your hand, or you are as good as dead, Aurelius," I warned.

Darkness seethed and smoked from my every pore as it clouded the room.

"As you've brought a captive human to the Court of faerie, it *is* our duty to make sure she gets back to the human realm safely. We have every right to take her, Mendax, and you know it." Langmure smiled smugly, clearly enjoying this.

The entire room was hushed, frozen and tense as they watched us. We had walked right into this.

"She comes with us. Let's go," Aurelius said as he moved Callie toward the door.

She was stunned as she stared at me. Far too weak to do anything against the strong fae male. Even if he had not had the strength gifted to fae royals, she was no match for him.

His hand snaked around her middle as he pulled her back against him and toward the door, his wings spreading wider the more his hand touched her body. He leaned down to whisper something against the crook of her neck, and the golden feathers trembled.

Seeing the other male touch her sent a thundering crackle of rage through me like nothing I'd ever felt.

Every vein in my body vibrated with the unbridled need to get him away from her. What if they took her away from me?

Letting out a snarl, I grabbed Langmure's head and ripped it from his body.

A loud crack broke the air as his spinal cord severed. Smoke flowed from my hands like a tornado, shredding Langmure's Seelie body and sending pieces of him everywhere. His gold blood speckled the room and every person in it.

231

I would *not* let them have her. War or not.

I shadowed behind Aurelius, now the only living Seelie prince. The room gasped and screamed, knowing how strong you had to be if capable of shadowing in the Court of faerie itself.

I reached out to grab Aurelius's throat, and he struggled to wrap his wings protectively around Callie. How saintly of him.

It made me feral seeing him attempt to shield her from me. She was mine.

He was the only one I would hurt.

"Enough!" shouted my mother as she walked closer to us.

She grabbed Callie and pulled her away from the Seelie. Even her grabbing Callie sent a bolt of protectiveness through me.

"We have every right to take her home, Queen Tenebris," he stated, staring at the human before he turned his attention to me. His wings strained as they were now spread so wide. "*You* have killed the crown prince of Seelie. *Over a human.* You have just started a war you will not win. You don't even have a king," he threatened, breathing heavily.

He was right, and I knew it.

I was going against the fae laws in keeping her captive. He had every right to take her and return her to the human realm.

I saw the lust in his eyes though. Humans were like an exotic prize to most male fae, and this was no different. He was taking her for himself.

"We are bonded," I stammered quickly.

"What?" The queen and Callie gasped in unison.

"We are bonded. NOW, Mother! Do it now!" I urgently demanded as I spared a glance at my shocked mother.

She was quick, though, and didn't hesitate for a second to grab both of our hands. She closed her eyes as the entire room darkened.

"No! Please! Stop!" Callie fought desperately to free

232

herself from the queen's grip as she looked between me and the Seelie.

I didn't care.

Even if only for a few hours of my life, she would be mine in every way.

My heart squeezed unfamiliarly at the thought of her being tied to me for the rest of her short life.

The room swirled and darkened as lightning flashed and thunder rumbled inside the room. The crowd screamed as smoke, thick and heavy, swirled like a squall surrounding everyone.

Energy crackled. I felt something swell in my chest with a shock. It felt like lightning shot through my system and straight into Callie's as it left us both struggling for air.

The smoke cleared, and the darkness in the room receded.

"We are bonded," I panted, freeing my hand. "She is my future wife now, Aurelius, and I *can* and *will* do *anything* to her I like," I said, stepping chest to chest with the Seelie prince with a deeply satisfied grin.

Something inside me felt filled, no longer hollow. It felt like an amber moon glowed through my skin.

"No! Please," Callie pleaded. She ran to where I stood and grabbed my arm, shaking it frantically. "Please! You can't do this to me! I want to go back! I don't want to stay with you!" she cried harshly, and something newly built inside me broke with her words.

Of course she wouldn't return whatever brainless feelings I had formed. She had been conditioned to kill me.

The Seelie had been right. I had just created a war over a *human*, and that realization finally unraveled me. Her poison had completely invaded me.

I felt unhinged with fury at the realization that I was falling in love with her.

I looked to my mother in a panic needing her gone more now than ever. "Start the trial now. If she completes them, she will be returned unharmed to the humans, bonded or not."

"But then ho—" the queen argued.

"Now!" The walls rattled as the room shook with my intensity.

Everyone flinched and hid except for the queen and Callie. Aurelius had already disappeared red-faced.

The human stared at me disbelieving, but I saw it. Hidden behind her tears and pleas, her angry fire fought to emerge. Fought to unleash itself upon me.

I knew in that very moment I was so deeply in love with her, and she would be the one thing capable of my demise. The weak point in my unbreakable armor. I stared at her, and it scared me to death. It scared me to death what I wouldn't do for her.

I clenched my fists so hard, I felt my knuckles strain in an effort to be free from my skin.

"The second trial starts now. The game is afoot," I growled at her as we shot daggers into each other's eyes.

She had ruined me, and I would make sure I ruined her.

CHAPTER 24

CALLIE

N O, Mendax, please!" I pleaded, but it was already too late.

The familiar swirl blurred my vision.

I braced myself for something hard and cold, remembering how I'd awoken on my back in the blood forest.

I squeezed my knees to my chest and wrapped the long fabric of my dress over the top of my head should I need protection. The soft crimson fabric was the only armor I would have.

I continued to have the sensation of falling. The muscles of my body shook from exertion at the tension of preparing to brace my fall.

Still nothing. I felt only weightlessness as I continued to fall.

"Look, toots, we are gonna be here all night if you stay under that dress," croaked a smooth voice creased with age.

Every muscle in my body tensed, waiting for the attack, but none came.

I slowly pulled the dress from my head and sat up apprehensively.

Rage still vibrated under my skin, but I tried to channel it into something productive that could save my life.

Mendax was a monster, and I couldn't believe I had ever doubted that.

Bonding to me just so that he could take the throne as king. He would never have to actually be married because his human bonded would be dead.

How stupid could I have been?

He didn't care about me ever. He only ever wanted me dead.

I would make him regret *ever* bonding to me, if I had to return from hell to burn him myself.

"It's a good thing I'm not tryin' to kill you or nothin' 'cause even an old woman like me could've by now. Just standin' there like that," the voice said. I opened my eyes and braced myself.

Not what I was expecting, though I don't really know what that would have been anyway.

The cave was large and arched over my head by at least another eight feet or so. There was no opening to be seen, no window or door. Just dusty brown walls that formed a deep, open cavern. It smelled like musty soil, but there was no soil or water to be seen, only dusty clay walls. It was dark around the edges, but not enough that you couldn't see. Large wooden torches were bolted to the wall of rock every few feet. Their tall orange flames flickered with a hiss, the—

It wasn't the torches that had hissed.

A large snake dropped into the middle of the room from out of nowhere with an angry hiss and slithered its black and green body to the edge of the cave's floor, attempting to find its freedom.

I screamed and ran to the long table in the center of the room and scrambled to the top, only realizing it was a table after I stood upon it, shaking.

I was *terrified* of snakes.

Nothing, and I mean *nothing*, scared me the way snakes did.

It's as if he had known that somehow. Known that this was what would break me.

I felt a flutter of foreign, masculine pride in the back of my head.

What? Was that him?

Holy shit. I could feel him, like a trickle of his emotions were entwined with mine. I could feel his anger, and it felt like spicy hot lava in the back of my mind. There was something else. It felt like…I don't know…sadness? I hadn't felt anything quite like that since—

Since *she* had taken the other half of my heart.

I would get home and get my friend back. I hadn't been through all this for nothing.

Bastard.

I tried to send my anger to wherever that spot in my mind was.

"Get off my damn table! Be a little self-aware human! No wonder you are in this predicament."

I froze, crouched on the long black table to look at the old woman.

She stood looking annoyed at the end of my long wooden perch. Deep purple robes hung off her round body. Wrinkles, deep and thin alike, etched across her golden tan skin. Her silver hair was pinned beautifully up in several knots atop her head, the same silver of the brows that furrowed in my direction above gorgeous brown eyes. She looked old, but in a goddess-like way, not in a haggard old woman way.

"Get off of my table before you knock off all of the potions," she scolded.

Her accent matched her robed attire sounding as if it were from another time entirely.

"Wh-who are you?" I asked as I eyed the snake in the corner.

It slithered at the wall but seemed content to avoid us.

Three more snakes dropped from out of nowhere with a soft thud, landing just to the side of the table.

237

I screamed, feeling the blood drain from my face. Was I going to pass out? After all of this. Everything I had been through just to have it all brought down by a stupid fear of snakes? I loved every animal, and I would never hurt a snake, but for some reason, they terrified me.

I felt a wave of relief and the muffled sound of laughter from a crowd in my mind.

He knew how much this was affecting me—he could feel it.

"The snakes are not your only worry, child. I suggest you get off this table and begin your trial before this room is filled with snakes. *I* can shadow myself out, can you?" the beautiful old woman asked.

"You-you don't understand. They are venomous snakes. I can tell by the shape of their head. Most nonpoisonous snakes have a triangular head, but these have a broader jaw. It-it's because of their venom sacks," I stammered, unable to focus. Pure fear had its grip on me and my decisions at this point. "Who are you anyway?" I asked again.

"I am the oracle, Lania. I am here to deliver your words of fate and task you with your second trial," she said calmly as if we weren't in a room raining venomous snakes out of thin air.

"An oracle? You're going to read my fortune for the second trial?" I asked incredulously before looking at the slithering reptiles along the floor. My body immediately began to tremble. Would they hurt me, or would they help me like the other animals? "What about the snakes?" I narrowed my eyes at the woman.

"Foolish girl, as the oracle, I am also the monarch of poisons." She put her arm on her purple-clad hip and motioned for me to get off the table.

The swallow stuck in my throat. The snakes had moved to the other side and seemed to be piling up on each other, likely for warmth in the cold cave.

"So you're poisoning me," I stated, looking at the seven various colored cups on the table, each filled with a different colored liquid.

"Yes, essentially." She looked down as if that made her sad. "My job today is not as oracle, but I have been blessed and burdened with both titles, so I will lighten my tongue. Death and darkness will haunt you well into the golden fortress disguised as home." She stepped closer, and her eyes glistened against the torchlight as she studied my face. "You search for what makes your heart whole. Remember, the viper warms himself in the daylight but finds his home in the dark. Above all else, remember to unleash the viper inside when you need it the most." With this, she bowed her head down and took a few slow steps away from me and the table.

"I don't understand any of what you just said," I announced, worried that maybe I had missed a clue she'd just given me.

She simply smiled. "You will soon." She began to fade.

The opacity of her robes changed before my eyes.

"Wait! You can't leave me here!" I screamed.

"In front of you rest seven unmarked glasses. Four of the glasses are poisons I myself have harvested with the intent of killing you. The remaining three glasses are filled with their antidote." She was barely visible now. "Take them in the correct order, and you shall live on and earn the chance to return home. But take even *one* out of order, and you will die a very slow and painful death. I would not dawdle in your decisions as this room will slowly be filled with venomous snakes as you have so aptly surmised," she sang.

"Wait!" I shouted after her, but it was too late, she had completely vanished, and I was now alone.

Alone in the cave with the snakes and an impossible amount of poison.

My mind began to spin as my hands grew clammy. Even if I poisoned the snakes, more would drop down. If I just refused to drink the poisons, the snakes would kill me.

Another two snakes dropped from the sky. These were solid black with rattles that shook wildly as they echoed a horrible melody of doom throughout the cave.

"Oh my god, I can't do this. I can't! Fuck!" I shook as I

clamored on the table again, careful not to tip over the silver stemmed cups.

I pulled my legs in to sit crisscross as I looked down at the line of cups.

"Okay, okay...let's see," I mumbled to myself, trying desperately to calm down.

One wrong move and I would be writhing in pain and then dead.

All right, the first cup looked clear. I lifted it, cautious not to spill anything with my shaking hands as I held it to my nose and sniffed, hoping for some type of clue. I don't know why since I didn't know what to look for. I set it back down and picked up the second chalice. This one had a beautiful purple liquid, but I could smell nothing.

The third chalice looked to be a beautiful rosy-pink hue and smelled warm and sweet, almost like...

My mind flashed to a patch of gorgeous pink flowers I had smelled at a hotel conference years ago—oleander! This was oleander!

My heart began to race. I knew botanical properties and their poisons. I had just assumed they would use magical toxins. Did they even use herb and botanical poisons? Had Lania, the monarch of poisons, done this to help me?

I scooted up closer to the cups before I hastily moved back in a nervous shift. This was crazy.

If I remembered correctly, oleander flowers produced oleandrin and neriine. Two incredibly potent cardiac glycosides. A single leaf could kill you, let alone an entire brewed cup.

I set the glass down and hurriedly moved on to the next cup just before another three snakes dropped to the table.

I screamed and felt a sharp bolt of worry. Wait, that worry wasn't mine. It was from Mendax.

Why would he be worried?

Probably worried I would figure out the task and get out alive.

240

Defiance and anger bubbled beneath my skin like lava. How could I have been so *stupid* to think he had started to care about me?

I couldn't believe I had let him touch me. *Taste me.*

My mind flashed with how insane his tongue had felt on—

Lust.

Pure blinding lust pounded through my mind from the monster himself. He could feel my arousal through the bond.

I shook my head and tried to clear my mind.

I would get out of here. I would get out of here and go home if it was the last thing I ever did.

I picked up the extra fabric from the train of my dress and wiped the sweat that beaded across my face before I heaved out a deep breath and picked up the fourth cup.

As soon as I inhaled, strong herbs assaulted my senses from the pale-green liquid. What was that? Fennel, crab apple, maybe? Chamomile? It smelled strong, like an over potent tea. I set it back down. Okay, out of four cups, I could only place one.

The fifth glass was also green, a bit darker than the last one. I held it up to my nose and braced myself for disappointment.

Carrots.

It smelled like carrots? What in the—?

What poison smelled like carro—

Water hemlock was in the carrot family and was incredibly toxic!

I immediately dipped the tiniest bit of my pinky into the green liquid and wiped it on the top of my forearm.

Within a few seconds, the skin began to redden and hive.

It was definitely water hemlock. I was certain of it. It grew along the park's wet meadows regularly and caused severe skin reactions from touching it.

I set the cup down and smiled at the poison, feeling slightly more optimistic.

Another snake, this one red with bright green stripes, fell

on the table and nearly knocked one of the cups over before I screamed and kicked it with my foot.

I needed to hurry. They were coming faster.

The sixth cup was filled with what looked to be another cup of clear liquid, but upon smelling it, I immediately placed lemon. Strong lemon. Unless it was poison masked with lemon, I had to believe that this was an antidote. Lemon juice was incredibly acidic. I filed that away in my mind as I set the cup down and continued to the final cup.

The clear-ish pale-green liquid looked similar to the others, maybe a bit lighter. Some sediment had settled to the bottom of the cup, and I squinted to see if it might lend to a hint. No luck. It just looked like small white dots. That could've been anything. I sniffed the liquid.

I gagged, almost dropping the cup.

It smelled like raw meat.

How disg—

Root something…snakeroot! I was shaking so hard I could barely see.

White snakeroot was an incredibly common poisonous weed with tiny white fluffy flowers! That could be what the white speckles on the bottom were from, and it smells like raw meat. Quite an unmistakable fragrance.

The plant was so incredibly toxic that people died just from drinking the milk of a cow that recently grazed on white snakeroot. That had to be what it was!

As if on command, at least five snakes fell to the floor with a sickening sound.

The floor was covered now with slithering hissing snakes.

My eyes clenched shut with fear as they slid over each other across the floor. Some were the size of a garter snake, but some were absolutely giant.

My god, what I wouldn't give to get out of this room and away from these creatures. I loved all animals and could even appreciate them, but some unfounded part of my body was absolutely terrified of these snakes.

Okay, there was no sense in wasting any more time.

I couldn't help but feel like the oracle had been trying to help me by giving me a few human herbs—

The humans.

Did Mendax still plan on taking over the human realm and destroying all the humans?

I growled in frustration at my chaotic mind as I tried to focus on the cups in front of my knees. I couldn't just leave the humans to be annihilated when I could have done something.

Okay, one problem at a time.

I needed to make it out of here alive, and then I would try and work a deal with Mendax or something. There had to be something I could negotiate to at least stall the humans' demise. Maybe as his bonded, he could no longer hurt humans—

Oh my god, could that be a thing? How would I find that out? He had bonded us in haste, so maybe he hadn't thought that through?

I smoothed the sweat-dampened hair from my face and tried to sort my chaotic thoughts.

With a deep breath, I carefully moved the third cup of rosy-pink oleander poison to the left, then followed suit with the white snakeroot that smelled like nasty raw meat and then the water hemlock that smelled like carrots. I was gambling that those three were what I guessed and were all poisonous. I moved the chalice of what I guessed was lemon juice to the right in my "antidote" pile and stared at the three ominous cups remaining.

A snake fell from nowhere and landed in my lap.

I screamed and tried to fling it off as I fell off the table onto the snake-littered ground.

My hoarse screams echoed through the cave, which only seemed to rile up the serpents that climbed around me as I scrambled, trying to get to my feet. For the first time in my life, I felt so scared I couldn't function. My body was shutting down from pure panic.

My eyes fell shut as the thick bodies of snakes crawled over me. How I hadn't been bitten yet was beyond me, but I would be soon. One can only huddle in a snake-filled room so long before they were bitten and killed.

Get up.

You're a terrible assassin.

I thought you had pull with animals?

Fucking Mendax! His voice was quiet and hard to hear in the back of my mind, but it was almost like I felt it more than heard it.

I sat up, furious. This was the last thing I needed!

Get out of my fucking head!

And I'm not a fucking assassin! Does a well-trained assassin roll up in a ball and wish for death surrounded by snakes, you idiot?

The nerve of that prick. I stood up and slowly moved to my previous perch atop the snake-free table of poisons fueled purely by annoyance.

I never said you were well trained.

I growled.

Get out of my head, Mendax! I hope if I do die, you feel every single thing through the bond. Every tiny ounce of pain from me being killed and gone forever.

Silence. Good. I lifted the unknown purple cup.

You have no idea the level of pain I will feel when you are gone forever.

Sorrow and anger, more potent than the poisons in front of me, flitted through the bond, and I sucked in a surprised breath.

More snakes fell.

I shook my head and tried to focus yet again. The purple liquid was beautiful but had no fragrance. If I were guessing by the opacity of the purple and the theme from the other poisons, it was botanical. Could it be an antidote? Like the other clear cup, it had no fragrance.

My mind scanned through the toxic flowers I knew of that came in that color. Aconite was the same purple, highly poisonous, and coined the Queen of Poisons, with the only known antidote being some mix of borax or something I couldn't remember.

I set the cup down and picked up the clear and fragrance-free cup. Could this be that? The blend of borax? It wouldn't have a scent, and it would be clear. I took a chance and moved my suspected borax mix to the right with the lemon juice and the purple I suspected as being Aconite to the left. If my shoddy guesses were correct, then that would be four poisons, all to my left and two antidotes to my right, with the strong herb-smelling one in the middle. It had to be some sort of antidote. It smelled like there were at least ten or so herbs mixed together. There was an old medieval antidote called nine poisons. I shakily moved it to the right.

Well, with four poisons, I would have to start with one of those.

I moved the Aconite to its own place, then set what I believed to be the clear borax mixture in front of it.

When the cattle in the study had consumed the white snakeroot, they fed them a diet rich in acidity to fight the toxins.

I set the pale-green chalice that I suspected was snakeroot next to what I hoped would be the borax mixture and then placed the supposed lemon juice next to that.

That left me with oleander, nine herbs, and water hemlock. Maybe.

Two poisons and one antidote, how would that work? If I took both poisons together, it would only up the toxicity to my system.

Had I heard the numbers wrong? Had it been three poisons and four antidotes?

I fought to swallow; my throat felt dry and sandy.

I must be wrong about something.

Was this not oleander? The rosy-pink flower? Was it an antidote instead?

A breeze wafted into the cave, obviously induced by magic since there was no opening.

The flames of the torches flickered wildly before all going out save for one.

The room instantly became more eerie and daunting, with only the slight hint of light that bounced off the many, many slithering bodies. The sounds of their hissing felt louder as my senses waged war against my mind.

I moved the questionable pink liquid to the end and prayed it was an antidote. There was no other way I would survive, even if, against all odds, I had guessed the others correctly.

I grabbed the first two cups in the line, what I believed to be the Aconite and its borax antidote. I brought the purple liquid to my lips as a tear escaped before I pulled the chalice quickly away.

What if I was wrong?

Poisons were horrible. At the rehab center, we had to deal with animal poisoning constantly. Animals get into weed killer or antifreeze. It was always horrendous watching the sweet creatures suffer.

And suffer they did. They nearly always died an excruciating death from it.

I so badly wanted to go home and see everyone. I vowed that after I made it out of here, I would somehow find Eli. I missed him so badly that sometimes it hurt.

I returned the cold metal to my lips and threw back the purple liquid, dropping the cup to the side of the table and downing the contents of what I prayed was to be the antidote. I threw the cup to the serpents with a loud clang and waited.

Instantly I broke into a damp sweat.

My stomach bubbled and gurgled its protest, but no pain came.

This was no place for a human, and I would do what I could to make certain the Unseelie never got to the human realm. The Seelie, at least, were good-natured and wanted to help.

I grabbed the next pair of goblets.

The white snakeroot and the lemon juice.

At least that's what I hoped I grabbed, the lack of light had made it impossible to differentiate the color of the liquids as it now just looked shiny black against the metal chalice's rim.

Down my gullet they went, one after the other. I would have given it more thought, but what sounded like at least a hundred snakes dropped to the floor, and it was all I could do to hurry. Were they dropping consistently now? I couldn't see very far around me because it was so dark.

I felt the nausea rise as a deep belch sounded. I was going to be sick.

Sick, but I wasn't convulsing, and that was a very good sign.

I was down to the last three.

The three that I was the most uncertain about.

One of which I wasn't entirely sure if it was even a poison or an antidote.

Something slithered across the table, and I had to shove its heavy body off with a thud. They were rising quickly, and they sounded absolutely furious if their rampant hisses were any indication of their anger.

I grabbed the water hemlock and the nine herbs. That left the questionable pink, which I first suspected was oleander, staring back at me.

It had to be an antidote. I couldn't end on a poison or it would kill me.

Either she had misspoken, or I had misheard the numbers, but that had to be an antidote. There was no other way this could work out. I was fairly certain of the others, more so after having tasted them and confirming a few, such as the lemon juice. Several of the botanical poisons reminded me of their flowers' smell, which also added to my confidence.

All but the last pink one.

I held the water hemlock to my mouth and swallowed it

247

down. They each tasted foul, and it took everything within me to force the liquids into my mouth.

I chased it quickly with the strong herbed drink and nearly retched. I had to stop and hunch over like a heaving cat before I could down the strong-smelling liquid.

I waited a minute. By now, the other poisons would have caught up and taken hold. Without looking in a mirror, I couldn't see the color of my tongue or the state of my eyes, but I checked my pulse and was just thankful my heart hadn't exploded yet.

Had I done it? Had I guessed them correctly?

The last pink chalice stared at me, daring me to lift it.

If I had miscalculated and this was poison, I would be dead within minutes.

I picked up the glass and fought back tears. The worst part of this one was I wasn't entirely sure. I didn't have a good guess. Just a hope and prayer that this was not my time and that it was an antidote.

The cold metal touched my lips, and I swallowed it in three big gulps. It was bitter with a sweet hint of flavor. With my nose close to the liquid, I smelled it again before I emptied the contents of the cup and threw it to the floor, awaiting the tension to leave my shoulders and confirm that I was right, and it was the antidote.

My fingers clenched the fabric of my dress tightly.

It was oleander.

It was poison, and I had no antidotes left.

CHAPTER 25

CALLIE

T HE LAST GOBLET OF LIQUID WAS POISON. NOT AN ANTIDOTE.
I grabbed a fist full of my hair at what I had just done.
I had miscalculated.

She *had* said four poisons and three antidotes.

My stomach immediately seized in a tight cramp, and I fell on my side still atop the table as I pulled my knees to my chest.

There were no more cups; nothing else was in the room but snakes.

My skin grew both too hot and too cold at the same time.

"You are monsters! This wasn't even a fair trial! You just wanted entertainment for your disturbed people!" I screamed, clutching my stomach as stabbing pain spread throughout my body.

I waited but felt and heard nothing from the crowd or Mendax.

"Well, congratulations, you assholes! You got what you wanted!" I cried as hot tears dribbled down to collect on the table below my face.

My voice was hoarse with wailing sobs of defeat. Panic surrounded my every thought.

"Go take the throne, you piece of shit! You're nothing but a monster, and that's all you'll ever be! Some day you will get what's coming to you!" I choked back a scared sob.

My mind was blurring together like I was underwater. Everything felt foggy and painful. I could feel things beginning to shift and move as my muscles started to spasm.

I was crying so hard now snot ran down my face onto the table and pooled beneath my face. Why was everything in my life so punishing? So agonizingly hellish and tiresome.

At least I could be with my mom and sister again. I would finally be able to hug them again after I died.

"I am so stupid. I wish I'd never seen those fairies, and I wish I'd never met Eli. I wish I'd never seen a stupid moth or mushroom in my life. I wish I'd never become a scientist. I wish I'd never made that deal. I wish I'd never met any fae ever!" I blubbered just before a sharp pain had me crying out as my stomach seized painfully. My mouth felt so dry.

My heart was beating so fast that it felt like a train was running through my chest. The hot tears continued to blur my vision.

"I wish I could go back to Willow Springs and pretend again. Just pretend everything is normal and okay and that... that is my life. I could date Cliff and settle down. I would hug Cecelia if I ever saw her again. I would hug Earl so tight and tell him to stay so far away from those stupid mushrooms." My blubbering was incoherent, but it didn't matter because no one was here. I would die completely alone.

Fight, lamb. Show me the serpent that I know you really are, Callie. Give me all the venom you've got.

He was encouraging me? How ironic.

Calling me a serpent. Couldn't he decide? A lamb or a serpent? A person couldn't be both.

If I was a serpent, I would have already bitten him.

I would have bitten him a thousand times before he threw me in the dungeon.

I would have filled him with so much fucking venom his eyes floated and his heart exploded—

That mouth of yours is making me hard with all of these venomous threats.

The venom.

Ohmygod. The venom.

I struggled to sit up. My stomach felt tight, and I was barely able to move.

The venom was the last antidote.

The last poison was oleander. It had lethal cardiac glycosides known as oleandrin and neriine that sped up the pulse to erratically high levels.

I rolled off the table with a crack as my back landed hard atop a lumpy pile of snakes. I grabbed the nearest one, my fears overridden by the last morsel of my will to live.

There was no more space left for panic. I was too full of desperation.

The thick black reptile was huge. My hand couldn't encompass his body, but I trailed it to the end and lifted hoping it wasn't his tail.

It wasn't. The large black snake widened its pink mouth before striking me in the chest just above my right nipple.

I screamed as the snake slithered angrily away.

The harsh sting had me clawing at my breast where the viper had struck. I felt the rush of venom surge through me like a bolt of electricity before it began its paralyzing effect.

Snakes used their venom to dull and sedate their prey, making it easier for them to consume. This would counter the poison's effect by slowing down my heart rate.

The collection of poisons in my stomach would likely be in abundance, hence able to burn off enough of the lethal venom to where I would only be incredibly sick, but not dead. Unless they didn't get me out of here in time and the other snakes bit me.

Before I could even move my arms out to collapse on the ground, the room whirled around me, and I was again back in the center of the ballroom at the Court of faerie.

This time I felt no cold marble floor beneath me like that of the last trial.

Warm hands shifted underneath my back. My eyes fought to stay shut. To go somewhere far, far away from all of this torture.

I was in Prince Mendax's arms.

I opened my eyes, prepared to fight, but instead, my body betrayed me. Every taut, sedated muscle grew heavier in his arms, and I found myself tucking into his broad chest, finding comfort.

It made no sense. He was the reason I was sent to the trial.

I knew he wanted me dead.

But something had cracked in him. I could see it in the way he stared at me.

As if I alone gave the oxygen that allowed him life.

He studied me as raw power flooded the space around him. His black wings of smoke spread so wide it felt as if the room struggled to contain them. Emotion filled the pools of sky-blue eyes studying my face. His dark brows furrowed, and his mouth was only a thin line with a look of shaken wonder on his face. I felt him tighten his grip on me as he began to walk, carrying me out of the ballroom.

Darkness fought to close the edges of my eyes again, and I prayed this was just the sedative effects of the venom and not my death.

"You are safe now, lamb. I've got you," he whispered with a trembling voice.

"She will be killed in the last trial, Mendax, no matter what you say. I will *not* keep a human in my bloodline. *I* run the next trial, and she *doesn't* make it out." The queen's cold shout echoed around us.

The clank of large doors being opened sounded at the same time a cool breeze hit me, but my eyes had already fastened shut. Only the warm feel of Mendax's body as he pulled me against him and the steady pace of his haggard breathing grounded me.

"I can lose everything, but not you. I can't lose you," he whispered so quietly I knew I wasn't meant to hear.

Pure warmth and protection radiated through my mind like a cocoon of sweet and cozy feelings.

It was from him, and it felt like a dirty, vulnerable secret I wasn't supposed to know.

"Get away from me," I growled as the oversized shadow gave me a predatory stare.

I had passed out sometime after we had ridden in the carriage and slept the entire way back.

I wasn't sure if the queen had ridden back with us, but in the few hours it took to get back to the Unseelie castle, it had become deserted. The night always seemed to be filled with shadows and smoke when I saw it, so I still had no idea what part of the day it actually was.

"Callie, I'm sorry, but this isn't a choice. There could still be a pocket of venom in the puncture marks, and I will not risk it," he gritted through his teeth, barely hiding his frustration.

"Funny words from the person who caused the venom," I bit out as harshly as I could. As if my words were the snake itself striking.

I edged toward the door of the room he had taken me into. I just wanted to get away from him and his sexy amber-smelling body.

I was exhausted, but I wasn't about to let him suck the poison out of my bite.

The bite above my breast.

He was the villain in my story.

The merciless shadow that felt nothing and cared for no one.

He had tried to kill me numerous times. He alone had caused me more pain and anguish than I had felt my entire life, and I would not forget that.

253

So then why did I find myself wanting more of him? Needing him?

I knew there was more to him than he let on. I'd witnessed kindness and gentleness from the horrifying umbra. After speaking to the maids, I knew he wasn't as bad as he made himself out to be. Or maybe he was, but not to me.

I should feel terrified and frightened by his presence, but instead, I found myself only wondering what he would feel like under my fingers. He had discovered how my skin felt—tasted.

I craved to know what his fae skin felt like under me—inside me.

I shook my head so hard my hair whipped the wall, and I silently begged my idiotic brain to right itself from these horrible, delusional thoughts.

He was the bad guy.

You didn't *care* about the bad guy. You didn't want to be *near* the bad guy. You didn't want to make the bad guy smile so hard that it caused something in your gut to ache.

You didn't fall into the bad guy's traps, and you certainly— *certainly*—didn't fall in love with him.

He ran his large hands over his face and through his silky black hair, attempting to harness his growing anger.

"I can impel you, Callie Peterson, remember that," he threatened as he stepped closer to me and the door frame.

"Don't you dare," I said through gritted teeth, suddenly feeling incredibly weak and helpless.

"The venom will get out one way or another, Callie. Either I call the nearest guard or suck it out myself," he threatened, taking another step closer. "But know that I'll kill the guard for touching you before his mouth has the chance to speak again," he growled as if the mere thought of someone else touching me made him a monster.

Only a few feet separated us now.

"Promise me," I whispered, all the fight leaving me momentarily as I made my plea.

I noticed his body relax slightly with his victory.

"Anything," he stated as if it physically caused him pain not to step into me and take me in his arms.

"Promise me that you will *never* impel me, that you'll *never* take my free will away," I pleaded softly.

"Done." He stepped closer, the movement fluid and graceful.

"One more thing, Mendax—"

"Malum," he whispered as he stepped into me, the front of our bodies pressing tightly together.

His eyes were full of heat as if an inferno fought to emerge from under his gentle movements.

My body stiffened, and I fought the urge to melt into him. I wouldn't allow it. I stepped into my footing and held my ground.

"What?" I asked, shocked. My more tender emotions recoiled with the realization of what he had just done, the power of the word he had just spoken.

"My true name is Malum Mendax, Crown Prince of the Unseelie Court," he whispered a little timidly, as if he were handing me a gun.

As far as the fae believed, he was.

"Speak my name from those soft lips, and I'll give you anything—everything—you could ever want," he whispered hoarsely against my neck as he struggled to swallow, and I could tell he meant it.

He lifted his face, and tender emotions filled his eyes. But only anger filled mine. I didn't want this. I couldn't do this.

"Let me leave, *Malum Mendax*. Forget the last trial and let me go home. Now," I said through gritted teeth.

His closeness was doing things to me I didn't want—things that were making this a lot harder. I accidentally inhaled, and the smell of spicy amber filled me like a hard drink making me tense with anger.

He is the bad guy!

His features sharpened as if he'd been asleep this whole

time and had only just awakened. He stepped back with a scowl.

"You will never leave me, Callie. *This* is your home now."

He stepped back farther, and his black outfit seemed to radiate shadows as his features grew tight. He tilted his head, making him look even more unhinged than his crazy words had made him sound.

"The trial is written in faerie law as a promise, and the queen has taken control of it. It cannot be stopped, but I will see to it that my—that you are unscathed."

"If I come out alive, then I get to go back to the human realm. That should also be written in faerie law, as you say. You promised me," I countered.

My eyes had begun to well up from exhaustion and frustration. My dress was the same from the trial, and it blanketed my frame, heavy and uncomfortable.

"That was before you were my bonded. Before I realized I can't live without you," he insisted as he crossed his arms. Challenge flashed across his eyes with a gleam.

"You tried to kill me after you bonded to me! I had no say in this! You have been trying to destroy me since I got here!" I shouted at him, suddenly feeling uncontainable.

The wariness from the trials ebbed away, replaced with anger, both with myself for feeling some morbid type of connection with him and with the monster himself.

He turned his back to me as he raked his fingers through his inky tresses in an attempt to calm himself. He looked barbarous. No longer gentle and sweet. It was as though the layer had finally cracked, and the creature left was fully unhinged and maniacal.

I recoiled slightly as the air shifted. The human prey in me began to panic with a new fear.

He was losing his control, I could feel it. I should be frightened, but some idiotic, lurid part of me begged to see what would happen if he did. Would he finally kill me? Or something worse?

"We may have both been trying to destroy each other, lamb, but rest assured, only you have succeeded," he snarled as he turned. "I have tried and tried to rid myself of you. I have never felt the things that you evoke in me."

He walked to the dresser that sat against the wall as if he needed the space between us or he would truly snap. He grabbed a glass decanter from the tray and poured the dark amber liquid into a small glass. Shaky hands held the glass as he replaced the decanter's topper.

"You will finish the last trial. I will find out what it is from my mother and make absolute certain that you are kept safe." He tossed back the amber liquid, emptying the glass. "And then we will be married. Then my burdensome suffering will finally end," he mumbled the last part softly.

I stepped closer to the door slowly, attempting to keep my movements undetected.

He was insane.

Gorgeous and alluring but cracked in the head all the same. I ignored a secret part of me that seemed to vibrate with the power I got knowing how strongly I affected him and the butterflies it gave me. He was the Unseelie prince. The most feared of the fae, and I, a little human, had somehow gotten to him?

"I *will* go home after the third and final trial. Your mother will see to it. I know she would never allow a human to take her throne," I said smugly as I watched a muscle tick in his defined jaw. He knew I was right. "I'll die before I marry you. I still hate you," I growled at him, not sure if I was reminding myself or him.

Something sharp seared painfully on my right breast. The bite mark burned like fire coal against my skin.

I startled and clutched my chest tightly with a hiss.

Mendax groaned and threw the glass against the wall. It shattered as he shouted out an angry roar.

"And I still want you dead just to rid myself of these nagging feelings! You are mine, and I will kill the entire world if it means keeping you," he snarled. "Which includes getting the trace venom from your wound!" He growled as he took a step closer.

His wings unfurled in large billowing half-moon shapes that trailed onyx smoke along the floor.

I gasped at the sight of his wings spreading wide.

And then I ran out the open door.

The hallway was dark, but that would only help him. He seemed to be made from the shadows. My bare feet slapped against the cold marble floor. I was almost to the end of the hallway. I knew where I needed to go, and I would do anything to get there.

I *couldn't* let him catch me.

I listened, expecting to hear footfalls behind me, but there were none. That didn't mean anything though. He was a master killer. He *enjoyed* it. He was probably silent and hidden in the shadows right now. Watching me.

The door to the left at the end of the hall was open. If my calculations were correct, there should be a set of stairs in there that would get me to the roof. To the portal Walter had said he knew was up there. I would find it. I had to.

The pain seared through my chest again. I wasn't sure if it was from the thought of Walter being dropped off the roof by Mendax or the trace venom, but it hurt like crazy either way.

I turned to run into the room but fell backward as I slammed into a black wall of muscle. Mendax had shadowed into the doorframe. Firm arms wrapped tightly around my waist, stopping my fall.

The front of our bodies pressed together, and my thin dress did little to buffer the feel of his hard muscles against my chest and shoulders. He was so large, every ounce of him chiseled and sculpted. The hard muscles of his abdomen tightened against me. My arms pressed against his biceps, feeling the hills and valleys of strength through his thin tunic.

The scent of campfire smoke and amber lacquered my senses as I inspected the sharp features of his face in a daze. His high cheekbones and sharp jaw looked so masculine when he clenched his jaw that way. Sky-blue eyes stared intensely at my mouth as if it were the key to the universe.

My eyes flickered as warm porcelain slid under the tips of my fingers. I hadn't even realized I'd reached up to touch his face. My pointer, middle, and thumb traced the line of his jaw.

My eyes widened at my need to touch him. Stabbing pain flickered like confetti over my right breast shaking me out of the lust-filled daze. What was I doing?

I pushed off his chest, having caught him off guard just in the right moment, and ran down the hallway to the large staircase.

Panic and pain set in halfway down the wide stairs, and I'm not sure what caused it, the venom or the all-consuming want to be consumed by him. The need to know what would happen if I let the villain touch me.

I released my grip on the black railing and ran for my life. Every part of it.

I ran from myself and my wrong and broken feelings as I clamored down the hard stairs, afraid of what truly would be my death if I didn't escape.

As I tiredly ran, the train of my dress caught the front of my foot, and I stumbled down the last several stairs with a painful thud. Every corner jabbing into my previous nearly healed injuries.

I scrambled to get up when I felt his still presence to the front of me. Close enough I could feel the power radiating from him as the smoke billowed from his wings. Close enough to see the look of helpless frustration written in the depths of his steely eyes.

"Please, Callie," he pleaded but didn't move toward me.

"Get away from me, you psycho!" I shouted, turning as fast as I could. I began to run back up the stairs I had just come down. I was so slow now. I knew, had he really wanted, he could have grabbed me.

I clutched my chest as I stumbled over the last step, seriously debating letting him suck the poison from my system if it meant all the nagging pain would stop.

I reached the top platform on my hands and knees and crawled right into a pair of strong legs. I jumped up with the last of my will just as he stepped into me.

Something soft and pleading in his eyes spoke to whatever was left of me.

He swept his leg and gently kicked mine out from under me at the same time as he grabbed me. I jumped a moment late, not having seen the embarrassingly slow attack coming.

Strong arms held me as he dipped me backward and pressed firmly against my front. His hand held wide at the base of my skull while the other wrapped around my waist, pulling me against him.

His breath ghosted lightly across my face, both of us frozen as we stared intensely at the other.

"I-I have tried so hard to eradicate you from where you now live inside me."

His words were so quiet and deep that I had to lean closer. I pulled myself up slightly to hear them, to feel them whispered across my cheek.

His words were shaky now, not the smooth, confident cadence I was used to hearing from him. "I would destroy anyone for you...anyone including myself," he whispered, slowly reaching out to cup the side of my neck in his hand. "Every fiber of you has desecrated me wholly." His voice cracked hoarsely. "The buttery texture of your skin has burned me with every touch. It's all I think about. I-I am consumed by thoughts of you day and night." His soft confession flowed from him in a plea.

I tilted my head up to find our faces were only a breath apart as he leaned over me. Before I realized what I'd done, I pushed my lips against his, my body refusing to take orders from my brain.

Soft velvety lips pressed against mine, gentle and tender,

filled with everything we were both afraid of. I reached my hand to the back of his head and snaked my fingers through his satiny black hair needing to feel it. The action elicited a deep groan into my mouth from Mendax. The sound seemed to set fire to my bones with a painful need to be closer to him.

Within a second, the kiss had gone from tender to a blinding frenzy as I righted myself against him, and we struggled to touch more. I pressed my body so hard against his that I whimpered into his mouth when the wound on my chest smashed against him. Without breaking the wildness of our kiss, he reached down and cupped my ass in each hand, lifting me up. My dress shoved around my waist as I tightened my thighs around his body as I felt everything press against him with maddening friction.

It was a flurry of wild, needing hands and lips as he held me in the middle of the hall.

I felt something hard press against me so I gasped and pulled away. My arms held onto his massive shoulders as I looked down at him in a lust-drunk haze, half expecting to see him holding a knife against me.

He was hard as a rock.

The feel of his cock dented against the thin triangle of fabric that covered my center sent warmth and desire flooding through my lower belly. He realized what had shocked me and licked his lips with a salacious grin.

My back slammed against the hallway wall. I felt him press his length harder against my barely covered slit as he pulled away from our kiss to watch my face. My eyes flickered shut at the sensation. I didn't care how wrong it was, I needed to feel him thrusting inside of me like I needed air.

He pressed against me a little harder with a deep groan, lifting my ass slightly, simultaneously causing a stroke of friction for us both. I bit my lip as I pressed my hips into him as though the fabric would incinerate and I would feel him inside me. Mendax's lips found my neck as he trailed his tongue and soft mouth across the sensitive skin just below the shell of my ear. His hand slid across the bare skin of my thigh as goose bumps erupted in their wake like a command. A deep moan escaped with the feel of his lips as they moved stealthily across my clavicle. Playful bites and trails of teeth raked across my cleavage.

Mendax lifted his head to look deep into my eyes.

"How does it feel?" he said, breathing heavily. "To know that I love you and that you have doomed me? That you and only you have the power to disarm and debilitate me. That *you*, a human, have dismantled every part of me and rebuilt it as a shrine in your honor." His pupils were blown out, eyes almost completely black now. He trailed his thumb across my bottom lip as he bit down on his own. "The way your mouth quivers slightly when you hold back your fiery words," he rasped seductively as he pressed his thumb into my mouth. "The spark that you hide has swallowed me whole." His strong hands skimmed across my shoulders as he shoved down the straps of my dress and exposed my breasts with a cold shock from the hallway's icy air.

Pain flickered through arousal, and I squeezed my locked legs tightly around his waist. He snaked a hand down to press over the fabric of my underwear. At the same time, his other hand gently touched the two fang pricks next to my nipple. My eyes flickered, and I failed to stifle a sigh as the touch of both places sent the most delicious mix of pain-laced pleasure through my body.

"Oh god, Mendax," I cried breathily as his fingers shoved aside the triangle of fabric covering me and pressed his mouth down to the bite. His tongue flicked across my hardened nipple as he stroked two fingers over my clit, causing me to jump and swear at the intense sensations.

I pressed myself against him, feeling the outline of his rock-hard cock behind his leathers.

He moaned, and the deep vibrations rumbled into my chest. Suddenly a sharp sting of blinding pain ripped from the skin under his mouth as he sucked at the bite. I shifted to get away just as his fingers dipped inside me.

I clung to him, unable to think of anything but the intense feelings that coursed through my body. My nails dented into his back as my head pressed against the wall behind me. The combination of pain and pleasure made me delirious. I writhed and arched against him, hoping he would give me more.

I froze with the realization he was sucking whatever residual poison out of my wound.

"Wait! Won't the poison hurt you?" I whispered, shoving his hard shoulders away to look into his face.

I should want him dead. Not feel worried about him.

He pulled his face back, and my breast popped out of his mouth. He looked up at me as though in awe.

"It will not hurt me, little lamb. You are the only thing that could hurt me now," he whispered as he stepped back and set my legs on the ground.

I readjusted my dress and tried to steady myself. I kept my hands to myself, afraid that if they so much as brushed the hem of his shirt, I would be unable to control myself again.

His large frame blocked me from stepping away from the wall. His soft blue eyes looked at me in a way I would have given anything to experience.

From anyone but him.

"You were never supposed to mean this much to me," he rasped, shaking his head.

"You are the bad guy," I whispered, and my breath moved the black hair that fell across his forehead. "You are filled with hatred and wickedness. You *enjoy* killing." My bare chest brushed against his, the conflicting emotions at war in my mind. None of any of this felt real. His hands found my waist, and I couldn't help but feel relief when they did. "I love sunshine and animals. I-I am human—I don't belong here. I need to leave," my soft whispers pleaded as he bent down slowly and joined our lips in a slow, sensual kiss.

All thoughts, rational or otherwise, left me. I was a puddle against his touch. It didn't matter how much my mind fought for what it thought was right.

"I *am* the bad guy, Callie." He pulled away from my lips just enough to lay his whisper upon them, never opening his eyes. "Which is why you will never, ever be free from me again."

He kissed my stiff lip, biting the bottom before he pulled back just enough to speak again. "I am selfish, and I like hurting people." A haggard breath left him. "It doesn't matter if you belong here or not. I won't spare even half a thought before I murder every person in this world if they get in my way. I would search the crevices of hell and every nook in between for you. The fae will beg you to stay, knowing that is what keeps their loved ones alive another day." He cupped the side of my face gently and opened his eyes with heavy lids. "And you aren't as good and full of sunshine as you would like people to believe, my little assassin. I see straight through you. It has my dick hard waiting to see what type of hellhound you truly are."

My blood thrummed through my veins with his words. He *still* thought I was an assassin sent to kill him.

He was nothing but danger, in every sense of the word, and I needed to get away before he snapped—any more than he already had. I started to push him away, expecting him to get mad, but instead, a hurt look flicked across his pale eyes before he stepped back.

"For the last time, Mendax, I am a scientist," I growled.

I hated this. I just wanted to go home.

A small grin tugged at the sides of his mouth. God, he was handsome when he smiled.

"I never said that you weren't a scientist, my love. The two things can exist at the same time," he purred. His wings pulsed with heat as they coiled their black smoke around my body. "You were sent here to destroy me, and you have succeeded, even if it wasn't in the way you intended."

264

I don't know what had gotten into me. But something inside me liked that he thought I was dangerous, not some Barbie doll idiot or some stuck-up boring scientist. He was enamored with me, the man who hated everyone, wanted me. The man who everyone feared, feared me.

I smashed my face to his, feeling his muscled chest with my palms.

What did it matter? I wondered when heat coiled in my belly and I pushed his back flush against the wall as we returned to a frenzy of hands and tongues.

CHAPTER 26

MENDAX

S O FULL OF NEED THE TINY WOMAN WAS AS SHE PRESSED against me. Not for long.

I was not a patient man, and I had hungered for this moment since the second my fingertips had grazed her soft human skin. *She is perfect.*

It didn't matter how much I tried to hate her. I pushed her away because I wanted to pull her closer.

I let her take control with the kiss, curious where my little lamb would decide to go with it. I wasn't normally patient, but for her, I would wait until the world froze over. I would do *anything* for her. Anything.

Callie kissed me hard, pressing every part of her soft body against mine, yet somehow there wasn't enough of me touching her.

I quickly rectified that by winding my fingers into her *unbelievably* soft hair and pulling her against me. Her soft moan as she flattened into my body almost made me come right then.

My heart slammed against my chest with delight—finally feeling full. All I had needed was this woman—this tiny, powerful woman's touch—and I felt like…I felt unstoppable.

Of course I had touched others; I was no stranger to bedding a woman. They shamelessly threw themselves at me, and a few times, I had played the game, attempting to feel something—anything other than a need to feel blood. But it never worked. The only thing that ever made me feel alive was killing. The feel of being the last person that creature saw before they left this realm. Hearing them beg, that was the only thing that ever made me feel anything.

Until now.

Her tiny hand crawled under my tunic, and I couldn't help but melt at the way her hands seemed to grow hungrier and erratic the more of my skin she touched. It was delicious seeing her need for me.

I did my best to harness my control, but it was taking more than I had.

All it took was one tiny, needy moan from her and I couldn't hold myself back any longer. Anything she wanted was hers as long as she was with me...and whether she liked it or not, that would be for forever. I *must* do something about her fragile human mortality—I could barely stomach the thought of her leaving me even in death.

I pinned her wrists to the wall above her head as I stepped into her, and my thigh parted her legs as far as her dress would allow.

I hovered just above her lips, unmoving. Her heavy eyelids fell as she panted. The fast up and down caused her cleavage to strain tight against the neckline of her dress. She waited impatiently for my lips to close the distance and touch hers. But I didn't. I hovered, relishing the feeling of control and the need I could feel pouring from her through the bond. She moved forward first to press her mouth against mine, but I pulled back, teasing her.

She huffed and tried again to capture my lips, but I hovered just out of reach. She pulled back, defeated, and I pressed my mouth to hers, letting her know I was in control. I couldn't hold back the approving moan that floated from my lips as I deepened the kiss and skimmed my fingers lightly down the arms that I still held above her head, down the velvety skin of her side, then down to her hip. She shivered in response, and I had to adjust myself. Iron blocks were not as hard as my cock in that moment. I've never been so strained as I watched my little lamb beg for me.

I wanted to torture her the way she had tortured me. The way that had stopped me from having the ability to think of anything else.

Grime and blood covered her filthy dress from the trial—

I shook myself out of the lust-filled daze to realize she hadn't had a chance to sleep or recover from her second trial. She hadn't even had a chance to bathe before I had pounced on her, unable to keep myself away from her any longer. Now that the poison and anything that could have been lying in wait was out of her system, I needed to get her cleaned up and rested. I would get a witch to finish healing the rest of her wounds from the first trial.

Mother had been furious when I told her I would not allow Callie to enter the third trial. The pieces just happened to fall together after I had forced our bond in my jealous rage. I killed the Seelie royal on neutral territory because he had wanted her, and the queen was rightfully furious with me for the war I had invoked.

But, in a second, I would do it all again.

When Prince Aurelius had tried to shuffle her away and take her to the Seelie realm, I could have burned the world down—and that's exactly what would've happened had he not stopped.

No one would take her away from me. Ever.

I would murder every Seelie bastard alive if I had to, and then I would steal their yellow sun from them just because my Callie admired it.

Mother would retaliate by sending her to the trial before she had rested and healed from today's burdens. No matter how much I needed to be inside her tight human body, it would wait until she was truly safe, for good. The queen was semi-barbaric like me, and I knew she would send her to the gridiron of the fates. She knew that would be the only place I couldn't help her.

We would see about that.

After this trial, I would make Callie my queen and dethrone mother. If she didn't go peacefully, that was on her, but either way, she would go. One way or another.

I lifted Callie into my arms and creased a smile so deep I felt it in my blood when she wrapped her tiny arms around my neck and nuzzled into my chest as I carried her down to our room.

"Where are we going?" she asked breathily, her body still thrummed with heat, and I could feel her arousal.

"To my room," I said, squeezing her against me as if she were a pet mouse that might drop down and run away.

"Are you going to fuck me, Mendax?"

I nearly dropped her and came in my leathers, but thankfully I did neither. The sound of her voice rough with need for me—*and only me*—was almost too much. How was I going to get her rested when all I wanted to do was throw her to the marble floor and bury my hard cock so deep inside her that neither of us would ever think straight again?

Goose bumps racked my body at the thought of how my tip would feel parting her. Sliding ever so slowly into her slick—

"She's dead, Mendax."

A snarl rippled from me as I turned to face the queen. Of its own accord, my smoke wrapped protectively around the beautiful human I held in my arms, shielding her from the queen's view.

"Then so are you," I stated without feeling a thing. All my feelings were held underneath the smoke of my wings by a tiny human form.

"*She is a human!* You don't even know her. You have brought a war to your people killing Prince Langmure," the queen seethed. "One fuck, and you'll be tired of her if you don't kill her in the process," the queen snarled. "You will not marry her, so help me."

Callie's body tensed against me with the queen's words. It sent a rage through me that I couldn't explain. I shifted my wings, making sure the smoke thickly shielded my love, and placed her protectively behind me. Her small hands bunched the fabric of my shirt as the smoke pulled her tighter against me.

"Still your tongue before I do it for you," I rumbled, barely controlled. Mother's eyes repositioned, seeing my seriousness. She took a step back, knowing I held no bluffs in my arsenal. "The next time you speak about my future wife in that tone, it will be your last. Mother or not."

The queen's eyes darkened. "She dies in the trial tomorrow. I will *not* stand by and watch you muddy our blood with a *human*. The same humans that ruined your father! The plan was to bond to her so that you could ascend the throne and *kill* her. Stop thinking with your dick and end her. You think she will stay with you? She will betray you the second she gets the opportunity. It's what humans do!" she snarled. "Callie, my deal still holds. If you complete the trial, I *will* return you to the human realm unharmed. You can die with your friends there once we take over." She smiled at the look on Callie's startled face.

I shadowed in front of the queen before she had a chance to blink. Power pulsed from me like a fucking storm.

She was my mother, which is exactly why it was so foolish for her to push me. She knew that I would end her—just as I did my father—should she get in my way.

She may be smart enough to be frightened of me, but she was still the Unseelie queen and smart enough to know that my darkness had bled from her.

A wicked smile tugged at her cruel lips.

"The entire realm will watch tomorrow as your human either dies in front of you at the gridiron or turns her back to you and runs away into her world." Her smile deepened. "Then you will finish the plan and descend upon the human realm. You will kill the rest of her disgusting kind, and the Unseelie fae will take their rightful place, owning both sides of the veil. The Seelie don't stand a chance." The pale woman beamed. Her dark hair glinted off the hall lights like a pool of black poison.

I thrust my hand out to grab her throat and crush it.

She shadowed away before I had the chance to collapse her windpipe. I could have easily followed her, but the thought of killing my mother and leaving my hellhound alone was unappetizing, to say the least.

I shadowed behind Callie and grabbed her hand, pulling her toward our room.

"Come, you need to rest before tomorrow. Bathe and pick which side of our bed your body prefers. I will explain what the gridiron of fates is."

After drawing her a hot bath and making certain she was safe and healed, I pushed a little magic into the bond to speed her healing as much as possible. I laid my softest tunic on the bed for her to sleep in and pulled the best men I had to guard Callie's room while I went in search of the information that I needed.

I hadn't even left the room before I wished I was with her.

CHAPTER 27

CALLIE

I SANK MY BODY DEEPER INTO THE NOW TEPID BATH AND WAGED an internal debate between letting myself relax or sinking below the surface and drowning. For a few seconds, the latter seemed like my best option and the only thing that would bring me relief from the pits of hell I seemed destined to constantly put myself in.

The water splashed up the porcelain tub and onto the dark marble floor with a slosh as I scrubbed my pink-tinged body for the third time.

I should be so disgusted by what happened in the hallway. The way his hands skimmed my skin and commanded every single need and desire into the goose bumps of my flesh before he made them erupt with tingles. The thought of his large palms skimming my body as if I were a map with a hidden treasure mark made me clench my thighs together.

I shivered and began to scrub my tender skin harder. The spicy, sensual scent of the soap only reminded me of him.

I scraped and scrubbed to the point of panic.

Not because I was upset that I had let him touch my body or clawed for him like a feral animal.

But because he had stopped and my mind would *not* allow

me to think of anything other than how hard his length had felt nestled against me. How close I was to having that ache sated. How *I* had caused that. Only a thin piece of fabric had separated us from joining.

I hissed. My skin felt as if it were being scrubbed from the bone.

The way his pale blue eyes looked when I had been unable to stifle back a moan.

He was crazy. An evil, psychopathic villain.

But when he kissed me, it was like the entire world melted away—like everything was right for just once. Like when you step into your home after you've been gone a long time. The second the smell of home and comfort hits you, the tension in your body withers away. The feel of belonging and comfort cloak you like a warm blanket.

That's how it felt when Mendax touched me, when he looked at me with three different shades of light blue eyes. I saw—no felt—what I meant to him.

He is the bad guy, I reminded myself for the trillionth time, but it didn't matter.

I craved him every bit as much as he seemed to be lost to me.

But soon, it wouldn't matter.

Hot tears fell from my eyes, lost in the sea of bath water as they dropped.

I had to leave here and see my family. Not my Willow Springs family, but my real family, and once I left this realm, I would never see Mendax again.

I climbed out of the cold tub. As I collected the fluffy black towel from the counter, I caught a glimpse of myself in the mirror.

Cold, red-rimmed eyes stared back at me with the sharpness of a dagger.

My wet hair hung in blonde clumps down my shoulders and back as water dripped from the ends, hitting the dark floor with small tip-taps.

I wiped the remaining tears from my face with the back of my hand and stared at my naked body in the mirror. Envy for Mendax overflowed with such angered fervor that I was surprised my skin hadn't turned green. He didn't have to hide any part of himself from anyone. He wore his darkness like a crown.

My eyes darkened with the hate and resentment I started to feel.

His people loved him for being him. An entire hidden world loved him for his darkness. He never had to fight being what he was, not once.

The liquid in the mirror rippled, and my mind instantly flashed back to Mendax's body pressed deliciously behind me as he had held my hand to the mirror. The searing pain that followed as the mirror that hated humans had burned my skin.

My head lolled to the side as I looked into the very same mirror now. The tight corners of my mouth pulled into a devilish smirk.

I lifted the mirror from its mount on the wall, the metallic liquid angrily rippling as I carried it to the now empty tub. I threw it in as hard as I could with a cruel smile.

The gold frame shook but remained intact as bits of the mirror shattered, sharp triangles and silver pools of liquid.

I grabbed one of the beautiful black candles from its holder on the wall behind me and prowled over to the dresser. I began to unscrew the silvery metal knob I had eyed since first entering this bathroom.

Still naked, I unscrewed one of the hollow knobs and smiled.

I walked over to the iron wall sconce that held the beautiful black candles and slowly scraped a bit of rust from the sconce into the hollow dresser knob.

Practically gallivanting back, I held the silvery metal knob—now loaded with magnesium—under the gold faucet.

I scraped the open edges of the metal knob against the

274

gold of the faucet. It took patience, but all I had to do was look into the broken shards and pools of the mirror that had hurt me, and again, perseverance filled me.

The last bits of metal from the knob itself, having been scraped off by the faucet, fell into itself as the knob acted like a small cup. I covered the top with my thumb and shook the magnesium and iron oxide together before setting the cap-like knob on the mirror with a heinous smile I couldn't control.

I picked up the black towel. My body was already dry so I quickly tossed on the large black tunic Mendax had left for me. His scent cascaded over my body with the cotton, and my nipples pebbled. He may as well have licked me all over with the way it made me feel to wear his shirt.

My hand grabbed the black candle, and I lit the towel.

I spared one last look into a broken shard of glass, wiping the dark look from my face and replacing it with the familiar, sweet smile. I threw the flame-licked towel onto the dresser cap and mirror that rested in the tub together and walked out of the bathroom feeling a sense of peace.

The bathroom exploded, bursting into giant white flames that licked at the walls of the bedroom.

I wiped off my smile and steadied my eyes as I greeted the shocked faces of four guards that had shoved themselves through the door. Their surprised eyes scanned me before they hung their mouths at the white flames coming from the fallen bathroom door. They couldn't speak as they looked back at me in shock.

Thermite bombs would do that to you.

"I think you might need a new mirror."

❧❧

"It's a good thing I have a fire mage and a brownie cleanup crew, or I would be very upset at my bathroom burning down." Mendax looked at me as a hint of amusement glittered in his beautiful eyes.

275

"I'm sorry again. I feel terrible. I just thought that if I propped the mirror up in the bathtub, it wouldn't be so scary. I didn't like being so close to it after it had hurt me." I shrugged. Some of that was true.

His warm eyes raked over me with a new adoration that made my chest swell.

What. The. Fuck?

I blew up his bathroom, destroyed a mirror that was probably priceless, and somehow he looked at me with *more* awe and admiration than he had before.

"Tell me again, hellhound, how that fire got started." His low, deep voice rumbled through my chest as he unbuttoned his dark shirt and tossed it to the other side of the bed.

His body was so sculpted and defined. Each muscle and cut showcased the killer he really was. His broad chest bore muscles I had never even seen on human men, and I couldn't help but stare. His stomach muscles tightened with a laugh as he caught me gawking.

He sat on the edge of his large bed and pulled me into his lap. My back pressed against his bare chest. The second his hands wrapped around my waist to keep me in place, I had to clench my thighs together. The motion caused a surprised squeak from me at the friction and lack of underwear I wore under the oversized tunic. I struggled and wiggled to get up from his lap, but that only caused his length to stiffen under me.

"Let me go," I grumbled but accidentally caught myself pressing more weight into the pulsing erection below me.

Why didn't I want to go? Why did he have to look at me like that? It made my stomach tie into knots.

"Never," his husky voice whispered across my ear.

The heat of his breath tickled my neck, and my lady parts responded as his lips moved to the curve of my shoulder and neck.

The hand not holding my waist cupped my left breast with a firm squeeze as a high-pitched noise I wasn't aware I

276

could even make shivered out of my mouth. My head involuntarily started to lean back to rest on his shoulder, giving him full access to my neck.

"You look exquisite when you come undone, my love," he breathed across the sensitive skin of my neck, and I had to squeeze my eyes shut to concentrate enough to speak.

I wanted more than anything to hate him, but my body wanted to do other things with him.

"I am *not* your love, you psycho," I purred back softly, my voice full of sultry venom.

His mouth pressed against the top of my shoulder, and I felt his teeth scrape and drag against my skin as he spoke.

"Go on then. Leave me." He stilled both hands that rested on my waist.

I didn't waste a second to question the opportunity as I tried to plant my feet and run from him, but still, his hands held me firmly against his lap and chest, locking me in place.

"I can't," I growled through clenched teeth as I felt his hands squeeze tighter around my waist.

His lips found my earlobe. "I just wanted to make sure you knew." He shifted my body to the bed and stood up.

Holy gods, was he handsome. Maybe just tonight—

No. *No!*

He was the bad guy!

I scooted back until my back pressed against the silky headboard and watched his eyes turn cold.

"You will return my affections, Callie. I suspect under that act of yours you already do."

He reached toward me, and I scooted to the side, away from his touch. The corner of his mouth lifted in a smile that crinkled the creases of his eyes as he grabbed the heavy blanket on the bed and pulled back a corner gesturing that he was going to tuck me in.

"I am not sleeping here," I said with a suddenly shaky voice.

He sat on the end of the bed and motioned for me to get under the covers with a firm nod of his head.

"Just the *thought* of sinking myself so deep inside you that I fill both your mind and soul is enough to make me come," his low voice purred. "But my need to protect you clouds my mind, and I will not rest until you are safe at the end of the last trial tomorrow."

I shifted my bare legs under the amber-and-cedar-scented sheets and attempted to do a better job of not showing my barely masked disappointment. I did need all the help I could get before the trial.

Before I left him and returned home.

The air hung heavy as our eyes communicated silently what neither one of us could say.

I swallowed hard as we continued to stare. Somehow emotions got tangled in what our eyes were telling each other.

I was scared of dying, and a part of me—a part I was ashamed of—didn't want to leave him. He was the only person that ever made me feel this way. Like I could show him all my monsters and he would only love me more.

It was an insane thought, but the ache in my chest at what I had to do tomorrow left me feeling a little unhinged.

I would never see him again after tomorrow; he would be gone forever.

Something reckless crawled up my spine. The way he watched me didn't help. His powers pulsed and radiated from him with every move.

Monsters of the scariest creation ran from him when he was near.

I'd seen him kill for no reason other than that he was bored. He commanded the entire realm of the most conniving and despicable fae, but yet somehow...somehow I knew whatever I would tell him to do, he would do it just to please me. Even in my wildest dreams, I couldn't have imagined anyone would ever look at me the way he did—villain or not.

I bit my lip, trying to force away the wild thoughts that flowed through my mind.

Then I sat up a little taller.

"Come here," I commanded seductively, wanting to test what I thought I already knew.

His eyes darkened instantly, and the corner of his mouth dimpled.

"This will be my last night with you before I go home or die and I—"

His face wiped free of any humor and back into the fierce Unseelie prince as he stiffened.

Before I knew it, he had grabbed my legs and pulled my body down flat against the bed, the tunic now scrunched up around my chest. My heart pounded in my ears. Had I pushed him too far? I knew he was deranged, but what had I done?

He hovered over me and pressed his knees between my legs. His arms had somehow grabbed my wrists and pinned them above my head before I could even register what had happened.

"No, you come here." His eyes darkened as his body hovered just above mine. He pulled back to blatantly run his eyes up and down my now fully exposed body. I watched as his breath hitched in his chest and his teeth pulled in a corner of his lower lip. "I am yours to command, my love." He pressed his soft lips against my cheek. "But I don't think you understand the capacity of the blade you wish to wield." Another kiss to my jawline. "It's true, you may possess me now, but I will haunt you until your mortal blood rises from its depths to feel my touch." He moved himself down and was suddenly ghosting velvety kisses across the inside of my thighs.

My legs were parted—my whole body displayed openly for him. I sent up a silent prayer that he couldn't feel my legs shaking with anticipation.

He looked up from between my thighs with a sultry smirk and deep need written across his face.

Mendax's hot breath tickled across my innermost thigh and center. He was so close to touching my skin.

But he didn't.

"Your body reacts to my touch like a forest fire." His whispered voice danced over my center before he pressed his mouth to the crease between my thigh and center.

I was shamelessly squirmy, now needing to brush against his mouth. He looked up with a dark look, his pupils completely blown out.

"You should be resting now. Such a naughty human." His hot breath accompanied a tiny touch from the tip of his tongue against my throbbing clit.

A sigh left my mouth as I reached out and grabbed a handful of his hair, not thinking. A hungry growl tore from his chest as he stared at me with barely shackled restraint.

Never had I responded to someone's touch like his. It was as if every trail of his fingers burned a memory that I would replay over and over again for the rest of my days.

"Tomorrow, you will go to the gridiron of fates for your third and final trial." His hands slid across my thighs. "It is the oldest and most controversial form of fae punishment." His thumb trailed up my center, and I pushed up just before it was gone. "It is where fate rules all and decides what your punishment truly should be." His mouth kissed my clit as a hand trailed up my stomach to grab my breast.

My back arched immediately in response, pressing into him.

God, this was torture! I needed to feel him.

My hand moved from his hair to his bouldered shoulder. Electricity surged between my legs at the feel of his bare skin until he dipped back down to take a deep swipe pulling my clit into his mouth.

A cry of pleasure flung from my mouth like an insult. I was panting harder now, as was he.

"The gridiron of fates is a large arena." His mouth trailed licks and kisses up my hips. "The queen and I will sit on our thrones and preside over the trial from the stands." His mouth had reached the lower edge of my breast.

His large arms caged me in as his abdomen and chest rubbed sinfully against my center. He began to pull back, and my legs shot around him to keep him in place. It felt like a part of me would die if I didn't feel his body pressed against mine.

A hard swallow moved down the column of his thick neck as his blazing stare burned through me.

I writhed against him,, needing release.

He bent down to kiss between my breasts. "So needy for me, little lamb," he murmured across my clavicle, and I had to turn my head away to stop myself from slamming my mouth into his, dying to taste him.

"There will be two doors inside the arena. Pay attention, you need to know this." He was breathing heavily now as he ground a small thrust against me.

"Please, Malum," I accidentally whimpered into his ear as I pulled him against me.

His wicked smile was that of a cat that had just caught a mouse. He pressed a finger to my lips to quiet me. Needing to make him regret his smug look, I sucked the finger into my mouth and swirled my tongue around it before he pulled it out. His mouth hung open before his eyes flickered shut for a beat leaving his mouth gaping.

If this was a game of wills, I would win; his reaction assured me of that.

He continued speaking as his hand reached between us to feel my wetness and glide into me in an act of sweltering retaliation.

I nearly came as soon as his fingers pushed inside me.

"As I was saying." He kissed the sensitive underside of my neck—the part that wolves showed their submission by presenting to their alpha. "In the arena, there will be two doors you must choose your fate from."

His fingers worked far too slowly in and out. My nails dug into his bare back, trying to make them move faster. God, I was so close already.

"Behind one door is your freedom, or so the queen has promised." Finally, his fingers moved deliciously fast as I panted like a dog in his ear. "But that is not your fate, I will see to it."

His pace slowed again, and I tried to make up for it with my thrusting hips. I could feel his hard cock stab into my thigh every so often, barely restrained by his pants.

"More importantly, behind the second door will be the most vicious and deadly creature they can find, and *only* the queen will know what door it is behind. Should you choose that door, the beast will immediately descend upon you and kill you so fast there is nothing you or anyone else could possibly do to avoid it."

Was he still talking? It sounded like bubbles inside my head. All I could think about was what it would feel like as he pressed himself into me. First, the tip would slide in, then slowly the rest of him before he pulled out and then in again. He was large, large enough that my body would need to adjust to him—but god, would it feel good.

"Are you listening, love?" He smiled as his face hovered over mine, watching me come undone.

I nodded, unable to think straight. "I want you inside me. Please," I begged.

His wings gently flowed out, and the black smoke curled around his back more like a blanket than wings. They flowed over my hands, where I'm certain my nails must've broken his skin, to glide over my body. The smoke held its own sensation entirely. I touched the smoke, swirling wildly, just like I had longed to ever since the first day I had seen them. It was unexplainable. You could feel them, and they could push back as hard as iron, but then my hand would push through other parts like normal smoke, completely at his will whether he wanted them to be a wisp or full-blown objects.

He moaned as I felt the two rectangular bases where the smoke joined at his shoulder blades. He shivered against me before pulling back with a boyish look. "They are sensitive," he stated as he leaned forward again, this time collecting my wrists above my head as he pressed them into the mattress. His deep strokes continued as his thumb circled me.

I was going to come.

"Please, I need you," I purred against his neck before finally reaching my head up to touch his mouth with mine.

His fingers slowed as the kiss grew tender. He lifted his body enough to watch me, and his hand picked up the pace. He moved his body to the side of the bed, and I waited for him to remove his pants like a hungry animal waiting for its meal.

His hand reached out to cup my face as he undid his buckle with the other. He leaned over my chest to bite my earlobe gently. My eyes slammed shut with delirium as he pressed into my chest so he could reach my pussy at the same time, needing to touch me.

"I need you so bad," I murmured through closed eyes.

Mendax kissed the sensitive skin below my ear as his fingers slammed into me. His thumb worked magic against my clit, and I saw fireworks. I was going to come.

Tension surged through my body on the edge of tipping over. I was about to—I was co—

He pulled away. "Remember that," he said as he removed his hand and stood up with a wicked glimmer in his eyes.

He turned and walked to the door as I sat dumbfounded and unsatiated in an angry, frustrated blaze staring at his back as he walked out the door.

Just before he closed the door behind him, he jutted his head inside and said, "Sleep. I want to invade your mind before I invade your body, my sweet lamb. I need to hunt down a few families. The beast keepers are refusing to speak to anyone other than the queen about which door the beast will be placed." He ran a hand through his tousled black hair. "I will kill every member of their family in front of them until they tell me what door the beast will be stationed behind. Callie"—his face looked so serious now—"look to me tomorrow, and I will tell you which door to choose." He held my gaze for a long moment before the door slammed shut, and I was left in an unsatiated stupor.

Could I even trust him to tell me the door that would lead to my freedom? He was the one who had put me in the trials to kill me. What if he still wanted me dead and this was all a lie? It's obvious he was a psychopath. Would he tell me the door with the beast just so I couldn't leave him? My mind swirled with torturous thoughts.

Could I trust him?

CHAPTER 28

CALLIE

I STOOD IN A SMALL, POORLY LIT ROOM OUTSIDE THE GIANT colosseum. Like every other time I had been outside in the Unseelie realm, the sky set at dusk, only light enough to see with the help of the leftover sun and moon that shone down and illuminated everything like a blue stadium light.

When I woke up that morning alone in Mendax's bed, I had a split second of disappointment. When I looked over to his empty spot, the bed still made with crisp dark linens, I immediately felt like something was missing. It was for the best, but I couldn't help but hate it.

I had never felt more confused about what I wanted than when I had watched Mendax walk out that door.

Part of me—the part that was left yearning—felt so angry and frustrated I had let myself fall under his spell. Another, much less intelligent, part of me felt a pang of sadness that he wasn't sleeping next to me on our last night together. It would be the last time I ever saw him.

The last time I would probably ever have someone look at me the way he did. Like I was everything to him. Like he... loved me.

I couldn't stay. That would be insane. Wrong.

It had taken me ages to fall asleep, completely engulfed with his amber spice lingering decadently on the sheets of his bed. I tossed and turned all night, filled with nerves and confusion. My body felt great though. Every wound, even the deep acid burns from the first trial, had healed completely. It was incredible.

I wasn't sure how I was going to choose the right door, the door without a human-eating beast behind it.

The queen was the only one who knew what was behind the two doors, and I had no faith in deciphering her facial tells. Besides that, I wasn't sure if she would take pity on me and rather I return to the humans or have me dead. I had a pretty good feeling it would be the latter, and that was what I would bank on if I was left with no other options.

I paced the small square room as the four guards watched me. I could probably take them out somehow and run, but that's not what I was here for, and I wouldn't know where to find a portal anyway. I hadn't seen Mendax at all today, and my gut clenched at the feeling that I was making a huge mistake. I grabbed handfuls of hair on either side of my head and pulled, begging to feel something that would ground me—something that would keep my mind on track with why I was here.

This was it.

I would leave one way or another, and I would never see him again. He would be gone forever.

A small scream shot from my chest that startled the iron-clad guards as I pulled at my hair.

I would not let him get to me like this. He didn't love me, he was just infatuated and mad.

I loathed him.

Didn't I?

I couldn't do this.

Yes, I could. I had family and friends I missed dearly— that I would do *anything* to be with again.

I sat in a rickety-looking wood chair and held my head in my palms.

Nothing in the Unseelie court was like I had initially thought. Even the weather. This morning I had been unable to sleep and rose extra early. My door was locked, so I tried the balcony. It was locked as well, but when I pulled back the heavy velvet curtains, I was able to see a bit of sun for the first time since being here. It seemed filtered and somehow more gray than what I was used to, but my skin sang at not having seen it in so long. The distant village looked...almost like a normal village. I could see shops and vendors, and they all looked shockingly normal.

The maids and the people I had met who hadn't tried to kill me had all been surprisingly kind and sweet. Sure many of them seemed to favor a bit of darkness, but that wasn't so different from humans. The only ones that seemed to really hate humans were the queen and the army controlled by the queen. Even Mendax wasn't the evil brute I had been told he was. Maybe—

I stood up and shook myself out of it just in time to hear a roar of something large and horrible a short distance away. The sound sent a shiver up my spine.

The beast.

If I chose the door with the beast behind it, I was as good as dead. I would have no weapons, no reaction time, and no advantage.

Mendax wouldn't let me die, right? He wouldn't.

I could see it in his eyes. He truly thought he loved me. Not just a faint dribble of love either. An all-consuming, soul-drowning love. I huffed, suddenly feeling trapped and frustrated.

He didn't even *know* me.

But it felt like he did. I wanted to hide in his giant menacing arms until this entire thing no longer existed. But of course, I couldn't do that.

I also couldn't go in there blind. I needed a plan.

I had no other options. I had to hope Mendax wouldn't choose the beast, still hoping to kill me. I wasn't so sure though. He had tried to kill me multiple times before. Whether or not it was because he was fighting his urge for me or not, he still very much had wanted me dead and hadn't succeeded. What better way than to lure me into a false sense of security? Could I be so sure now that he wouldn't rather I were dead than leave him? He definitely seemed the type that would rather kill even his bonded love instead of setting her free.

No, he would never set me free. I could see that in his beautiful eyes when he watched me. He would die before he'd let me go home.

A loud roar and applause from a crowd in the distance, somewhere past my confines, elicited a string of curses from my mouth. It was almost time.

He was arrogant. He would be confident in thinking he could stop me before I was actually set free.

He would tell me the door with my freedom and then stop me before I could leave.

Right?

A knock at the door sounded, and my chest leaped with the hope that it was Mendax. I told myself it was simply to find out what door to choose, but I knew better.

A short man with a brown bowl cut motioned for the guards to collect me.

It was time.

I wiped away the tear that fell from my eye. My legs shook like a branch in a rainstorm as the guards led me out of the small room and guided me to a giant iron door clad with large bolts and a humongous circular knob. It took two men to open it and one to shove me in.

I took a few steps and gasped at the giant colosseum surrounding me. It was huge. Rows and rows of stands all filled with excited, shouting fae.

My feet faltered as I walked on the rusty-brown dirt toward the center of the arena. I felt like a tiny ant in the center of the vast structure. The crowd shouted and cheered loudly at my entrance, and I spun to take in the scene that surrounded me as it blurred.

Like an electric shock to the back of my head, I felt his eyes on me. I spun to the right to see the queen and prince in their ornate black thrones sitting on the lowest level above the arena's stands. Our eyes snagged each other's like barbed hooks as we silently communicated in a way only those with an unspoken connection could.

I'm so scared.

I won't let anything happen to you. You're safe.

The queen looked a little perplexed herself, but I couldn't understand why. Would she take pity on me because her son loved me? No...no, I knew she wanted me dead. She wouldn't risk having a human in her bloodline.

She rose from her throne, and the crowd silenced with eerie quickness.

"Callie Peterson, your mortal fate is no longer in the hands of the Unseelie court." Her voice echoed through the stands as every person hung on her smoothly spoken words. "The fates will decide if you are truly good and deserve to be spared," she coughed out under her breath. "Or if your human soul deserves to die a most painful death."

The crowd lost it. Cheers echoed, but I also noticed a few that looked angry at the sound of my death speckled throughout the crowd.

"Behind one door lies a monster, hungry and starved for human blood, created specifically to hunt the humans. Behind the other door lies a portal that waits in anticipation to take you back to the human realm."

The people went crazy with applause.

My hands trembled as I stared up at the Unseelie queen. My nervous fingers found the V-shaped scar on my finger. My toe dug into the sandy dirt, unsure of how to steady myself for what was about to happen.

She waved her graceful arm out to the right, and the black shimmer of her twig-like crown and dress caught the moonlight at just the right angle to sparkle like it was alive. I looked in the direction she pointed to see two giant arched doors made of iron, one next to the other at the end of the arena. They were huge, easily twenty feet tall. My breath caught at the thought of how large the monster was that would be on the other side. My eyes shot to Mendax in panic.

His calm, confident expression told me everything I needed.

He knew exactly which door held the beast and which held my freedom.

I wiped my sweaty hands on the brown pants I wore and nervously patted at the folds of fabric until I felt the dagger I had swiped from one of the guards as we had walked here.

I cracked my neck to each side with a deep breath. This would all be over soon. All of it.

"Choose your fate, human," the queen bellowed with a smile before she sat down in her throne to the wild chanting of the loud crowd.

I stole a look to Mendax in a silent plea.

Which door do I choose?

His face was calm, his breathing steady. I watched as the onyx leather draped over him lifted and dropped with somewhat calm breaths. His steely eyes took me in as a muscle in his jaw clenched and his hands gripped the armrests of the black throne tightly.

His head nodded, so slight a movement I wouldn't have caught it had it not been for his glittering black crown catching the moonlight. He nodded at the door to the right, and his eyes clung to mine.

Would he send me to the beast or the portal? That was the real question. I stared at each door for several moments, trying to listen for noises from the beast or anything that would help me decipher which door held my freedom. The crowd jeered impatiently, hungry for a massacre.

I stood between the two doors, my eyes trained on the right one.

What if it was my freedom?

What if it wasn't?

Warm tears fell from my eyes. No matter how hard I bit the inside of my mouth, I couldn't seem to stop them.

This had to happen. All of it.

I stole a glance back to Mendax on his throne.

His body was tense now. Was that a tell of some kind? His full brows creased slightly as he ran a pale hand over his face. He was nervous.

Worry and adoration poured through his stare. I could feel his anxiety through the bond.

Maybe it would be better if the beast did devour me.

I walked in front of the large door to the right before thinking better of it and stepping back a few feet.

As soon as the door opened, I would run to the portal and leave before Mendax could get to me. He would never just let me leave; he would be at the portal to try and stop me. But I had to leave—this was the only way.

I would have to be fast. One last goodbye.

"I choose this door," I said with a tremble in my voice.

The queen nodded, and a vile smile slowly painted her lips.

The look made my stomach drop to the floor.

Thuds and creaks sounded as the door slowly rose.

I didn't hesitate. The second I saw her face, I began to run toward the opposite side of the arena, slowing my pace only enough to rip the dagger free from my pants.

I turned back, and my face paled.

Its red back brushed the top of the opening door as its huge body pounded in.

It was the wrong door—Mendax had told me the door with the beast.

He wanted me dead after all.

I readied my stance against the ground as every step of the creature's enormous feet sent earthquake-like shivers into the stadium floor.

It had the body of something between a T. rex and a snake. Was it a dragon? It didn't look like anything I'd ever seen before.

The crowd gasped in loud waves as the beast sauntered in angrily.

What appeared to be old blood covered its large body, and it had larger legs in the front with an odd bend to the elbow. In the front, a barrel-like chest seemed to protrude out a bit. Sharp thorn-like scales stuck out at least three inches and lined the beast's chest. Several of the thorns were also on the razor-sharp ridge of his back and down every leg.

The blood drained from my face as its eyes locked onto mine and it began to pick up speed, running straight at me. A loud snarl and high-pitched cry made my bones recoil as the sound shot forth from its hideous mouth. The bellow allowed me to see the two rows of razor-sharp fangs that lined its gigantic dinosaur-like mouth. Everything about it reminded me of a dinosaur wrapped in lethal thorns. The same sharp spikes framed its face and hooked backward from its long nose to the back of its head. From there, it formed a thickly scaled neck. Snake-like black eyes glistened hungrily at me, daring me to move.

I was backed up to the doors I had entered from on the opposite end of the colosseum when a deep crocodile-like rumble sounded from the creature's chest, and it raised its hackles, readying itself for attack.

I raised the dagger, upset that my animal gift hadn't worked on it. It didn't seem to hold the same weight here as it did in the human realm for whatever reason. Nothing seemed to like me here.

Not even Mendax apparently.

Its body tensed, and I flinched as I waited for the strike, wondering how fast it would take to eat me. I steeled my nerves as I firmly squeezed the smooth gold handle of the dagger. The familiar feeling of a blade coating me like a forgotten shadow.

The beast went for me.

My eyes flinched tightly closed as my body tensed so hard I heard a crack at the back of my jaw. I waited to feel the first sting of pain that would come from its warped talons or needle-sharp teeth.

I opened my eyes in horror to see Mendax's large back suddenly in front of me—wings spread the widest I'd ever seen them—as he snarled back at the beast with a sound that rivaled the beast's gruesome noises.

My breath threatened to fail me at the sight.

No! God no!

Everything inside my soul died and reincarnated, feeling his smoke push me gently back, away from the beast.

He had shadowed in front of me, taking the attack— saving my damned life.

I stole a quick look at the queen, who screamed and pounded her now inky black hands and arms against an invisible barrier into the arena. Black smoke billowed angrily from her, threatening to choke out the shadow guards that surrounded the entire first level as she screamed for her son. She looked at me with a stare that could have killed me all by itself.

He had put up some kind of shield to keep her and everyone else from entering.

She had known her son would find out about the beast and tell me which door would keep me alive.

Queen Tenebris had switched them again. Much more the diabolical queen than I had given her credit for.

I should have never, ever doubted what my family told me about them.

Loud screams and bellows from the crowd blended with snarls and growls as the beast swiped abnormally dexterous claws at Mendax. The prince blocked each strike easily with the help of his now firm smoke. The dark prince sent a sharp stab of what looked like black lightning into the monster's chest with a simple flick of his hand. Tension and rage poured from his black armor-clad body. The look on his face was nothing short of white-hot wrath. The red-scaled beast began to flinch backward from Mendax's strikes. The small action brought a further onslaught of violence from Mendax. The warrior bent his head down a fraction and eyed the enormous beast in front of him like his gaze alone could cause the heathen to combust. The insanely intimidating fae looked at the monster in the most horrifyingly nightmarish way possible as a corner of his mouth pulled into an eerie smirk, and it dawned on me that Mendax hadn't even been trying to hurt the beast yet. He had been playing with it, letting out a bit of his anger. The hair on the back of my neck rose at the sight before me.

Dark, evil magic crackled in the air like lightning.

My eyes caught the still-open door where the beast had entered, and like the coward I was, I ran for it.

I couldn't do this—I couldn't. Even if it meant I could no longer go home, that I left half of my heart, I couldn't do this.

Gods, why hadn't he just let me die! I wouldn't be so tormented.

I spared a last look at Mendax and the beast. Tears streamed down my face, hot with terror and sadness, as brown dust from the arena flew around us like a tornado. Mendax's eyes happened to catch mine at the last second. His sharp eyes hardened with an edge of pain as he took in my tears, my stance.

Do. Not. Follow me. My eyes pleaded with his as I tattooed every feature of his beautiful face into my memory and prayed with everything I had that he stayed where he was.

I took off like a cannon. This was the only way to truly save us both.

Cold air shredded my lungs in deep gasps as my legs pumped harder with each stride that hit the dusty brown floor. With every hard slam to the ground, the open door drew closer. The deep blue of night had settled outside of the gridiron's lights. The ominous moonlit freedom beckoned me through the other side of the large door frame. I would run out this door and to the portal of the door to the left and be free forever. The guards were behind the barrier Mendax had put up so they wouldn't stop me.

Tangled blonde hair whipped across my face, blocking my vision as my side slammed into the ground with the force of a bus. I was grabbed around the waist and lifted with such force my bladder let loose a little. Unmerciful claws dug their harsh tips into my skin. The monster had apparently realized I was the only real prey inside the arena and had given up on Mendax.

Blood-red scales and thorns on the beast's face were so close I could smell the musty reptilian-like odor emanating from its mouth as it squeezed me painfully in front of its face. Black eyes as empty as a puddle sparkled in front of me with hunger. The heat of its open mouth hit my legs as I whimpered out what would have been a scream of terror had my lungs not been crushed in its massive grip.

With haste, it shoved my legs in its gaping mouth, the fabric of my pants tearing and slicing alongside the flesh of my leg as it slid across the beast's sharp teeth.

The red devil stilled with half of my body already in its mouth. I felt it slowly grab me again and pull me out, and the action caused another rip of skin and fabric on my right leg as I was pulled free from its damp mouth.

I tried and tried to loosen the beast's grip. It pulled me out of its jaw before setting me on the ground so gently that I thought I must have already been dead and dreaming.

As I looked into its black eyes, I saw a smoky-looking sheen. As soon as I was set safely on the ground, it stepped away from me as if hypnotized.

I glanced to the right to see Mendax, only a few feet from me, as still as a statue staring wickedly at the beast.

Mendax looked to me, and for the first time since I'd met him, he looked terrified as his blue eyes were full of emotion. His gaze quickly changed as his pupils grew somehow darker.

He looked back to the beast and thundered a war cry that made a vein protrude in his neck and forehead, his face now contorted into undiluted rage.

The creature stared unfazed at the prince, his face expressionless as if he were some kind of zombie. He deftly lifted his sharp claw as if he were a puppet being commanded and—

He was a puppet being commanded.

Mendax was impelling his mind.

It was unfathomable to see someone hold such control over anything, but to see him so effortlessly inside the mind of a beast the size of a house felt incomprehensible. The prince's body was tight with furious tension. I watched, terrified, as his muscular shoulders settled ever so slightly. The beast held up his giant claws before digging his talons deep into his chest with a sickening crack, tearing through its rib cage to pull out a present for his puppet master.

Without so much as a whimper, the zombie-like monster dropped to its knees, a cavernous hole that leaked inky black gore now resting in the middle of its protruding chest. Its hand opened to dump its beating heart onto the ground as it slumped to the ground in a lifeless heap of red scales and black blood-coated claws.

The wet heart shuddered once more before going as still as its owner that lay next to it.

I couldn't believe it. My human brain fought to block out the information.

"She switched the doors at the last minute, Callie. I-I almost lost you," he shouted at me. "Every one of them will pay for it, that I promise. I will never be without you, Callie, never." Fear snaked through his tender voice, cracking it.

The amber lights of the stadium flickered across us, and the open night air tossed our hair gently in different directions as silent muffled sounds from the audience and queen still trying to get passed the shield echoed against the still night.

I shuddered, the taste of rancid betrayal on my tongue.

Tears streamed down my face as salty reminders of corruption, trailing into the corners of my mouth before running off my chin in a waterfall of deceit.

God, why had he followed me!

I studied the door before I readied myself. I knew I couldn't outrun him.

"I'm so sorry, Malum," I whimpered softly as the tears blurred my vision.

Our eyes locked, and he ran to me, his face wrinkled with anxiety as he pulled me against his chest. The tears fell harder at the deep swell of comfort I felt pressed tightly against him.

I closed my eyes and forced myself to do what I had been sent here to do this whole time.

CHAPTER 29

MENDAX

L IKE EVERYTHING ELSE TO DO WITH CALLIE, I NEVER SAW IT
coming.

The iron blade dug deep into the flesh just below my wing.
The exact spot I had shown my love where to end me forever.

I shouldn't have been surprised, but I was.

Her soft body pressed against mine like a hug.

Her face was stoic, trained, even as I took in the wetness
in her own bloodshot eyes. My breath hitched with the feel
of the deepening blade.

She had delivered my killing blow.

Still, she didn't move, her body tense as she continued to
hold on to the blade. I fell to my knees, unable to stand any
longer. Callie dropped with me, unable to pull herself away
as if some force kept her against me.

"You were right about everything, Malum," she cried,
holding onto me tighter.

The sting of using my true name as she buried a blade in
my body was its own unique torture.

I opened my mouth to speak, but no words came out.
Her eyes held mine as tears fell from her face and landed on
the dirt of the gridiron's floor.

"I was sent to kill you, but not by the humans." She twisted the knife, literally and figuratively.

Callie moved back and shifted to stand above me, leaving the knife lodged in my back. Her wheat-colored hair blew in the wind as she stared at me, still crying. Her face looked torn between wanting to help me up and wanting to run from me as fast as she could.

"I knew you had a spark inside you, Callie. I just hadn't thought it'd end up being a whole fucking inferno," I stated.

My body was growing weaker with every second, and talking was hard for a lot of reasons. Every part of me wanted to pull her to me, still needing her beside me. My soul ached for my last breath to echo off her cheek as she held me tightly.

Two tears fell from her face and onto my chest as I struggled to stay kneeling below her. Her hard exterior cracked further with every breath of life that left me.

"You understood me like no one else." Tears streamed down her red face as she took a few steps backward. Pure regret filled her eyes as she wiped them with the back of her hand. "It seems my fate is to have an incomplete heart no matter what I do." She took a few more steps toward the opened door.

Blood rushed in my ears. I had to stop her—she was going to leave. She was going to be gone.

"Callie, I need you. Please. Please don't go. Wait! Wait to go until I'm dead so that I never have to feel the pain of you leaving."

"You're still the villain, Malum. You will always be the villain. Queen Saracen was right," she said, her voice shaky now as she took another step away from me toward the door.

My blood stalled in my veins, more from the sight of her leaving than the blade in my back.

"You're looking pretty evil yourself right now, darling," I rasped, wiping the black blood from my lips as I fell to my side. My cheek hit the ground with a crunch. My eyes still clung to her, refusing to squander my last few moments of watching her.

"No one expects an angel to set the world on fire," she said as a flicker of desperation passed through her eyes. "I'm sorry. I had no choice—it was the only way—"

She shook herself and wiped her tears on the back of her hand again as she straightened her posture. She took one last long, yearning look at me before she turned with clenched fists and walked out of the arena door.

"Nooo!" A scream ripped from me, overfilled with agony and every last bit of rage I held as I watched her walk away from me.

I wouldn't let her get away. I would never let her get away from me. I couldn't go on without her. I refuse to be without her ever again!

I honed in on my mind, reaching into my powers and pulling up the ability to impel her. She would not leave me, I would make sure of it, and when I got her back, I would show my goddess exactly what it felt like to be my queen. I would let her take everything from me she ever wanted.

Electric heat coursed through me with the strain of my power. One call to her and she would return where she belonged at my side. Forever. She would be lucky if I ever took the chains off her pretty throat again; I would tie it to my own.

"Callie Peterson, return to me," I commanded, infusing my power into the words.

She paused, her head turned to look me in the eye. Yes.

"Callie, return to me *now*, please." My voice cracked with the surge of power I sent through to her name.

The vixen holding the threads that tied me together smiled sadly. She turned from me and walked away. Completely unaffected.

No! No...*No!*

Callie wasn't her true name. The goddess had given me a false name the entire time.

My head collapsed against the ground with shock.

She was good. She was *so* fucking good. Better than I had

given her credit for. I clutched at her tooth hanging from my neck. My palm closed tightly around it as I settled further into the quiet, and it made me feel that she wasn't all the way gone from me.

She would never be free from me. Never.

By now, the dark army had broken through the shields as my powers and I weakened. They descended upon the gridiron floor like ants.

"My lord! Men, kill her now!" the captain of my shadow guard shouted before my smoke reached out just enough to wrap around his ankle and pull him to the ground with a sharp tug.

I winced at the pain the effort had caused.

"No one touches my future queen but me unless they want their head cut off," I whispered to the fallen man.

He looked shocked, his face full of puzzlement. "But my lord…she just…we need to get you to the healer now. That was a killing blow," he said with a pained crease of his brows as two others helped him up and began to fuss over my body.

"It would be if I was a normal fae, but I am a Smoke Slayer." I lay back and closed my eyes with a smile.

I was no fool; I had seen through her innocent act the second I had laid my eyes on her. She was a goddess filled with the power to maim. She overflowed with a pool of darkness that matched my own. She was absolutely perfection in every way.

Of course I wouldn't have shown her my real points of weakness.

No, I would heal, and when I did, I would hunt her down. She would lead me to whoever had made her do this, and I would kill them long and slow for whatever pain they had caused her. Then I would stop at absolutely nothing—*nothing*—until she was mine forever, my queen. There wasn't a person I wouldn't kill or a world I wouldn't destroy to get to her. If anything, this only made me want her more. I wanted to give her darkness a home—a place to crawl inside of and corrupt. She *belonged* with me.

A hard smile creased my lips and crinkled my eyes as my vision faded to black.

CHAPTER 30

CALY

THE SHARP, BITTER SMELL OF ANTISEPTIC MIXED WITH UNDER-tones of soaps and harsh cleaners drifted into my nose with a hard inhale. Intense fluorescent light burned the back of my eyelids as I struggled to open them. Everything was sterile, crisp, and white. An array of beeps and voices rang loudly in my ears, overpowering my senses in the span of a second.

A grid ceiling with little brown specks and large rectangular panels of lights encompassed my vision.

I sat up abruptly, and at the same time, someone grabbed my arm. Something plastic covered my face, and I flung it off. The elastic band caught under my ear as my heart pounded through my chest.

"You're okay, calm down, honey. You had a bad accident, okay? You're at Michigan Springs Hospital. Can you tell me your name? What can you remember?" a pleasant yet robotic voice questioned.

"I'm Callie Peterson. Proud environmentalist and biological technician. I-I was walking through the forest to get my microscope when I stumbled upon an anomaly of luna moths and a perfect circle of destroying angel mushrooms. I live at 4313 Sassafras Road, Willow Springs, Michigan—"

"She's up! Oh my god, she's finally waking up! Get every-one in here!" a familiar voice shouted from the corner.

I turned my head toward all the voices. My head was pounding so hard.

I was sitting in a hospital bed with bands and IVs riddled across my wrists.

An older man in a lab coat gently pressed me down so my back hit flush against the hospital bed again. "Take her easy there, champ, you've been out for a while. Now just take a few deep breaths for me, and your family and friends will be in shortly. Your grandpa Earl just went to grab the others."

A cold stethoscope pressed against the warm skin of my chest. I looked down to see my body in a stiff blue hospital gown, not a beautiful black ball gown.

I pulled the stiff cotton blanket up to my chest, feeling uneasy. Something was wrong.

"Where am I?" I asked the graying man before a small swarm of familiar faces filtered into the room.

"Now I'm sorry, but we can only have a few in at a time, this will be too much for her. All vitals are stable and looking good," the doctor stated before he smiled tightly and walked around the crowd of people and out the large door, closing it behind him with a click.

Cliff and Cecelia stood at the end of the hospital bed. Each had grabbed ahold of one of my feet and held it, the warmth of their hands squeezed as the movement shifted over the rubber-bottomed socks I wore. Several others from the park and Willow Springs had gathered around my bed. A few girls from town stared glossy-eyed at me, their golden hair nearly washing them out completely from view under the harsh lights. Several of their faces were puffy and red as if they had been crying a lot.

The second I saw them, everything inside me shattered. They all looked so bland, so unremarkable, so…plain.

So human.

Not like the faces of the gorgeous fae—

304

Earl stood to my other side, shaking slightly in his feeble frame as he dabbed his eyes with a whitish-gray handkerchief.

"It's all my fault—the whole thing—I'm *so* sorry, Callie." Earl blubbered into the handkerchief as he pulled the worn ball cap from his head and twisted it in his hands.

"We can't seem to get ahold of your mother or sisters, we used the contact info on file, but it seems to go to a disconnected line. Your family must be so worried," Cecelia mumbled as she squeezed my foot in a motherly sort of way.

"What happened? What's going on?" I asked.

Dread and madness coiled around me. In the back of my mind, I knew the words I would hear.

"We found you in the woods behind your house, you were surrounded by destroying angel mushrooms, Callie. It turns out they have the highest toxicity that has ever been recorded in fungi. The whole town is in an uproar with all the scientists that came in taking samples and removing spores," Earl said as he crossed his arms over his chest, pacing back and forth. "I'm so sorry, Callie. This is all my fault."

"It is. Don't you think you've done enough? You ought to wander down the hallway to the psych ward and stay there," Cliff bit out aggressively at Earl.

Everything felt so unfamiliar. I couldn't remember anything. It was like I had popped into someone else's life, and none of it clicked into place.

A nurse I hadn't realized was next to me cleared her throat. "The mushrooms toxicity clouded your system so aggressively that it nearly killed you. Had this man not found you when he did, I'm afraid you wouldn't be alive right now." The small dark-haired nurse pointed at Earl.

Cliff practically growled at the foot of the bed.

"Enough, I'm sorry, but this is too much for the patient. One at a time," said the tiny nurse in blue scrubs as she ushered the crowd toward the door. "Callie, sweetie, who would you like to stay first? Just one, please."

"Umm...Earl, I suppose," I mumbled, trying to piece things together.

Flashes of the beautiful fae prince showed through my tired mind. I thumbed the V-shaped scar on my thumb, still trying to remember.

The room cleared reluctantly, and the nurse followed behind, leaving Earl and me alone in the hospital room after she kindly showed me the buttons to call for her should I need anything.

I felt tired, and a sting on my leg caused me to move uncomfortably on the hard bed.

Wait—

I moved my leg and felt a sharp, grating pain. The same exact place the beast's teeth had scraped over my skin. Wait—

Suddenly everything clicked into place, and I remembered everything.

I grabbed a cup of tiny ice chips and filled my mouth as I steadied myself.

"Calypso."

I choked on the ice at the sound of my real name and dropped the large cup onto my lap, spilling small crystals of ice everywhere.

My mouth hung open as I looked back to see Earl leaning against the white wall toward the foot of my bed. His demeanor was completely different. Suave confidence replaced the shakiness and feeble nature, and his voice had a familiar smooth tempo.

"What did you say?" I asked, shaken.

"You didn't think I'd just leave you to this enterprise all alone, did you?" Earl asked as he smoothly pushed off the wall and took a lazy step toward me.

He was like a man possessed. Not Earl at all.

"Who are you?" I asked, glancing at the closed door, feeling more and more unsure of everything by the minute.

"I was shocked when you didn't figure out it was me." He laughed, and the sound caused a flash of memory to dance in my mind.

It couldn't be.

He stepped closer to the bed, his face still old and haggard, but the most charming and boyish smile overtook it. "I couldn't let you do it alone. I was worried you wouldn't find the portal if I didn't help, but once you got close, I panicked and tried to stop you. That never should have been your task. Fuck, Cal. If she knows I meddled, she won't keep her end of the agreement." Earl's voice sounded so young now as he shrugged boyishly and tucked his hands into his jeans pockets bashfully.

"Wh—" No. It couldn't be. There was no way.

"She's irate about him killing Langmure. The queen will probably give you the other half of your heart just for killing Mendax after what he did to her son. If you ask me, you've more than proved your allegiance," Earl whispered as the edges of his face grew blurry.

I pushed back farther on the steel bracketed bed. My head pounded like a drum as my tongue flicked through the empty space of my missing wisdom tooth.

There was only one person—

I gasped as Earl's blurred body quickly shifted to a much taller, more handsome man. Tan skin and tapered muscle made the contrast from the frail man that much more shocking.

Prince Aurelius of the Seelie court stared back at me, his eyes brimming with emotion.

"You tricked me, Aurelius," I said through gritted teeth feeling none of the bite I forced into the words.

His handsome smile dropped instantly. "Come on, Aurelius?" he pleaded. "Call me Eli like normal. You know Mom couldn't find out I was helping you, or we would never be able to prove your allegiance and get her to return the other half of your heart. It's the only way she would let you, *a human* might I remind you, come live in Seelie with us." His charming smile beamed for an instant before his looks grew more serious. "It's a good thing I did help you too, remember?"

I crossed my arms, full of anger. For a few moments, I had prayed that maybe none of this was real. That maybe I could wake up and actually be a scientist that worked for a park in Willow Springs.

"What I remember is that a fox tried to stop me from going to the portal in the forest," I said, suddenly feeling a barrage of feelings I was uncertain of.

He ran his hands over his face and mouth. "What do you want me to say, Cal? The thought of my best friend—my *very mortal human* best friend—going to the darkest, most evil side of the veil had me uncomfortable. Sometimes I don't have the best control over myself in my animal form around you."

Heavy silence filled the sterile room.

"You finally got to see what animal I shift to though." He chuckled hard, and the sound almost relaxed me. Almost.

"It wasn't that impressive," I said, fighting a grin.

When I was ten, Aurelius made the mistake of telling me that because he was Seelie royalty, he could shift into other forms, and an animal was one of them. I begged and pleaded for years, frustrated that I wasn't allowed to know what it was. Royals shifting in front of humans was a big no-no and severely punishable.

"Was it *not that impressive* when I stopped your mortal heart from ending after that piece of shit killed you? Some garbage training my mother gave you. You weren't even on the other side for five minutes before you were dead." His voice suddenly lost all laughter. The seriousness of it was unsettling. He seemed so much...older than I remembered him. He continued, "Had I not—"

A loud knock sounded at the door, and we both froze.

"You doing okay, Callie? Need anything?" The small nurse popped her head through the crack of the door, and her eyes immediately roamed over Eli's larger-than-average human frame full of muscle and golden skin.

I held my breath, waiting for her to ring an invisible alarm

308

that would have the entire hospital coming to take Eli away from me again.

"I'm good, thanks," I said, smiling a false smile. I was so good at them now.

She winked at me and gave the barely passable-for-human fae a longing once over before she closed the door again. My face steeled once more as my eyes shot to Eli's.

"What do you mean he killed me? I thought I was just injured? Did I die? What did you do to save me?" The memories were foggy but still there. "You licked me and cried on me!" I said with the initial intention of finding out what had really happened but also teasing him.

His frozen face stopped me completely.

"You remember it?" his whisper laced with panic.

I nodded wearily, and his amber eyes seemed to thrum with magic before he bent over the bed and grabbed my hands.

"Tarani was with me, I–I was taking her back home from beyond the veil, and I had to make sure you were okay."

The panic in his voice set my blood pumping in overtime. I swear I could smell the faint scent of smoke from the forest that night. I was so tense.

"What did you do?" I asked.

The feel of his hands around mine unsettled me for some reason. It didn't feel right. The smell of smoke filled my head enough that I had to sniff to clear my nose.

"I will not jeopardize my baby sister, Cal. I never should have taken her with me to the Unseelie realm, let alone have her witness—" His voice cracked, filled with pain and regret.

"What did you do, Aurelius? Why would Princess Tarani be in danger now? You both left the Unseelie realm safely—I don't understand," I whispered as I tried to pull my hands free, but he held firm.

For some reason, the action made my senses flare, and a tiny swirl of anger floated in my mind. Normally I would be comforted by his touch?

"I-I just couldn't lose you, I couldn't," he said as he squeezed my hand tighter, pulling it up to his cheek.

It was oddly intimate, and I shifted uncomfortably, wanting to pull away.

He's my best friend, like a brother to me. This was weird, and I didn't like it. Burning wood, like the scent of a forest fire, was everywhere. I sniffed again.

"What did you do?" I asked again, pulling my hand back, losing my patience.

"You can never tell anyone, *anyone*, what you saw me do. Do you understand? It will result in mine and Tarani's death…and likely yours as well."

My breath hitched, and my eyes began to water uncontrollably at his words. I had never been close with Tarani or Langmure, only the queen and Eli, but I still cared about what had happened to them.

He squeezed my forearms so hard I thought it might bruise. I looked away, attempting to school my features.

I had already told the Unseelie prince.

For the very first time, a tiny bit of me was glad he was dead and couldn't hurt my family.

I opened my mouth to make my confession to Eli and to tell him that he was hurting my arm, but when I looked up to meet his eyes, they were filled with horror as they stared at me.

Minuscule wisps of black smoke moved from my skin before dissipating into the air.

"Oh, my sun—" His mouth gaped open with shock. "His powers—"

He flung my arms from him in pure terror as we watched the smooth velvety tendrils emit themselves from my arms and hands.

As soon as he stopped touching me, the smoke ceased.

We looked at each other in silent alarm.

"Maybe it's something that happens when one of the bonded dies," I said, knowing in my gut it wasn't true.

I swear I could feel a distant amusement that didn't feel like my own.

"Yeah...maybe," he said, staring at me as if he'd never seen me before this moment.

I quickly tried to change the subject.

"Do you think your mom—Queen Saracen—will really let me live with you guys in the Seelie court now? That she will return what's left of my heart?" I asked my best friend, and I couldn't help but feel a little sad.

It wouldn't matter. Not now.

The half I did carry had died with Mendax.

I flinched at the thought of him hunched over with my blade still lodged in his back.

Perhaps it was because Queen Saracen had taken too much of my heart as a down payment? We had all agreed that she would hold a piece of it until I showed my allegiance— maybe she took enough to make me truly vicious.

I felt vicious. Dark.

I wonder how much I could've loved him with a whole heart?

"She's not evil, Calypso. She's not Unseelie," he growled. His amber eyes darkened slightly. "She already blessed you once, Cal. What do you want?" Eli said indignantly.

His skin glowed under the lights. He had dulled it slightly with a glamour as the Seelie always did when they walked among the humans, but even with the dimming, Eli stood out like a god among men.

"Taking half of my heart is hardly a blessing, *Aurelius*," I bit out, using his full name instead of the familiar Eli I had called him since we were kids.

"That's not what I'm talking about, and you know it. Besides, you offered that yourself as a show of your serious- ness when you asked to live with us—with me." His honied eyes grew tender for a moment. "I'm talking about the animal blessing. That's a Seelie royal trait that she bestowed upon you after you saved her in that field. To be honest, I thought it would help you out more than it has." He suddenly

311

found something very interesting on the floor. "Had you not been there to save her against Queen Tenebris, she would have never survived. You saw how tiny she had grown—how much power she had lost fighting the Unseelie queen." He worried the bottom of his lip.

He loved his mother so much—we both did. After my mother and sister had died when I was ten, I had no one.

Queen Saracen often visited then, her and Prince Aurelius. Always thanking me for saving her that day. Their kindness was unmatched in my times of need. The queen even went so far as to dispatch one of her wet maids to take care of me when my mother was gone.

They were the only family I'd ever known.

But fae and humans were very different.

Eli and I quickly became best friends spending all our time together well into our teenage years. Queen Saracen often commented on how cute it was. That is, until Prince Aurelius kept skipping his royal duties to come be with me, the human.

Fae customs were very different. They don't believe in humans entering their realm without a title of ownership or unwavering proof of their allegiance. So when a few years passed and I had practically gone mad trying to figure out how to find a portal and see them again, Eli's mom, Queen Saracen, threw me a bone.

I wasn't just a human hoping to live in the outskirts of Seelie. I had wanted to be as close as possible to my fami— to the queen and Eli as I could be. Which meant a human paying allegiance to the royals. Much different stakes than paying allegiance to a commoner.

I didn't care though. I would pay any price to be with the only people I had left.

I pleaded until the queen accepted. As any fae did, the queen had enemies, and somehow along the way, I ended up being trained to execute her killings in the human realm. I was human, and therefore, her kills in the human realm were overlooked as she wasn't breaking any fae laws.

312

Most fae in the human realm were easy to kill. They never suspected it of me, and over the years, I had stopped using brute force and started to use my science background to help make the kills easier. It's why I had taken so many classes on botanical poisons.

I didn't care. I would have done anything for them.

I *had* done anything for them.

Eventually, it led me to Mendax. He was my final test of allegiance, my big fish to freedom.

She gave me no details of when or how it would happen, only that I needed to distract and kill the Unseelie prince to get back at his mother, Queen Tenebris, for nearly killing her in that field when I was a kid. It was poetic. It was my final payment and ticket to the Seelie court, where I would be made whole again, heart and soul, quite literally.

"So that whole time you were Earl, you couldn't have found one single time to be honest with me? How though? They all knew you?" I pointed at the door, thinking of all the small things I should have picked up on but had missed.

"It's a glamour, Calypso, a little bit of magic in their minds," he said as if I should have known.

"I've missed you so much since she quit letting you come to the human realm." I huffed angrily, and suddenly all my frustration felt clear and loud. "How do you think I felt seeing you at the faerie court? The first time I see you in years, and it's sprung on me like that? There?" I shouted at him.

I was angry for being kept in the dark. It had an aftertaste of betrayal in and of itself.

He was in front of my face and grabbing my arms before I could even register, he had moved.

"Do *not* talk to me about the tortures of that night, Calypso," he snarled, and I found myself suddenly unfamiliar with the man in front of me. My childhood best friend was replaced with an angry titan. "I had to school myself the moment my eyes landed on you in that ballroom. It took everything—*everything*—I had not to run to you and hug you, to take you away from that...that devil! Do you know what it did to me watching that monster bond to you? To watch him kill my brother and then attempt to kill you?" He was shouting now. "I had to watch you in the trial the *entire* time and act like it was fun!"

I immediately regretted whatever I said that had gotten him so upset. "It doesn't matter now," I reassured him. "The bond is disintegrated, and Mendax is...dead." My face fell with the horror I couldn't seem to mask as I said the words aloud.

I tried to push it from my mind, but the feeling sat on my chest like a heavy iron weight.

I had killed several fae, so I knew that to kill a creature as powerful as him, I would have to get close. Close enough that he would let me see all of his weaknesses.

I just had no idea I would become one.

Eli's amber eyes darted back and forth between mine as they studied my face.

"He is dead, right?" he asked, suddenly looking weary and unsure.

"Mendax is dead." The words crackled in my throat as if my own body refused to believe them.

"You're sure? Because if he's not dead like you promised and the queen and I take you to the Seelie court, it will be your death, and there's nothing *anyone* could do to stop it, Calypso."

I nodded.

Eli continued to stare at my face. "Good. Now come with me to the Seelie castle, and we'll get the queen to make that heart of yours whole again."

WANT MORE BLOOM ROMANTASY? CHECK OUT

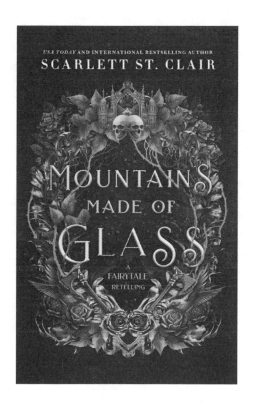

CHAPTER ONE
The Toad in the Well

*The goose hung suspended by its feet from a low limb, bleed-*ing into a bucket. Each wet plop of blood made me flinch, the sound inescapable even as I chopped wood to feed my hearth for the coming storm. The air had grown colder in the few minutes I had been outside, and yet perspiration beaded across my forehead and dampened all the parts of my body.

I was hot and the blood was dripping, and the strike of my ax sounded like lightning in the hollow where I lived before the Enchanted Forest. I could feel her gaze, a dark and evil thing, but it was familiar. I had been raised beneath her eyes. She had witnessed my birth, the death of my mother and father, and the murder of my sister.

Father used to say the forest was magic, but I believed otherwise. In fact, I did not think the forest was enchanted at all. She was alive, just as real and sentient as the fae who lived within. It was the fae who were magic, and they were as evil as she was.

My muscles grew more rigid, my jaw more tense, my mind spiraling with flashes of memories bathed in red as the blood continued to drip.

Plink.

A flash of white skin spattered with blood.
Plink.
Hair like spun gold turned red.
Plink.
An arrow lodged in a woman's breast.
But not just a woman—my sister.
Winter.
My chest ached, hollow from each loss.

My mother was the first to go on the heels of my birth. My sister was next, and my father followed shortly after, sick with grief. I had not been enough to save him, to keep him here on this earth, and while the forest had not taken them all by her hand, I blamed her for it.

I blamed her for my pain.

A deep groan shook the ground at my feet, and I paused, lowering my ax, searching the darkened wood for the source of the sound. The forest seemed to creep closer, the grove in which my house was nestled growing smaller and smaller day by day. Soon, her evil would consume us all.

I snatched the bucket from beneath the goose and slung the contents into the forest, a line of crimson now darkening the leaf-covered ground.

"Have you not had enough blood?" I seethed, my insides shaking with rage, but the forest remained quiet in the aftermath of my sacrifice, and I was left feeling drained.

"Gesela?"

I stiffened at the sound of Elsie's soft voice and waited until the pressure in my eyes subsided to face her, swallowing the hard lump in my throat. I would have called her a friend, but that was before my sister was taken by the forest, because once she was gone, everyone abandoned me. There was a part of me that could not blame Elsie. I knew she had been pressured to distance herself, first by her parents and then by the villagers who met monthly. They believed I was cursed to lose everyone I loved, and I was not so certain they were wrong.

Elsie was pale except for her cheeks which were rosy red.

Her coloring made her eyes look darker, almost stormy. Her hair had come loose from her bun and made a wispy halo around her head.

"What is it, Elsie?"

Her eyes were wide, much like my sister's had been at death. Something had frightened her. Perhaps it had been me.

"The well's gone dry," she said, her voice hoarse. She licked her cracked lips.

"What am I supposed to do about it?" I asked, though her words carved out a deep sense of dread in the bottom of my stomach.

She paused for a moment and then said quietly, "It's your turn, Gesela."

I heard the words but ignored them, bending to pick up my ax. I knew what she meant without explanation. It was my turn to bear the consequences of the curse on our village, Elk.

Since I was a child, Elk had been under a curse of curses. No one agreed on how or why the curse began. Some blamed a merchant who broke his promise to a witch. Some said it was a tailor. Others said it was a maiden, and a few blamed the fae and a bargain gone wrong.

Whatever the cause, a villager of Elk was always chosen to end each curse—some as simple as a case of painful boils, others as devastating as a harvest destroyed by locust. It was said to be a random selection, but everyone knew better. The mayor of Elk used the curses to rid his town of those he did not deem worthy, because in the end, no villager could break a curse without a consequence.

Like my sister.

I brought my ax down, splitting the wood so hard, the blade cracked the log beneath.

"I do not use the well," I said. "I have my own."

"It cannot be helped, Gesela," Elsie said.

"But it is not fair," I said, looking at her.

Her eyes darted to the right. I froze and turned to see that the villagers of Elk had gathered behind me like a row of pale ghosts, save Sheriff Roland, who was at their head. He wore a fine uniform, blue like the spring sky, and his hair was golden like the sun, curling like wild vines.

The women of Elk called him handsome. They liked his dimpled smile and that he had teeth.

"Gesela," he said as he approached. "The well's gone dry."

"I do not use the well," I repeated.

His expression was passive as he responded, "It cannot be helped."

My throat was parched. I was well aware of how Elsie and Roland had positioned themselves around me, Elsie to my back, Roland angled in front. There was no escape. Even if I had wanted, the only refuge was the forest behind me, and to race beneath its eaves was to embrace death with open arms.

I should want to die, I thought. It was not as if I had anything left, and yet I did not wish to give the forest the satisfaction of my bones.

I gathered my apron into my hands to dry my sweaty palms as Roland stepped aside, holding my gaze. Elsie's hand pressed into the small of my back. I hated the touch and I moved to escape it. Once I had passed Roland, he and Elsie fell into step behind me, herding me toward the villagers, who were as still as a fence row.

I knew them all, and their secrets, but I had never told them because they also knew mine.

No one spoke, but as I drew near, the people of Elk moved—some ahead, some beside, some behind, caging me.

Roland and Elsie remained close. My heart felt as though it were beating in my entire body. I thought of the other curses that had been broken. They were all so different. One villager had wandered through the Enchanted Forest and picked a flower from the garden of a witch. She cursed him to become a bear. In despair, he returned to Elk and was shot with an arrow through the eye. It was only after he died that we learned who he was. The next morning, a swarm of sparrows attacked the hunter who had killed the bear and pecked out his eyes.

There was also a tree that had once grown golden apples, but over time, it ceased to produce the coveted fruit. One day, a young man wandered through the village and said a mouse gnawed at its roots. He claimed if we killed the mouse, the fruit would thrive, so our previous mayor killed the mouse, and the fruit returned. The mayor picked an apple, bit into it, and was consumed with such hunger, he gorged himself to death.

No one else touched the fruit of the tree or the mayor who died beneath its boughs.

There were no happy endings, that much I knew. Whatever I faced after this would surely lead to my death.

READING GROUP GUIDE

1. Callie is a scientist, and her career is one of the most important aspects of her life. Why do so many people underestimate her? What does this say about being a woman in the scientific community?

2. Earl seems to know something that Callie doesn't know about the mushrooms she is searching for. Do you think Callie should have trusted him?

3. Callie falls through a fairy ring and becomes ensnared by Prince Mendax. He tries to kill her, but she is revived by a golden fox. Does her love of animals mean something more in the world of the Fae?

4. A creature called the Bog is sent after Callie while she is imprisoned in the Unseelie Court. Why is this creature's death by Callie's hand so important in representing her strength to Prince Mendax? Do you think the Bog's death gives Mendax a different impression of her?

5. Why do you think so many of the animals and shape shifters of the Fae realm want to protect Callie? Is this a hint at something Callie possesses?

6. Mendax begins to fall in love with Callie. Why do

you think there is such an attraction between them despite Mendax constantly trying to kill her?

7. How does Callie continuously keep surviving the trials? Do you think her training as a scientist helps her in the faerie realm?

8. Callie begins to feel things for Mendax that she feels she shouldn't, yet this doesn't stop them from becoming close with each other. Do you think Callie and Mendax's relationship is real or is it based on lust? What makes it seem real?

9. In the final trial, it comes out that Callie is not who she says she is. Were you expecting this? Thinking back on the book, were there signs that Callie was not actually just a human who had nothing to do with the faerie realm?

10. Earl is actually Prince Aurelius, who also happens to be Callie's best friend Eli that she has mentioned throughout the book. Do you think Callie, or Calypso, will still be obedient to Queen Saracen or do you think her love for Mendax is stronger than she thought?

ACKNOWLEDGMENTS

I really want to thank my family for all of their patience and support during the writing of this book. If it weren't for my amazing husband, none of this book would have happened. Thank you for always pushing me to follow my dreams, no matter how wild they are. Shout-out to my kids. I am so lucky I get to be your mom. Special thanks go out to every single person who reads this book. You are making dreams come true by giving it a chance. If it were not for you, I'd have to wear real...non-sleep clothes to work every day, so for that, I am eternally grateful.

★Cue play-off music★

Last but not least, thank you to everyone at Bloom Books. I am truly honored to work with such an amazing and talented group of people. You are all so appreciated.

...and mic drop.

ABOUT THE AUTHOR

Jeneane O'Riley is a #1 bestselling author of whimsically dark and romantic fantasy books. Her love of storytelling began as a small child, dreaming up glorious fantasies to fall asleep to. As she has grown older, her love of storytelling remained, but the tales grew more dangerous and full of toe-curling tension.

She is a hobby mycologist and nature enthusiast who resides in Ohio, at least until she can locate a proper bridge to troll, or perhaps a large tree spacious enough to hold her smoke show of a husband, her Irish wolfhound, pet dove, and, of course, her three children.